SYMPHONY

SYMPHONY

Jude Morgan

ST. MARTIN'S PRESS   NEW YORK

SYMPHONY. Copyright © 2006 by Jude Morgan. All rights reserved. Printed in the United States of America. No part of this book may be used or reproduced in any manner whatsoever without written permission except in the case of brief quotations embodied in critical articles or reviews. For information, address St. Martin's Press, 175 Fifth Avenue, New York, N.Y. 10010.

www.stmartins.com

Library of Congress Cataloging-in-Publication Data

Morgan, Jude, 1962–
    Symphony / Jude Morgan.—1st U.S. ed.
        p. cm.
    ISBN-13: 978-0-312-36951-4
    ISBN-10: 0-312-36951-4
    1. Berlioz, Hector, 1803–1869—Fiction. 2. Actresses—Fiction. I. Title.

PR6113.O743 S96 2007
823'.92—dc22

2007033902

First published in Great Britain by Headline Book Publishing,
a division of Hodder Headline

First U.S. Edition: December 2007

10 9 8 7 6 5 4 3 2 1

For Don Astley

'She inspired you, you loved her and sang of her; her task was done.'

Franz Liszt, letter to Hector Berlioz, 1854

Prelude: March 1849

A lunatic asylum: yes.

Healthily situated on the clean heights of Montmartre with the city of Paris seething and smoking below, Monsieur Blanche's Asylum for Lunatics has a not unpleasant appearance. A high stone wall and plane trees enclose a substantial house in ruddy brick and stone with a sun-dial mounted on the gable, and cream shutters at the many windows. No bars. Monsieur Blanche – who has a high reputation – does not believe in restraints unless absolutely necessary. Inmates wander the neat gardens, sit in quiet thought on the timber benches. Still, a lunatic asylum: from somewhere comes a wild, sexless and despairing scream, that goes on and on as if the screamer has no need of breath. It hangs in the air.

We won't linger. We'll pass swiftly into the tidy wallpapered parlour where Madame Blanche is preparing to go on a visit.

– I hope this is one of her good days, Madame Blanche remarks to her husband, as she ties on her bonnet. Sometimes I'm afraid she hardly knows me.

– The paralysis? asks Monsieur Blanche, who is going over his correspondence at the bureau. No improvement?

Madame Blanche – plump, berry-eyed, miniature clamour of keys at her tight waist – shakes her head at her bonneted self in the mirror. – No. I did have hopes of some feeling in that right side by now . . . Her doctor has tried the electrical treatment, but I have seen no effect.

Monsieur Blanche's gentle face darkens in a grimace. – Mere quackery. I was reading a paper by some charlatan who tries the electrical treatment on the *faces* of lunatics. The electric rod, apparently, alters their expressions and renders them more pleasing. Electro-physiognomy, he calls it. Quackery. Well, as long as she is as comfortable as possible . . .

– Oh, she's well attended. Madeleine and Joséphine are very good.

1

A miracle to find girls so honest. There are a thousand who would trade on such a place.

– She'll be glad to see you, my dear, even if she isn't able to express it.

– I hope so. Though I think there is someone she would be much more glad to see . . . Well! One does what one can in this life. The rest we must surrender to God.

Madame Blanche administers a sharp dry kiss to her husband's cheek, puts on her gloves, and goes forth.

But in the cool whitewashed hall she stops as an unthinkably gaunt young man, yellow-pale, bursts out of the stair-shadow and comes at an anguished stooping sidle to hover beseeching at Madame Blanche's side.

– What is it, Claude? Be quick, now: you see I am going out.

– Yes, Madame, yes. Please, will you look? Only one look. If you will please look . . .

The young man's fascinating unfleshed hands, as long as her forearms, open prayerfully to present a calfskin notebook. Madame Blanche takes it up. She pours out a precise measure of patient attention as she turns the leaves.

– Very good, Claude. I see you have written several pages more today.

– Five. Five, gasps the young man, hunched, with a smile like wire.

– Then you have been working very hard. And you, are you happy with what you have done?

Receiving the notebook back with a look half regretful, half possessive, the young man shakes his head.

– Not happy. Oh, there are touches – here and there fine touches. Still, it is not what I had *here,* insists the young man; and his fingers map and clasp his skull.

– Well, nothing worthwhile is easy. But I'm glad to see you are working hard. Now, Claude, I must go.

The young man droops backward, a grasshopper courtier, gathering the precious notebook to him. Madame Blanche always takes the trouble to look at Claude's work, though neither she nor her husband can make anything of the close-packed lines of jagged, looping, unreadable script. Probably no one can. It is a species of shorthand: a script, and a language known only to Claude. He is writing an epic poem, so very exalted that French will not do, no earthly tongue will do. He has filled fourteen of those notebooks so far. It is his occupation, or vocation. His parents have washed their hands of him. They regarded this behaviour as mere weakness, and wished Monsieur Blanche to cure it. Monsieur Blanche does not undertake to cure: console and classify, those are the duties of his profession. The parents intended Claude for a lawyer – as if, Madame Blanche remarked to her husband with wintry humour, anyone can understand *their* language. But the main thing is for Claude, it occupies him: it fills him, so to speak. And after all, as Monsieur Blanche commented, we don't know: his poem may be the greatest masterpiece ever made, if one could unlock it.

An old bow-legged porter opens the gate in the wall, and soon a steep, winding, unpaved lane takes Madame Blanche up – a little breathless – past a windmill, past stone walls bellied with age, past white-stepped and green-shuttered cottages, and over a muddy crossroads to the Rue St Vincent. Her face grows sombre as she approaches the house.

A pretty house, though, vined and ivied right to its hipped red roof, and privately, even secretively, nestling in its walled garden of pear and apple trees. Spring has given these the merest dusting of green: hence, perhaps, the feeling of delicate suspension about the place – a chalk drawing one might smudge at a touch.

– Good day, Madeleine. How is your mistress today? May we see her?

– Oh, good day Madame Blanche, come in, come in, says the young maid at the door, bobbing, welcoming. I hope you have not been caught in the rain –

– It has not rained, though it will later. How bright you've made the hall, Madeleine: where did you find such flowers?

– They're from the garden – the south side. Madame chose them herself.

– Ah, then she has been out?

– Two days ago. She was able to sit out for a little time. Since then – not so good. The speech especially. But not bad, not very bad, Madame Blanche, I'm sure she will be happy to see you . . .

A large drawing-room: well-furnished, and yet somehow uncomfortable, because this is one of those rooms where everything plainly has its place. The rug geometrically placed in the centre of the lustrous floorboards: the table with its sharply folded newspaper, spectacles, water-jug, and single glass shining like a great tear, and with the very table-cloth hanging as symmetrically as a painted theatre-curtain: the embroidered fire-screen, the foot-stool, the twin chairs of striped upholstery that seem to carry on their own exclusive conversation; and

3

most of all, the woman seated in the high-backed *fauteuil* before the broad French windows.

There is so much white spring light, and her silhouette is so sharp, so bold and solid, that they seemed locked in contention, as if one would eat up the other.

Madame Blanche goes to her. – My dear, how do you do? Let me kiss you. I'm glad to see you enjoying the sun, such as it is. And Madeleine tells me you have been outside . . .

Madeleine, the maid or nurse, has quietly resumed what is obviously an accustomed station at a little sewing-table in the corner, and Madame Blanche bends over the woman in the window, holding her hand and talking in soothing tones of little mutual matters. And the woman – is she happy to see her visitor? Or does Madame Blanche, unwittingly, intrude upon the fierce privacy of illness?

Well, look first at the hand Madame Blanche is holding. Not the right: that is a nerveless upturned claw. The left is rigid, its whiteness broken only by the smooth arc of a ring, but it is a very beautiful hand. And as Madame Blanche talks the beautiful fingers, with effortful slowness, tighten around hers.

– Monsieur Blanche sends his compliments, by the by, my dear. He was hardly able to stir last week – a gouty condition: but he dosed himself and is quite well again. Has Dr Desroches been to see you lately . . . ?

Is she, was she, a beautiful woman? To judge one must push aside the veils of her affliction: the heaviness of immobility, the distortion of expression on the right side of her face where an invisible paw seems to rake the flesh. And one must solve the equation of contradictions: an elegant lady of forty would possess such a hand, but the muslin cap and the severe wings of slaty hair belong to the stolid matron, likewise the plain stuff dress and plaid shawl. Yet note the cameo-clasp bracelets and delicate silver pendant of intertwined flowers – personal, young, Romantic. And then there are those eyes.

– What's that, my dear? Forgive me, try again, says Madame Blanche as the woman who is many women stirs, fights with a tremor, and forces a murmur between her frozen lips. Tea, did you say? Ah, I thank you, my dear, but I do very well as I am, and I won't take poor Joséphine from the kitchen – is today not your laundry day? Oh, yes, I have a prodigious memory, you're right: my curse, Monsieur Blanche calls it – but you know what men are for remembering, or forgetting I should say . . .

Those eyes. Restless: even when turned politely on Madame Blanche, their gaze is liable to drift back to the window. But this – sidelong – is the best way to see them: huge eyes, suggesting the entire shape of the eyeball as the evening crescent suggests the whole moon. Intense eyes: one might try the old image of lamps, but no – stale: besides, there is no light in them. They do not even truly look outwards. The garden, the spring buds, the pretty walk between espaliers – they seem only to be things convenient for the gesture, the form of looking. The real gaze is inward – down other perspectives, surely longer, stranger.

And surely for ever closed off. The woman seems to listen to Madame Blanche's mild talk of this and that, but her replies are vestigial, mewing murmurs and nods, and a hoarse sigh at the back of the throat identifiable – at some dreadful distance – as laughter. And it is not long before the woman makes a signal that is unmistakable and final. She leans her head back and closes the remarkable eyes: covers their shadows. Madame Blanche is prompt.

– Well, my dear, I must not tire you. And doubtless Joséphine will have your soup ready soon. You still find your appetite returning, I hope, my dear? Splendid. It has been delightful to see you – oh, and I must remind Madeleine to try the rosemary oil again. Just a little on the wrist and temples – I'm sure you found it soothing, did you not? . . .

But the woman makes no motion now. She might be asleep. And perhaps even kind brisk Madame Blanche, tittuping to the door, cannot conceal her desire to be out of this tidy blank room, away from the cold frame of light with its dark stencil of paralysis.

Outside she sucks in fresh brash air; and turning back to Madeleine in the porch says, pensively: – Well, she has had worse days. Of course she will never again be as she was. I don't suppose he . . . ?

Madeleine shakes her head.

– Hey, well. Goodbye, Madeleine. Remember the rosemary. Look, I was right: it's starting to rain.

Remember.

Rosemary – that's for –

What is it? What is she? Who is Sylvia, that all her swains — *no, wrong, prompt, prompt, damn it* —

And here is long-faced doleful Joséphine taking away the untasted soup from the table at the woman's side while buxom red-armed Madeleine crushes a little rosemary in a pestle, freeing the green imp of scent.

Rosemary. Sylvia. Who is she, that all . . . who is she?

The nursemaids busy themselves with practised movements, passing and repassing, dancing the sickroom minuet.

Ophelia. That is she, I. And I, of ladies most deject and wretched, That sucked the honey of his music vows —

— What is it, Madame? Would you have water? Or the cordial? The fire-screen?

— The drawer, I think she means the drawer.

Come, night; come, Romeo; come, thou day in night . . . No, wrong, wrong, where's the prompt —

— She's agitated, poor soul. I think it's the company that does it. Is this what you wanted, Madame?

A miniature portrait is placed into the woman's hand — or someone's hand, some giant hovering at her side, whose hand is modelled on her own, obliging giant who brings the portrait closer to her eyes. Up from a well of longing looms the face.

My lord, I have remembrances of yours.

— Is that it, Madame? Something more?

— A question. See the frown, that's for a question. What — which — ?

— When, it's when.

Come Romeo —

— When will he come again? Oh, Madame, I really can't say.

— Don't upset yourself, Madame. Let's try a little of the rosemary, it'll calm you.

There's rosemary, that's for remembrance.

— She wants to weep, poor soul, but she can't make tears any more.

Too much of water hast thou, poor Ophelia, And therefore I forbid my tears . . .

That's for remembrance.

I remember.

I have no voice. Will you hear me?

PART ONE

Ophelia

1

First there was her father murdering her mother.

First there was this, the struggling and the screaming and her father's shoulders high with the damnable effort and the plunk, plunk, plunk of the curtain-rings as her mother grasped and clawed at the bed-curtain as she sank, as she sank, and still the screaming.

The screaming is me.

And now her father, interrupted in his work, looks over his shoulder and frowns at her. In pure irritation.

No, not that scene, not first. Change it. Roll up that drop.

First, first, the other father. The true father. She sees his shoes – which shows what a tiny girl she must have been in this scene: but also she always got such a feeling of him from those shoes. Big broad black square-toed squeaking things. You could have set a pair of fat hens in them. Rusty stockings and old-fashioned knee-breeches too. Not that that was so uncommon where they lived.

'These shoes will outlast me,' she heard him say once. And he was never silly, not he, not the other father, but she nearly thought him silly for that. Shoes didn't last. She was always having to have new ones.

First – but perhaps the witches came first. (She believes the witches always come first. There, at the back of things and in the root and source, they lurk.) But *he* could always keep them at bay – her other father.

She called him so sometimes, when she forgot.

'Father, we went on such a walk and I found such a big mushroom, bigger than anything—'

'Did you, my dear? And did you pick it? You shall show me. But a moment first, Harriet, and recollect yourself. I think you mean no harm: still you should not call me Father, you know, for that name belongs to someone else.'

She tried not to pout, pouting.

'Come, Harriet, never tell me you've forgotten your father? You're too big a girl for such forgetting, I'll swear.'

(How old is she here? Try six. She has a sense of hair down, white drawers instead of petticoats, much dexterity with her hoop: of tears infrequent but not to be quickly got over; they lodge.)

'You saw him in January. Your mother and brother too. They came on a visit.' Gentle, sorrowful reproach in every soft furrow of that face. 'Now, I know you remember.'

She squirming, liking the talk with him, the tender attention: not liking the subject. Then the outburst: 'But I live with *you.*' There was more: she would take him by the veined hand and lead him over the vastness, the endless acres, of her love for him. But she had no voice, for that.

'Yes, Harriet, and I am very happy it is so. But you must understand, your father is not able to have a settled home, because he is a player—'

At that word she rose in puny revolt. 'I play. *Children* play.'

'– and so he must travel about the country,' he went on, eyeing her sadly, 'and as when you were very small that did not seem to suit you, it was agreed that you be brought up here under my care, until—'

'Yes – I know. Let me show you the mushroom.' She became a breeze, blowing it all away: because she could not bear that *until*.

Let me show you the mushroom, let me show you my father the player. He, too, is big: fleshy in an unwholesome way: not quite believable. Here he comes in his beau's riding-coat and boastful hessians (so different from those shoes). Artful hair, weathered cheeks, a summoned smile: arms open – to show the breadth of his chest, of course, that windy rafter-rattling chest, not to welcome or embrace.

Did she remember, ever, an embrace? In truth, no. His hands went about her shoulders, and then there was a sort of measuring pat down her arms and hips. She saw men at Ennis market do something similar to horses they thought to buy: would she do?

Oh, exit, Father, for now. Enter again the one she must not call so, her guardian. The Reverend James Barrett, Pastor of Drumcliffe and Dean of Killaloe. And to her confusion there were others who called him Father: the Irish folk of the town, that is to say the Catholics or Papists. They had their own priest but still they were warm to her guardian: sometimes brought him their troubles or sought his advice. Thank you kindly, Father. Not what you properly called a Protestant minister but he didn't mind.

'When you are as old as I am,' he said, to a visiting lady, 'you begin to see that how things are called does not greatly matter.' The lady talked of founding a charity school for the labouring poor – or deserving poor: which should it be? She was very grand, very high. Fine kid gloves up to the elbow and a bandeau about her head, which gave Harriet the horrid fancy that she had been hanged and cut down. She did not much care for the lady all in all. Perhaps because she had made her guardian talk of being old – and at that Harriet wanted to stop her ears.

Old: that was the Widow Glasheen, who was always to be seen spinning at her cottage door at the foot of Church Row. On walks with Nurse, Harriet would go to give her good day, touch the spindle and run her fingers round the wheel-spokes, peep in fascination at the ancient face: no bigger than a turnip it seemed beneath the great mob-cap. The Widow Glasheen had so many grandchildren and great-grandchildren it was higher than she could count; but she could name them all in a piping sing-song. 'Biddy and Michael and Rory and Thady, Connor and Brian and Rory again, Nonie and Patrick, Molly and Dan, Biddy again . . .' It went on: Harriet could recite it all. Her memory worked that way.

Which greatly interested her father, when he visited.

'Such a memory, my little Harriet! Say it again, now,' and then the measuring hands. Measuring eyes too. The look of a man given too much change in a shop and hoping it will not be noticed.

But the Widow Glasheen – the day came when she was not in her place at the cottage door. A crack in the world. What had happened? Nurse found out.

'Dead, Miss – dead as a herring. Her neighbour-woman found her so last night, still sitting at her wheel, God ha'mercy.'

Harriet howled. The first thing that was not right.

'Why, Miss, what's all this whillaluh? I only hope I may go as quick and quiet. Don't you know she was monstrous old, and don't you know that old people stand always at grave's edge? Now hush, for the widow-woman's sake. If you cry too soon or loud for one that's died, you wake the white hounds that come and snatch their soul away.'

Her nurse, Bridget, was full of those tales. Harriet hated the thought of the white hounds taking the Widow Glasheen's soul: she hated to walk past the deserted cottage, and turned her eyes away. But it was something else she was really turning her eyes away from.

'Very good, Harriet. Very good. Now you may put away your book.' Her guardian, after hearing her read her lesson. He rubbed the bridge of his nose: the light seemed to shine through the papery skin of his hand. It was not very good: she had made mistakes, stumbled through it. But she could not allow the knowledge that he had fallen asleep.

Old: no, she could not allow that.

Walking with Bridget, she ventured on the question.

'Old, Miss? To be sure he is. I'll say this, he's a good deal older than *me*.' With a conclusive nod, Bridget brought everything back to herself. But here we are in the market-place now: her favourite part of their daily walk. Ennis was no poor, moiling little town. You might find more fashion in Waterford, but no more thriving and bustling: here a market-wife tumbles her basket of cabbages straight from her head on to the stones, and there flash the painted panels of the departing coach, Cork–Limerick–Kilkenny, with the barefoot boys running behind to hazard their lives on a grab at the bars, and there the farmers make obeisance round the mystic three-legged scale where the potatoes are weighed, and here the young blades practise their lounging under the portico of the courthouse, and wish they dared call out to the young ladies in trim spencers and bonnets, deliciously conscious as they trip by to purchase their lace and exchange their sentimental novels.

The townspeople made a pet of Harriet. She was the Reverend Dr Barrett's little girl, and – everyone said it – fetchingly pretty besides: that rich black cluster of hair: oh, those eyes. A wolfhound put its questing nose into her neck: come away, ye brute, and don't scare Missie. Troublous, she stared at a pig having its back leg tied: look ye, Missie, it doesn't hurt him at all, never ye get in a flustrum over it. This was nice – and discomfiting. Harriet did not like having attention called to her. She feared being looked at.

The Reverend Dr Barrett's little girl – but also Mr Smithson's little girl.

William Joseph Smithson was well known in Ennis. Almost an adoptive son of the town: he came from elsewhere, but Harriet could not say where precisely. ('A gentleman born, mark you,' he would grumble proudly in his cups, 'the Smithsons of Gloucestershire.' He was certainly English, as was her mother. But who knew the Smithsons of Gloucestershire? They were as remote, as legendary, as the last of the Mohicans.) And just there, down Cooke's Lane, past the grim gratings of the House of Correction, was another place from which she turned her eyes.

It was a theatre.

'What's amiss with you that you won't go down here?' Bridget, tugging at her unyielding hand. 'Is it the House you're afraid of? Well, it can't hurt you if you're a good girl. It's when you're bad that you've to fear the Bridewell. Then it's a different matter . . .' And she went on again to conjure the horrors of the House, where you had to stand all day in fetters and beat hemp until your arms were half out of their sockets, and you slept on a plank bed covered with straw and made water in a pail with everyone looking.

But it was the modest building a little further on, it was the Theatre Ennis, or Mr Smithson's Theatre, that Harriet Smithson shrank from.

A maltings once. It still had the chimney. But some years ago, when he was temporarily settled at Ennis, Mr William Smithson, the most celebrated actor-manager of the south of Ireland, had leased the building and fitted it out with a stage and a pit and a gallery seating two hundred. 'With his own hands,' Bridget would reminisce admiringly. 'Never had such a thing in the town before. Not that it was any manner of good to me, mind. The cheapest ticket was a shilling, and I worked in the bleach-yard then, and it was all I could do to keep myself in stockings.'

Her father's theatre, then, in a way. Whenever his travels around the country brought him back to Ennis he mounted a short season there: that was when the visits happened, the hands on the shoulders, the assessing. And whenever Mr William Smithson was in town, Bridget would make much of her to people in the market-place.

'Yes – here she is, his own little girl. Don't you see the look of him in that face? Why, it's even a wonder she wasn't born on that very stage, for she was all but peeping out. Will you hear it . . . ?'

Harriet had heard it many times, always with dislike. The very week

13

before her birth, Harriet's mother had gone on stage at the Theatre Ennis for a benefit performance. 'Oh, she did not play much of a part, I believe,' the Reverend Dr Barrett had told her, 'more of a token appearance. There was a musical piece with a scene of Vesuvius erupting, I seem to recall; oh, and *Romeo and Juliet*.' About the theatre he spoke, as ever, with mild forbearance. Some men of the cloth were severe upon the morality of dramatic entertainments, he said, but not he. 'Men do far worse things in this world, Harriet, than stepping upon a stage.'

She listened: trusted: as ever, believed. And yet. She did not like the theatre, did not like talk of the theatre, and could not speak of it or explain it.

The Reverend Dr Barrett's filmed eyes saw much, if not all. He drew conclusions. She must have unpleasant memories of theatre life in infancy, before coming to live with him (which she did not, for all before him was vacancy, void before creation) and he thought to dispel them by taking her to the Theatre Ennis himself.

Not when her parents were performing: he sensed her resistance to that. It was another travelling company. 'It appears that they have had the honour of playing before all the crowned heads of Europe, to an acclaim as universal as unparalleled. Goodness me, *all* the crowned heads.' He snuffled humorously, perusing the playbill. 'Well, with such accolades, we can hardly refuse *our* patronage, my dear.'

Harriet could not, would not refuse him anything. Perhaps he, if anyone, could dispel the cold fog of misgiving about that building in Cooke's Lane. The place where something, she felt, was waiting for her.

With her hand in his she entered the dark door and let the theatre swallow her up.

Smell of orange-peel, sawdust, hot fustian and bodies. The smoky air and the roar of voices smothered her: it was like when she had slipped in the bathtub and gone under: her swamped senses sang hideously for release. Their seats in the pit were only yards from the stage. Curtain, obscenely large: when she had had the ulcerated throat her fever had made just such titanic distortions of her bed-furniture. An explosion of drum and cymbal stopped her heart, then scurrying fiddles and flute made it race. Some hidden giant lifted the curtain. Something went out from the audience, a surge or lunge of attention: on the backless bench Harriet braced her tense shoulders against it. A terrace, a palm, a sea:

they were there, and not there: she squinted in distress, trying to make sense of them, until the man in the sky-blue coat and tight pantaloons swept in shouting.

Oh, that man: the shiny white face with the old neck beneath, the restless stamping back and forth, the sudden booms and hootings into the audience. He was the son of a baronet who had been captured by Barbary pirates, which he was glad of because so had his lady-love a year and a day ago, though he was also being pursued by a lady he did not love who was disguised as a page, and whose breeched legs brought fierce whistles from the gallery . . . He was this but he was also someone else, someone whose gaping mouth lapsed into a nervous pinch between speeches. It was somehow like when Harriet looked at things with her eyes crossed: soon you felt queasy.

The breeches lady was very gay and sang about being carefree, but she had hollow, shadowed cheeks like Mr Keogh the consumptive who was wheeled about Ennis in a Bath chair. By contrast the other lady was notably plump, especially about the middle, and when she rushed on stage into her lover's arms there were more whistles and laughter and a voice shouted from the gallery: 'Sure you're too late, man, she's already been had!' But later she thought her lover was untrue and she wept, and Harriet could see the real tears, glistening tracks on the red-and-white face-paint. She turned her head away.

'There, my dear. Never mind. It's all pretending.'

All pretending. The comic manservant took a resounding tumble: his body smacked the boards. Everyone laughed at him, as they would not laugh at someone who had really hurt himself. Or would they? Was that the dark secret of this place – that it brought out the worst in you, like the shebeen-houses out on the Loughrea road where, Bridget said, men broke each other's heads with bottles? The old-young man vanquished the pirate captain in a clattery swordfight, then made a speech about British liberties. There were a few subdued whistles. All pretending.

And pretending was wrong. She knew it: she had pretended a stomach-ache to avoid her arithmetic lesson, and though her guardian had surely known he had let it pass; but her own punishment came with the sickly, cheating feeling that rose in her afterwards, which was as bad as a stomach-ache. Pretending was a sort of lie: and it was a lie that Harriet felt all about her in this noise and swelter.

Perhaps it was a grown-up matter, one of those unreachable things on the high shelf of adulthood, like the shebeen-houses: like the rasping jokes that greeted the announcement of a grand tableau-transparency to end the entertainment, representing Nelson falling on the deck of the *Victory*: 'Show us him falling on Lady Hamilton!' Though there were other children here who seemed happy enough.

'Yes, very much, thank you,' she said, when her guardian asked if she had enjoyed it, as the blessed moment came to leave, to step out of the shrill fug and into cool, truthful air. Blissfully she acknowledged returned realities, the horse-puddles in the street, the beggar-woman advancing with black-grained palm and propitiating smile. Her guardian dug deep.

'God bless you, Father.' The hand snapped shut, the old expert eyes already scanning the crowd.

'Home now, Harriet?'

'Yes, please.'

Oh, yes, please. God bless you, Father.

Harriet skipped. She did not expect to return.

'No, I believe she is positively averse to theatrical entertainments altogether,' Harriet overhears her guardian say to the visiting grand lady.

'Not in the blood, then. Well, some might say that's a blessing. Oh, the Smithsons are a decent enough sort of people, I know, but still all too often the stage is the mere anteroom to the bordello. I speak plainly: you know I always do. And so I don't hesitate to say, my dear sir, that you look tired: are you overtaxing yourself? I've said before, a man in your position need not preach more than half-a-dozen times a year.'

Harriet could hear the patient smile in her guardian's voice. 'I am honoured by your concern, but you know I am like an old carthorse – take him out of the shafts and he drops.'

Harriet ran away then. She could see the horse falling.

Then there was the mad boy with the broom.

You didn't see him about Ennis very often. When he did appear it was a minor occasion, like the arrival of the itinerant ballad-singer. Children gathered.

The last time Harriet saw him, she was taking her morning walk not only with Bridget but with her guardian. Another occasion: lately he did not stir much from the house.

Surprised, cordial greetings. 'Morning, Father. We've seen but little of you. Is it sunshine you're hoping for? There's a terrible Noah's-ark in the sky.'

'Oh, just taking my stick for a walk, Casey.' A long breath. 'The poor fellow was pining.'

The mad boy – who might have been nineteen or twenty from his size, but it was the size of a boy writ large, a wrong size – was the youngest of the large brood of Murphy the linen-draper, who had pots of money, according to Bridget, but was the most close-fisted man in Ennis. The old man trudged the country lanes picking up kindling, with an old great-coat fastened round his neck to avoid wear on the sleeves. 'If I had his money,' Bridget said, 'I'd lay it out on a new suit of clothes at least.' She set her jaw. 'And more beds besides. There's not enough in that house, judging by that poor half-saved gossoon.'

What did she mean? What did beds have to do with the mad boy? Harriet had to ask, knowing the response.

'Hush now! You shouldn't ask such things.'

In the market-square the Reverend Dr Barrett had to sit down on the bench outside the coaching-inn. 'I must get my breath,' he said. 'You run about, my dear. As long as you keep Nurse in sight.' It was a bright day and the market-place was busy, but there was a particular commotion over by the courthouse portico. Harriet went to look.

There was the mad boy with his broom, and all about him the usual excited gaggle of children. Bridget let her play with other children as long as their necks were clean, and Harriet knew several of the gleeful faces that turned to her.

'He kissed it!'

'Timmy Byrne told him to kiss it and he did! You never did see!'

The broom was an old besom, almost worn away from being dragged everywhere by the mad boy. It was his companion. Sometimes he cradled and stroked it: sometimes put its smooth handle close to his cheek and talked to it in a confiding mutter. He never seemed to mind the audience of children and youths that followed him about. When they laughed at him he laughed too, a deep, honking laugh like a donkey's bray.

'Kiss it again! Like it's your sweetheart!'

The mad boy did it, chuckling, then looked round uncertainly at the reaction. Children were screeching and dancing on the spot. Harriet wanted to move away, but some fascination kept her there watching the mad boy. And, after all, he seemed to be enjoying himself too.

Then a big prentice-boy, hulking in leather apron and breeches, did something new. He snatched the broom from the mad boy. The donkey-laugh changed to bleats of distress as the prentice-boy ran in a circle around him, holding out the broom and then snatching it away.

Soon others were joining in. They tossed the broom between them, sometimes right over the head of the mad boy, who ran fruitlessly back and forth, groaning on one long note. The laughter grew louder and harder. A butter-woman came over and cried shame on them, but no one heeded her: other adults were stopping to look, to grin and laugh. Still Harriet could not move, though she did not laugh, and dreaded the broom's being thrown to her: she didn't know what she would do.

Then her guardian's hand was on her shoulder. 'Go to Bridget, now. Quickly.' Breathing hard, he waded in among them. The laughter fell away. The prentice-boy had hold of the broom again, and he glared mutinously at the Reverend Dr Barrett. Then he dropped his eyes. The Reverend Dr Barrett took the broom from him. He handed it to the mad boy, who was making a bubbling, sobbing noise, and told him to go home.

'I do not at all mind you playing with other children, Harriet,' he said afterwards, when he had breath. 'But not games like that: not ever. I will not have it. Do you understand?'

It was the only time he had ever spoken severely to her. Oddly, she did not feel bad: she felt loved.

About a year later the mad boy died of a brain-fever.

His father finally untied his purse-strings for the funeral, which was a grand affair: black plumes, mutes, red cloaks, a closed carriage following the hearse in slow procession through all the streets of the town. No child could be denied the treat of seeing a good funeral: Harriet took her place with the rest.

Instead of watching the procession, she found herself watching the watchers. All along Chapel Lane and up Market Street they stood, doffing hats, bowing heads, looking solemn. Some dabbed their eyes with handkerchiefs, or set up a wail as the cortège passed. And some of these, Harriet noted, had laughed and mocked at the mad boy and his broom.

All pretending.

She was not sure how long it was since her parents had last come to see her, but certainly she found herself a good head taller against her father's waistcoat. She felt different this time too: not quite so abashed in their company. Curious, even.

'Being engaged for a short season in Galway, we thought to take in dear Ennis along the way. The company have gone on ahead – one *hopes* to a warm welcome. In the past we have not found that town greatly appreciative of our efforts.' William Smithson pushed back his thick, greying hair with both hands, a uselessly large gesture. 'But there, my dear sir, you will be the first to acknowledge that Irish society is not what it was. Sad result of the Union! Where are the *ton* now, where the men of education and refinement? Shifted over to England, to London and Westminster. All too often now the commercial class set the taste, and I fear they are *not* discriminating.'

'It is much to be regretted that so many of our great estates now are owned by absentees, who never set foot in the country,' the Reverend Dr Barrett said. 'Society is diminished, as you remark, sir; and what is worse, many poor labouring people suffer, through the neglect of these estates, and the corruption of intermediary agents.'

'Oh, to be sure! The condition of the peasantry is very shocking. Such poverty and ignorance. I was only remarking to Constance the other day – was I not, my dear? – on how my heart bleeds, actually bleeds, at some of the sights we see on our travels.' Her father's long face grew longer, his brow crinkled, his lips twisted with pathos. Meanwhile his big, careless feet tapped a miniature jig on the rug. His body, Harriet saw, was giving him away: it showed when you were lying.

Her parents had come to dine, bringing also Harriet's brother. And this was the first time he took shape as such in Harriet's view. Though he was scarce eleven he looked older: he stamped about with grand carelessness, a small reproduction of her father. He travelled with the company, appeared on stage, and loved it. They could hardly have been greater strangers to one another. His name, she recalled with difficulty, was Joseph.

19

Today was different.

'Look. Look, isn't that funny? We're both the same.'

With ungentle hands Joseph thrust her towards the pier-glass above the parlour mantel and then, realizing she could not see so high, hoisted her effortfully up in his arms. He had lost a front tooth practising for a sword-fight and she, in the natural order of things, had just lost one too in the very same place. 'Look. Show your teeth. Ugh, you're heavy. There, see? Both the same.'

Harriet experimented with a smile. The mirror, encasing a curly-haired little girl and a big curly-haired boy, presented her with a new idea. She was not invisible. People could see her all the time just as she saw them. She did not stand outside the world: she stood relative to it. Fear melded with fascination.

Relatives. Before they had only been seasonal interruptions, like Christmas evergreens or colds, as quickly forgotten. Now Harriet began to wonder about them. Her mother, with her warm, scented, absent kisses, her abundant flesh that she somehow carried gracefully as if it were a padded costume: were all mothers like her? The Reverend Dr Barrett smiled on Mrs Smithson: Harriet had heard him commend her sound Christian principles. She had the first inkling that what he did, he did for her mother's sake.

Not her father's. Her father: there was the biggest wonder of all, this man, whose voice bounced off the wainscoted walls: even to hear him scratch his head was to be deafened. The linen at his cuffs was a little frayed.

'Without Mr Pitt we are sadly adrift,' he was saying, and made drifting motions with his hands. 'There seems as little hope of peace as of victory.'

'They say he was a shocking toper,' put in Joseph. 'Six bottles of port a day, that's what I heard.'

'Oh, the private sphere has no bearing on a man's public life,' her father said.

'It does if he's drunk,' Joseph said; and gave Harriet a wink of collusion. She did not know where to look.

While Joseph was to dine in candlelight with the adults, Harriet was deemed too little. A distribution of kisses, and she was despatched to find Bridget, milk and oatmeal, the rites of bedtime. But she hesitated outside the parlour door. She had half a mind to peep in and return Joseph's wink.

Instead she found herself listening, unbreathing.

Her guardian's voice: 'And now tell me, my dear madam, how does Harriet's little sister? I have hesitated to address such a tender question . . .'

'Bless you, Dr Barrett, you needn't. The fact is, we are in high hopes that we may raise her after all. She has quite begun to thrive with the new wet-nurse – well, if not to thrive, then to do a good deal better.'

'I'm so very relieved to hear you say so. And the – the trouble?'

'As to that, the doctor says we can only wait and see.'

'Which means he does not know.' Her father's boom. 'Like most of his profession, the one thing he is certain of is his fee. For myself I am optimistic. Air is what is needed: good air is all, and the air of Waterford cannot be bettered. I only wish I could say the same of the receipts there . . .'

'Well, you're a quiet little mouse tonight,' Bridget said, as she slipped on Harriet's night-rail. 'Did a fairy steal away your tongue?'

Harriet turned from her and extinguished her burning face in the pillow.

'Dr Barrett tells me you are a good scholar, my dear.' Her father, the next morning. He had called to take Harriet out for the day. A fine jaunt we shall have, he said, and it might well take in a visit to the pastry-shop . . . She hardly heard him for the clamour of questions in her head. Now he strode beside her, high-chested, heartily sniffing. 'I am pleased. Of course, there is more to life than book-learning.'

Cooke's Lane: of course he would come here. He stood before the doors of the theatre and sighed. 'A wandering peripatetic like me cannot expect a home – but if I have one, this is it. A poor thing, but mine own. Now, Dr Barrett says you went to the theatre and did not like it. Can this be so?'

'No, Father. I did not like it.'

'Papa, you must call me Papa. I asked Dr Barrett for the name of the company – but, dear me, his memory . . . Some wretched strollers fit only for the barn trade, no doubt. Ah, when you see your papa perform, it will be different. Your mama too, though she prefers to take only the occasional role nowadays. And Joseph, he shows great promise: and so well grown he has even been able to take walking-gentleman parts. Do you know what a walking-gentleman is, my dear?'

Harriet didn't want to know. As he strode on she kept her ground and asked his back: 'Papa, what is this about my sister?'

He stopped: stared down, as if a cat had suddenly barked like a dog.

'My dear Harriet – what is this? I have said nothing to you about a sister.'

'I heard it. Last night.' Now she felt ashamed, knowing that listening at doors was bad. But there was no reproof, as if he found that, at least, quite a natural thing to do.

'Come, my dear.' He coughed and demanded her hand. 'The fact of the matter is, you must have misheard.' As he spoke there was a curious hitch in his step, as if he was physically eluding some slight obstacle. 'Your mother's sister, perhaps. We were certainly talking of her. She lives at Bristol, you know, married to a tradesman there – oh, in a very genteel line, mind you . . .'

She could see he was not telling the truth. But it had taken all her will to pose the question: interrogation was beyond her. She could only submit to his overbearing custody. But the sister followed with her: the undreamed possibility that had become her dreams.

'Not hungry?' Her father had taken her for what he called a nuncheon at the coaching-inn where the family were staying. He thrust veal-and-ham pie and coddled eggs under her nose. 'This is very fine fare, you know. Specially ordered for a special occasion.'

'Perhaps it's too rich for her,' said her mother, eating contentedly.

'I'll have it,' Joseph said, lunging.

'No, no,' her father pronounced. 'If Harriet does not choose to eat her portion, it shall be sent back.'

'That's not fair!'

Her father sprang up, deftly and even casually hitting him round the ears. 'Comport yourself decently, sir. Is this a bear pit?'

With tears in her throat Harriet forced herself to eat. The sound of the slaps shook her. Her mother clucked her tongue, chewing: Joseph scowled and grumbled, her father raised his hand again. The old waiter came into the room with wine, sniffing back a dew-drop. Joseph sneaked a slice of pie from her plate. Her father, noticing, took no notice. Wind shrilled through a cracked pane, bringing a noisome aroma of stables. Her father poured wine and drank at it in eager, sucking gulps, as if he were eating it. Joseph balanced a spoon on his nose and her father began laughing uproariously. None of it made any sense.

Outside, a crash and a yell. Joseph flung down his knife. 'What's that?'

'Ask permission before you leave the table, boy,' her father grunted. Joseph was already at the window overlooking the inn-yard.

'Oh, look, Papa! The funniest thing you ever saw! They were trying to back that horse into the shafts and instead it's tipped that curricle right over.'

William Smithson joined his son at the window. 'Oh, dear, dear,' he said, laughing richly and tolerantly. 'And now those poor dunderheads have got it stuck fast in the arch. See that old fellow scratch his poll. Aye, my friend, you must think it out. Dear, dear. A likeable people in many respects, but quite hopeless.'

Harriet found her mother was smiling towards her in a conspiratorial way: these men and the things that amuse them. Kind eyes, Harriet thought. She wondered about her little sister's eyes; and then froze on the precipice of speech.

'What is it, my dear?' Her mother followed Harriet's downcast gaze. 'Oh, is it these? My bracelets? They're pretty, aren't they? That one is pearl, you see, and that one coral. It grows under the sea, though I confess I don't know how.' She gave a timid laugh: Harriet glimpsed as a distant flash the idea that her mother was a little afraid of her. 'You shall have many such pretty things when you're grown.'

'Mama, will you tell me about my little sister?'

Her mother stopped in the middle of a breath, then glanced about her in a mildly perturbed way, as if she had put down a pencil and now could not find it. 'Sister . . . My dear, where did you hear such a thing?'

'I heard it yesterday when you were talking. I asked Father – Papa – but he said I was mistaken but I know that's not true.'

Her father was still at the window, chuckling over Irishness.

'Yes,' her mother said simply. 'You have a little sister. She was born last February. I had rather a bad time and – well, never mind that. Her name is Anne – which is a pretty name, don't you think?' But a glance at Harriet's face showed there could be no diversion. 'She is with a nurse at Waterford.'

'Why?'

'Oh, bless you, you must know a woman can't be nursing a baby when she goes about the country as a player. We put you to a wet-nurse for

23

your first year. Joseph too. Mind, with Anne it must be longer, I'm afraid, because she is – not very strong.'

Last February. Harriet calculated: there had been two visits since then.

'Why didn't you tell me?' She was no longer surprised at her own boldness: she was so far out in daring now she was beyond sight of land.

'Well, my dear, because she was so poorly. We really thought we wouldn't raise her, and – Lord, this is very disagreeable to talk about. We didn't want you to be disappointed, hearing you had a sister and then – then if she didn't live. Oh, but she is improving a great deal now. Her legs are shockingly thin, poor creature, and I think her back is not quite right. But we have hopes.'

Sister Anne. Thin legs, bad back. It was too much to take in now, but Harriet could feel the preparing of great spaces for it in her mind.

'When will I see her?'

Her mother didn't answer. Her father had turned from the window and was regarding them with kingly sternness.

'Really, Constance. I hardly think this the proper occasion to talk of that matter.'

'Yes, my dear,' her mother said, with placid resignation. 'I'm sorry.'

'All in good time, Harriet, all in good time,' her father said, resuming his seat at the table and taking up the wine bottle. 'As I told you.'

And now Harriet would not have been surprised to see him make the bottle disappear up his sleeve. You could get away with anything, it seemed: it was all in the way you did it.

'My little sister.' After her parents had gone Harriet could not stop talking about her to Bridget. 'She's at Waterford. I'm going to see her some day.'

'Hush now, don't be talking so much of what you want. Your luck will run out. It sounds as if she's a poor thing, a cripple most likely. I wonder what your mother did when she was carrying her. Mrs O'Shaughnessy got into the boar-pen when she shouldn't, and her boy came out with a snout for a nose.'

Superstitions, her guardian would tell Harriet: don't believe them. 'I doubt that Bridget believes these old tales, really, but she finds a relish in them.' He smiled. 'Like that toasted cheese she's so fond of late at night, when it gives her such dreadful dreams.'

Superstition: mere tales: not truth. 'You know the truth given to us by our Lord,' her guardian had said, 'and you are always safe in that.'

And so she was – up to a point. In his house, yes, and in the streets and lanes of Ennis likewise, among familiar faces and kind words. But on the witchy walks – that was different.

Once a fortnight she and Bridget went on a visit to a former servant of the Reverend Dr Barrett's who lived in the country south of Ennis, taking a basket of provisions, and coins in a muslin bag. Out of the town things changed. Bridget changed: became witchy.

She was a trim little body with a round, pursy, high-coloured and eager face, as if she were always running a slight fever. Out in the country a new and dark animation came over her. Bridget could read only with difficulty, but out here she scanned the land, conned it, fluently interpreted. This was where she came from.

'Oh, our cottage was miles away from any town. I didn't know of such things. I'd never seen more than five houses together when I first came to Ennis. Where I was born you saw not a light after dark from Dan to Beersheba. If so be as you were late coming home from the field, and the night came down, you might as well have been under a blanket. And that's when you've to beware, for the pooka will come out of the darkness, looking like a horse, a terrible one, but you follow him, thinking he'll lead you somewhere, and so he does – down deep into the bog where no one sees you, light or dark, till everlasting.'

Witchy: there was no other word for it.

'Look now – I wonder whose field that is? Farmer Sullivan's, I fancy. Well, he'll come to grief. He's dug up that fairy-mount. That's the end of his luck. I knew a man back home who dug up a fairy-mount in the corner of his field, because he couldn't turn the plough for it, and he tried to ask pardon, but it was no manner of use. His childer dropped one by one into the grave.'

Superstition: old tales. Harriet tried to keep her guardian's sane, kindly voice fixed in her mind, but out here it faded, out here among the piercingly green fields and the shack-like smoke-filled cottages with the dunghills before the doors and the black-armed turf-cutters watching her pass with a slow stare. Out here you must always give good day to an old dame going by, not because it was good manners but in case she was a witch.

'Not that it's always the old ones. Witches can be young and beautiful – the wickedest ones. That's how it is with these folk – you can't tell.'

Fair is foul, and foul is fair.

And before they rode to their Sabbath, they bathed their feet in the blood of a slaughtered babe, but blood was the key to them, because if they put a *geas* on you the way to undo the curse was to scratch them and let their blood . . . Bridget's cheeks shone the more she talked of it. And there was no stopping her, much as Harriet wanted to: she hated the witches like all unavoidable facts. Just to mention them was to bring their intent profiles stencilling the moonlight on her bedchamber wall.

Yes: the witches came first, after all.

You do not believe in witches?

Be assured, they believe in you.

Oh, all was well again when she got back to the house in Chapel Lane, where the chesty ticking of the clock made sense of time, where the walls were measured in leatherbound books, creaky, a little musty, wise, like extensions or editions of her guardian himself. Still, you knew that other world was out there, vivid under a confused sky. Shut it out: draw yourself up to the study table where the Reverend Dr Barrett gently corrects your recital of the kings and queens of England, speaking of Queen Anne and George I reminiscently, as if he had known them.

And then – it must come – that odd solitary breakfast with the cook-maid helping her to what she called a slice of pig, and looking at the clock (its crooked smile) and muttering about the master being late (failing, failing) and calling out to Bridget what to do, what should we do?, and then the heavy, so heavy thump on the floorboards directly above, some-thing falling but not falling surely, almost as if something very large has been *thrown*, and then the clatter of feet up the stairs and Bridget shrieking out to the garden for Patrick the daysman, help, help, and then no more.

No more.

I cannot choose but weep to think they would lay him i' th' cold ground.

On the day of the funeral Bridget bathed and scrubbed her mercilessly, as if there were some possibility of defilement. 'You must bear up,' she kept saying. 'It's hard, I know. Even *I* find it hard. But still.'

Yet Harriet was, apparently, bearing up. A cousin of the Reverend Dr

Barrett's, deaf, gouty, and hard-breathing, had come over from Dublin to take temporary charge of the household, and fuss over the will; and though he looked on Harriet as a minor nuisance, like a kitten under the feet, he did remark absently: 'The child bears up very well.'

So this, Harriet thought, gazing at her black-clad reflection, was what bearing up looked like. The eyes in the mirror stared at her, somehow, while fixing themselves far away.

Bearing up, then, must be this: the feeling of perfect frozen stillness, so that to raise your hand was a wrenching and unnatural event. It was not being able to sleep or eat, and the small placid tone in which she heard herself decline the food. It was the presentiment that there must be a crack or a hole somewhere at hand down which she was to throw and extinguish herself, since there must surely be something *provided* to make this bearable.

All of Ennis turned out for the funeral. The shops were shuttered. Protestant and Catholic priests walked in the procession after the carriage containing Harriet and a primping, nagging Bridget and the gouty cousin, who complained of damnable twinges. She saw some people in the streets weeping, as they had at the funeral of the mad boy. Perhaps that was not bearing up. It certainly looked very easy and relieving: pleasant, almost.

She did not remember the funeral. Afterwards, at the silent house, Bridget reproved her for not bearing up after all. She couldn't tell what had happened: only that her throat was sore. She lay on her bed and slept for twelve hours.

Her father stood before her in the hall. His face was raw with cold and his restless hand smoothed and raked at his windswept coiffure until at last, with an air of concession, he let it be. 'My dear,' he said. 'My dear Harriet. We came as soon as we could. But it was a shocking road from Kilkenny, quite a disgrace . . . Such a dear good man. You must be greatly – greatly saddened. But still, you know, he was eighty, a good age, a very good age – and a good man . . .' He seemed to cast about for something better than these dismal scatterings of consolation. Then her mother appeared in the doorway, burdened; and he made a triumphant turn to her. 'And look,' he cried, 'we have brought your little sister.'

Her mother came forward, and lowered to Harriet's eyes the tiny, sharp-chinned, straw-haired scrap who was nothing like any of Harriet's imaginings. Strange, then, the almost prosaic unsurprise that possessed her: oh, yes: of course: it's you. As if she had known her all her life.

And then, though her father stood by with the flourishing look of a vindicated man, though Anne's thin arms stretched out for her, Harriet suffered a mutiny of revulsion that drove her, running and sobbing, into the empty parlour: to the fading, failing traces of the man who could *not* be replaced.

She wept for so long that her mother left off patting her and began patting herself, sighing again and again: 'Dear, dear. I don't know.' Harriet did not intend, could not envisage ceasing to cry. It was only when a little clammy insistent hand began to tug at her, as if to urge her off the sofa, that she began to gulp, gasp, acknowledge life as a possibility again. Her sister circled her: Harriet heard the teetering asymmetrical footfalls. Hot breath huffed her hair: Anne trying to peep at her. And the hand tugged.

Harriet did not want the hand. But, then, you did not want to feel hungry or thirsty. Everyone understood that. Everyone recognized, like a starkly clear reflection, the face of need.

2

In the quiet house on Chapel Lane, the lawyers' clerks and the auctioneer have departed, and the old quiet has become absolute stillness.

For Harriet, everything has become motion.

'The company.' Her father introduces them at an inn on the road to Tipperary. 'Mr Dillon, the Low Comedian. Mr Partington, the Old Man. 'Mr Cadell, the Juvenile Lead.' Harriet stares dully at these people: fidgety, flashy figures, bowing and curtsying and blowing kisses at her in a way that seems to her — she can think of no other description — not serious. Her father explains, to her vast indifference, what each one does — their line of business, he calls it. The Heavy Father plays villainous roles, tyrant kings, hard-hearted guardians. (A plunge of her heart at that word.) The Juvenile Lead, young heroes and lovers. Through her dense misery a little thin puzzlement seeps. Mr Cadell the Juvenile Lead is very nearly as old as the Old Man. He has a lean, pinched, baleful face and a stoop; and he looks at her father as if expecting at any moment to catch him out in some tremendous lie. That part, at least, she can understand. After their showy greetings, the company seem to share Harriet's uninterest: they are absorbed with a continual shuffle of places, unspoken communications and secret jokes. 'Modesty should forbid me to mention it, my dear, but for the sake of completeness I must add: the Tragedian, your humble parent.' A brief clap: very brief.

Like the noisy meal in the inn dining-room, like the sleep in the itchy inn bed with sister Anne burrowing and whimpering beside her, like the clattering breakfast in the pewter-grey dawn and the thawing of her numb fingers before the niggardly inn fire and then, again, the road.

The road is not so much a thing as a state, a condition: above all, an absence. There is no stillness: no rest or order: there are not even days of the week. There is only passage, and you get so used to it that fixed places – the inns, the scant townships and hamlets along Ireland's sunken spine – seem anomalous: as if they, too, have just stopped moving, or are about to start. Sometimes the road itself is good, at other times a mere firmer spot in the bog. Here and there Palladian mansions materialize on the horizon, slowly turning their symmetrical profiles about. The company moves at a lumbering pace. The Smithsons travel in an ancient, unsprung carriage, and the precious scenery and props go in a wagon, but most of them walk: the Singing Chambermaid, who is heavily pregnant, rides a mule, and Mr Cadell the Juvenile Lead has an old nag, as spare and sullen as himself. There are several children in the company, robust and theatre-born, who will run alongside the carriage and stare boldly in at Harriet, seeming to wonder what she is doing there.

Harriet wonders that too.

'You'll get used to it, my dear.' Her mother, vainly battering herself against the wall of Harriet's silence. 'It's right and good that you mourn poor Dr Barrett. But these things happen. It's only natural. And, after all, it has made us a family again.'

Again? thinks Harriet: how, when we never were a family?

At inns and posting-houses her father exerts himself greatly in *bonhomie*, seeking needful information: when is the date of the next race meet? Is the local magnate still old Lord Killairn (mean, unwelcoming) or the young heir (spendthrift, worth cultivating)? Sometimes he will borrow Mr Cadell's horse and ride on ahead to solicit mayors and worthies and distribute playbills.

'What, Cadell, d'you fear the mare won't be safe with him?' Harriet hears someone say, as they stretch their legs in the inn-yard. 'The old villain's a good horseman, say what you will.'

Mr Cadell's long dry sniff. 'I don't fear for the creature's *safety*. I just have fears whether I shall ever get her *back*.'

Another absence: warmth. Harriet always feels cold, as no one else seems to. No, there is one other. Her little sister Anne, past two but absolutely undimpled, fleshless: perpetually she huddles against Harriet, bony as an umbrella. Harriet tries to warm the chickenish hands between her own. This is something she can do. Likewise singing to her, helping her perform her lopsided terribly intent walk, undressing her for bed. (Still the quick catch of the breath as she pulls up the shift and sees that taut-skinned hump over the left shoulder – but getting used to it, getting better.)

'It does my heart good to see you taking to each other so,' her mother says. She is a woman for whom everything is very quickly all right. Harriet tells herself: She is my mother: she is kind and wants to help: I must love her. She gets it by heart, like a hard sum.

There is not much else to get by heart. There are only play-books on the road – dog-eared, tissuey from thumbings, covered with scribbles and crossings-out. This vaguely affronts Harriet: she would never have done that to the leathery treasures in her guardian's library. One day the memory of those, and her distaste for the play-book lying open on the table, and the eternal coldness in her bones all come together. She is in a frowsy inn-room: her father is downstairs arguing over prices with the landlord: Joseph is muttering to himself as he rehearses some nonsensical business with a walking-stick: Anne is whining. Harriet reaches out for the play-book – or it reaches out to her – and marches over to the fireplace with it. In it goes: the wan fire begins to leap and crackle; Harriet reaches out exultant hands.

'I saw you.' Joseph is at her side, flushed and righteous. 'I saw you do that. That was *The Magpie*. We've only got a few of those. I shall tell Father.'

And now Harriet, too, crackles: flames. 'Tell him. He's your father. He's not mine. My father's dead.'

She has never heard her own voice so loud. Too loud to hear the squeak of the door, where her father stands, with a braced look like a man in a gale.

'Yes, Harriet,' he says, in what is, for him, a small voice. 'Now, he is.' And turning away, he places his hand on his heart. A gesture she knows is called theatrical. What she does not know is whether that makes it real or not.

Dublin: for a long time on the road there had been talk of it among the company, and it made them more chattery and excitable than ever. 'Of course, things will be different in Dublin . . .' 'I only feel I really come *alive* when we do Dublin.' Mr Cadell spoke loftily of the many people there he would look up: he made it sound faintly unsavoury. Her father had the panels on the ancient carriage repainted. The intimations of grandeur even reached Harriet through her private shadows, and she felt rather disappointed at the place she saw when the carriage halted and her father, a little drunk, put out his head and began an impromptu apostrophe: hail bright queen of something-or-other. It was only a riverside village after all.

'Bless you, my dear, this isn't Dublin. This is only Chapelizod,' her mother told her.

'And yonder bright sparkle, yonder silver thread, Harriet, is the blessed Liffey, that leads to the heart of the blessed city itself,' her father said, lurching back into his seat. '*There* is discernment. There are pits and galleries worthy of the name. There are, God forgive me as a gentleman born for dwelling upon it, but there are receipts.'

And such a hugeness of habitation, of tall spires and ship-masts and houses that seemed, incredibly, to rise almost as tall, of wheel-clatter and stink, scaffolding and shop-fronts, building and selling, rich people in silks and poor in rags squeezing for the same walking-space, that after a while Harriet could not look. It was like having the experiences of a week in a minute.

Her father had already written to secure lodgings for the family and he made a great fuss about them. 'This, I hope, will be something like. We have *made do* for long enough.' Harriet, growing wise, took this to mean he could not really afford them. They were better than usual: a set of undamp rooms above a tea-dealer's shop in Fishamble Street. Her father was all a-twitch, clumsy with concentration. There was much at stake for him, Harriet gathered, in mounting a season in Dublin. The audiences here were used to the best, her mother told her: in the summer touring companies came from Drury Lane and Covent Garden. Names that meant nothing to Harriet, but her mother's voice turned hoarse as she pronounced them, as if they were holy places. Harriet surprised herself in feeling sorry for her father when he set out for the theatre early in the mornings, humming, pale, unseeing. Though she did not go out much, she could see a good deal from the window. Those people, thronging and purposeful and at home in their great city: her father, with the bald spot on the top of his head, diving into the harsh tide.

Her mother was taking one of her rare roles, so Harriet was often left alone in their lodgings with Anne. They were nominally in the charge of the company carpenter's daughter, a moony girl of fourteen who functioned as a maid-of-all-work; but she spent most of her time downstairs trying to attract the attention of the tea-merchant's prentice-boy. There was a certain peace in these days, a peace of absorption. Fretful Anne required much amusement, and that prevented thinking. Harriet cradled her sister's head through her restless, effortful naps, invented games, built satisfying constructions out of the battered chairs and musty tablecloths. Sometimes Anne's gaunt baby face would loom worshipfully at hers, as if she dreamed of but could not yet aspire to a kiss.

When the strange man came into their lodgings, there was at first only annoyance at the interruption, the breaking of the fine-spun threads of play and solicitude.

'Well! There's a charming picture.' He stood smiling pleasantly down at them, a ruddy man in riding-coat and boots, smelling of outdoors. All the same Harriet felt he was not pleasant. 'These must be the offspring.'

The carpenter's daughter was behind him, all in, as Bridget would say, a flustrum. 'I tell you he's not here—'

'So you do, and likewise you won't tell me where he is, and no doubt you've got your orders, and never mind.' Still smiling, tapping his riding-crop against his leg, the man stumped through to the bedrooms. 'Halloo!

Mr Smithson.' When he came back he was a little flushed. He's been looking under the beds, thought Harriet: and she wanted to laugh and cry at the same time.

'You can't come in here like this,' the carpenter's daughter was saying, near tears herself. 'It isn't right—'

'Oh, there's a lot of things that aren't right in this world, Missie. I could tell you a thing or two, only I won't.' The man picked up a chair, placed it with a slam in the centre of the room, and sat on it. 'Anyhow, he lives here, and a man must always come home, and so I'll wait. You don't mind, do you, my dears?'

Harriet said: 'What do you want?'

'Why, I want to see your father.' That smile, so unpleasantly pleasant.

'What about?'

'About the recovery of a debt,' the man said, as if to an adult. 'I made Mr Smithson's acquaintance the last time he was in Dublin, and it has left me thoroughly out of pocket. And a little out of temper too,' he said, with a laugh, and a sharp crack of the riding-crop against his boot.

Anne began to whine. Harriet hoisted her up.

'I've got to change her clout.'

'Quite the little mother!' The man took out a clay pipe. 'Go your ways, then, my dear.'

Anne's clout did not need changing: only the situation. Harriet could not bear it. She could not bear the man, the smiling, the gentle menace. With Anne in her arms she ran down the back stairs and out into the streets.

'Crow Street. The theatre in Crow Street. Can you tell me—?' Shyness had to be forcibly overcome: like the desperate last tug that brought a baby-tooth out of its socket. The man with the riding-crop wanted her father and it was not good, not good at all: she had to find him, warn him. 'If you please, can you tell me—?' An old woman gave her complicated directions that sent her wandering among reeking quaysides, while the birdlike weight of Anne became a sack of coal. Luck or blind instinct brought her at last to a street where her father's playbills were pasted on every wall.

The theatre: she stood trembling before the porticoed doors. She had never been inside such a place since that evening in Ennis. The curious dread rose in her, mixed with resentment: this was the skewed world she had exchanged for the Reverend Dr Barrett, the books and creaking shoes and rightness. But still she must go in, must find her father: when no one came to her knocking at the locked doors she ran down the alley at the side. She knew there was a thing called a stage door. (And a green-room: surprising how many things she knew that she did not want to know.)

The stage door was like a dirty secret at the end of a dark passage strewn with refuse. Inside, a maze of darker passages, tripping her up with sudden unaccountable ramps and steps – but the smell, there was no mistaking that close greasy smell, and that was what led her, gasping, exhausted, till she burst into a tallow-lit room. Several mirrors displayed wild yellow portraits of her face. A red velvet robe lay on the floor like a dead man. Mr Cadell, dressed as a soldier, was sitting over cards with the Low Comedian.

'The point is, something *can* be made of Cassio – a great deal – but depending on the production. With his lordship there, it's *all* the Moor. Cock's life, did you hear him rant over Iago? Such imbalance . . . Hullo.' Mr Cadell looked round with unfriendly surprise. 'What do you do here?'

'If you please, where is my father?'

'On stage, my dear,' the Low Comedian said, in his thick brandy voice. 'It's a full dress. We're nearly done. Sit and wait for him, if you like.'

'Damn it, child, you can't go through there,' Mr Cadell called after her. 'Don't you hear it's a full dress . . . ?'

Past painted battlements (all pretending), into what she knew (hated to know) were called the wings, the ache of her arms and the grizzling of Anne and the thwack of that riding-crop and the theatre-smell coalescing in her mind. The prompter, old and arthritic, could not get up from his stool in time to stop her. Harriet passed through a bright membrane of candlelight into a bedroom, rich with brocade hangings but opening on one side into nothingness like a cliff-edge.

And here, after all, is where it begins: her father murdering her mother on the rich bed, pressing the pillow furiously over her face while she fights and screams and the curtain rings go plunk, plunk, plunk: here it is.

Harriet did not drop Anne: there was that much to be said. She managed to set her sister down before the screams went into her and out of her, echoing in the great dark beyond the cliff.

Afterwards, when they had calmed her in the green-room, her father knelt carefully beside her and held out the back of his hand. 'I know what it is. It's this. It's the blacking, that's what alarmed her.' He rubbed with a wetted forefinger. 'See? It's Papa underneath, my dear.'

'I told you,' her mother mildly murmured, 'there's no need to cork-up for a dress – it's such a nuisance to get off, for one thing.'

'And I told *you*, my dear,' her father said, through gritted teeth, 'that I must have it for the Moor, if I am to work him up properly before tomorrow. It transforms. And here is poor Harriet proving it – isn't it so, Harriet? You were frightened by Papa's black face?'

Not really: not in the way he meant. The blacking did not so much mask him as emphasize him. It unleashed something terrible, potent, and also real. That was what she had screamed at. Not the lie but the new, suffocating truth she had breathed in that place.

'A nuisance,' her father was saying, rubbing irritably at his cheek with a handkerchief. The blacking, or herself? She had a notion. But when she stammered out the story of the man with the riding-crop, he was all alertness.

'What manner of man, my dear? Think now: describe him to me.' She obeyed. The fantastical idea came to her, as he thoughtfully listened and patted her hand, that her father was pleased with her.

'Who is it?' her mother asked. 'Not McBride? I was sure you settled up with McBride.'

'Not McBride.' Her father straightened up, snatching off his tight, curly wig. 'Damn. Damn his impudence, I mean. Don't fret, Constance, it's no great sum. Look'ee here, as I've things to do, you must carry through to the end of the act without me: have Roderigo walk through the part. Mrs Beale, will you bring a little of your excellent cordial for Miss Smithson? I'm obliged to you . . .'

On his way out her father picked up the red velvet cloak, folded it carefully, and tucked it under his arm. Watching, Mr Cadell thinned and thinned his lips, as if with difficulty refraining from a vastness, an infinity of comment.

The man with the riding-crop was gone when Harriet returned to their lodgings that evening. So were the coffee-pot, the sugar-tongs and her mother's writing-case. Everyone avoided speaking of them, like the deceased.

★   ★   ★

'Well, plainly it still does not suit her.' Her father. Every word was audible through the thin walls of their lodgings. Harriet lay still, breathing Anne's sweet-sickly hair. 'And one cannot afford to have such scenes as that repeated. She will only be a hindrance.'

'It is a great pity,' yawned her mother. 'I thought we were rubbing along quite well.'

'I confess I am disappointed.' A pause. 'It seems I was wrong.' But he did not sound as if he believed that, quite.

Nor did Harriet understand, quite. But she clasped at one certain comprehension.

'However shall we manage the Venice scenes without the Duke's robe?' her mother said suddenly.

A pettish slap of a pillow. 'Constance, I believe you take pleasure in vexing me.'

Harriet put her hands over her ears, thrust away the vision of the struggle on the rich bed, and curled herself round her joyful knowledge: there was to be an end, at last, to the road.

After the cold, coolness.

Harriet was put to school in Waterford, where cool maritime light attended to the pale, genteel faces of townhouses and unhasty ladies strolled in shade through the quayside colonnades. A cool time. Madame Tournier's Academy for Young Ladies was healthfully situated for air and breezes. The Frenchness of Madame Tournier only went as far as the prospectus: all the tradespeople called her Mrs Turner. The coolness in the house was also partly due to damp. It was fascinating to watch the progress of the wallpaper in Mrs Turner's parlour, which was slowly detaching itself in graceful little spirals. Probably this was reflected in the fees, manageable even by Harriet's father.

Cool the globe under her fingers, cool the demure crocodile walks in wind-whipped muslins up to the fort and back: cool the undemonstrative friendships with other girls, glassy with anxiety about their tradesmen fathers. Even time seemed to lose its intensity: a year, two years passed like a refreshing shower. Cool the voice of the equine lady who took them on a sedate trot through the neat parks of light literature: Addisonian essays and heroic couplets passed forgettably by. Then the lady, incredibly, got married, and her place was taken by a dowdy beetle-browed woman who threw them into confusion by telling them not to sit up so straight. She said it was not natural – like the Pope she took from their hands and replaced with Shakespeare.

Harriet looked into *Hamlet* with mixed feelings. It was a play-book, and from it rose the heat and babble of the company and the road – all the things she felt to be blissfully far off. But the new mistress did not care for it as a play. 'Mere actors are not to be trusted with words such as these. This, *this*, is poetry.' She spoke of pity and terror and sublimity. The other girls smothered giggles: she was so mannish: Lord, such a fright. As for the Shakespeare, it was monstrous dry: they preferred their pillow-hidden novels. But Harriet found herself reluctantly wading into these dark waters. Sometimes the rhythm of the verse seemed to enter her and cause some inexpressible alteration, like the unplaceable change from having a headache to not having one: a lift, a waking. To her surprise and dismay, she wanted to weep at the death of Ophelia. She had never wept at anything that was not real: morality prodded her for it. But such sadness and beauty: she groped in perplexity, tight-throated.

> 'There is a willow grows aslant a brook
> That shows his hoar leaves in the glassy stream;
> Therewith fantastic garlands did she make
> Of crowflowers, nettles, daisies, and long purples
> That liberal shepherds give a grosser name,
> But our cold maids do dead men's fingers call them.'

'If you please, ma'am, I don't follow.' The girl's face shone with solemn mischief. 'What does it mean by the "grosser name"?'

The beetle brows came down. 'There are certain references in the Bard that must for the sake of propriety be omitted.'

Just as they thought: there was a soft fizz of glee. Harriet felt cheated. She wanted all of it – even as she recoiled. For she knew there would be eager talk in the bedrooms tonight, talk of the sort she did not like. Older girls lifted their shifts and disclosed alarming transformations. Harriet, colouring, withdrawing, had been called a prig. Was it that? It appeared to her a simple practical matter of dislike. When her breasts began to swell, she felt encumbered: she preferred the easy, serviceable body of the child, not this tricksy matter of weights and balances. When her first menses came, early, she had learned enough from the bedroom conversations to know what was happening. But she said nothing, except to Mrs Turner, to whom she had excruciatingly to apply for clouts.

'You saw your mother at Christmas, did you not? One would have supposed she had the foresight to make the appropriate preparations.' But this was said with no more asperity than usual. Mrs Turner was a dour, square-chinned matron who took a dim view, or a cool view, of the world in general. Her one enthusiasm was the war in Europe, which she followed with a strategist's attention. Every Saturday she would have the girls to tea in her peeling parlour, where she would inform them in detail of the latest successes or, presently, reverses of Bonaparte. Who was, she notified them, Antichrist. They listened, mesmerized by the way she rubbed her hands up and down her thighs while she talked.

It did not prevent her teaching the language of the Antichrist, French: no young ladies' academy could do without it. This was Harriet's worst subject: it all sounded to her as a meaningless gasping and honking, like a cold in the head. Mrs Turner shrugged. 'Never mind, Miss Smithson. I do not anticipate that a knowledge of French will be absolutely required of you in your future life.'

Meaning, meaning, of course, that her parents were players and so in time would she be. How little you know, Harriet thought. One or two of her schoolfellows were well-bred enough to sneer at her theatrical connections, but most found the very idea thrilling and pumped her for colourful stories.

They were disappointed. All far away: all gone.

There were the family visits: also a couple of short holidays spent with them in Waterford or Cork. Her father had grown more florid and loud, not so much entering a room as arriving like a coach-and-four. And yet there was a stretched look about him: a man eking himself out, spreading his substance thin. Her mother was growing stout and a little deaf, though it might have been deafness of an elective sort, to shut out unpleasantness. Joseph sprawled and put up long booted legs everywhere, permanently cross: the world affronted him. Harriet tingled with relief when they were gone: tingled, too, with inevitable guilt. Not that they were displeased with her. She was, as her mother said, such a boon to little Anne.

Her sister had been placed again with a nurse in Waterford, and so Harriet was able to see her on Sundays and half-holidays; and soon, when she was old enough, Anne was to attend Mrs Turner's school. And Harriet was to Anne as the rising and the setting of the sun. Harriet was perfectly sure she did not merit this adoration, but that was beside the point: what mattered was the need, and she must satisfy it. Often after a long time spent with Anne her hands would actually feel empty, while her mind filled with the question: What am I for?

Then: a comet, revolution. This.

'Girls, stop a moment. Observe Miss Smithson. Again, please, Miss Smithson. There – *that* is the way.'

Mrs Turner, presiding over dancing and deportment. Harriet had never been very attentive to these arcane mysteries: elegance, a graceful carriage, the correct way to enter a room. But now the other girls are to draw back while she walks, turns, curtsies, adopts the first position of the cotillion, second position . . .

But no, *don't* observe Miss Smithson, because that is precisely what she has always dreaded: the eyes raking her, the exposure. Yet Mrs Turner must be obeyed.

'Now observe the fluency. The true bend at the waist – not like a pair of compasses. *That* is the style.'

And now they will all hate me, thinks Harriet with resignation. But nothing can dim the force of this revelation. It comes from nowhere, absolutely unexpected: for who ever thinks about the way they move? It occurs to her that she does have a habit when out walking of giving a little cough to warn people that she is behind them: they never seem to hear her approach.

Call it a gift, then – but a gift like some unwieldy piece of furniture delivered to a little house: the question is what to do with it.

Well: perhaps this.

Enjoy it.

It may be among the list of sinful things, this solitary revelling in the self, but no matter. Creep down with your noiseless tread to the big schoolroom, swept and empty in the late summer evening: position yourself before the long looking-glass where the cold maidens are drilled in deportment: bow, turn, sweep, catch your own eye by surprise, study the infinite play of expressions. Play. Perform.

Only one thing can break the spell. The thought of Anne, and how she will appear in this mirror.

At first, when Anne joined the school, it was not as Harriet had thought or feared. The girls stared, but were not unkind. After all, Anne was not pretty or significant: one could feel rather pleased with oneself next to her, with that back, that teetering limp, that goblin face. And Mrs Turner excused her dancing and deportment.

But there was a walled garden behind the house, shaded by apple-trees, where every afternoon the younger girls were permitted to run about. Anne, who could not run about, nevertheless insisted on going there. Naturally Harriet went with her. Keen scholar of expressions as she was, she did not know how to interpret the look in Anne's great eyes as they followed the other girls, leaping and skipping. She could think only of the hunter's glare of a cat: birds on the lawn.

When it came, Harriet was ready.

'Poor little Humpty,' a girl cried, twirling by the bench where they sat, 'she can't play with us.'

'My sister's name is Miss Anne Smithson,' Harriet said sharply. 'I know *your* name, and I think you would not like it if I called you by a nasty one instead. And I can think of one, you know, very easily.'

But Anne rose to her own defence: rose screaming, furious, and deadly. 'Get away, little beast!' she yelled in the other girl's face. 'You tell lies and I know, and what will happen to you is your nose will drop off and your teeth will rot and your eyes will fall out and you'll *die*.'

The girl trembled and melted away. Anne turned her face to Harriet, with the old worshipful look restored. 'Harriet, can we play a game?'

Those sedentary games: chore and challenge. Harriet's imagination must conjure scenarios and narratives, settings and characters, and integrate them with that walled garden and stuccoed house. Such a pressure of make-believe sometimes left her exhausted. And she must never break the interior rules. They could spend years as prisoners of the wicked baron, and they could at last escape by poisoning the gaoler, and where they got the poison from was Harriet's pocket, and she had had it all the time but had forgotten about it, and they could pacify the baron's mastiff with a mutton-bone from, yes, why not?, the same pocket – but Harriet went wrong in the flight from the castle, which involved them running full pelt to the drawbridge.

'I *can't* run,' Anne moaned. And though Harriet tried to suggest that in the game they were not themselves, and could do anything, it was no use. Anne presented her with a silence of stony wisdom. You could never be anything but yourself.

Couldn't you . . . ? The games, wearisome as they often were, stirred something new and perturbing in Harriet, whose emotions had always been clear-cut, solid: this was formless. It went nowhere. It was, she supposed, longing.

'Let's play pretend.' When Harriet's invention ran out, Anne would gamely make this beginning. 'Let's pretend . . . let's pretend we're witches.'

'No.' Harriet tried to snatch back her sharpness. 'No, please, that's . . . I'm too old for that game, really, Anne. Something else.' Not the witches, even now. Especially now. There was too much of the witch in Anne's bony face, too much of the real showing like a skull through the skin of make-believe. She was beginning to see that pretending was a serious business.

That instant convulsion of fury sent Anne hurling against her, feebly slapping. 'You're horrid, Harriet, horrid. I hate you.'

'Well, it doesn't matter, because I still love you.' And this was true. It had nothing to do with being lovable. It had nothing to do, Harriet decided, holding her squirming rioting sister against her altered body and watching the sun spear and flood the apple-trees, it had nothing to do with anything.

'I may positively assert that this is the end,' declared Mrs Turner, dogmatic slippered foot on foot-stool, newspaper in hand, 'the end of Bonaparte.' Rub, rub. 'The Antichrist has been comprehensively defeated by a combination of armies in the vicinity of Leipzig. No phoenix, I think, may arise from such ashes.' The parloured young ladies stifled their yawns in seed-cake. It was October 1813, and it was all monstrous tedious, and Harriet, lounging with new-found confidence on the *chaise-longue*, was as absent as any: thinking only of the nuisance of tomorrow, when her father's company were to arrive in Waterford to give a short season at the theatre. Not thinking of downfalls and phoenixes, certainly not in relation to herself, not at all. We never do.

3

'It's the wrong season.' William Smithson slammed his palm down on the table. Probably he only meant to tap it, but the brandy-bottle at his elbow was having its effect. 'The wrong season entirely. Summer's the time for Waterford. Now the town's half empty. And the half that are left are senseless brutes.' He glared at his wife, who was mending a costume by the light of a tin candlestick. 'The wrong season, I tell you.'

'You've chosen the wrong pieces,' said Joseph: big as his father now, high-coloured and high-strung. 'No one wants *Venice Preserved* here. They're too genteel, or think they are. They'll only suffer it if you throw grand duds at them. Scenes and machines. Look at our execution scene. The wheel is a carriage-wheel. You couldn't break a rabbit on it. No wonder they laughed.'

'When you have led a company for as long as I have, you may perhaps pronounce on these matters,' his father growled. He tried to focus his red-rimmed eyes on the papers in front of him. 'I swear the ticket-takers are swindling us . . . The piece is sound, sir, absolutely sound. Why, when I gave it for my benefit in Dublin—'

'That was Dublin. And that was years ago.' Very young, Joseph, very merciless. Not that he was exulting: it was only the pleasure of picking at a scab. 'It goes on too long, it drags. Especially without cuts. And especially when you keep trying for points.'

'Shut up. Shut your mouth, you bastard.'

Said almost despairingly, as if the nagging voice were inside his head and not across the other side of the room. Once, Harriet thought, her father would have got up and struck Joseph: but time passed, time wrought. Joseph folded his arms, watched his father dispassionately. She spoke, partly to dispel the poisonous silence.

'I'm sorry, what are points?'

'Speciality of an *older* school of acting,' Joseph informed her. 'Whenever you see a grand speech coming, stomp to the forestage and make a great meal of it. Strike a pose. The audience are supposed to applaud. Supposed to, mind. You'd learn these things, Harriet, if you'd put aside your precious sensibility for once and come and see us.'

'I thought it was Papa you were quarrelling with, not me,' Harriet said, surprising herself. But she felt so peculiarly older, translated to this new plane where you said and did things without the continual dread of consequences. Perhaps it was being out of the schoolroom – Mrs Turner had granted her and Anne a week's holiday to be with their family – and perhaps, too, the lateness of the hour. It was past one in the morning, and she realized she had never before been up at this time.

'It will be better tomorrow,' her father said, pushing away the papers. '*She Would and She Would Not* is no masterpiece, God knows, but it always pleases.'

'It does if Hippolyta is young and spicy and pretty,' Joseph said relentlessly, 'but unfortunately our Hippolyta is Miss Cornwell, who looks ready only for tea and penny whist.' He paced up and down the room, which did not take long: these were very cramped lodgings, and while Anne shared her parents' bed Harriet was having to sleep on the sofa, which smelt of unspeakable things. 'We need a change. Fresh pastures.'

'"Fresh fields, and pastures new",' his father corrected him. 'Milton.'

'You see?' threw out Joseph, vaguely but with venom. Old, old. 'Why don't we cross over to Bristol, the West Country? Be done with Godforsaken Ireland.'

'Godforsaken Ireland, as you call it,' said his father, 'is where we have a name.'

'I know. That's the trouble.'

William Smithson held his great head, the head of a seedy caged lion, and began to laugh. 'My dear boy,' he rumbled appreciatively, 'if only you could be so amusing on stage, we would not be in such trouble.'

An unexpected victory over the young cub: Joseph turned scarlet and stormed out of the room. Good at that, Harriet noted.

Her mother yawned and stretched, as if tired by a long, pleasant chat.

'Things always look better in the morning,' she remarked. 'I'm for bed. Oh, is this the only candle?'

'It would seem likely,' Mr Smithson said mordantly.

'I'll leave it then. I can make do. Don't tire yourself sitting up, my dear: remember the morning rehearsal.'

'How could I forget?' He sat back and stared at Harriet. '"Tomorrow, and tomorrow, and tomorrow, Creeps in this petty pace from day to day . . ." Shakespeare, my dear. I doubt you read Shakespeare, at Mrs Turner's?' He did not wait for an answer. 'Well, how goes it there? I am a shocking papa, I know, I have hardly asked how you do. Mrs Turner gives a good report of you . . .' He looked wanderingly around him, as if he had just woken up. 'Apologies for the quarters, by the by. Best that could be managed.'

'I do very well, thank you, Papa. Tell me, is the company not thriving?' Exciting, too, this directness, as if anything could be said, any door flung open.

'We are a little pinched. Receipts are—' He stopped, as if there were simply no word for what receipts were. 'But we have weathered worse storms. I will be candid. The heart of the matter is, *I* am a little stale of late. There is a want of tone, of elasticity. Begging my infallible son's pardon, it is *not* the piece, which is as strong as a horse. Let me give you a little: you shall judge.' He stood up, stretched out a hand. '"Tell me why, good Heaven, Thou mad'st me what I am, with all the spirit, Aspiring thoughts and elegant desires That fill the happiest man? Ah! rather why Didst thou not form me sordid as my fate, Base-minded, dull, and fit to carry burdens? Why have I sense to know the curse that's on me? Is this just dealing, Nature?"'

His trembling, outstretched hand closed at last on the brandy-bottle. He started, and for a long time did not cease, to cry.

'Good God,' Joseph said, coming upon her in the wings the next morning, 'so someone does listen to what I say. Harriet the Puritan has come to see us at our devil's work.'

'I've come,' Harriet said. 'Nothing to do with you.'

He followed her gaze to the half-shadowed stage, where the Young Lady, Miss Cornwell, was attempting to be playfully innocent. The strain was evident.

'Pitiful, isn't it?' he said, in an undertone. 'Moderate the gestures, madam, for God's sake, and stop addressing the sky. We're not at Drury Lane, alas. Of course you know, sister, you would judge the effect much better from the pit.'

'It would be too dark to judge anything, as you only use full lighting for the dress.'

'Learning, aren't you?'

She ignored him. She was quietly absorbing her own victory, and registering its limits. She was in a theatre. Her nostrils twitched with the remembered smells. What she had shunned was all about her, yet here she stood securely with her feet on the gritty boards: no crumbling bridge, no chasm beneath. Finger of disappointment pressing her. There must be something more, or why had it always mattered so?

The wardrobe-mistress thrust a bulldog face at them. 'Where's Mr Smithson?'

'Lord knows.' Joseph groaned. 'He said he had to go somewhere. He'll be back. Well, Harriet, what is your opinion of these our revels? Hell, I'm sounding like Father.'

'I confess I have never seen anyone who was thinking show it by gripping their temples and walking up and down,' she heard herself say. 'When you're thinking, you don't tend to do anything, because you're thinking.'

'What a relief. I was suspecting you of being some sort of changeling, but now I know you are of the true theatrical blood, because you're being a cat.' Joseph measured her startled expression, then smiled. 'Of course, you're absolutely right.'

That night her father went to bed mellow and genial: *She Would and She Would Not* had gone over pretty well, all things considered, the afterpiece had been much applauded, and there was another bottle of brandy. From somewhere in Harriet's malodorous sofa-tossed dreams there came a ferocious knocking. It was a door: it was morning: the door was theirs.

'I shall most certainly not see them.' Her father – sight to be avoided after first unavoidable glance, blue jowls and flowered banyan and pale hairy ankles beneath – was firm with the carpenter's daughter. 'We shall meet at rehearsal. Tell them – tell them there is no need for an earlier colloquy.' Harriet's mother translated. The carpenter's daughter muttered away down the stairs. Something wrong, something wrong like the smell of burning: coffee was drunk in an air of pretence, everyone trying not to sniff.

Then Joseph lounged in late, demanding: 'Who was that making the infernal racket at the door?'

'Some of the company,' his father said, eyes on his coffee.

'What the devil did they want at this hour? They should be getting ready for dress.'

Mr Smithson slid out of his seat. 'Harriet,' he said brightly, 'will you come a walk with me? Down to the quays, I think. Take a chestful of air, expand the pipes.' He was out of the door and down the stairs with surprising speed. Harriet grimaced at her wild hair in the looking-glass, flung on her pelisse and followed. So did Joseph's sardonic stare.

'Ah! Waterford has its charms as a prospect, if not a financial one,' her father said, striding on. 'I am informed by one who knows that yonder bridge is no less than eight hundred feet across. And I am beguiled by visions of our delightful Irish somehow building it – getting half-way across, perhaps, and then cheerfully remarking, "Well, that will do . . ."' Harriet, you have lived largely retired from the world, but I fancy you are not ignorant of its ways. You observe: heavens, I notice the way you observe.' He stopped and rested his unsteady hands on the wall overlooking the harbour. He would not look at her. 'My dear, it is entirely possible that you will not be able to stay at Mrs Turner's for the next term. In fact it is profoundly possible. There is a shortfall . . . a matter of fees.'

Harriet turned this over. She found some regret, not much surprise, and a measure of fear: so there was to be another new chapter. What was in this one, and would life always be so inscrutable? But her chief emotion was pity: for her father's embarrassment at having to tell her this, for the staggerings of a man obliged, even for a little time, to throw away the crutches of untruth.

'Of course you are pretty well grown now, and schooling must end at some time. In my day it was not uncommon for girls to come out at fourteen – I know your mother had her first ball-dress at fourteen, and—'

'I shall be fourteen in March, Papa.'

He jumped, as if he had forgotten she was there. 'Quite so. We shall – we shall have a party.' He seemed to find something so fatuous in those words that his eyes bulged, stricken, as if the tears of last night would spring again. He said, in a bark: 'I wish to God you would reproach me.'

'Well. It's true I thought I would be staying at Mrs Turner's a little longer. But I am not ignorant, as you say, Papa: I do know about the money troubles.'

There were coarse shouts from a waterside tavern behind them. Her father pursed his lips fastidiously. 'Pretty situation for a gentleman born. Perhaps that's my trouble. Too much care for the *art* of the stage. And I spend too much, on flats and built-stuff and rehearsal time, and all the public wants is a vulgar farce and a jig by a woman in tights. Also I am not a good father, and I am not saying that so you will contradict me and make me feel better about myself. Consolation cheaply bought.' Now he looked a little nonplussed at his own candour. 'I think theatre people generally are indifferent parents. Family life needs a centre, and we have no centre. We roll about like marbles on a table-top. Forgive me, my dear, I'm liverish, and that always makes me talk like a sensible man instead of a fool. I shall be my usual self later. In the same spirit, I would like to know that you do not despise me or what I do.'

'The Reverend Dr Barrett once said to me that men do many worse things than stepping on a stage.'

He looked at her with hangdog curiosity. 'Do you still miss him?'

'I often think of him,' she said, after a moment. 'Will always love him, or his memory. But I'm not—' She sought a word, and found one peculiarly right. 'I'm not bereft. On the other hand, I do wonder what is to become of me.'

'Get used to that, my dear Harriet. That continues until – well, I won't say the end. I'm not that liverish.' He shook himself in grim humour. 'You needn't wonder that, or fear it, you know. This is another thing I didn't mean to say, but you could do well – you could do very well in the family profession.'

The flinch was very nearly, not quite physical. 'No, no. I don't – well, I don't know anything about it.' Something said to drown the shrillings of alarm.

'Don't you? What, for instance?'

She cast about. 'Built-stuff. You talk about that, but I don't know what it means . . .' And don't want to. Yet she waited for the answer.

'A rather crude expression, simply signifying pieces of carpentry that form movable parts of the scene: columns, banks and whatnot. Ours is rather meagre nowadays . . . But these things are easily learned. Not so the other things, the intangibles. Voice. Mrs Turner tells me how admirably you recite. You have presence, stature, grace, expressiveness of feature—'

'Don't – Papa, please don't.'

He studied her. 'Your mother is an actress, Harriet. And you surely don't think her anything less than a lady.'

Unworthy: it flashed between them. 'I've told you, Papa, it's not a question of shame. I simply do not think I could possibly . . .' Well, she had wandered blindly into this new place of honesty: why not open her eyes? 'I'm afraid.'

His scalp lifted: he seemed to find those words so enormously telling that he was swamped with responses. But before he could choose a reply, his name was called. Bellowed.

'Smithson! Mr William Smithson, you bastard!'

The voice was Mr Cadell's. The noisemakers in the tavern were members of the company, and now they came spilling out, the Juvenile Lead at their head: staggering, some of them, but still making for her father with some purpose.

'A deputation,' her father murmured.

'Mr William bastard Smithson, most celebrated actor-manager-bastard in the south of Ireland.' Mr Cadell made a grovelling bow. 'How goes it in the land of the cheating, swindling, lying bastards, hey, Mr S, how goes it?'

Her father drew himself up. 'You are drunk, Mr Cadell. So are you all, it seems. A curiosity, as you should be at dress. I suggest you go directly to the theatre, and we'll say no more about it.'

'And we'll say no more about it!' parodied Mr Cadell, very chesty and *pomposo*. 'But that's just the trouble, you see, my dear sir, no one ever does say anything *about* it, and so you get *away* with it.' Passers-by were stopping to gape: Mr Cadell appealed to them. 'D'you know him? Sir, madam? The celebrated Smithson, currently to be seen in the celebrated farce *Venice Preserved*, not that it was writ as a farce, you understand, but under the celebrated bastard Smithson things take a different turn—' Her father made to move away, but Mr Cadell stepped in front of him. 'Come, my dear sir, you're not shy of an audience, surely? Thought you'd be glad of one, they are so shockingly hard to come by for this pissbegotten company—'

'A company that will dispense with your services, Mr Cadell, after this exhibition.'

'Ah, but it won't, you see, because there goes your Pierre and you know well you've no one else to take the part, isn't it so?'

'If Mr Cadell goes, I go too.' The Old Man, Mr Partington: he looked grim and ill with drink. 'I've stood by you before, Mr Smithson. I've notions of loyalty. But this is too much.'

'Come, come,' said her father, reaching for heartiness, 'if you have a legitimate grievance, then I shall hear it, but the street is not the proper place. Let's adjourn to the theatre—'

'The street is the very place!' cried Mr Cadell, his voice rising to a new note, fluty and perilous. 'For one thing it is where we shall all end up under your direction, my dear sir, and for another it is the perfect place to *reveal* you. I'd say unmask you, but do you know what's under the mask?' He gestured to the appreciative little crowd that had gathered: a play without buying tickets. 'Another mask!'

'Better go home, my dear,' her father whispered to her.

'No.' She put her arm through his.

'The grievance, well, let us say grievances, and I would tire your patience if I were to enumerate them all, but how about not being *paid* for two months? Does that not strike you as a legitimate grievance? And on top of that—'

'Dudded,' said Mr Partington. 'That's what rankles, Mr Smithson. That's why we're not at dress, because there is no dress. It's a scandal.'

'Dudded, in the picturesque language of the profession, means deprived of one's costumes, usually because one's esteemed manager has taken them to the pawnbroker's,' shouted Mr Cadell, whirling, strutting.

'A temporary difficulty – requiring the raising of a little capital . . . a little . .' Her father's lips moved: the lines would not come. His face was all cavernous shadows. Old, old.

'So I have nothing to wear, and very soon I shall have nothing to eat.' The waywardness of drink took Mr Cadell from flamboyant irony to fury in a second. He loomed, towered. 'So tell me, Smithson, what I have to lose by breaking your bastard head for you?'

'Please, Mr Cadell, stop, for God's sake. You don't know what you're doing. Please. I know you're angry, I know you feel badly used, but consider a moment. You have nothing to lose, but surely nothing to gain. He's my father and I love him and I can't bear to see him abused – but I know he has made mistakes, and he knows it too.' This was Harriet, or someone who had taken possession of her: stepping up to shield her father, turning open-armed to the drunken stares, pitching her voice above the noise. 'And you, Mr Partington – everyone – I know you have been loyal. My father knows it, and he truly appreciates it – don't you, Papa?'

'None better,' he said huskily.

'And if he does not express it, perhaps that's because he has so many things to think of – and I know this sounds as if I'm excusing him. Well, I am, and I'm asking you to excuse him too.' She had managed to fix Mr Cadell's eye. His fleshless jaws worked away. 'Even if he sometimes does bad things, he is not a bad man. And if you'll go to the theatre, I know he will sit down with you and talk of these matters, and – well, that's all I can say. I don't know how they can be solved. Only not this way. Please.'

Mr Partington grunted and wiped a hand across his face. 'Well, begging your pardon, I've got to go and be sick. Come on, Cadell, you've said your piece.'

Mr Cadell resisted, for a moment, the firm tug on his arm. 'Hiding behind a slip of a girl, Smithson. I salute you.' He gave another sardonic bow. 'You've surpassed yourself.' But he went, with the rest of them.

'Very charmingly done, my dear.'

Her father had maintained a perspiring silence throughout the walk back to their lodgings, while Harriet felt peculiarly faint: as if a load of bricks had crashed beside her and missed her by inches. Now, on the doorstep, he turned to look at her: placed his hands on her shoulders. 'Very charmingly done indeed.'

'But I meant it, Papa.'

His smile was worldly, fond, unreachable. He turned to go in with a spring in his step. 'That's what made it so charming.'

It was, if you like, seduction.

Harriet, along with Anne, was taken out of school and rejoined the company on the road, but her father said nothing more about her taking up the family profession. He seemed merely glad to get out of Waterford in one piece. A moderately successful benefit night and the sale of her mother's jewellery had kept them solvent, or less insolvent than before. The costumes were taken out of pawn. The actors' wages were now only one month in arrears. Mr Cadell was quiet: a marked man.

There was something Harriet could do, if she didn't mind: help with the copying of parts. She wrote such a fair hand . . . Then there was Joseph's memory, his great weakness as a player: it would be a great help if she could aid him with learning his lines. So she sat up late with the play-book on her knee while Joseph faltered and cursed. She was usually at least a page ahead of him. The lines simply ranged themselves in her mind, neatly as the beads of an abacus.

It was, if you like, seduction, if the essence of seduction is that you are not aware of being seduced, but think you are doing just what you want to do. And as audiences at Kilkenny were sparse, and there were more doctors' bills for poor ailing Anne, Harriet wanted to help in whatever way she could: she wanted to.

'I wish we had something fresh to offer them,' Joseph said, sighing over the receipt-book. 'We need fresh blood.' It sounded like butchery. Harriet shivered, and went back to watching the rehearsal, and fretting at the limp outcries and fumbling business.

The play-books changed to her, or she changed to them. Among them were several pieces of Shakespeare: *Romeo and Juliet*, *Hamlet*, *As You Like It*, others. They were her father's favourites: he knew them and touched them like old love-letters. At night he liked to read them by the fireside. This was not the running-through of cheap farces: this was reverence and rite. Harriet, already smitten at school, joined him. She remembered the taste of that liquor, and she wanted more, and in no time she was a toper.

'Shall we have *Romeo* tonight, Harriet? Act Three? I'll read the Nurse. There's the fiery-footed-steeds speech – oh, that's a jewel.'

> '*Give me my Romeo; and, when he shall die,*
> *Take him and cut him out in little stars,*
> *And he will make the face of heaven so fine*
> *That all the world will be in love with night*
> *And pay no worship to the garish sun.*'

'Sweetly done – sweetly done, my dear. It's in the rhythm, you see? Like the pulse in the wrist. You feel it and don't feel it.'

They were very comfortable with each other, Harriet and her father, on these evenings, when they were not themselves: strange. He read Romeo with tender restraint. When she watched him in the theatre, he shouted and ranted. If only, she thought obscurely, the fireside could be brought to the stage. At night she dreamed Shakespeare, was not even sure she did not recite Juliet in her sleep.

It was, if you like, seduction.

And soon it is becoming part of you, soon it is as if she has always known these things. The etiquette of entrances and exits, the complex chess-moves of stage directions: up stage, down stage, left centre back, down right centre, prompt side, opposite prompt, scissor cross. The dressing-room partitioned by chalk-marks on the floor, and the Walking-Gentlemen playing dice and the Heavy Woman opening her powder-box and drawing out, like hairy delicacies, the mouseskin eyebrows that make her face, and the Singing Chambermaid suckling her baby: skin-bloom on her breast, white-lead on her cheeks. Smell of wax from the lighting-store: smell of steam and moth-balls as the laundress plies the iron on ruffs and brushes out brocades. Harriet wanders among it all, trying to remember other things, entranced, reluctant. Is this what they mean by 'in the blood'? Fresh blood. One of the Walking-Gentlemen waylays her behind a flat and tries to tell her things about her body: her sharp reaction leaves him quite unfazed, as if he has merely asked her what the time is. From the wings she watches Miss Cornwell making heavy nothing of the grief of Lady Anne in *Richard the Third*, and quietly fumes. Has the woman never wept? Doesn't she know what weeping feels like? Lady Anne keeps making gestures with a large handkerchief, and Harriet longs to snatch it from her.

But when you have got it, Harriet, what will you do with it?

'Well, no one else is by, my dear, it's just you and me. Mother and daughter, like a pair of old gossips – I declare it's thoroughly pleasant!' Mrs Smithson has grown more cosy, vague, sentimental and obliging as she puts on flesh: she is like a warm cushion that someone has been sitting on. 'So just be easy. Let's try it, and see how you go on. Lucy is a smallish part, but it has a pretty effect. I played it many a time in my prentice days, though I'm only fit for Mrs Malaprop now. Remember the nice business with the books – only don't drop 'em. Lord knows, I did that too.'

For a time a haze of reminiscence veils Mrs Smithson while her daughter, meaning nothing, meaning only to entertain a possibility like a remote relative who will stay the night and be gone, enacts the maid in *The Rivals* behind the closed door of a panelled wormy inn-room on the Wexford road. But the haze lifts, for there is a professional inside the genial dumpling, and the cushiony eyes spark and take notice.

'Dear me,' her mother chuckles at last, 'I shall have to retire.' And laughs, wonderingly.

Gone, now, the fireside evenings, the convivial sipping of Shakespearean wine. Harriet and her father stand in a new relation. He trains and drills, she balks and resents. They hate each other cordially, while remarkable things happen, hardly remarked amid the tiredness, the ferocity, the acrid dust of the threshing-floor where the grain of her vocation is laboriously beaten out. They do it for hours.

'Breath, Harriet, remember the breath. Breathe, damn it. Stop hunching. *Breathe.*'

'I am breathing. How do you suppose I'm alive? Though, Lord knows, I wish I wasn't.'

'Save the self-pity, my dear, for your début: you'll need it then.'

'What début? I'm not going to do it, I hate it. Papa, I can't do it.'

'I'm well aware of that, God help me. Again, second scene. Cross, pause, then above the couch.' Snaky hiss of impatience. 'Behind, it means behind, you should know that.'

'It's stupid.'

'It is not alone in that. So. Now, opening speech, and breathe, in God's name breathe . . . Better: better.'

'. . . Papa, why am I doing this?'

'Because you can, Harriet. Stop crying. Oh, come here. Because, my dear girl, hush, don't you see? You can.'

Small part in a half-hour afterpiece, experimentally staged in the yard of the inn where they are staying. So far she has only pitched her voice into empty theatres during rehearsal-time: now comes a new discovery to be assimilated. A mass of people soaks up your voice and then throws it flatly back at you. Harriet has to think on her feet, but that is life now: her days are a bruising tumble of discoveries. Twenty minutes in, and she has learned that the voice must go over their heads, so that it falls on them like rain. A growling old fear dies without a whimper: the faces watching. If you could see them all, the terror would flatten you, but that's just it: you can only see one face at a time, and if your eye does alight on one, that is the one you must speak to, convince: as if you were seated by a fireside.

End, and applause, and her father niggling and fault-finding in her ear; and yet his face glows, he is drinking her in. Harriet wanders about, numb: it's like when you've been lying on your arm and it turns into a dead tingle, except this is her whole body, all her senses – there is dimness, voices fade and flutter. Her father is extolling the family genius: blood, blood. He says something about a duck to water, or water off a duck's back – she is too weary to make sense of anything, can only sink, sink into a chair with the water bubbling up around her.

And now it is Dublin, and it is a soft, light afternoon in May of 1814, and events are rushing downhill towards us. In the city chop-houses mercantile men scan the damp newsprint and chew over the new truth: Napoleon is deposed and – surely safely – deposited on Elba. Time for a new world. Harriet, sick, pacing backstage, trying to remember how to breathe, thinks of Mrs Turner, with her campaign maps and her thigh-rubbings: the old world, dying. The playbills are printed, the costume subjected to last-minute pinnings and prinkings. Now there is only the new world to be ushered into being: only now the delivery, the straining birth. In Crow Street the Theatre Royal has opened its doors, and the footmen have crowded in to save their masters' seats, and Mr Smithson's company, by permission of the royal patentee, are to present Mr Reynolds's comedy *The Will*, featuring the début performance of Miss Smithson in the role of Albina Mandeville.

Backstage everything is going wrong. There is a tear in one of the flats, the carpenter has gone missing, Mr Cadell is drunk, and Mr Smithson is roaring at everyone. In other words, normality.

Harriet sits before her mirror, and inhabits her circle of candlelight. Another discovery: now, she wants her mother. But Mrs Smithson is in the green-room still striving to pacify Anne, who has had an apocalyptic fit of temper on finding that here at last is a time and place in which she cannot follow her sister. Anne concludes these rages by curling into a hedgehog ball that she maintains, silent, stricken, long beyond the usual sulks of children. Harriet stroked her hair, whispered to her: but she had to leave at last. There are cobweb touches of guilt: Harriet brushes them away, thinking, After all, I am doing it for her, for the family, to help and save, to keep us going. But she knows she is not doing it for any of these things – if she is going to do it at all.

For there is still the stage, and as she pictures it, vast and rippled with candlelight, she sees not boards but water, murmuring and hungry. How can she emerge from the wings into that without floundering, falling, going under?

Drowning.

There is only one way. She cannot frame it as such in her mind, for the mild shade of her guardian will not let her blaspheme; but if the curtain that is about to rise reveals a stage of water, she will simply have to walk on it.

EPISODE IN THE LIFE
OF AN ARTIST

First Movement: Reveries, Passions

Largo – Allegro agitato ed appassionato assai

Eight hundred miles away, across two seas, and about an hour later, Dr Louis Berlioz descends the steps of the *mairie* in the little French town of La Côte St André and wonders about the mind.

Specifically, he wonders about the mind of the man beside him – whether he has got one. Dr Berlioz has been awake for twenty-four hours, and though professionally accustomed to missing sleep, he is a little giddy with fatigue; also, after the stuffiness of the town-hall chamber, with the breath of cool sharp air that funnels down from the mountains and into his lungs. Which perhaps accounts for the way the man at his side swells and dances in his vision: a big, paunched man in white uniform, sash, cockaded hat, plume, boots, spurs, gloves, braid, tassels and whatnot: a man who momentarily becomes, to Dr Berlioz's weary eyes, a huge grotesque puppet, mouthing, mindless.

'It is necessary to be certain. You understand. It is necessary, always, to be certain. It is a difficult time. I understand. But you understand, it is necessary . . .' Perhaps it is partly the man's inadequate French that makes him sound like an automaton. But Dr Berlioz is too tired to be charitable, and inclines to the view that the man is an idiot.

'I must be certain, you understand. What pretty girls you have here.' Dr Berlioz cannot answer. The girl in question, hurrying across the dusky square on a late errand, is Cécile the baker's daughter, and as plain as a sparrow. 'Mind, it is not necessary for you to be proud of that. I have seen pretty girls everywhere. Not only in France.'

Dr Berlioz, though a proud man in many ways, is not proud of anything just now. As he has told the puppet, now shapeshifting back into a colonel in the Austrian army, he simply wants to go home. For the past month the white uniforms have been a familiar sight in the town. There are twenty thousand infantry and cavalry encamped on the plain below the slopes, and officers billeted on every house big enough to take them. The victor's privilege: the Emperor is deposed, the Allied armies are all over France, and now we must feed our enemies.

They are not so bad. There are grumblings about the exactions of money, food, and fodder; and the other day Monsieur Buffevent the mayor made to Dr Berlioz a quiet little joke about the neighing of the Austrians' horses, and how difficult it was to distinguish from their uncouth language. But the two officers quartered in Dr Berlioz's own house are thoroughly pleasant fellows, one of whom is busy carving a wooden rattle for the doctor's newborn daughter. (Please God spare her. This goes through Dr Berlioz's mind like an involuntary spasm, without belief. He is a rationalist, a free-thinker. Sometimes it seems like the freedom to despair.)

So, not so bad: if only the colonel would let him get back to that house, to embrace his anxieties, instead of detaining him with these nothings when their business is over.

'Well, this is talking of things past. Enough of that. Now we can forget, and live. It is necessary to live.'

'It is very necessary to live. Tell me, Colonel, have you any notion how long you will be here?'

'God knows. I am only a puppet.' Did he really say that? He did. Dr Berlioz feels dizzy again. The mountain breeze brings a whiff of roasting meat, from the encampment. It does not so much rouse his appetite – he suffers from poor digestion – as remind him that he must eat. It is necessary to eat to live. The colonel puffs out his pink cheeks. 'I can only say I hope it will be soon.'

In spite of everything, a lance of sympathy goes through Dr Berlioz. After all, he can go home eventually, but the Austrian officer has no real home here, and is, perhaps, lonely and bored. It is terribly hard, this habit of understanding: it takes something out of you.

And suddenly it is as if the colonel is bored with himself: with a click of his booted heels he stalks away. Dr Berlioz is free to walk home, and to think about the mind – as a distraction from thinking about the difficulties awaiting him there. His life has been occupied too, taken over by a regiment of troubles.

The mind: is it the same as the brain? A nice physiological point, which, as a very good doctor (studies in Grenoble and the Paris School of Medicine, several essay prizes from medical societies, manuscript of a medical treatise half finished in his desk drawer), as well as a free-thinker untrammelled by the dictates of religion, he is well qualified to ponder. He has seen human brains. He well remembers, as a student at a dissection, the egg-like lifting of the sawn skull-top; and the memory has been refreshed this very day. A young Austrian cavalryman, deeply drunk on the local Rocher liqueurs, mindlessly whipped his mount to a gallop down the steepest of La Côte St André's steep streets. He doffed his shako to a watching lady, lost his balance, and was hurled out of the saddle to shatter his fair head on the paving-stones. (Legacy of the Revolution, those paving-stones, the time of proud civic renewal: *ancien-régime* mud might have saved him.) Dr Berlioz was at the *mairie*, taking as a member of the council the turn of duty imposed by the occupiers, and was sent for at once. He did what he could, which was nothing. For several minutes the cavalryman blinked at Dr Berlioz, unpained, while the cream-red juice ran from the modest hole. End of a brain, or a mind.

Hence the long interview with the colonel, who must laboriously establish that this death of one of his soldiery was truly an accident and nothing more sinister. That was not likely, in La Côte St André. When the Austrians arrived they demanded that all weapons be handed over, but the resulting pile was not large. The townspeople – and for this Dr Berlioz respects them – have always been more attached to living than dying. Oh, he has seen the convulsions of the last twenty years shiver through them, like a mild fever: seen the medieval church half knocked to pieces during the Revolutionary atheism, then painstakingly put together again when Napoleon restored religion: has seen the young men go off to fight for the Emperor, plucked from dusty-cool farmsteads and mills to die in flyblown blazing Spain or stiffen in Russian snows. It is one of the interesting things about the mind, he considers, that it is so flexible, like a trusty old carpet-bag into which you can fit anything. Even the cautious folk of La Côte St André let off fireworks for Napoleon's birthday and celebrated his victories. Now they despise him. Dr Berlioz despises him too, for the mess he has made, though admitting his strategic genius: he does not except himself. His own mind is as baffling and contradictory as any.

Indeed, he would hazard that he has at least three minds. One: the doctor's mind, and the scholar's mind also, like a clean, shining instrument: moving easily amid the webs and symmetries of anatomy and the varied and capacious books of his library: an instrument for reaching conclusions. Two: the mind that must concern itself, often happily, sometimes painfully, with the transactions of living – with his property, from the meadows and vineyards and barns to the broken red tiles on the house roof, and above all with his family, those mysterious others who must be loved and balanced: picture a raft that he must navigate while ensuring that each of them distributes their weight evenly. Yet all of this is negotiable for Dr Louis Berlioz, who is a man of intelligence, firm character and generous principles, much respected in the district in a way the English sawbones never is: in Ireland, indeed, he might be a priest.

But the third mind, that is different. It discovers black canker in the sweet heart of a flower. It contemplates the woman he married and sees past the beauty and vivaciousness to long dry avenues of disappointment. It assesses La Côte St André in its pottering mountain-girt retirement and declares it not a home but a lair for an old toothless beast to lurk in. (Dr Berlioz is thirty-eight.) It prompts him sometimes to dose himself with opium so that, just for a while, he can simply exist in the world instead of clinging to it like a man on the outside seat of a bucketing coach. It proposes tremendous solutions: it invites the void, flirts with the idea that nothingness is better, somehow more *right*, than being. And this mind Dr Berlioz does not know what to do with. It ought to be cured, perhaps. He cures bodies: Uncle Claude, the *curé*, presumably cures souls: no good.

One day, he tells himself, it will all be resolved. There must come a day – at least one day – when old problems have been dealt with, and new ones have yet to arise, and there is a beautiful equilibrium. The trick is to recognize it when it comes.

Just short of his house – not so much large as substantial, like a solid reputation expressed in timber and stone – Dr Berlioz stops dead. His heart (he has seen human hearts too, handled their yielding, squidlike weight) misses a beat, then does a timpani roll before assuming a quickened rhythm. Someone is waiting for him outside the house. Even in shadow the slight high-shouldered form announces his son, Hector. There must be news and it must be bad. Hector steps forward into the light of the porch-lamp: Dr Berlioz almost stumbles into it.

'Hector, what is it? Tell me.'

'What is it? Oh, Papa, nothing — I just wanted to see you. I knew it was past time for you to come home, so I came out to wait. Pardon the impudence, but you look terrible, Papa. I'm sorry, did I give you a fright?'

Dr Berlioz shakes his head, taking deep breaths. 'You'll bring me to grey hairs, my boy.'

'Of course, what else are sons for?' Hector says cheerfully. 'They kept you very late — what was it? Another requisition of onions? I swear those Fritzes live on them.' Hector keeps still even less than most boys of eleven, so the lamplight attempts only a sketch: thin mobile planes of face beneath a profusion, a *bale* of light hair: eyes that jab. 'Monique has saved supper for you. And Monsieur Favre called, wanting, he said, some more of his usual for his little trouble in the basement. I nodded very wisely as if I knew what he meant. Actually, I do know what he meant.' A grin like a flash on a keen blade. '*And* Mama is much better tonight, and the baby has fed well. I thought you would like to know.'

'Thank heaven.' Another spasm. Just for now Dr Berlioz will happily concur in, if not believe, the idea of heaven. His new daughter has been sickly and his wife weak since the birth, and there has not been enough milk. Relief shakes him. He feels like weeping, as he often does, though he has not in fact shed a tear since he was younger than Hector. 'Thank you, Hector.'

'Heaven first, then me. I suppose that's fair. And now how are *you*, Papa?'

'Me?' The lamplight presents a sketch made from a different angle: his mother's fine nose, humorous, stubborn lips. Dr Berlioz feels such love he wonders how he will cope with it, like a sudden fortune that may prove a burden. 'My dear boy, I'm a doctor. No one is supposed to trouble about how *we* are.' He smiles: he has a long, grave, noble face, on which a smile appears like a confession: you almost feel you should not be seeing it. 'But I do very well, thank you, Hector. Only a little tired. Let's go in.' And he places a hand on his son's shoulder. The hand is heavy, but it is lightly borne. One of those moments of equilibrium, perhaps. The trick is to recognize it — before it goes.

*　　　*　　　*

Ask about the Berlioz family in their district of the province of Dauphiné (south-east, mountainous, rather curmudgeonly, with Geneva and Milan much nearer than Paris) and there will be general agreement. Dr Berlioz, to be sure: a fine man: Monsieur Tourine the turner will tell you how the doctor stayed at Madame Tourine's side when she had childbed-fever and never slept a wink, and brought her from the brink of death, and then waived his fee. And Monsieur Tourine's neighbour, whom everyone calls Old Hébert, and who totters on two sticks down to the Esplanade every evening to play an unbeatable game of *boules*, will tell you about the doctor's father: now in clovered retirement at Murianette but in his day a masterful bull of a man who made money, never missed church, and was marched to prison by the Revolutionaries singing psalms and reminding his servants to take care of the walnut-trees. Go down to Grenoble, the local metropolis, and you will find the name of Berlioz still elicits approving nods: yes, to be sure: lawyers, very much respected in the town, very much respectable. That, indeed, is the theme that is subject to numerous variations, but remains recognizable: a respectable family. God, yes.

Ask one or two of the sociable ladies of Grenoble who are acquainted with the Berlioz family, however, and the respect will be coloured with a regretful titter. Yes, Dr Berlioz, a perfectly admirable man, and with property not to be sneezed at: but, my dear, where he chooses to *live* – have you *seen* La Côte, and more to the point have you *seen* the bonnets there, or what pass for bonnets? And their menfolk will chuckle, swinging and cradling booted legs, and protest that, well, it is a healthy spot, after all, though heaven knows (they believe in heaven), they couldn't live there themselves. And the ladies will exchange significant glances, and wonder aloud how poor Finette can bear it.

'Finette, what are you doing?'

Madame Berlioz – Joséphine, Finette – descends the stairs for the first time since her *accouchement* and stands triumphantly in the doorway of her husband's study.

'What a beautiful day. Let's call it the first day of summer. Have you breakfasted, my dear? I shan't believe you if you say yes. And our guests? Heaven knows, there's nothing wrong with *their* appetite.'

'Sit down. No, don't sit down, go back to bed. You're not strong enough—'

'Not strong enough for half the things I want to do, but strong enough to make a start. I will sit down, though.' Madame Berlioz gives him her most brilliant smile. He notes the puffy post-natal flesh, the swollen feet pushed into kid slippers. His emotion is a sort of diagnostic tenderness edged with impatience. 'The little one has fed well again, my dear, and she's quite peaceful. Nancy's sitting with her. Do you know what she said? "Will she always be my little sister, or will she catch up with me one day?"' She laughs her high, breathy laugh. 'And I am coming to life again. God is doing wonderful things.'

Dr Berlioz has nothing to say to that. 'Rest, my dear. If the milk is coming, that's because you are resting.' But he does not expect to succeed. He knows that shining look. He wonders again about a wet-nurse, but breast-feeding has been orthodoxy since the Revolution: Frenchwomen must be so many she-wolves, suckling a new generation of Romuluses and Remuses. 'Is she sleeping? I should take a look at her—'

'She is sleeping, and entirely beautiful. And it's high time we made arrangements for her baptism. I've been thinking of godparents. One doesn't want to exclude Félix, but the soldier's life is so very un-settled . . .' Madame Berlioz pales and closes her eyes.

'There. This is what comes of getting up too soon—'

'Just a moment's faintness, my dear, it passes. I shall make myself far worse if I lie there fretting. I must see Monique about the laundry. I must be part of things again. Is the hay all cut?'

'It is,' says Dr Berlioz, sitting back in resignation. 'And it has all gone to feed the Austrians' horses. And we are desperately short of fodder.' Suddenly he wants to pour out all his troubles to his wife, to lean on her: but they are not like that. He has a sharp vision of their wedding day: white wintry light on the walls of the little hillside church near her father's house, enshrining a tall, slender, richly beautiful woman: the prep-aration of a great purpose. Momentarily, as she glided towards him, he was terrified by her otherness. It was wild as a footpad springing murder-ously at you out of the darkness: the urbane tongue wants to say: *There must surely be some mistake.* Now, eleven years and four children later, he finds he still wants to say it.

'Well, the Austrians cannot stay for ever. In fact, I have a feeling they will be gone very soon.' She claps her hands briskly. 'We shall weather the storm, my dear: God will provide. Now, tell me about Hector. He's all smiles when he comes up to see me, but there's something behind them.'

'Oh . . . I fancy it's his schooling. He doesn't say much about it, but I think he's bored. The seminary is not what it was. It seems there are only a few masters left, and all – all past their prime.' Besotted old priests, he wants to say. All his talk with his wife is marked by these omissions and ellipses: matrimonial censorship. 'I think it stifles him.'

'Well, well, my dear, all this shows how absolutely right I was to come down, because we have so many things to discuss.' She folds his hands in hers: hot, he notices, but not clammy. He realizes a part of his mind (which one?) has been bracing itself for childbed-fever, agony, even death. That's him: there is always a lookout in the crow's nest, scanning the horizon for disasters. Knowing this, he suddenly feels abject before his wife: before the faith he despises, the stubbornness of simplicity. He stoops and kisses her hands.

The thing about Joséphine Berlioz – convent-educated, provincially pious to her pretty fingertips, just made for the caressing of missals and rosaries and the primping of proprieties – is that she is often right. Soon afterwards, the Austrians strike camp and march away, leaving a blighted plain like the site of a vast picnic. The puppet-colonel comes to say goodbye to Dr Berlioz and – actually with tears in his eyes – to say what a great pleasure he has found in his acquaintance. The new baby is baptized: Adèle. And while Dr Berlioz carefully absents his thoughts from the ceremony, he is pleased to have it done: now he can give a name to one of his anxieties. Finette, out of bed and busying herself, grows stronger. The storm is weathered. And there is something behind Hector's smiles, and it is the monastery school: he is bored, restless.

'It isn't the Latin. It's the way they make it seem like – like sorting out a pile of dead leaves.' The blue eyes search his father's. Blue eyes, and this reddish-gold hair: somehow a tigerish combination, a face to be glimpsed in a thicket. 'How can you be interested in something if you feel nothing for it?'

Dr Berlioz only nods, judiciously. He is at his most reserved when he is most moved, and just now there are surges within him. A wave of memory confronts him with his young self, confronting his own father, declining to study dreary law any more. *Tell me,* his father demands in an advocate's boom, *tell me in what this disgust consists. I want to know, as it must therefore include* me *as well . . .*

'We must think of this, Hector,' Dr Berlioz says, and goes to consult the thermometer outside his study window, as he does every day. There is an element of ritual in this, though he is the most scientific and least superstitious of men: a suggestion that if you don't keep your eye on the temperature, it will go wild, freeze, boil: turn to storm.

By the way, ask the housemaid, Monique Néty, what she thinks of Madame Berlioz – if you can intercept her tireless figure somewhere between the laundry-attics and the root-cellars – and she will turn to you her splendidly broad-cheekboned face, like a mob-capped squaw, and as if you had asked her a question of stupefying obviousness, like what colour blood is, she will say: 'She is a saint, of course.'

At Grandfather Marmion's house in mountainside Meylan, where the Berlioz family always spends the late summer absorbing the benign air of the Isère valley, Dr Berlioz accompanies his father-in-law on a tour of the gardens – extensive, obligatory. Nicholas Marmion made money early as (inevitably) a lawyer and, widowed early too, his daughter safely disposed of in marriage, decided to retire early. Here, on the steep green slopes, he has cultivated a polite taste for poetry, some elderly mannerisms and, above all, his garden. He is eloquent in plantings and blackfly: a frail seedling frets him like an ailing child. Dr Berlioz, conscientious proprietor of a goodly parcel of farmland and vineyard, is interested in husbandry, but not that much. He respects his father-in-law, but not that much. He believes there is something fundamentally wrong with any man who devotes himself to one thing only: it makes you a miser of the personality.

Still, there is plenty of good sense in Nicholas Marmion, when his attention can be loosened from graftings and cuttings, and Dr Berlioz values these visits when family matters, important matters, can be aired and shaken and folded. They appeal to the sense of responsibility that ticks perpetually like a watch in his breast. In fact, you would have to go a long way to find a more thoroughly respectable sight than these two, doctor and lawyer, strolling the shrubberies in stiff cravats, discussing matters of the here and now with the far frosted peaks dreaming at the sky. And only in Dr Berlioz's mind is there a part (which?) that drifts up there with the cirrus and the gleam.

'They're gone,' says Dr Berlioz, of the Austrians, 'but they have left me out of pocket to the tune of one thousand two hundred francs. And others have fared worse – those who can least afford it.'

'Well, let's hope that's the end of it. I confess there was a time when my heart used to pound just at the name of the Emperor – dear, dear, old habits, Bonaparte, I mean – but after a time, one finds that the heart is simply not *meant* to pound all the time. The world couldn't go on. Regular rhythms are best. Look at nature. And look at that oleander – I swear it's not thriving . . .' Nicholas Marmion darts a shrewd, shadowed glance under plumy eyebrows, looking nothing like his daughter, the endlessly luminous Finette: Dr Berlioz cannot say why he finds that a relief. 'What, do you suspect that won't be the end of it?'

Dr Berlioz shrugs. 'Oh, everyone speaks well of the King, of course – never mind what they really think. *I* speak well of the King, not because I suppose him any sort of angel, but because the mere fact of him promises order and peace. The trouble is, I think people have grown used to not loving order and peace, and loving their opposite. They have been given this appetite, and if someone were to feed it . . . It is, if you like, seduction.'

'This someone can only be Bonaparte. Who is out of the way. They say he is very happy on Elba, inventing new flags and drilling his two dozen troops.' Nicholas Marmion tenderly stoops to interrogate a flower.

'Perhaps . . . Do you hear anything from Félix?'

'I hear he is alive, and still loves the Emperor – which is as much as I ever hear from him. Some new scars to add to his collection, no doubt. Oh, he'll carry on: he's too much the soldier to leave that life now, be it for Bonaparte or Bourbon.' Nicholas Marmion holds a bloom to his nose, inhales, and looks as dizzily refreshed as if it were a glass of brandy. 'Children, my dear Louis: it is painful when they surprise you, and painful when they don't. Just painful, really.' Dr Berlioz casts about in his mind for some reference here to Finette, to his marriage: but his father-in-law adds swiftly, stalking on: 'Thank heaven for you and Joséphine. Félix will never settle down. You and Joséphine, thank heaven, are settled.' Dr Berlioz bleakly imagines, for a scented, grass-bruised moment, the heaven that must always be thanked. How different I am, he thinks, without pleasure. 'And now the new shoot,' adds Grandfather Marmion, fingering a sticky-looking plant: after a moment Dr Berlioz realizes what he means.

'Adèle. Yes, she is thriving.' A tiny pause before this, like a gambler who knows his stake is lost anyhow. 'Thank heaven.' There, it didn't cost that much.

A mutter, from pointless greenery. 'If only this would.' And so that is just as important, thinks Dr Berlioz, with a boiling behind his eyes: but he waits till the boiling subsides to a simmer. After all, he thinks, everyone must have a pride and joy: after all.

'Three girls,' says Grandfather Marmion, straightening with a sigh, a sigh that expresses long futures of negotiations, selections, dowries: like an acquisition of land that will require a lot of fencing and draining before it pays. 'Still, there's Hector. Bright, I think. He gave me some sort of lecture about old dodderers who think the heart is made of grammar. Or something. I can't really tell what Hector's talking about sometimes.'

You wouldn't, thinks Dr Berlioz, entirely without rancour. 'His schooling is not going well,' he says temperately. 'The monastery school at La Côte is – well, it's a shambles, and they say it will be closed altogether soon. I think –' and how strange it is, sometimes it takes those words spoken aloud to alert you to what you do think '– I think I shall teach him myself.'

And with those words Dr Berlioz becomes aware, for the first time, of the sun on his back: how warm it is. He carries that warmth into the house, where his brood, his lovely anxieties, are gathered in the long drawing-room. Nancy, the little lady: Louise, the little gypsy: Adèle, the little enigma, on her mother's lap: Hector lying on the rug, arms behind his head, raptly gazing up at the beams as if they were the open sky. Perhaps he feels the warmth too.

'Hector, my dear, must you treat your grandfather's house like a Turkish divan?' his mother chides him.

'Good for the spine,' Grandfather Marmion says. 'Let me hold that beautiful little girl.'

'Aren't I beautiful, Grandpapa?' demands Louise.

'Of course you are, and you know it.'

'Well, yes,' concedes Louise.

'It's a sin to be vain,' puts in Nancy. 'The priest says so.'

'Only because he's ugly,' snaps Louise: and Hector, eyes dreamily closed, utters a laugh at the ceiling.

'Papa, what has become of your neighbour, dear Madame Gautier?' Madame Berlioz asks. 'She usually calls on us.'

'Visiting her family in Grenoble. She returns next week. I wish she would look to her garden when she does. Wretched climbers everywhere.' Nicholas Marmion's scissorlike fingers twitch.

'Oh, would that be the Duboeufs? I often hear of them. They say the daughters are turning out prodigious beauties and breaking all hearts.' Finette gathers the baby back into her arms with the comfortable smile of someone who has put all that behind her. 'But I did hear something unfortunate about the eldest. She was seen at the theatre. I hope it isn't true.'

Hector opens his eyes. 'Why?'

'Because the theatre is a place of irreligion and immorality,' his mother says seriously, informatively. And sincerely: no hoot of hypocrisy in her voice. 'It may appear harmless in itself, but there is nowhere that leads more swiftly to perdition.'

'I was rather fond of the theatre in my youth,' sighs Grandfather Marmion. 'Of course you're right, my dear, it won't do, especially for a young woman.'

'The Church will not even allow actresses to be buried in consecrated ground,' Dr Berlioz says tonelessly, stalking to the window. The sun is gone from his back now. 'Presumably the moral contagion continues in the grave.'

Hector, sitting up, looks from his mother to his father: utters again his high, broken laugh.

'No laughing matter, my dear,' says his mother, gently, 'when it is a question of the immortal soul.'

From Louise: 'What's immortal?'

'It means living for ever,' her father says, with a touch of distaste.

'Oh! Well, I'm going to do that anyway,' Louise says, and Hector bursts upward laughing, grabbing her and twirling her about. 'Me too,' he says, 'me too, little gypsy.'

Dr Berlioz looks on in pain and pleasure, and summons the sun again, thinking: I shall teach him.

★   ★   ★

The Hundred Days: retrospective, of course. No one knows, when Napoleon evicts himself from Elba and arrives in triumph on France's southern doorstep, that it will be a hundred-odd days until he meets his nemesis at Waterloo. But an appropriate term: it makes days seem different to number them like that, instead of dividing them like bundles into neat weeks and months. They seem to rush headlong at you, like an army.

They rush at Dr Berlioz, and nearly crush him.

In March Napoleon arrives in Grenoble to general acclaim, then proceeds north, passing within two miles of La Côte St André. Dr Berlioz steadfastly refuses to join his neighbours rushing to the high-road to watch, nor does he allow Hector to go: this is sheer adventurism. He sees the dancing of excitement in his disappointed son's eyes; but for himself he sees the dancing of flames, the stripping of fields, the blast of war. Blast Bonaparte, in fact: blast these so-called men of destiny, forever clambering up on the cardboard steed of heroism and trying to remake the world in their image. Dr Berlioz loathes the uncontained. It is a family joke that he cannot bear to see loose threads hanging from his wife's workbox, and must always tuck them fastidiously in.

Two weeks later comes the news of Napoleon's entry into Paris. Dr Berlioz despairs, or nearly: we do not know despair till we truly know despair, as he will. Finette is sick with anxiety for her brother, Félix Marmion, lieutenant in the Lancers and veteran – at twenty-eight – of campaigns from Cádiz to Borodino, and now rushing to join the Emperor's colours: how much luck can he have left?

Then the damp spring pokes a poisonous finger into the throat of little gypsy-haired Louise, as it does with several children in the town; but they get better. Louise develops an abscess in the pharynx, and writhes on a double spike of sepsis and suffocation. Is it better or worse when you, the father, are also the doctor? Trustful, Louise does not cry when he tries and fails to lance the abscess. It is a bright morning, pearly from a cleansing shower, when Louise dies. Her sisters weep, baffled: Hector goes about white and stumbling: Madame Berlioz screams, then turns to ardent consolatory prayers for her daughter's soul. Dr Berlioz, silent, feels himself going dry, thin, like a biscuit: about to snap.

At last Finette comes to him after a long session with the priest, glowing and uplifted. 'I know she is happy,' she tells him. 'I know.' And she seizes his hands in hers. He kisses them, not knowing what else to do. Having taken several grains of opium, he finds the hands look fascinatingly like a giant's: nails as big as spades, or coffin-lids.

In June comes news of Waterloo, and another fifty thousand deaths to add to that quiet little one in La Côte St André. There is no working out of such a sum: no answer makes sense. After the battle, another military occupation: this is getting ridiculous. Dr Berlioz misses the puppet-colonel. This time the troops quartered on the district are vengeful and demanding: the townsfolk go hungry while the commandeered wagons haul bread and beef to the encampment: Cossacks ride about on sprees, smashing and burning. Even Finette cannot bring herself to say that this will pass, though she believes it. Meanwhile in his country house at Murianette, Dr Berlioz's father begins to die.

As in life, as in defying the Revolution from prison, as in hammering the table with square fists while his quaking son told him he did not wish to be a lawyer, old Monsieur Berlioz is bullish in the face of death. 'Well, tell me,' he barks, lying purple and swollen in a tented bed. A gouty condition, with strangury and stone: the kidneys, those admirable engines, are running down. Is it better, or worse, to be the doctor when you are also . . . ? 'I suppose it can't be cured.' Said without complaint: the old man respects his son now, as much as a father ever can. In July he rouses from lethargy to reach out. 'Come, Louis, let me shake you by the hand. I'm not sure I shall be able to, presently.' It can't be cured: still a thousand devils shriek Dr Berlioz's failure to the skies. He loses his father on a day of August heat. At his request the maid throws back the shutters, turning the bedroom into a tank of light in which the body of his father floats. He looks as if he has just stopped doing something: which he has.

Surprising by-products dug up along with the new ores of grief: a change in yourself, in your position in the world. When your father dies, Dr Berlioz finds, you are no longer a son: so you are more than ever, more than anything, a father yourself.

As it is August, Dr Berlioz's family are at Grandfather Marmion's. He joins them there. Grandfather Marmion composes some verses in honour of the dead man. Finette holds her husband's head for a long time on her breast. Though dearly wishing to offer it, she refrains from religious consolation. Love is blind, but it sometimes sees.

Grief is an island, and usually the waves will beat you back if you try to reach it. Hector keeps paddling valiantly towards him, and Dr Berlioz is grateful; but he knows it is no use, not here, not now. There is consolation to be had, as there has been all through this horrible year, but it is special and fixed.

It is the teaching and the learning.

It is those precious hours in the library of the big cool house at La Côte, when Dr Berlioz and his son sit down to their lessons. The nearest word, anyway, for a species of mutual discovery. Dr Berlioz does not thrust Latin at Hector like a bowl of gruel to be swallowed anyhow. He opens his beloved Virgil, talks about the story of Dido and Aeneas, makes it a matter of passion and significance; and the passion and significance are in the language, which is beautiful and difficult, as most worthwhile things are difficult. And Hector, after bridling and balking, all at once plunges in, a horse let into a knee-high meadow. (So much for those besotted old priests, Dr Berlioz thinks triumphantly, guiltily.) The atlas? Certainly, open the atlas, let your mind roam around those delineated and imagined countries. French style, let us read La Fontaine. You did not notice the style? Then it must be a good style, because you were not aware of it. It is, if you like, seduction.

This is what keeps Dr Berlioz going: these sweet slices carved from the bloody mess of life. Seeing in Hector the remote reflection, like a lighted ripple at the bottom of a well, of all that he loves and believes. Everyone, after all, must have a pride and joy.

History, geography, languages: in time, of course, there will be medical science also, as that must be the crown of his education. Hector's intelligence and compassion mark him out as a doctor, even leaving aside family tradition. But in the meantime music also, of which Dr Berlioz is a fond amateur. He shows Hector the stave, the notes: the rudiments. It contributes to the sum of a gentleman's education, no more. Dr Berlioz loathes the uncontained.

And Hector?

You must be quick to catch him. He is always on the point of going somewhere, doing something. He is not shy or secretive: he is just simultaneously obvious and hard to perceive, like the drifting bubbles in the fluid of your eye. See them? Once you fix them, you have to stop seeing: you lose the world.

Quick, then. It's Saturday: no lessons. Down the stairs – odd stairs in the Berlioz house at La Côte, turning back on themselves, run down them like this and your feet must dance to their curious dotted rhythm. From the kitchen, a smell, like the lashing of a sweet whip – new-baked bread (and beneath it so much, for the grain is from their own fields, thus you *eat* your home as well as live in it) and Hector is appreciative of this, the sense of it goes through him like his own branching veins – image from the medical textbooks his father has begun to leave open in the study: it is, if you like, seduction – but no food, today is not an eating day, it is a being-eaten day. Being eaten by emotions, and if you want to know what they are, well, then, you are truly seeing through Hector's eyes, because he does too. Out: plashy steep main street, a cooper's wagon straddling it, splayed wheels, crunch and rumble, tumbled thump of tubs. Grey and cool, rain and cloud mixed up with dashes of undercooked sun, an ill-made soup of a day, but there are times when only outdoors is tolerable, when any four walls make a casket.

Damp rank meadow, canopy of weeping oaks, but a sufficient bed for thoughts: book in pocket, for when he needs to slip the leash of self. For now the view does everything. He is in love with distance. He throws all his senses at it. His self resounds and rebounds from those purple slopes: this is what it is like to be an echo. Below, at the limit of the shimmering plain, the taut horizon sends out to him a plucked note, plucking him: he vibrates with it.

He is twelve years old. A time of intensity: often forgotten. But look at his face – he will never forget it, or lose it. Sometimes he conceives of his life as a narrative, a tremendous account of every experience moment by moment: though no book could ever be large enough to contain it.

A minute within Hector: thus. Grass stems at his feet a jungle, his boot a rocky outcrop. Fancied jungles of Ceylon and Borneo: his finger tracing their seductive shapes in the atlas: one day I will go there. And there – past the twanging ring of horizon – oh, a noose to throttle you – beyond: how far Paris? Should know. Uncle Félix would know, been everywhere, thrill of Uncle Félix, home again at Meylan, survived Waterloo, charmed life – yes, but all lives are charmed if we did but know it – sound and smell of Uncle Félix, wonder when he will ride over, scraunching leather, brandy, pomade on the moustache, Nancy giggles tickled at his kiss, God, Louise, dear God, poor Louise, why, there must be a reason? Despair.

Tastes like mould (that night he slipped down to the kitchen ravening in the dark – the bread powdery blue on his tongue), yes, he knows despair. She is much with him today – she, the vision, the one, Estelle, it means star, what else could it mean? This is winter, she is summer. *At regina gravi iamdudum saucia cura.* Virgil, Queen Dido, gnawed by the pangs of love. Shame of, without warning, weeping as he translated, Papa, thank God, pretending not to see. Estelle, would he see her again when summer came (will it ever come?)? When they go to Grandfather at Meylan will she be there, will she look at him? Dread, longing, like standing on the crag by the tower and looking down, you want to fall, to know the falling. Hungry after all, gnawing, pangs. Stupid. Wish to have no body, just to be an emanation, a movement in the grass. Run away to sea. But then no Estelle, no star: not that she can see him, we see the stars, they don't see us. What it must be like to die for someone. What it must be like. What everything must be like.

Thousands of feet above La Côte St André, a layer of cold air from the mountains encounters a mass of cloud, and the undecided day gives way to a downpour. It causes Mayor Buffevent, caught out in it, to develop a chill, which quite ruins his voice for his address to the farmers' association. It causes Dr Berlioz to thank his own foresight in spending eight hundred francs on a new roof, and then to worry about that eight hundred francs. And it causes Hector to run indoors, where in sheer boredom he begins rummaging about in cupboards and drawers. And finds something.

'You know me,' says Félix Marmion, 'I would have cut off my right arm for the Emperor. But there it is, he's gone. I'm fit for nothing but the army, and His Royal Fatness will still need one of those. Besides, I'm a soldier, not a politician. Also I have debts. My God, what debts!' He smiles in admiration of them, revealing the split lips that give him the look of a slashed portrait. A sabre cut from the Spanish campaign. Lucky with that, Dr Berlioz's professional eye observes: an inch deeper and it would almost certainly have splintered nose or jawbone, the splinters probably thrust inward into flesh, resulting in sepsis rapidly becoming general in the heat and dirt of Spain . . . He arrests himself in the act of hypothesising the death of his brother-in-law, of whom he is fond. Next to resplendent peacock Félix – the red trousers with the blue stripe making his

75

swaggering tallness seem to go up and up for ever – Dr Berlioz is a sober rook. But the two men respect each other: neither has anything the other could possibly want.

'Who is in charge of commissions now?'

Félix laughs largely, scooping up the new puppy that is trying to chew his boot. 'My dear Louis, no one is in charge of anything. It's chaos. Oh, if anyone's pulling the strings, it will be some stiff-necked *émigré* still weeping over Marie Antoinette – or more likely his mistress. What can we do? Just have to wait for the new world to take shape.'

'Again.'

Félix laughs, the cheerful yelp of a man who enjoys laughing for its own sake. 'My dear man, you're a cynic.'

'Take another glass of wine. On the contrary, I'm an idealist.'

'Comes to the same thing. It's all about disappointment.' Félix takes his wine like a dose, over in a second. 'You know, you ought to get over to Paris once in a way. Open your eyes.'

'I was not aware they were closed,' says Dr Berlioz, who often finds himself exaggerating his thin-smiling dryness when with Félix, perhaps because it amuses him. Inside there is a hollow note like a gong. Paris, where he might have done great things: or failed to do them.

Félix Marmion puts down his glass, cocking his head. 'Who's that playing *Malbrouk*?'

'Hm? Oh, that's Hector. He found an old flageolet in a drawer the other day. Forgot I had it. He went around making such a damnable racket blowing into it that I undertook to teach him how to play it, just for some peace. Funny, it all came back to me straight away.'

'Oh, it never leaves you. Did I tell you I carried my fiddle in my pack all the way through Russia? Probably I did. Great resource when there were no women about. Well, he's certainly picked it up quickly.'

'Hector picks up everything quickly,' says Dr Berlioz, with a quaver of possessiveness, as if gathering something to him that might be stolen.

'Rotten tone, though,' says Félix wincing. 'Probably a crack. I shall be in Grenoble next week: I'll see if I can find him a new one. So, he's a bright fellow: what's to become of him? Finette was talking about having a priest in the family – but there, bless her, she wants everyone to be a priest.'

'Oh, he will follow my profession, of course,' Dr Berlioz says absently, savouring his wine.

'Ah. Have you told him?'

Dr Berlioz, looking into the endless redness of the wine, finds himself looking also into a vast surprise.

After a moment: 'Oh, he knows,' he says.

'Hector's in love.'

Perhaps mothers can never take this seriously in their sons. And Joséphine Berlioz has, with her son, a frequently teasing way – possibly because of the profound, God-haunted seriousness with which she really views him, his soul, his future. Jokes only matter to those who see life as a joke. This, this dumb smarting adoration of Estelle, pretty granddaughter of Grandfather Marmion's neighbour, sharer of the little outings and parties of the Meylan summer – well, it is nothing. You would have to shift the world off its axis to think otherwise: and Madame Berlioz's world is entirely fixed.

'I can quite understand it,' Madame Berlioz goes on to Madame Gautier, the neighbour, grandmother of the beautiful girl dancing round the long, summer-lit drawing room. (Beautiful girl, Hector would cry outrageously, if he were not brooding as only a thirteen-year-old can brood in the far corner behind the fire-screen, what does that mean, or *not* mean?) 'Estelle is the most delightful creature. Such a glow – I feel old, old!' Madame Berlioz laughs her pleasant husky laugh. 'She must be, what, eighteen now? Well, I doubt you will have to wait long, Madame Gautier, I very much doubt it. You'll soon see her respectably settled. Oh, look at Félix. Really he is shockingly bold – and still wearing his spurs too. But he does dance so very elegantly. These girls don't seem to mind his scar at all – I do believe they like it. Dear, dear, poor Hector, such a face! Off he goes.' Madame Berlioz and Madame Gautier co-operate in a chuckle. 'Oh, to be young again!' Nobody says that who really wishes it.

The haystack throws a shape of shade that is onion-domed, Moorish: exotic. The right shape to contain the prostrate form of Hector, whose thoughts are exotic in the true sense: foreign, foreign to all that surrounds him in Meylan and La Côte and all their piffling provincial kin. He does not yet understand this foreignness, which is partly why he is so brutally unhappy.

It is something to do with clash and paradox. Thus, he wants to spit Uncle Félix on his own sword for dancing so blithely with Estelle, yet he loves his uncle Félix, and admires him for that very dash and swagger that made him whisk the laughing Estelle on to the floor. And it is not as if he could even contemplate dancing with her himself: he would whimper and shrivel. Nor does he actually want her to love him in return, in the sense that one can only want the truly possible: he cannot expect the mountains or the trees, or the stars to love him, and she is no less than them. (And part of them. That cherry tree in his grandfather's garden where she gripped the trunk with one hand and swung herself idly about, humming and thinking: it makes him weep: often he stands leaning his cheek against the bark, once even dashed his brow against it and bled.) And though he cannot laugh at himself, there is a part of him that can conceive the possibility of doing so, some day: laugh at the fact that he adores her pink half-boots and can even be thrown into a miserable frenzy by a glimpse of the same shade of pink in a ribbon or nosegay, at the way he reverently separates her perfect Christian name from her less-than-perfect surname, beefy Duboeuf.

No laughter now, though: no harmonizing of the raging discords. And no possibility of going back into that house, to expose himself to the sympathetic grins. He will have to stay here for ever, that's all. But bewildered and helpless as he is, Hector grasps one nettle of impossibility, one thorny paradox, without flinching. Thus: he cannot and never will be able to talk about these feelings to anyone. Yet if he does not express them somehow he will die or go mad. His future is predicated on a conundrum.

The light fades: monochrome seeps into the valley. Hector sits up.

'One cannot,' he says aloud, with an air of profound pessimistic discovery, 'sit under a haystack for ever.' He trudges back to his grand-father's house, where Nancy skips around him in the hall.

'Hector's in love, Hector's in love.'

'When you're asleep,' he assures her smilingly, 'I shall cut off all your hair.' In fact he is very fond of his arch, prim little sister, and begins, in so far as it is possible, to feel better.

Hector's in love. Well, let us say rather that he has begun to be. In both senses.

★   ★   ★

Ask Estelle Duboeuf – daughter of a dyspeptic but doting Grenoble tax-collector, spirited, pretty, eloquent great eyes, nervous mouth, not as sure of herself as she would like to be – what she thinks of Hector Berlioz, and she will say, after a moment's puzzlement: 'Oh, Monsieur Marmion's grandson, to be sure. Well, I scarcely know what to think, as he has hardly ever addressed a word to me. Yes, I exaggerate. I know he has a sort of taking for me, or thinks he has. It is rather sweet to have a boy admirer. My friend Félicité in Grenoble has one. He makes her little paper boats and then runs away blushing, can you imagine? Of course you mustn't tease them too much: they take it to heart.'

Sounds in the Berlioz house.

Upstairs the squalling of a baby, at once powerful and thin, like a trapped bee fizzing against glass: this is Jules, the newest of Dr Berlioz's beloved anxieties. From the study, the groan of a patient being examined, and Dr Berlioz's calm voice murmuring reassurance. From the central courtyard, a competitive chirruping that resolves into Nancy and Adèle, inventing a complex game as they go along. From the kitchen, great clankings and sousings, the yip of a pestering dog, oaths. From the drawing-room, the idle tapping of riding-crop against boot as Félix Marmion waits for his sister to come down.

From Hector's room, a new sound begins. It throbs, then leaps: it chases about the house like a silvery elf. Félix Marmion stops tapping to listen.

'Well, Félix, all alone?' At last Dr Berlioz comes in. 'We're neglecting you. You must stay to dinner in recompense.'

'Finette went up to feed the baby. That must be Hector playing – but that's surely not a flageolet.'

'No, we procured an old flute for him. Leaps and bounds. Very capable, isn't he? So, you are a warrior again. Let me wish you well, as long as it doesn't mean wishing for another war.'

'Oh, the old crowned boobies won't allow that . . . Listen, I do believe that's an air of Boieldieu's. I remember dancing to that tune with a very pretty girl. Come to think of it, she was rather plain, but you know . . . Where does he get his music?'

'Anywhere he can. Lately he's been haunting the National Guard band. Not that there's a great deal of musicality to be found there.'

'Félix, forgive me, I simply hadn't a moment.' Joséphine Berlioz floats in, kisses her brother. 'How are you? You *look* well.' This is her frequent greeting, accompanied by a long glance of kindly dubiety – as if seeing much more but withholding comment.

'Little screech-owl gone to sleep at last, has he? Doesn't sound as if *he*'s going to be a musician.' Félix chuckles at her solemn bemusement. 'I mean like his brother. Hector the musician.'

'Lord, Félix,' says Madame Berlioz, fanning herself with her hand, 'don't even say it in jest.'

Félix laughs again, but laughs alone. Meanwhile the elf of silver flits about them, as if frantically searching for a way out.

Sunday afternoon at the Esplanade: *boules*, best clothes, strolling and gossip in the lime-tree walk to the sound, or rather the noise, of the National Guard band. Dr Berlioz and Mayor Buffevent perambulate in conclave, nodding to everyone they know. As they know pretty well everyone in La Côte St André, there is a great deal of nodding, so much that they resemble a pair of solemn ducks.

'How's your silkworm crop this year?' puffs Monsieur Buffevent, conscious of being stout and short-winded. And look at Berlioz, not an ounce of fat on him. Mind, the fellow never eats.

'Fair. But prices being what they are—'

'I know. All this trouble in Lyon. Plots and factions. We are addicted to conspiracies. Or they are – more sense in this part of the world, thank God. No, our crop was hardly worth the trouble. Madame Buffevent wants to give it up altogether. I say to her, "You'll miss the occupation. What will you do?" "Good works," she says. I try not to laugh.'

'Really, this band,' says Dr Berlioz, turning with a frown, 'I never heard such a wretched noise.'

'Not exactly doing us proud, are they? Of course, it would help if they had more instruments. I don't know where the horns have gone. With the horn-players probably. How's your boy? They tell me he's well up in music.'

'He spends a good deal of time on it. Too much time, I'm tempted to say, but then that's partly because he's teaching himself. I was wondering whether we could get a professional man in to take charge of the band – depending on funds, of course . . .'

'It's possible, yes, it's possible,' puffs Monsieur Buffevent. In fact, there are certain discrepancies in council funds that he is anxious not to have revealed. He will make them up before he retires, of course. Still, for now he wants to appear accommodating.

'One might make it more worth this person's while by engaging him for private pupils also,' Dr Berlioz goes on. 'I would certainly contribute. There's not only Hector, but Nancy, I think, has an inclination to learn a little music. And there must be others in the town.'

'Surely. Not a bad notion. I've heard the Rochers talk about piano lessons for their girls. Yes, I'll look into it. I might subscribe myself. Give Madame Buffevent something to do.' Monsieur Buffevent, who will die within the year and have his eyelids closed by the man at his side, wheezes laughter. 'Good works indeed.'

The new music-master is from Lyon, and his first impressions of La Côte St André are not greatly favourable. While shaking hands with Mayor Buffevent and declaring himself delighted, he runs through a gloomy inventory in his mind, thus. Typical smug provincial hole: three thousand people, of whom two thousand nine hundred and fifty mere clods: forty-five or so professing or pretending to profess a polite interest in music as an elegant accomplishment: perhaps four or five talented amateurs, knowing only second-rate salon trifles, yearning for more but doomed by the place they live in. Nothing can come from here. He has a son who is also a musician, and in his temporary despondency he curses family tradition and wishes he had set the boy to any other occupation.

Still, it's a living. Fortifying himself from a flask of brandy, he goes to hear the town band.

Madame Clappier, to her friend Madame Berlioz: 'My dear, I declare there's quite a different *look* about your Hector lately. If he was a girl, I'd say it was green-sickness.'

Hector's in love.

Oh, yes, still in love with Estelle, the star of his summers: but not only that. Her rival for his heart is something she could never imagine, though she has heard him play the flute and sing at Monsieur Marmion's evening parties. Nor could she imagine how they are fused together, she and her rival: indeed, in Hector's mind they are a single essence. It would be altogether too strange to think of.

And he is strange, now, the boy-admirer growing tall, deep-voiced, losing the undecided features of adolescence and wearing instead a face that seems to matter: aquiline, lean and deep-shadowed, not so easy to change with a glance or a teasing word. It is a face that can cut its way through a crowded room like the prow of a ship through sea. He does still adore, but the adoration is strange too, and no longer mute. Walking with him, or rather being followed by him, up the mountainside above Meylan, Estelle gives a squeal as he suddenly runs like a goat to the lip of a crag.

'Don't go so near the edge – you'll fall!'

He stops and regards her. 'Would you care?'

'Why? Do you want me to care?'

'Of course.' He gives a peculiar confiding smile. 'I want you to weep for me.'

'What a horrible thing to say.' She half turns: this is the moment for young beaux to stammer out apologies; that's the way the game goes.

Instead: 'Is it?' he says seriously. 'But it's such a beautiful idea.'

Then he springs away again, scrambling up to the ruined tower.

She frowns up at him. 'Don't you ever stop moving? I don't know how you can be such a fidget.' Dear God, she thinks, there is the voice of the mother I shall be.

'I don't know how other people can stay so still.'

Just a boy after all, gangling, full of quiddities. Still, Estelle thinks, I'm so glad I shall never be in love with him.

'My dear, a new flute?' Finette pauses with the dripping spoon half-way to Jules's mouth. 'But he has a flute.'

'Not a good one. This is to be of red ebony, from the best instrument-maker in Lyon.' Dr Berlioz pantomimes encouraging bites at Jules. He is always relieved when Finette finishes breast-feeding: he finds he is fonder of her. Something to do with the Madonna, perhaps.

'Well, you're the best judge, of course. But really, isn't this taking it a little too far? What with the music lessons, the guitar lessons—'

'Those we may discontinue. But the flute he shall have.' Dr Berlioz kisses his wife's sleek hair. 'Trust me, my dear. I know what I'm about.'

★   ★   ★

'No no no no. Please. Not that. Scribble on something else.' Dancing over her with dainty anxiety, Hector manages to snatch the paper from Adèle's sticky fingers.

'Why?'

'Because it's important.'

'Adèle, go and play elsewhere,' instructs Nancy, who is thirteen, and has a fastidious horror of childhood. 'Is it a love-letter?' Serious, not mocking, not at thirteen: it is all becoming tremendous to her. 'My friend Emma is in love with you.'

'Is she?' Hector laughs at the thought, then stops, assaulted by the vision of Estelle standing on the cliff-path, smiling down at him with amusement. 'Well, it's not a love-letter. It's just music.'

It's just music. It's music – just. Hector, who has never had a piano lesson, never heard an orchestra, hardly knows what he is doing when he laboriously translates the sounds in his mind into that inky-spiky code. That's why no one is alarmed by what is happening inside Hector. Just music. Madame Berlioz sings nursery songs to herself when sewing: Dr Berlioz is still fond of a tune: Uncle Félix plays a sprightly fiddle when the ladies suggest a carpet-dance. You see, it doesn't matter. No suspicion then that the likeable youth moving among them is a changeling. They do not spot the goblin tail because they cannot imagine it.

For the goblin, it isn't just music. That is one of the thoughts that is becoming unthinkable.

A neighbour clearing out lumber comes across a bundle of music paper. Hector's the one for music, isn't he? Keep it, keep it. Among the yellowing lavender-smelling sheets, Hector finds a sheet set out for full score.

He gazes. Twenty-four staves: they extend like magic wires far below him. Hector on the edge of the crag, wanting to fall.

Dr Berlioz finds he has been watching the hands of the study clock, waiting for them to reach nine precisely: which is, he tells himself, absurd. They are at home, not in a counting-house. But it is such an important day, such an important moment: somehow it needs an horological honour.

'Hector? Will you come in here, please?'

He comes, ruffling the riotous hair. He will never go bald, Dr Berlioz's mind (which one?) notes absently: you can tell by the way it grows straight up from the scalp. Absurdly again, Dr Berlioz is trembling.

'Hector. The time has come for you to begin your medical studies.'

Slightly dream-like feeling when you finally say something you have been preparing to say for a long time. You almost wonder if you really said it.

But he must have, because Hector replies.

'Is it?'

The tone is of sheer surprise: the last thing Dr Berlioz expected. Suddenly the doctor has a feeling of being behind thick glass: he even begins to speak more loudly.

'Certainly. Certainly it is time. You have made excellent progress in your general studies, and those we shall continue. But above all you display a questing intelligence, and I think your mind is in a state of readiness for the close and thorough disciplines of medicine. It is at once the most exacting and the most worthy of professions, and one that it has always been my hope to see you pursue. To *help* you pursue.' Dr Berlioz pauses expectantly.

'Yes. Well, yes, I know.'

'It may be that you doubt your aptitude for it – perhaps, even, your inclination. That's why I mean to start now, before any formal training. I want to introduce you to medicine's first principles – to open it up to you, if you like, as I hope I did with the glories of Virgil.' Dr Berlioz has a shivery presentiment that his son is going to say: *But that's different.* He hurries on: 'The *Treatise on Osteology* of Monroe is the best beginning. This volume. My notion is that you begin to familiarize yourself with it at your own pace, just as with your other studies.' He opens the great volume at an illustration and turns it on the desk towards Hector.

His son's eyes flick down at the flourishing curlicues and volutes, the dispassionate architecture of anatomy, then flick up to his father again. 'Yes.'

Just that. Dr Berlioz has a sensation of floundering – but, ah, here is dry land. 'By the by, I have ordered the new flute you wanted. It should be here at the end of the month.'

And now a spark, if of a smothered sort. 'Thank you, Papa. Thank you.'

Dr Berlioz waves a hand, granting himself a smile. It is, if you like, seduction. 'Your cousin Alphonse is also intended for the medical profession, and may be joining us in our studies. Well, I have a patient to call upon, so I will see you at lunch. Thank you, Hector.'

Dr Berlioz wonders what he is thanking his son for. Only when Hector is out of the room does he notice that the medical treatise is still on the desk. Dr Berlioz rubs at his breastbone, where his old indigestion announces itself again like a tiresome caller. Looking at his watch, he finds that it says ten to nine. He glances at the clock: ten past. Well. One of them must be wrong.

'My dear fellow, it simply doesn't work.'

The music-master has scraped together – appropriate phrase – a quartet to bring light to the bourgeois darkness of Sunday evenings in La Côte St André, and they have agreed to try over a composition of young Hector's.

Well, they try. Difficult to play when you are racked with laughter.

'I'm sorry. I'm sorry, but you're trying to run before you can walk. This – this is like someone trying to write a poem in alexandrines when they hardly know any French. Never mind. You've cheered us up.'

Hector, close-lipped and burning, gathers up the sheet music. But: at least he said poem.

'Occiput,' says Cousin Alphonse. 'It's occiput. We did it last week. Can't you remember that?'

'I suppose I could,' says Hector, 'if I wanted to.'

Dr Berlioz, exasperated, has left them alone with the skeleton. Hector rattles his pen-nib along the rib-cage. Moderately satisfying sound, to accompany the others in his head.

'I tried to whisper it to you.'

'Was that it? I thought you were stifling a fart.'

Alphonse laughs, as he does everything, warily. He is solid and conscientious and has a habit of tucking in his chin as if afraid it might offend someone. He is also, thank God, a fair violinist.

'Shall we try the Pleyel tonight?' Hector says urgently.

'Not tonight. I need to get through another chapter of Bichet. Nerve tissue.'

'What exquisite bedtime reading.' Hector fans himself with his scribbled and decorated notes. Oppressive summer: no air. He has no air.

Suddenly he has a vision of wrenching off the skeleton's head and running outside and kicking it like a ball down the street. Why would he want to do that? But, then, why would he want to do this? Feeling dizzy, he starts laughing.

'What is the matter with you?'

'Exactly.' Now he feels tears basting his eyes. From the skeleton the dry sockets stare pitilessly back. 'Exactly. What is the matter with me?'

At Meylan, during the tour of the frenziedly fertile garden, Grandfather Marmion interrupts himself in a disquisition on blackfly and gives Dr Berlioz a sharp look.

'Well, obviously this is preying on you. Just how serious is it? Will he really not obey you?'

'I don't want it to be a matter of obedience,' Dr Berlioz says, with a wince. 'But yes, it is serious, as he still insists he absolutely dislikes the medical profession and will not apply himself. Oh, he gets by, because he has a good brain, but Alphonse is far ahead of him. It's the attention he pays to music. I don't mind that in itself, it rounds a man off, gives him diversion and solace – but this is excessive. He is – not there.'

Grandfather Marmion sniffs. 'In other words, he's being pig-headed.'

No, thinks Dr Berlioz, though in a moment of temper he said that very thing to Hector the other day. 'It requires a good deal of patience. A certain degree of aversion is quite natural at first: doctors don't do pretty things, after all. But you overcome that. You see differently. I'm waiting for him to realize that – that this is his future. And a good one. Yes, a good one. Whereas the music—'

'Music is not a future. Not an occupation, not a profession – unless you count leading a dancing bear as a profession. He should know that, or else he's a fool. I'm sorry, Louis, but you can't indulge him. He needs to understand what's at stake. Think of what you've built up, and what your father built up. *He* should think of it, not waste his time with silly dreams. Your time also, by the way. I don't know: the young.' Nicholas Marmion draws his secateurs from his coat-pocket, as if prepared at once to deal with the young: to dead-head them.

'It will pass,' says Dr Berlioz. 'He will come round.' It is dismaying when he hears his own thoughts voiced by Grandfather Marmion: they sound different outside his head. All you built up, all your father built up

— yes, he is proud of it, proud in the same nervous, watchful way that he is proud of his children. And suddenly he sees it all, the property, the farm, the vineyards, the orchards, the security, the name — all this is the yoke he bears on his shoulders. Pride in that yoke too. Shrug it off? No, never. Imagine that. Just imagine it.

Rows are relative. Some families scream at each other all day and go to bed genial. The Berlioz family are not like that. Today's row between Hector and his father was more tremor than earthquake, but it has left everyone white-lipped. Madame Berlioz gathers her daughters to her. 'Come. We must pray. We must say a prayer to the Virgin for poor Hector.'

Adèle, in husky enquiry: 'Why, is he dying?'

Madame Berlioz chews her lip while her eyes sadly dream. 'He might as well be.'

'Hm. Not bad.' The music-master lays down his violin-bow and peers again at the score, as if suspecting an optical illusion. No laughter this time. 'No, really. There are oddities. But it does work.'

Hector, arms folded, says quietly: 'Of course it does.'

Sometimes, now, before the day's lessons, Dr Berlioz takes a grain or two of opium. It doesn't show; and it helps him to cope with the feeling.

Which is a sort of pressure, or resistance. Hard to explain. He remembers, when Hector was a very small boy, playfully closing the study door on him, or not quite, and then feeling the tiny determined push as Hector sought to get in. Oh, dear, I can't shut this door, I wonder why. And still that pressure on the panels, feeble yet concentrated, so that in the end the child won: you couldn't stop him without sending him flying, and that you couldn't do.

Something like that. Even as Hector buckles down, learns his basic anatomy, remembers the occiput, Dr Berlioz senses this resistance, and is saddened. Or increasingly saddened, as there is a new notch on the tally of grief. Little Jules did not survive his third year. The harvest of infants, regular as the vintage. Dr Berlioz does not believe that use is everything. It grinds and abrades, getting closer all the time to the agonizing quick.

I have buried one son, thinks Dr Berlioz, listening to Hector drearily describe scapulae and fibulae. I shall not, he thinks, with unaccustomed sharpness and bitterness, I shall not bury another.

'Is that a love-letter?' asks Nancy, with diminished hope but augmented respect – for her brother is now eighteen, smells of shaving-soap, makes chairs creak when he sits down: has moved beyond her.

'I wish it was. It's my passport for leaving Isère.'

'Oh, God.'

'Don't let Mama hear you say that, but yes: oh, God. Write to me in Paris, won't you?'

'If you write to me. You probably won't. You'll be busy dissecting, or whatever it is.'

Hector makes a face: not quite in jest. 'That's what it is.'

'Adèle keeps crying. I think she knows. Hector, you will behave yourself in Paris, won't you?'

He laughs. 'Why? What else would I do?'

'All sorts of things,' says Nancy, decidedly. 'All sorts, in Paris.'

'Well, I'll remember that when I'm sitting there listening to some everlasting lecture on the secondary symptoms of gout.'

Nancy donates a kiss, then sits down with a flump of skirts. 'You must listen, though, Hector.' Her mother flits across her unfinished face. 'You know you must listen.'

Stowing the passport in his pocket, patting it, scrutinizing the fireplace, Hector is a long time answering.

'Oh,' he says at last, 'I'll listen.'

PART TWO

Juliet

1

THEATRE ROYAL, DRURY LANE

This present Tuesday, 20 January 1818

His Majesty's Servants will Enact the Celebrated Play of Mrs Cowley:

THE BELLE'S STRATAGEM

With new Scenes, Dresses, & Decorations

THE CHARACTERS BY:

Mr Stanley *as Doricourt*: **Mr Dowton** *as Mr Hardy*:
Mrs Glover *as Lady Racket*:
and for the first time upon the London stage
Miss Smithson from Dublin *as Letitia*

THE PROLOGUE TO BE SPOKEN BY MR STANLEY
THE EPILOGUE TO BE SPOKEN BY MISS SMITHSON

To Which Will Be Added a Musical Entertainment called
THE FOOL OF FORTUNE

2

'Always remember,' her father said, before she left for England, 'if the audience love you, they love you for what you do, not who you are.'

Remembering, pacing the dressing-room, tasting fear like pennies on her tongue, Harriet thought: But what if they don't love you? What if they don't notice you? And − picturing again the vastness of the Drury Lane auditorium − what if they can't even *see* you?

Eliza's half-painted face quizzed her from the mirror. 'Where are you going?'

'Guess.'

'Not again.'

But no, not again: she would only bring up bile. She snatched up her cloak.

Previously, when the nerves had hit her, she had gone away from the backstage to mingle with the audience, to remind herself that they were people. It had worked at Belfast, where she had joined the company of Montague Talbot − aristocratic, eccentric, with the face of a dimpled infant and a voice of refined silver. ('Your destiny, Miss Smithson, lies in comedy. Do not subject your admirable instrument to the ravages of rant and the blight of bombast. Sparkle. Scintillate.') It had worked at Birmingham where − alone, in a strange country, with her heart aching for Irish voices and her mother's cushiony reassurance and even her father's vinous snuffles − she had joined the company of Robert Elliston, whose name alone was enough to make a seventeen-year-old novice tremble. Elliston was the biggest man outside the London patent theatres: big, too, in ambition and energy. Alone in a room with him you found yourself flinching, wanting to shrink like a mouse into the wainscot. A big drinker also, even by the standards of the English theatre, where Lady Teazles slurred and staggered through the Screen Scene and sozzled Othellos fumbled with the pillow while wondering which of the two Desdemonas to smother. ('Your destiny, Miss Smithson,' Elliston told her, exhaling flammably, 'lies in tragedy. The twittering of comedy is very well, but your art will only mature – no, say *combust* in the crucible of grief and pity.' Next day he forgot her name.)

Obstacles successfully overcome. And even when facing the committee of Drury Lane, she had contrived a similar technique to galvanize her paralysed legs and unglue her tongue. Forget the anteroom with the baleful authors cradling their manuscripts and the terrible old leading-man with desperation shining through his rouge: forget the ultimate power of the yawning, snuff-taking, bosom-eyeing gentlemen into whose presence she was ushered. Look instead at the little histories written on them, the things that made them mortal. The deep shaving-nick on that one's chin, which must surely mean that he shaves himself, which must mean either that he cannot afford a manservant, so not so grand after all, or prefers to do such things for himself, so a certain individuality and humanity there. Or the fat one who has the loudest voice, but who looks uncomfortable wedged into the Windsor chair: was he fat also as a boy, and was he perhaps teased for it, and is he really shouting at you or shouting down the other boys who mock him still in the recesses of his mind?

Again it worked – but perhaps now it wouldn't work any more, perhaps it had run down like a broken watch, because everything about Drury Lane was so immense: even the wilderness of booming passages and stairways she had to traverse to get to the stage door. Fearful temptation, once she broached the sweet open air, simply to carry on walking and let London consume her and turn the début of Miss Smithson from Ireland into a thing that never was. Strange Disappearance of Irish Actress: A Mystery Unparalleled. And then forgotten.

She wandered along Russell Street. I cannot do this: how did I get here? Perhaps I fell asleep in my little bedroom in the Reverend Dr Barrett's house, and everything since has been a long dream. She imagined London as she had seen the map of it in print-shop windows, densely wriggling with streets and courts and alleys, and then a tiny pointer representing her position outside Drury Lane theatre – and it made no sense, it was a glaring anomaly. No one else seemed to feel this. The fruit-sellers and sausage-vendors, the gilded ones in carriages and their mufflered coachmen, the lamplighter and the sprawled drunk – they all knew why they were here. Even the hollow-faced drab, worn past hope and care –

she knew best of all, perhaps, how she had got here. Very possibly she had started out as an actress.

Harriet made herself stand and gaze up at the front of the theatre. Always being rebuilt at more heartbreaking expense, it now had the lofty look of a temple, all pediments and pilasters. Harriet thought: The whited sepulchre. She knew a great deal about the world of the theatre now: knew it, she supposed, in the way you knew a member of the family, where disappointment and friction and even mistrust did not preclude love. (She did not and could not suppose it was the way you knew a lover: not yet.) It was a small world and this was its centre, this and Covent Garden just down the street. Here the crown was kept, and you were allowed, at least, to reach out for it. And now she was here Harriet could not do it.

A great pity, she thought, as she drifted numbly up the steps and into the lobby. All that work wasted: all the things the audience never saw. With Elliston's company she had had to learn forty different roles, sometimes four or five in a week. Every moment outside the theatre was spent reading and memorizing – every moment except for the singing-lessons and dancing-lessons and voice exercises, and her own punishing studies behind locked doors struggling to find the one interpretation among the many imposters that offered themselves so plausibly to her, the stilted, the arch, the extravagant, the muted, the merely adequate. 'My dear Miss Smithson, there really is no call for that,' Montague Talbot had chided her. 'You'll only take the freshness off.' Like most of the grand actors, he only turned up for one rehearsal and took no notice of what his fellows were doing in a scene: he had carried on as Romeo when his Juliet had fainted. But Harriet had a reason for her intense preparations: it was doubt. She had always doubted she could do the thing she did (and here was the proof, skulking in the lobby) and so she crammed and sweated in recompense. Even when taking a bow to warm applause, she had the lurking feeling of someone travelling without a passport.

And now the old trick was not working. The lobby was full of early arrivals, but she found she could not refresh herself from the well of humanity here. The men were either sleek young bloods, cherry-lipped and cold-eyed, or liver-spotted *roués* creaking in stays, and they were here for the women. The muslin sisterhood, as they were called. Everywhere bare arms and powdered *décolletage* and the slither of filmy gowns. Harriet looked for a way out and could not find one. A waxy-pale semi-nude with a swan neck turned to face Harriet. Her breasts might as well have been carried on a tray. She stared Harriet up and down with mixed hostility and puzzlement. I'm on her territory, Harriet thought, with sick hilarity, and turned to flee. She had to squeeze so tightly past a young beau that her belly brushed his taut pantalooned buttocks. 'You can do that again if you like,' he said, peering into her face.

The dressing-room looked almost domestic. The wardrobe-mistress was prayerfully pinning up the hem of Mrs Glover's gown, and Eliza was warming her slippered feet at the frugal fire while taking a nip from a flask.

'Where have you *been*?' she hissed. 'Stanley's been shouting the place down.'

Where have I been? I don't know. Harriet checked her paint in the mirror. How did I get here? I don't know either. I only know there's nowhere else to go.

First thing to hit her, the noise and heat. She did her best during rehearsals to picture the enormous place filled, but nothing could have prepared her for this, the sheer weight and force of that peopled space. There is the population of a good-sized town out there, in the pit receding into distance, in the boxes rising five tiers high, and they are all talking. And fanning, and fidgeting, and craning, and moving around: and the vast mutter of it goes up like great wings and beats around the domed ceiling.

First thing to do, quell the absurd suspicion that it is all a mistake, that this really is a town going about its business with no interest in that peculiar lit space to one side. They will look and listen – but you must make them.

Now it happens. Now you must not so much concentrate your mind as divide it into three minds, all working simultaneously. The first is the mind that works like a muscle, like blinking or digestion: the mind that has memorized your lines and cues, entrances and exits, stage directions and business. If this one does let you down, there can be momentary confusion or disaster: but Harriet's seldom does. Then there is the mind that is alive to the chances of the moment: to Mr Dowton starting out in weak voice – signal it with your eyes, raise your own tone, get into harmony, that's it: to the raucous party in the second left box, who if you show you notice them will feed on it: to Mr Stanley omitting a line, realizing it a lip-licking moment later, never mind, go on: to a surprising audience chuckle at quite an ordinary piece of business, must remember that, emphasize it.

And then there is the third mind, and all you can say is that it does not really belong to you at all. This mind turns you into Letitia Hardy, the very English heiress, destined to marriage by parental arrangement with your childhood friend Mr Doricourt. But he has travelled long on the Continent, and returning finds you disappointing beside the foreign temptresses he has known. Well, as you are plunged passionately and immediately in love with him – Doricourt, that is, not blustering double-chinned Mr Stanley who plays him – this is where the third mind does its work, transforming the real into the ideal, so you must prove to him that he is wrong. Which will require some laboured absurdities in the story, but no matter: only dig down to the truth of it, where we all feel that if the beautiful, disdainful he or she could really know us, appreciate us, feel our ardent burning on their skin, they would be converted: they would and must love. And so you go about it, cleverly and wittily, as we would all wish to: you play with his emotions: first you disguise yourself as an awkward hoyden and put him thoroughly off, and then you meet him incognito at a masquerade and ensnare him with all the roguish charm and vivacity you know you possess. And when the masks are finally off: Aha, you see, Mr Doricourt, they were both me. So can you be so sure of your impressions? Do you truly know your heart?

And Letitia certainly is a romp, who finds fun in her intrigues, as do the audience (the third mind never forgets them; in fact in the end it lives or dies by them) but still she, you, are also steeply, fearfully serious – because this is love. And if you convince as both the hoyden and the temptress, make people laugh and admire, is that not because you are wholehearted in your pursuit of that love? Why else go to that trouble, unless to claw down your unreachable star?

So laughter is a turning at a fork in the road, and to follow it is to bear in mind the turning you didn't take, the dark one where the tears are. What looks easy is hard. A feeling of something learned, something added to the sum of self and all selves and all total possibilities, as audience applaud and curtain descends – except then it is like those moments of profundity in a dream, quite lost or else nonsensical at waking. Letitia ceases to exist, the third mind goes out like a candle. Now all is feverish practicality.

'I knew that entrance was not timed right. Miss Smithson, don't you think? He should come in *bang*, sharp, else the laugh is spoiled . . .'

'Can't abide this new gaslight. Glary. I shall have a megrim tonight . . .'

'That first fiddle's out of tune again. How did he *get* the job?'

'Who did he fuck, you mean? I'll tell you later . . .'

Discomfort of dried sweat down your neck, under the powder. Manager yelling at Eliza for a missed cue. Clatter of preparation for the afterpiece. Hefting of flats. Wardrobe-mistress crooning over a torn train. Mutual compliments, like poison darts, flying about the green-rooms (second green-room only for Harriet, proportionate to her salary). Congratulations to Harriet on a triumphant début – but this is the theatre, who knows what that means? Well, nobody booed. And, against all probability: I can do this. Indeed, the one thing she does know, as she accepts and drinks her very first glass of champagne, is that for good or ill she cannot do anything else.

Remarks elicited from members of the audience leaving the Theatre Royal, Drury Lane, Tuesday, 20 January 1818.

Mrs Arthur Fellowes, of Great Coram Street: 'Yes, it was a pretty enough entertainment. The piece is rather in the sentimental style, but none the worse for that. Miss Smithson, yes, admirable, very spirited. From Ireland, I think? I thought I detected a touch of the brogue.'

Mr Arthur Fellowes, solicitor: 'Quite. Quite so.'

Mr Philip Wye, gentleman, of Twickenham: 'Oh, it served, you know. No discredit on the players, not at all, and the young Irishwoman was excellent – but, dear me, such tinselly stuff as is wanted nowadays. It'll be horses and rope-dancers next. Of course it's all about money – I hear the place is shockingly in debt. But what has happened to our theatre? Where is Shakespeare? Where is grandeur and nobility? Mind, I'm old enough to remember Garrick, you know. Garrick's Lear, that was something to see. Nothing like that nowadays.'

Mrs Walter Dunstan, of Highgate: 'I was half wearied and half diverted, which is about as much as I expect from a play. The dresses were fine, though nothing out of the common. Dowton's comportment I thought rather vulgar. Miss Smithson, rather too eager to please, though half-way pretty when dressed to advantage.'

Mr Walter Dunstan, broker: 'On the contrary, Miss Smithson is a remarkable beauty, with the most expressive eyes I ever saw. I only hope her beauty may not hold her back in her profession.'

Mrs Walter Dunstan: 'Well, my dear, as your failing sight is so unaccountably improved, perhaps you will be good enough to look for a hackney.'

Mr Robert Rose and Mr Nicholas Crossley, clerks, of Holborn: 'Uncommonly good. Prodigious, all of it. Miss Smithson, which was she? Uncommonly good anyhow. The gaslight especially. Never saw anything to compare with that gaslight. Beg pardon, rather tipsified.' (Laughter.)

Captain Wilcox, Sixteenth Light Dragoons: 'Never better entertained in my life. The bit at the masquerade, that was capital funning. Smithson, yes, that's the name, ain't it? Delightful creature, delightful. Why do you ask? Do you mean she's, you know, available? Oh, sorry – only, she is an actress, after all.'

European Magazine, January 1818, noticing Miss Smithson's début:

> She is naturally graceful in her action, but perfectly capable of
> assuming the awkwardness which some of the situations required
> . . . The speaking voice is rather distinct than powerful, and she
> gave the song of 'Where are you going, my pretty maid' in a style
> more remarkable for humour than sweetness. The Minuet de la
> Cour was substituted for the song at the masquerade, and in it
> her fine figure and graceful movements were displayed to
> advantage.

Eliza: she is an actress, after all, and it is in those terms, if not in those words, that she rationalizes the tangled personal life about which she makes Harriet her confidante.

Eliza Pembroke is her stage name, possibly also her real name: she is equivocal about that. 'I don't see how anyone can have a *real* name,' she says vaguely. She is engaged at Drury Lane at two pounds ten shillings a week in minor walking-lady roles – which, she says, suits her, as her memory is rather unreliable. Eliza is unreliable generally, which has probably hindered her from getting on in the theatre as she might, since she is sculpturally beautiful and has a good voice. But, then, this isn't, she insists, what matters.

'My sweet love, I don't know how it is in Ireland, but here the theatre is a matter of bed and board. Or bed and bawd, different spelling, you know. I don't say you *can't* be virtuous and do well – only that I don't see *how*.'

On Sundays, when it is fine enough, they walk from their lodgings in Catherine Street to stroll in St James's Park: quite good friends, though not understanding each other in the least. For Harriet, Birmingham seemed nothing remarkable after Dublin – even rather provincial – but London is a daily dismay to her: magnificent, exciting, but altogether too much, and with a strangely fictional air. From the lives of the kings and queens that the Reverend Dr Barrett used to narrate to her, to the play-books that have been her main reading for the last four years, everything she has learned about is suddenly there around her, as if sprung life-size from her head. There is a real Tower of London, a real St Paul's, a real Monument: the actual Ring where Mrs Pursy rode in *The School for Scandal*, the genuine Eastcheap where Prince Hal caroused with Falstaff. She is glad of the anonymous greenness of the park, to take off the continual pressure of wonder.

For Eliza the park is a place of delicious anguish, because of the possible presence of admirers – present, past or potential. Her neck is perpetually twisted. If *he* is here today, she will simply die. If *he* isn't here today, she will also simply die. The *he*s are haunters of the stage door, whom, as the theatre season progresses, Harriet often passes on her way out – at first with mild puzzlement, then realization, then irritation as they begin to flourish bouquets and puff out their chests at her. The thing is, they don't even know her.

'Well, they never will, if you don't speak to them and give them a bit of encouragement,' Eliza says, in her sweetly reasonable and husky way.

'But I don't want to encourage them.'

'Ah, that's because you think it's the road to perdition and what-not. And it's true, you have to be choosy. But you can do very well for yourself. Look at Mrs Jordan. Hooked herself a royal duke. Smart villa at Bushey. That's how high you can go.'

'He didn't marry her, though. I hear she died without a penny.'

'Well, you have to take your chances. Oh, sweet Lord in heaven, that's him, that's the one who said he was going to take prussic acid for me – no, no, it isn't. Same forehead, though.'

Harriet said: 'Mrs Glover was telling me about Susan Boyce.'

'Who?'

'Exactly. She was an actress at Drury a few years ago – when Lord Byron was on the committee. He took her up for a while. Then dropped her. The last Mrs Glover heard of her she was living in a garret on poor-relief.'

'Oh! Yes, I've heard of her. But she was riddled with the pox, you know, it was common knowledge.'

The pox. Harriet knows, in a way; but during these walks with Eliza she seems always to be taking steps into a greater knowledge. Wading into it, in fact, and not liking the feel of it.

'Besides,' Eliza says energetically, 'that's not so very bad, you know, hooking Lord Byron, even if she couldn't manage him. Do you think he really did it with his sister? I knew a girl who regularly did it with her father, but that was a sort of duty. I think it was the back-passage business that did for him, more likely. It hurts a bit, they say, but then at least you don't get pregnant. If you're a woman, I mean. Old Sol Vincent – used to play a Speciality Singing Countryman at the Haymarket – he did it with a different man every night of the season before going on. Picked 'em up in the Strand. Said it improved his wind. Turn this way, turn this way, that's the one who gave me the necklace.'

'Surely not,' says Harriet, looking. 'He's with a lady and two little children.'

'My dear girl, you are a scream – a scream beyond anything! Are they gone? The wife is a perfect pig of a woman, you know. Makes his life a misery.'

'This is what he's told you, of course.'

'And he has strong doubts that the children are his . . . Harriet, do you mean to tell me you've *never*—'

'I don't mean to tell you anything at all, my dear Eliza, because it's entirely private,' Harriet said, with a nervous laugh to drown the word *prig* ringing in her mind.

'Well, that's just what it isn't, in the theatre. You'll see. Some day you'll wonder why you're not getting any good parts, and you'll discover that they're always going to the manager's mistress – or else you have to be the manager's mistress to get them.'

'I can't believe that's always the way.' She was thinking – with mingled embarrassment and something she identified as respect – of her father. None of that, thank God. If there had been, she wondered, would she have been put off the theatre as a career? Not that she had ever really chosen it: somehow, it had chosen her. Suddenly she found herself asking: 'What's he like?'

'Who?'

Harriet nearly said, 'All of them,' as that was in a way what she meant. He: the person who could occupy such a large part of your life, without your feeling you were being evicted from yourself. 'The necklace man.'

'He is an altogether charming and delightful gentleman,' Eliza said, and then with no change of tone, 'though a bit of a bore. Ugh, look at those odious puffed sleeves! Are they really coming back in? She looks as if she's exploding.'

'Eliza, do you think it's true what Letitia says? "'Tis much easier to convert a sentiment into its opposite, than to transform indifference into tender passion." To go from hate to love.'

'Lord, Harriet, that's only in a play. It's got nothing to do with real life, believe me.'

Occasionally her brother Joseph was in London, and would drop in unannounced at her lodgings, bringing with him his own bottle of brandy. He would drink most of it without visible effect, meanwhile prowling the walls of the room as if measuring its dimensions, talking irritably and volubly. He had been restlessly involved with various touring companies all over the country. 'Everywhere,' he said, with satisfaction, 'except bloody Ireland. D'you hear much from the old 'uns?'

'Mother writes me regularly. She wants to come over and see me at Drury. I shall have to explain to her they're not giving free admission orders any more and she'll have to save for a ticket.'

'Penny-pinching pisspots. Place needs a good shaking-up. They should never have given the management to a committee. Half a dozen muttonheads do more damage than one. Not that the Garden's much better. More circus than playhouse. Mind, they're only following public taste, which is witless and execrable. Result of a witless and execrable age.'

Joseph stopped, as if grimly wondering how far he could follow this: then shrugged and resumed pacing. 'I hear Father's drinking himself to death.'

'Mother says his . . . his health is not good.'

Joseph coughed out a laugh. 'Dear Mother. She's been using these euphemisms so long she's forgotten the real words. When the old man dies she'll say he's temporarily indisposed.'

'You're very hard, Joseph.'

'No, I ain't, sis. I'm soft as butter, and that's my trouble, and that's why I look like this.' Joseph had attained a diabolic sort of handsomeness, but his skin was muddy and his eyes bloodshot. 'So how do you get on at Drury? How much are they paying you, and who's in your way? I suppose Fanny Kelly still gets all the plum parts.'

'Three pounds a week. I've had some good roles. I can't complain. Well, only about my voice. You have to pitch so loud in that theatre. At the end of the evening I can hardly speak. I keep trying to do as much as I can with gesture, without—'

'Without looking like an old barn vag rolling his eyes, eh? Or Father, in other words. Oh, you'll do well, sis. If not, you'll have to push *la* Kelly off a cliff. Or coquette it with the manager, if they ever appoint a proper one.'

Harriet tried to ignore that. 'Do you think Father is really ill? I mean, should one – go and see him?'

'One may do as one likes. For myself, I'm not particular. I could never do anything right for the old cuss. The annoying thing about parents is the way they *hang on* into your adult life. Nothing else of your child-hood does. You don't carry your hoop and satchel about with you. Whereas this . . .' Joseph impatiently twitched his big shoulders, looking very much like his father as he did so. 'Well, what about your summer? Shall you tour? Good opportunities at Margate, I hear.'

'I haven't decided yet.' But now I have.

'So tell me more. The second act – was there a sag? Did you find there was a slackening of attention? I know the *Belle* inside out, and I always feel the second act must be *galloped* through if it is to hold together . . .'

William Smithson wanted to know every detail of his daughter's début. Breathing effortfully, tremulous hands gripping his knees, he listened entranced. Sometimes he pushed away the invalid's rug and took a few thoughtful, tottering steps about the room, as if playing out the scene in his mind.

He did not, Harriet thought at first, look so very bad. Then she realized that familiarity was deceiving her. She had expected to see her father, and there he was: even if he was sitting hunched in an armchair like an old man. Even if his face bloomed with veins. Even if he seemed to have no jaw. Bit by bit she assembled the sad and unrecognizable reality. In the end she held on to his eyes, which were unchanged. And they did kindle at the sight of her – oh, yes, God knew what she was to make of it, but William Smithson feasted on her presence.

It was doubtful that much feasting went on in these dingy Dublin lodgings, though the family were getting by, somehow. 'My infirmity', as her father put it – the drinking, the stroke that it had caused, or the combination – prevented him working, but her mother was taking the odd role, and all in all . . .

'All in all, what keeps us going is you, my dear,' her mother crowed, 'your fame! Drury Lane at eighteen! And in the dear *Belle*. I've played Letitia in my time, but between ourselves I always found it a strain. I'm not good at animation.'

Mr Smithson turned a sickly smile to and away from her, then continued quizzing Harriet. The masquerade, was it well staged? And the afterpiece, did it suit? A theatrical programme was like a good meal, the courses must complement one another . . . Soon she was telling him of her other roles. He sat back, shawled, gaunt, wry, a little dribble at the corner of his lips. Somehow she was reminded of a Pope or Inquisitor. William Smithson, the great liar, now far above lies.

'*The Innkeeper's Daughter*,' he grated. 'I don't know it. But I have a strong presentiment that it contains at least one thunderstorm and one murder.'

'And a ruined church,' Harriet said, smiling faintly. 'Oh, and a shipwreck. But it does work very well.'

'So does a dose of senna. Oh, I've perpetrated worse things in my time, no doubt. But the patent theatres resorting to such stuff . . . Where is our Shakespeare? What about Mr Kean? I read that he has returned to the stage, and I'm glad for it, though one gathers that he is rather less than a gentleman.'

'He has played Othello and Richard the Third this season, to much acclaim,' Harriet said – primly and neutrally, to conceal her excitement.

Kean, the wild and incandescent, the greatest actor of the day, had been a presence in her thoughts that she had tried not to think of ever since joining Drury Lane. It was like being in a room in which you knew that something tremendous, perhaps shocking, was hidden in a drawer. She had seen him about, several times. He was small, swarthy, unimpressive. But she was not fooled by that. She knew about transformation.

'Well, there's hope, then, perhaps,' grumbled her father, reaching mazily for his glass of cordial: or that was what they called it. '*The Innkeeper's Daughter*, indeed . . . Desdemona!' He pronounced it with abrupt, intense emphasis, right at Harriet, like a rich curse. 'For God's sake, Harriet, they must give you a fling at Desdemona. I see it. You have it. The absolute innocence – not that Desdemona was technically innocent, being a wife—'

'Oh, my dear,' Mrs Smithson protested, chuckling and pink, 'this is really not proper—'

'But I tell you she *is* innocent,' he shouted, with the cornered ferocity of illness, pounding the chair-arm, 'innocent in the true sense, that is the essence of her character, she is innocent of evil, not innocent of all that other – mechanical business of the flesh, which means nothing.'

Mrs Smithson, folding her generous arms, looked at the sooty grate with an oddly dejected expression; and then Anne, who in spite or perhaps because of her limp had a way of slipping silently into a room like a ghost, announced: 'They are the same, Papa, it's scriptural. It's a point of faith. The flesh and the devil. If that's what you mean. Which it is, I take it.'

Anne: she had this way of sliding her remarks in, like someone sticking pins into a pincushion – or flesh. To be with her was to be sombrely conscious of allowances and concessions: here was a young girl who was without health, looks, occupation, freedom, cheer, warmth, prospects – only this new censorious religion, which made her yet more difficult to love. For two hours after Harriet's arrival Anne refused to look at or speak a word to her sister. Then she came and put her face close to Harriet's, rather in the way she used to when hoping for a kiss; but this was to subject her to the ultimate scrutiny, the great delicate eyes roaming every inch of Harriet's face. Searching, Harriet felt, for lies.

'You left me,' Anne said at last.

'Heavens above, child, Harriet went to England to make her fortune,' Mrs Smithson had cried. 'And she's very near done it too. You ought to be glad. What an odd thing you are!'

Harriet said: 'I'm sorry.' Why? Because, in spite of everything, love required it. Anne had nothing, and you had to give to her.

And now Anne came and sat close by Harriet's side, claiming her hand, clasping and pressing it as if she would make it part of herself.

'Please, my dear, not another homily on the wickedness of the stage,' her father rasped. 'I've told you, it is an entirely mistaken idea, and also highly disrespectful to your mother and sister.'

'I don't believe Mama's wicked,' Anne said, and turning her vast gaze on Harriet: 'I don't believe you're wicked. But lots of wicked things do go on in the theatre. Everyone knows it. You can't deny it.'

'It depends what you mean by wicked,' Harriet said.

'No, it *doesn't*!' Anne hissed, and Harriet felt her fingers almost crushed. 'That's exactly where you're wrong.' Suddenly a confiding smile. 'But as long as I can trust you to be good.'

'Anne, really,' her mother clucked.

'Yes, Anne, you can,' Harriet said. You had to give to her; and besides, it seemed an easy promise to make.

She became aware of Frank Cope half-way through the new season at Drury Lane. At first, he was a voice.

The committee having run the theatre into the ground, they had cast about for a manager, or saviour, and had got a Kemble. It sounded good. The Kembles were the royal family of the theatrical nation. Mrs Siddons, the dowager queen, was in retirement now, and her brother John Philip Kemble had lately taken his last stately bow (Joseph: 'Pah – the man who put the anus in *Coriolanus*'), but there remained two brothers, Charles and Stephen. Charles was a respected actor of classical parts and a firm upholder of the dignity of the profession. Stephen was an enormously fat gouty windbag – he could play Falstaff without the padding and also without getting a single laugh – who had been farmed out to the provincial circuit. The committee appointed Stephen.

Still, they also engaged Harriet for the season at five pounds a week. And Stephen Kemble tried: he even recruited new blood, including a young Walking-Gentleman named Frank Cope.

That voice. She first heard it when the company were rehearsing an after-piece melodrama. Harriet as the heroine was lying on top of a trunk in a drugged sleep while the villain did something nefarious to the lighthouse kept by her godfather, her real father being a smuggler due for repentance (my child, my own) in the last scene. The actor playing the hero was indisposed that day – 'Caught a dose,' Eliza had informed her, 'got to go for his mercury treatment' – and so the unknown Mr Cope was called on to deliver his few lines in the scene. Mostly exclamations and what some play-books, to Eliza's infinite merriment, called ejaculations: but this voice did something with them, this ringing, reaching tenor with a shiver of tension in it. The drugged sleep meant she could not see the voice's owner, but that didn't matter: she enjoyed the voice like a piece of music. She wondered when she would hear it again.

It was a sharp winter. She had new, solitary lodgings in Russell Street – Eliza had come to a domestic arrangement with her latest admirer – where she had to pay for coals and candles. In an anxiety of thrift she would go to bed early under a heap of blankets, though she had lately suffered from insomnia: the needle of her mind would thread through the long night, waking, dream, waking, dream. If she had been reading or, more rarely, rehearsing Shakespeare, she found herself to her amazement dreaming in blank verse. The bed floated, carried on some potent tide of unhappiness she could not account for. She would tiptoe to the window to open the curtains and look for dawn. Frost-ferns would be stealthily flourishing on the glass. She wondered what it would be like to watch them, from beginning to end, making themselves.

Well, this is comparable, perhaps: the steady growth of Frank Cope on her consciousness.

A crowd scene. 'Mr Cope, if you could stand at the rear of your group, as you are the tallest – up centre, so. And all of you, try to show a little more animation: this is an execution, remember.' A glance. Tall, slightly angular figure, sweep of light fair hair, amused lips.

Overheard in the green-room: 'I hear they're going to try Mr Cope in *Where There's a Will*. Yes, the singing part – apparently he has a pretty voice.'

Encounter with Mr Cope in the backstage corridors: he doffing his hat and civilly making way for her. 'Miss Smithson.' He knew her. Long legs, long fingers: very Walking-Gentleman. Not knowing what to say in return. Saying nothing, no doubt appearing haughty. Not that it mattered.

Encounter with Mr Cope at the stage door. 'Miss Smithson, I wanted to say how very much I admired your performance last night.' Utter surprise – theatre people never said anything like it, except during fencing-matches of irony and malice – which must have shown: he smiled. 'Yes, oddly enough being on the stage has not quite destroyed my enjoyment of going to the play, though no doubt the time will come. I was in the pit.'

She hesitated, then found herself asking prosaically: 'Could you hear me?'

'Every word distinctly. Some might say that in a piece like *The Robber's Bride* that is scarcely an advantage, but you transcended it. I am only a beginner, but I have heard it said . . .' He paused, as if she had been about to say something: had she? 'I have heard it said that the pit is the only place worth pitching your voice to, as the gallery are only interested in looking at the scenery, and the boxes only interested in looking at each other.'

'That may well be so, sir.' It was some sort of answer, anyhow: she felt like an infant struggling with her first words. And now the exit, haughtier than ever, though she believed she was the least haughty person in the world. She just didn't know what to do.

Unwise mention – no more – of Frank Cope to Eliza: instant opening of floodgates. 'Oh, you're there, are you? Well, about time. Everyone knows he has the most prodigious taking for you.' Panicked splutterings from Harriet: she had performed in front of three thousand people, but at that *everyone knows* all the old fear of being looked at welled up. 'My dear love, why the fuss? We're only flesh and blood, after all. Even you, and you know I mean that kindly. You might do a lot worse. He has quite the most elegant figure – actually a gentleman born, they say, though of course his family won't own him now he's on the stage. Only a Walking-Gentleman, to be sure, so there's no *advantage* to be got, but then some kisses pay for dinner and some pay for themselves, as I always say. Do you want me to speak to him? I could—'

'No, no. No, Eliza, nothing of the sort. You are quite on the wrong track. Please, forget all about it.'

Eliza studied her with beautiful and absolute incomprehension. 'Well, but do you like *him*? That's the point.'

'That's not the point at all. Please forget it.'

Which was what she said, as such frigidities were all her infant-tongue could manage: but inside she cried with honest appeal, What do I do? What does anyone do?

How could she find out whether she liked Mr Frank Cope? Going to the linen-drapers in the Strand to buy material for shifts (save, save), she looked about her while pondering the question. She saw women of her own age – call them girls in truth – trailing in the wake of masterful mammas, and in her mind followed their carriages back to townhouses in the squares, beheld the white waistcoats of substantial papas, eavesdropped on their plans for an evening party: which young gentlemen should be invited, who was eligible, was that a sincere interest on the part of Mr Blank . . . ? And she felt helpless. At twenty years old she lived alone, paid her own bills, and ate at carefully selected chop-houses where her solitary state would not expose her to being thought a prostitute: the mamma-girls would shriek and wilt at such a prospect. Yet they confidently strode well-lit paths while she wandered in a fog.

Spring brought an end to the frost-ferns, the gnawing anticipation of having to find work during the summer closing of Drury Lane, and a note from Frank Cope delivered to her lodgings, commending her last performance, and asking her advice on the speaking of blank verse. She stared at it for several seconds as if it were a snake, then threw it away.

The next day came the letter from her mother.

The expected letter: the letter that had existed, really, since she had parted from her father in Dublin last summer, felt his blundering dry kiss and smarted at his bony hand clamping her arm and trying to say, too late, too much. Without thinking about it, any more than you think about the water you must drink to live, she had posited her life about this letter. And water was apt. The letter announcing her father's death was rippled, crackly with tears. No doubting their reality: her mother was not that good an actress. In the midst of her own grief, which was featureless and dry, Harriet was humbled by this: lately it was continually being impressed on her that she did not understand love.

3

The Bristol coach was late, and in the warm coffee-room of the Blue Boar Harriet fell into a doze containing a superb dream. Her father was not dead after all, and some fantastic luck had come to him, such as Bridget used to tell her the fairies might grant. Proudly he displayed to her the elegant figure of her mother, eyes glinting with wisdom and understanding; and the equally elegant, straight-backed, symmetrical figure of Anne, who said tenderly to her: 'This is the way it was meant to be, you see.'

The noise of the coach woke her. The dream sloughed off as she stepped out to the inn-yard: it felt like being gently flayed.

'There she is!' Anne, being lifted down from the coach by the porter, cried out as if to a saviour. 'Harriet, Harriet!'

Garlanded with ill-wrapped packages, puffing and sighing, Mrs Smithson gradually descended. Dropping things, she spread out black-sleeved arms. 'Oh, my dear Harriet, what shall we do? Whatever shall we do?'

Rhetorical question of the bereaved. Except her mother's moist, frightened eyes seemed to beseech an answer.

Harriet knew what to say. She knew now, also, why she had been saving. The dream disappeared altogether: or went to the place where forgotten dreams go.

'Come home with me,' she said, 'of course.'

Anne burrowed into her. 'Oh, yes. For always.'

Well: a family again, of sorts. (They had always been 'of sorts'.) 'Dear Lord, my love,' marvelled Eliza, 'you can't take that on your shoulders. They'll wear you out. They'll turn you into an old woman.' Eliza was leaving the stage to live with a man she called her 'protector', though it was hard to see what he would protect her against – men like him? But the family business wasn't so bad. Mrs Smithson was tearful and reminiscent, ate to console herself and groaned through the night with grieving indigestion. She was going to look for theatre work, she said, as soon as she was steady. Anne seemed quite content, absorbed as she was with an omnivorous curiosity that found no titbit beneath its notice. What play are you in tonight? Shall you wear those shoes? Where do you get them? How do you clean them? Where do you keep the brushes? Harriet realized, coming home to lights and talk, that she had been lonely. After a while she found that she was still lonely. But that altered nothing. Responsibility, she discovered, was a sort of drug. Just before the start of the theatre season she had fasted to keep herself employably slender – nothing but potatoes mashed with vinegar – and soon had found herself taking pleasure in the discipline. It was the same with supporting her family. There was something compelling about being severe on yourself.

For more room, she shifted lodgings again: but she was used to that, so much so that once on leaving the theatre she had said to herself: *I'll go home now.* And then, after a stupefied moment: *Where is it?*

So: no time, with her demanding charges, for thinking about Frank Cope. A relief. She did write him a note of apology in reply to his: regrets, too busy, and so on. She wrote it three times before she sent it. Well, the season was nearly over anyway – and after the summer, who knew? The life of an actress, she was learning, was a series of such precipices. Just hope not to fall off. There was no one to catch you.

'Why do we have to go to Margate?' There was a new edge to Anne's habitual plaintiveness: an assertion of rights. 'We're settled here. I like it here.'

'I do too. But in the summer there's no work in London.'

Anne glowered. 'I wish you didn't have to work.'

Really for the first time Harriet considered that, and recoiled. God, she didn't. Vacancy yawned at the thought.

'Tut, Anne, don't you know your sister has a very promising future? We're lucky, greatly lucky to have her. Not many young women could support a family respectably.' Newly roused from a nap, Mrs Smithson smacked her lips in distaste at the wine she had drunk and stared at nothing. 'The only other way is to marry a rich man. Which is what my mother and father wanted for me. No, thank you. I chose my William for love. And I never regretted it. I'd do it all again. Everything.'

Harriet had never conceived her mother as a figure of romance. Intriguing, if unsettling: Mrs Smithson seemed far away from her. 'Would you really, Mama? Everything?' Or: is that how it is, how it should be?

Anne chuckled bleakly. 'Well, you can't do it again, Mama, so there's no use in talking of it. Anyhow Harriet's not going to do *that*. Marry a rich man. You're not going to marry anyone, are you?'

'Not even as an alternative to the wicked stage?' Harriet said lightly, feeling heavy.

Anne did not so much dislike teasing as refuse to acknowledge it. 'If you were to get married, I don't know what I should do.' She gave the question a moment's sharp thought. 'Die, probably.'

Margate, like most genteel watering-places, offered a neat little theatre and audiences who were sedately appreciative as long as they knew the play already and had some nice costumes to look at. Mrs Smithson doffed her mourning, refreshed her memory, and managed to get a place in the company along with Harriet: they played together once in *She Stoops to Conquer* as Mrs Hardcastle and Kate, mother and daughter. Harriet bit her tongue at her mother's fluffs and lapses, and thought how unutterably strange life was.

In their seafront lodgings – first pair back, upstairs an Italian singing-teacher with a painfully audible love life, downstairs a fierce landlady florid and aromatic with gin – Anne lurked and waited. 'The sea air!' Mrs Smithson had cried at first. 'Lord, my love, it will do you a power of good!' One turn along the promenade, among Bath chairs and blanched consumptives, was enough for Anne. 'I loathe being with cripples.' So she stayed in and read the Bible, sometimes glancing darkly up as if she had come across something terribly apposite.

Joseph descended on them, as ever unannounced and unsentimental. 'Bear up, Mama. He was an old rogue, but he had his qualities, I dare say. People do go, though, and it's no manner of good getting upset about it.' He slept on the sofa, snoring and muttering bits of *Macbeth*. To Harriet's surprise, he sought her out alone in the green-room one evening when their mother was not playing.

'Listen, sis. I've had brandy so I'm serious. Can you really, you know, manage those two harpies? Only you're earning more than me, and I'm always flitting from place to place, and so it makes sense. But if – you know—'

'I can manage very well, Joseph. Which is what you wanted to hear.'

He grinned at her, wolfish and unhappy. 'Been thinking of trying America. Long way, though, and I get seasick. Well, I've never been to sea, but I'm convinced I would be. Look, I've got news. They're going to appoint a proper manager at Drury Lane, and the bids are in. The likely one is Elliston – in fact I'd say he's a certainty. So I say unto you, look sharp. He'll remember you, won't he, from Birmingham?'

Dubious, Harriet recalled the flamboyant Mr Elliston: the way he would sometimes glare impatiently past her, as if she were an inconvenience that had got in his way. 'Probably,' she said. 'Possibly.'

'Which, which? Well, I know what you mean. Opportunity, though, sis. Seize the whatsname. Of course they say Elliston's a shocking character. Drink and – what's that delightful term? Debauchery. Ever see any of that?'

'He was – what's that delightful term? Volatile. But in truth I never saw a great deal of him. He tended to shout us into position, then go off to shout at the wardrobe-woman.'

'Ah. Just wondering, you know.' Joseph took a coin from his pocket and began flipping, spinning, paying unnatural attention to it. 'Only if he does get Drury Lane, would you say he's the kind that has to be . . .' he hovered, a bee without a flower '. . . persuaded? No, call it charmed. Charmed.'

'What would you say if he were?' Not fencing: she wanted to know.

'Be damned to him.' Joseph spoke with startling urgency, teeth gritted. 'And anyone else of the sort. That's all I'm saying. I'm not trying to turn fatherish on you. God, I know how the world wags, and so do you. Just keep out of that, sis, because you don't need it. You'll get on without it. Is that what I'm saying? I suppose it is.'

'Thank you for the advice, Joseph, and I hope I shall never need it.' She was so embarrassed that there was nowhere to go except further into frankness. 'It's not the same for men, is it?'

'Ha! Dear God, no. In truth we can do pretty much what we like. Which, by the by, is not as satisfying as it sounds.'

'Do you think you'll marry? Have children? Mama was being vaguely wistful about grandchildren the other day.'

'Marry, don't think so. Too much the fidget. Besides, it always seems to me like – the end of dreams.'

Harriet laughed. She realized she was very fond of him. 'Isn't it supposed to be the beginning?'

Now he laughed, and in his eyes she glimpsed a tremendous unhappiness, and knew he would never tell her about it. 'Only in plays.'

She took the coach to London on her next free day and went to Drury Lane, where she half expected Elliston to be already installed. Not yet, the porter told her, with a solemn wink, but he had been there several times talking with the committee. At a Covent Garden coffee-house she paid for pen and ink and wrote Elliston a short letter, presenting her respects, saying she would be most happy if honoured with any communication from him relative to her engagement at Drury Lane next season . . . She grimaced: it sounded anxious and needy, but so she was; there were only a few weeks left at Margate, the new season loomed, and unpaid bills were clawing at her mind. Stepping out into the piazza, she found Frank Cope walking towards her.

'Miss Smithson – this is a great pleasure.'

And it really looked as if it was; which was why she presently found herself strolling about the Garden with him.

'A prudent move,' he said, when she told him about Elliston. 'He's certain to be the man. Is he such a Tartar as they say? No, don't tell me, I must just commit myself to the hands of Fate. Which have been rather rough lately. Oh, I picked up a few bits at the Haymarket, but mostly it's been a matter of slicing my bread very thinly. I don't mind it,' he said, laughing at her expression. 'I've only myself to consider. You, on the other hand, have dependants. I call it admirable, what you're doing, Miss Smithson – which sounds horribly soapy, though it's true. You don't come across much family loyalty in the theatre – wonder why?'

'Our eyes tend to be fixed on other things, perhaps.' Her eyes were fixed on his boots, very pointed and slender. She wondered if they pinched, and wondered why she wondered.

'The arts of the stage, no less. "Players, sir! I look upon them as no better than creatures set upon tables and joint-stools to make faces and produce laughter, like dancing dogs." Dr Johnson. I can quote so accurately because my father was always quoting it at me – before he disowned me altogether. Acting is a sort of art, though, don't you think? If rather a low one.'

'I don't think it's low.' She recalled her long-ago hatred of the theatre: the pact she had made with herself on entering it, the collusion with necessity and gift: and somehow now she had arrived at a new feeling for it – love. Was that how it was, then?

She felt Frank Cope's scrutiny on her, like an unscreened fire warming her cheek. 'Have I offended?'

'Not at all.' She was brisk. 'It's what many people believe. But I say it depends on the material. There's very little you can do with *The Spectre Bride* and *The Demon Nun.*'

'You're making that one up.'

'I was the demon nun. Walled up in the third act. When you're playing in such stuff you can only do your best with it – except you can't do your best, that's the trouble. To call on your best you need something fine, hard, something difficult to rise to.'

'Like Shakespeare? Must pass on to you this vivid memory: pair of ladies leaving the theatre after *Hamlet*, one asking the other what part she liked best: "The comic jigs between the acts," says she.'

'I'm afraid we often do him a disservice. My father was a great lover of Shakespeare, but he would sometimes put on mangled versions because people didn't want any other.' Father: *was*. Past tense. It kept coming back to you like a jab in the stomach. *I cannot choose but weep to think they would lay him i' the cold ground.*

'You have played him a good deal, I should think.'

'Not as much as I would like. Sometimes in Ireland. *As You Like It* and *Richard the Third* with Mr Elliston.'

'You're too modest. This is really why I addressed you that rather impertinent question about the speaking of blank verse. On the few occasions I've done it I come out ranting.'

'So do most of our actors.' She was rather shocked, but refreshed, at the note of assertion in her voice. 'I think the most important thing is to follow the rhythm instead of resisting it. Not exactly forgetting that it's verse, but realizing that our language does have that sort of rhythm. When we are excited, or angry, or wretched, we tend to speak with a pulse.' (Anne the other day, when her mother had made a mild joke about her temper: 'I *hate* you, *stop* it, *can't* you *see* my *pain*?' Harriet had noticed the iambic pentameter with fascination, and guilt: perhaps art made you cold, using everything, all grist to the mill.)

'Never thought of that. But the line-endings – how do you mark them, how do you avoid sing-song? And how do you bear all this in mind without forgetting your lines or walking into the flats?' He laughed suddenly. 'I don't expect answers, Miss Smithson, because if I was any good I would already know them. I'm just wondering aloud. Actually, I think I'm only fit for demon nuns.'

'No, no. You have a very good voice. It was the first thing I noticed about you.' For a shaken moment she considered what she had just said: the moment became a pause that on the stage would have been hugely pregnant. 'The voice can be trained, of course, but still there is only the instrument God gave you,' she hurried on primly.

'I can't pitch, though,' he said, after his own pause. 'Above a certain volume I crack ridiculously. Which is about enough of me, I think. How do you go on at Margate? Much company in the town?'

Walking, talking. The sun and the colonnades made precise geometries of brilliance and shadow: moving from one to the other you had to resist the urge to stretch and step as if over a threshold. Curious and alarming, all of it. Caution, caution: that was as immutably a part of Harriet as being right-handed. Still, only walking, talking. She must go soon, yes, soon. He begged her first to give a sample speech from Shakespeare: let him feel the pulse. She obliged.

It is, if you like, seduction.

Mr Robert Elliston took up the lease of Drury Lane in September. He looked at the books and the company contracts for last season. Then the letters went out. Harriet was performing a week's engagement at Bristol when she received hers.

'As a measure of necessary prudence he is reducing the numbers of the company by forty,' Harriet said, tossing the letter down.

'Yes?' her mother said, on such a stupidly hopeful note that Harriet wanted to scream at her. Instead she took some deep breaths.

'I am one of the forty, Mama. Never mind. I shall find something else.' That night she missed several cues, through being swamped by cold waves of alarm. The audience didn't notice: they were waiting for Madame Saqui to do her rope-dance in tights.

Another letter – from Frank Cope. How had he found out she was at Bristol? She put the question away.

The celebrated Elliston is part wise and part fool. Wisdom enough in dispensing with *my* services: utter folly in not availing himself of *yours*. Well, depend upon it, he will rue. (How's that for a theatrical locution?) Now I hope this will not be taken amiss: I have contrived to get an engagement at the Royal Coburg (walking-gent of course), and I took the liberty of mentioning the

name of Miss Smithson to the manager. He knew it: he was interested: *very* interested. There is no doubt of an offer – if *you* are
interested. Again, if this is an unconscionable presumption, pray
forgive it. Tempted to sign myself the Demon Nun, instead of what
I truly am, your obedient servant . . .

'Who is that letter from?' Anne demanded.
'Really, Anne,' puffed Mrs Smithson, 'that is no concern of yours.'
Oh, yes, it is, said Anne's look.

The Royal Coburg. Hard to think of a grander name: it almost seems
to wear sash and epaulettes. Elegant new building too. Unfortunately it
is situated south of the river, in malodorous Lambeth, and you must
run the gauntlet of dark lanes and pickpockets to get to it. Once there,
it depends on your expectations whether you will be thrilled or
disappointed. The speciality of the house is *burletta*, which, perhaps
appropriately, sounds like someone being sick. You shall have music –
that is, jigs and hornpipes and sentimental songs – and spectacle: battles,
horse-riding, dogs leaping from burning towers into barrels, choruses
of brigands, cataracts, flights of doves. You shall have melodrama –
wicked uncles, deathbed repentance, virtue triumphant – and
pantomime: tumblers, acrobats, a slapstick King of Egypt with a whistle
for a voice. You shall have Miss Smithson in *Beauty and the Beast*,
descending on a cloud-litter in a Turkish costume of silver gauze. You
shall have the opportunity to throw as many oranges as you like, as it
is standard behaviour in the Coburg audience. A play? Well – you know,
you can't have everything.

'This,' says Frank Cope to Harriet, as they wait in the wings while the
robber's bride performs a clog-dance, 'this is rather a hell-hole, isn't it?'
And he slips his hand into hers.

It could be interpreted as a gesture of solidarity. It could be.

*I had never held a man's hand before. It doesn't sound like much. But think –
think about hands, and touching. How many people's hands could you touch even
for a short time without discomfort – or without feeling, this is important, this is
intimacy?*

I was very young. Younger even than my age. Lately I have slipped the other way. The clock of my heart and the clock of my body have never shown the same time.

I envy people who are synchronized, who are always their proper age. They have the secret of easy living.

'That man called today,' Anne said. 'I sent him away.'

'Why did you do that?'

Anne was always ready, at any moment, for confrontation. 'Because you weren't here, and *I* don't want to see him. I told him so. What does he mean by it? Coming here as if he's—' Her sharp chin quivered, and she spluttered. 'As if he's *something.*'

Lately Frank Cope had taken to calling at their Lambeth lodgings to accompany Harriet to the Coburg. The dubious character of the neighbourhood made it generally acceptable, if not to Anne. The social call was new.

'There was no need to be rude,' Harriet said, turning from Anne's glare: sometimes it afflicted her like the light-scribble that heralded a migraine. Her stockings were wet from a downpour. She went into the bedroom, but Anne with her swift hobble pursued her.

'You'll get yourself talked about. Is that what you want? You know about actresses and their reputations. At this rate you won't be the exception. You'll make yourself a by-word.'

Harriet took off her stockings. Anne watched her hungrily. The well-turned shape of her own legs made Harriet feel guilty. From guilt she rebounded to cruelty. 'My dear, you're being absurd. I do believe you're jealous.'

Anne said, scarcely opening her lips, yet very distinctly: 'I do believe you're a whore.'

It was after rehearsal. Harriet was about to go home when she found Frank Cope calling to her from the end of the green-room passage.

'Look here. See what I've found.'

The room was dark except for a thin ooze of light from a high window. Fantastic shapes reared in the gloom. Harriet sucked in breath as a finger touched her face: no, a cobweb.

'What is it?'

'Prop store. Your eyes will adjust in a minute. Another prop store, I mean – must be things they're not going to use this season. The question is, when would they ever be used? Look.'

Look at this, and this: after a moment's hesitation she joined him in examining, disbelieving, crying out in hushed hilarity. 'If you ate a pound of cheese before bed you couldn't dream it,' he said, holding up a stuffed snake wrapped round a busby.

'Pure Coburg. Essence of Coburg,' she marvelled. 'Oh, dear Lord, that's not what I think it is—'

'Human rib-cage.' He rapped. 'Real bone, I think, not plaster. This I can't fathom – musical instrument?'

'Something for a torture-chamber, I'd guess.'

'Ah, this one I've worked out. See? It's a fish you climb inside. Why not?'

Impromptu scenes suggested themselves. They became breathless with laughter.

'In token of our gratitude for destroying the man-eating fish, I present you with this. It is the sceptre of Isis. Also it cracks nuts.'

'A thousand thanks. Yet no, I've been tricked! 'Tis the poisoned egg-beater of Hecate!'

'Yes, puny man wearing a Chinese gong-hat, and 'tis my revenge for turning my father into this wooden peacock. Now take up thy hookah and vacate my dominions . . .'

'We really should write it down. Take it to the management.' He came close to her. 'It would work.' From being unable to breathe for laughing, she was suddenly unable to breathe for his mouth. There was an instant of sheer puzzlement – what was he doing?

Kissing her. But it felt like being stiflingly chewed. She pulled away, tried to make a joke about cutting this scene; but it was as if he were no longer aware of her, or that aspect of her. With his smile clenched, like a dog with a stick, he began clawing and rubbing at her body; somehow he raced at it, as if there were a bet or challenge: how quickly could he touch it all? Fending him away with her hands, squirming backwards, seemed to do no good: rather, he grinned as if this were the expected and even appropriate thing, then got her fast in his arms and propelled her backwards on to something that was like a hard couch, or soft coffin.

She would never have believed slender Frank Cope could weigh so much. In fact, she still did not believe it: any moment it would be revealed as a joke, a romp. Then he did things to her neck with his tongue, and she believed it. She cried out: 'Stop it. Get off.' She tried to use her fists, but he blocked them with one forearm and then whipped up her skirts like a tablecloth. 'No.' He caught her hand and pulled it down to his loins, pressing it to some part of himself that was as outrageous as the clutter around them, a shifting and swollen excrescence. 'No.' She was screaming now. When he tried to cover her mouth she bit, hard. He yelped and jerked back: then slid off her, his face changing – actually laughing a little.

'Well, well. I take the point. My apologies, if you want them. But really, I have never been wrong before.'

She stood, quaking, brushing and brushing at her clothes, brushing him off her. 'Bastard.' It was the first time she had ever spoken the word.

'Tell me,' he asked, rearranging his hair, 'who are you saving it for?'

'Not you, not you.'

'Well, obviously. But who? A manager? Elliston? I may be mistaken, but I believe money is his particular vice. The point is, they don't like it any better if you're virginal. Less, probably, because you don't know what you're doing. Just a little advice for you, if you are looking to sell it.'

'You are so vile.'

'Oh, come,' he snapped, getting up and irritably twitching his shoulders. 'You're an actress. How are you going to play Juliet, in the unlikely event you're offered it? Juliet got fucked at fourteen and loved it. Naturalness, that's what you aim for, ain't it? How natural is Juliet with her legs crossed? Hey, well.' He went to the door. 'Let me know if you want the instruction after all.'

In bed that night she wept, silently – absolutely without a sound. Yet soon Anne was at her bedside, as if she could scent the salt tears.

'It's that man,' Anne said, and then vehemently: 'It's that *man*.' The change of emphasis arraigned all men, everywhere. Harriet sobbed and moaned. Anne stroked her hair, heaping and handling it like treasure. 'I told you. Now you know. Was he horrible to you?' She seemed to drink in, to inhale Harriet's mute, shaking response. 'Well, now you know. And it's for the best. Now it's just us.'

★   ★   ★

Spring: the Royal Coburg season came to an end. When she left, workmen were beginning construction of a vast curtain made of sixty-three pieces of mirror. 'It'll probably bring the ceiling down,' she heard Frank Cope say to someone in the green-room. Civil, faintly ironical nods were all he had for Harriet now. She prayed never to see him again. She could not help seeing him in her nightmares, but those, she thought, would fade.

A summer in Dublin kept them afloat, but London was the centre of her world now, and September found her back at Drury Lane, seeking an audience with Robert Elliston. Crossing Covent Garden she steered clear of the colonnades: shun that darkness.

Darkness into light. Elliston, wearing for some reason a costume wig, grandiloquent, bright-nosed, greeted Harriet like an old friend. Miss Smithson, to be sure, where had she been hiding? Taken on at three pounds a week: and please be aware of the new system of fines and forfeits. She was back on the ladder, if a couple of rungs down.

Back in the melodrama-pantomimes and lyrico-extravaganzas. No rope-dancers or glass curtains, at least. Or not yet. 'Elliston's thrashing around trying to find something that will draw,' Joseph commented. 'So don't despair. In the end he might even try theatre.'

Darkness into light. At last Elliston got his draw. Enter Mr Edmund Kean.

Or, as it should be, *Mr Edmund KEAN.*

Who is Mr Kean? Nobody much, if you were to pass him in the street. Not tall, not handsome, not graceful, not even very well made. You might just notice the deep-set burning-black eyes – and then you might well give him a wide berth.

One thing: he is not like any other actor. Some of the old school still swear by Mr Hill's *Essay on the Art of Acting*, which enjoins patterning your postures after ancient statues – to look noble, just stand there like the Apollo Belvedere. But Mr Kean never stays still for a moment. Others prefer to be themselves – that is, sterling gentlemen who happen to be portraying Hamlet: never forget that under the costume I am an unimpeachable good egg. But nobody could think Mr Kean a good egg. His private life is all over the scandal sheets. As for a gentleman – Mr Kean has no bearing, no carriage, no orotundity of voice. His background is shady – bastard, foundling, gypsy, no one knows. He rasps like a crow and scuttles unpredictably about the stage. And nobody can take their eyes off him. Harriet, watching one of his rare rehearsals, finds her eyes stinging: she has forgotten to blink. Numbly she goes home and remarks to her mother: 'I've been doing it all wrong.'

Drink and (of course) debauchery have kept Mr Kean from the stage for a time, but now he is back and the Drury Lane management raise prayerful eyes: give us this day some decent receipts. No demon nuns for Mr Kean: he is a Shakespearean, and a titanic one. Ladies have fainted away at his Othello. (And been kindly revived in his dressing-room later.) The leading actresses of the company, Miss Kelly and Madame Vestris, who sit on the best roles like fierce hens, plume themselves in readiness.

And then Mr Kean drops in to watch Harriet rehearsing a rather dismal little farce called *Not So Good As She Should Be*, and growls: 'I want her.'

'Where are you from, Miss Smithson?' Mr Kean prowls about his dressing-room, trying on wigs. 'No, don't tell me. Ireland.'

'How did you know, sir?' Not, she pleaded inwardly, the brogue.

'I have second sight, my dear madam.' He gives his sudden, intimidating blast of a laugh. 'And it was on the bill at your début. I remember it. Yes, I see all, I remember all.' He glowers at himself in the mirror. 'No, the black one, I think. So, what have you been doing at Drury? Trash, no doubt. Simpering for simperers. Where did I put the black wig?'

'Just behind you.'

'I remember everything that's *important*.' Mr Kean has an odd, asymmetrical, fascinating mouth, in which a smile and a sneer co-exist. 'We shall return this great barn, Miss Smithson, to the glories of the legitimate drama. Sounds plaguey dull, doesn't it? "The le-git-imate dra-ma".' He rolls it out in a Kemble voice. 'But you and I know better.'

Harriet wonders, Does he really have second sight? She is sure Bridget would have run from him. 'There will be Shakespeare, sir?'

He advances close to her, blue-chinned, brandy-fumed. 'What do you like best in Shakespeare, Miss Smithson?'

'Tragedy. *Othello. Hamlet. Romeo and Juliet.*' At that last one, a bitter tremor.

'Not much for you in *Hamlet*. Well, Ophelia, for what she's worth. Desdemona, though, there's a part. Do you know Lady Anne in *Richard*?'

'Very well. I have often played it in Ireland—'

'Ah, but this isn't Ireland.' He holds her at arm's length. 'You are remarkably beautiful.' Before her heart begins to sink he adds: 'Nay, don't fret yourself, Miss Smithson, I have quite enough affairs to be going on with. I'm thinking of effect. I want pain and grief from you, madam –' his fingers dig like wire into her arm '– and they are ugly. They distort. They wrench.'

'I know.' She does not flinch, from that grip or from those eyes. 'I know that.'

Forget the three minds. Acting with Kean, all you have are nerve-endings.

There are scarcely any preparations. 'Preparations kill,' he says. 'Preparations are tyrants. Genius is liberty.' Also his rakehell private life precludes rehearsals, as he is scarcely alive before three. First, *Richard the Third*, with Harriet as Lady Anne to his Richard. Her first Shakespeare in London: all day her scalp tingles, her palms moisten. Then Kean arrives at the theatre, late, scowling, bloodshot. He calls her to his dressing-room and talks to her over his shoulder: 'Don't shout. Don't flutter your hands. And don't do anything clever. It's me they come to see.'

She tries, really tries not to feel stung. He is liverish, and many actors are snappy before the performance, from tension. She paces the green-room, regulating her breathing. But a finger of unhappiness keeps prodding at her shoulder. Don't do anything clever. How are you going to play Juliet? My apologies, if you want them. She smells again the dust of that prop-room.

Kean has crackled through the first scene in the time it would take a Kemble to clear his throat. He lurches into the wings, still Richard, still fierce and devilish, and looks her up and down. 'Damn it, I'm not usually wrong, but I wonder . . .' He shrugs and jerks his thumb. 'Well, go on.'

She goes on, somehow. Everything has left her: breathing, preparation, the nicely calculated balance of grief and pride with which her Lady Anne is to follow the King's hearse. She is stranded: all she can do is remember her lines. I belong in the Coburg really: demon nuns and performing dogs. How are you going to play Juliet? Don't do anything clever. I have never been wrong before. Damn it, I'm not usually wrong . . . Papa, I wish you were here. Why? Because you never disappointed me. The house is full, but she cannot turn her face to it: she imagines a great curtain of sixty-three mirrors, all terrifyingly reflecting her. She fixes her gaze on the hearse.

'Lo, in these windows that let forth thy life
I pour the helpless balm of my poor eyes.'

Anne's tender, covetous hands stroking her hair. That man. That *man*. Naturalness, that's what you aim for, ain't it? Well, well.

'If ever he have child, abortive be it,
Prodigious, and untimely brought to light,
Whose ugly and unnatural aspect
May fright the hopeful mother at the view . . .'

Her voice is shaking. Let it.

Enter Richard. He springs on the scene like a pouncing cat: 'Stay, you that bear the corse, and set it down.'

It's me they come to see. True: the whole house shivers. Don't do anything clever – like getting drunk every night and morning, and forgetting where you put your wig.

'Villain, thou know'st nor law of God nor man:
No beast so fierce but knows some touch of pity.'

Don't look at him. Don't do anything clever. Kean circles her, palms out, his face a piteous, beseeching mask. A mask. All pretending.

'Fairer than tongue can name thee, let me have
Some patient leisure to excuse myself.'

My apologies, if you want them. She finds herself stepping back from him, though she had prepared to stay down left until the ring business. He darts after her, exultantly. She does not know what to do.

'Fouler than heart can think thee, thou canst make
No excuse current but to hang thyself.'

Bastard. Not you, not you. Kean turns cryptically, teasingly from her, not saying his line. She follows him with baffled eyes. Is he trying to throw her? Are they that self-adoring, these great actors? Let him: she is just as much a professional as he . . .

'He is in heaven, where thou shalt never come.'

She is supposed to spit at him later in the scene, but she spits out the words so violently that, yes, spittle rains on Kean's face. He beams as if it were summer rain.

'And thou, unfit for any place but hell.' Oh, you devil.

In the wings after the scene, Kean hoarsely chuckling with his wiry hand on her shoulder. 'Not enough to be professional, you see, Miss Smithson. No danger in it. The moment, the moment is where we must live.'

She gasps into her hands. 'I could never keep that up. It's too . . .'

'Too much like life. Which you can't prepare for either.'

And now, Desdemona.

Harriet wishes her father could see her: accepts he cannot. She has a quiet faith, but she cannot imagine that you are allowed to look down from heaven into theatres.

Yesterday in Covent Garden she bumped into Eliza, very pregnant and not very well dressed. Happy, though, apparently. Her new protector was a lawyer. Or, rather, a lawyer's clerk. Eliza laughed blurrily. 'But he is so *very* handsome. And after a while – I don't know, you just can't do without it.'

Kean's Othello is frightening. From the beginning you feel that he might kill you: even his tenderness is threatening, a love like a ray through curved glass, burning as it concentrates. (Is that how it is . . . ?) In Desdemona she cultivates stillness, the steadfast rock to his tempestuous sea. Sometimes Kean himself seems to fume at her passivity – but, then, she is learning from his example. The moment, the moment. Desdemona, her father said, is innocent. And who more innocent than she? She makes herself flint to spark him. When he murders her, it is with all the desperation of impotence. Though she makes sure to turn her head to one side when the pillow descends, still she can hardly breathe for a minute. She can hear the sweet stricken hubbub from the audience: not unknown for men to jump on the stage and try to rescue Desdemona. Dying, sensing the groan of the house like distant thunder, she feels more triumphantly alive than ever before. And indeed, is it possible to feel more alive than this? Frank Cope, Eliza, are you not after all monstrously deceived?

Joseph, in the green-room, months later: 'Felicitations on your triumphs, sis. I've been reading all about them.'

'You must be reading very old newspapers.'

He laughed. He liked her tart. 'Yes, as it happens. Abroad. Would you believe where *I've* had my greatest triumph? Well, turned a profit anyhow. Amsterdam.'

Joseph was managing a touring company. Harriet wondered about him as a manager: he had the temper, but he seemed to lack the essential touch of shiftiness.

'Amsterdam? What do you play?'

'Usual repertory. Actually no, some serious stuff. Middleton, Rowe. Even *Hamlet*. It goes over, believe me. A lot of your Dutch burghers know English – but even without that, it does go. You have to make it work, that's the thing. You have to make them feel it.' He fingered the playbill for tonight. '*The Chinese Sorcerer*. Ah, that deathless classic of the drama. Any elephants in it?'

'Only Mrs West.'

'Tut, naughty. And what are you?'

'The Emperor's niece. Princess O-me.'

'Oh, my . . . What's Elliston playing at?'

'He's trying to make good the theatre's debts, I suppose. These things pay, Joseph, you know that.'

'Aye, but do they? He must have spent a fortune on sets and refitting. And now I hear he's poaching these notables from Covent Garden. Young, Liston. I doubt they come cheap.'

'No. But they draw.' Harriet took a sip of wine: a new indulgence, to be carefully hidden from the under-manager, a malevolent toady who went around counting candle-ends and looking for infractions. 'They were turning them away from Mr Liston's first night.'

'I hear he has to dose himself with laudanum to keep off the horrors. Comedians are always a little mad. Personally I hate them. Anybody can raise a laugh. Just fall over.' He stretched in a hound's yawn. 'So. You, in the meantime, have to make do with O-me the Chinese whatsname. What happened? Last season, *Othello* with Kean. Excellent notices. Now this. Did Kean drop you? I know he's a queer fish.'

'Mr Kean has done everything possible for me. He plays in my benefits, he chooses me from the company whenever he can. But even he can't alter the management—'

'And besides which, he's always half-seas-over, or running after his fancy-pieces, or running from his creditors. And the old harpies still cling to the best parts, no doubt. *La* Kelly still ruling the roost? I told you, you'll have to do away with her. Put some ground-glass in her brandy. I hear she drinks like a fiddler's bitch.'

'You hear a lot, don't you?'

He grinned. 'Lord, yes. Make your hair curl, if it didn't already. Nothing about you, though. I mean that in the best sense. No breath of scandal et cetera. How do you do it?'

'I cover my traces very well,' she said, making a face.

'No, I'm serious. You amaze me. Looking after gobbling old Mama and that poisonous little sister the fairies gave us. I feel appropriately guilty, by the by. Is it – you know – bearable?'

'If it weren't, how could I bear it?'

He contemplated her sombrely. 'Do you remember – whenever it was – asking me if I would marry?'

'Oh, Joseph! Who's the unlucky woman?'

'Be off with you. No, I'm thinking of you. Tell me, is that what's putting you off? Being prop and stay to Mama and the imp? Because if so, don't let it. I doubt I would stand them for a fortnight – but I would try.'

'You must have heard something I haven't. Who wants to marry me? I must start reading those scandal-sheets. Or are you matchmaking?'

'Pooh, I only know theatre people. For God's sake, don't marry one of them. Look, what I mean is someone will come along, surely. You've got talent, charm, beauty. Pause for mutual cringe of embarrassment. Now that's over, think about it. Are they holding you back?'

She emptied her glass. 'You talk as if there's nothing for me but marriage. I am a regular player at Drury Lane, Joseph, and I do have good roles, not just these bloody double-damned Chinese princesses—'

'Never heard you swear before. Harriet, I'm being realistic. Fanny Kelly's still going to be doing Lydia Languish from a Bath chair. Nothing shifts 'em once they're at the top – except when some pretty piece jumps into bed with the manager and suddenly she's got a début.' He frowned. 'I suppose I'm saying I want you to be happy.'

'I shan't marry.' His eyebrows went up at the fierce edge in her voice: she sought to soften. 'Thank you for your concern. But after all, dear brother, I am *wedded* to my *art*.'

They had a laugh together then. And she wondered whether Joseph, observant though he was, could guess that deep down she meant it.

4

But you have to live with this: the longing.

Longing for what? What is longing ever for but the intangible and unnameable? It is somewhere in the night-smell of coal-smoke and fog and suppers as she walks back to Great Russell Street after the theatre, and in the sounds: the clank of the sausage-vendors shutting up their ovens, the first rumble of the vegetable-carts, the pointed tap of feet ascending steps to a front door. The thump of the door, closing on the world.

It is somewhere in the lowered young eyes of the City clerk at the chop-house who always lingers over his small plate of *à la mode* beef for a solitary, precious hour: somewhere likewise in the self-possession of the flautist in the Drury Lane orchestra, thin as his flute, coat shiny at the elbows, who always arrives early and plays sad, beautiful airs to himself and the great receiving emptiness of the auditorium – a shepherd in a gilded and plastered grove.

And on summer tours it shimmers in the hayfields and in the distant towns that sail into view, a flotilla of roofs, cathedral spires like great masts. It is there in the provincial theatres, in the excited family in the dusty, peeling box: that look, in the gangling boy and the big-chinned girl, of an unexpected goodness. On the road it is in the ambling gait of the turnpike-keeper coming out of his toll-house still chewing his dinner; and in the wonder that quite randomly you were born yourself and not him, and what it must be like to be him: what it must be like. What everything must be like.

★   ★   ★

Curious episode. Just before the 1824 season, Harriet found herself boarding the Dover packet to France.

The sea was choppy, and she strolled the deck to a wordless chorus of vomitings. Frequent crossings between England and Dublin had given her strong sea-legs, but she had her own inner queasiness about this odd enterprise. Joseph had taken a company to France, and had begged her to come over, if only for a few nights, to bolster its prestige. She had agreed because he was her brother, but several of her fellows from Drury Lane gasped, urged her to make her will, recommended a breastplate under her costume. 'Come back soon, my dear. And try to come back alive.'

Exaggeration, of course: but still. A hopeful manager had taken English drama to Paris last year and narrowly escaped a riot. Shakespeare was an abomination: the English were theatrical Wellingtons, invading French culture. The audience threw harder things than oranges. Joseph, before his departure, was breezy. 'Oh, they've got to forget Waterloo *eventually*.' Still, he settled for a season at Boulogne and Calais, which were full of English expatriates.

'Ghastly old dandies hiding from their debts, mostly,' Joseph said, when he met her at Dessein's in Calais. 'They still dress like Brummell and talk about Prinny. It's a fantasy. But they're starved for theatre. Also the French do come, some of them.'

'With pistols?'

'No, they just spit a lot. How'd you get on at the Customs House? Not too much fondling? Capital. Welcome to France.'

Memories of Mrs Turner's school, the Napoleonic maps and thigh-rubbings, and her own doomed tussle with the French language. But now she was here, none of it seemed quite real – or, rather, it seemed not quite adequate. Calais reminded her of a dingier Deal, and Boulogne of Brighton. She heard people speaking French, but the feeling that they were acting was reinforced by the readiness with which innkeepers and post-boys dropped into English. She almost expected the narrow chalky streets to wobble like backdrops.

At Calais *The School for Scandal* received polite applause, and at Boulogne it was followed by an invitation to supper with some wealthy expatriates who talked Westminster politics over the roast beef. In her room at the Hôtel de l'Europe Harriet learned her lines, then threw open her window to smell the sea air. Just sea air: no different. Then from somewhere below sprang the sound of a row. A male and a female voice skirmished, then broke out in volleys of fury and obscenity. Harriet did not understand a word, but her fascinated ear followed it all, the rapid staccato of accusations, the gruff rebuttals, the swear-words spluttered out as a child desperately scrabbles for and throws stones. Underneath it all she detected tears. When they came at last, in mutual desolate hoots, it seemed as right as a piece of music returning to the keynote. The tears that rose to her own eyes made an interesting coda.

The whole French episode was a mere novelty, she felt, though when they parted at Calais Joseph was nervily exhilarated. 'Receipts not so bad, not so bad at all. You know, it has possibilities. A break from stodgy old England, anyhow.'

'When we were in Ireland, you always longed to get to England.'

'Did I? I suppose I did. Wish I had your memory. No, I don't, because I imagine it doesn't tend to make you happy, eh?' He kissed her: unprecedented. 'Thank you for supporting me, sis. Miss Smithson of Drury Lane, you know, makes a difference. Don't let them grope you too much when they row you out to the packet. I know what they're like. A knitting-needle discourages, so I hear.'

'You hear a lot. Where will you go now?'

'Not sure, not sure. Thoughts of Brussels. Oh, I'd plump for Paris, but – probably not wise.'

Not wise at all, Harriet thought, kissing him, now there was a precedent, in return. Interesting episode, but really, she thought, gulping at the Channel wind, there was nothing here for the likes of them: nothing at all.

Drury Lane, nadir of winter, and Harriet has been again rehearsing Lady Anne in *Richard the Third*, again to be played with Mr Kean, though the great man still disdains most rehearsals. Incredible cold of a huge, empty theatre at this season, so you chatter through your lines like a revivified skeleton and exhale clouds at every cue. Someone has asked for a stove, and received Mr Elliston's usual response nowadays, which is a wild kick in your direction and a slurred suggestion that you seek alternative employment. After rehearsal Harriet remains behind on the bare stage to try some directions that make more sense than the manager's: becomes aware, in the giant grotto of shadows that is the auditorium, that someone is sitting there.

'Miss Smithson. How goes it? Come, come.'

Mr Kean is sitting there in the pit, or rather, the seats being backless, lolling. Below the famous eyes his face is relegated to a few angles and twitches. He takes her hand: actually, it is a masculine shake, preparatory to business.

'So. Are you ready for Richard? Or I should say, are you ready for *my* Richard?'

'Why? What are you going to do?' She is used to Mr Kean's unpredictability, but she would like to know which unpredictability to expect, or not expect.

'Do? Survive, I hope.' He looks sick and yellow, the ugly-beautiful mouth never more ambiguous. 'Anyway, you know. All I'll say is, plunge on regardless, it's the only way.' He flings himself back, peering as if trying to see her round a screen. 'You do *know*? Don't you read the scandal sheets?'

'No, I don't. They're a great bore. I have read about it in the *The Times* – the court action, that is—'

'*The Times*, most scurrilous scandal sheet of them all. True voice of a puling hypocritical nation. The kingdom of cant. *The Times* would have me hung, drawn and quartered, preferably in reverse order.'

Of course she knows. Mr Kean has long been having a public affair with Mrs Cox, the wife of a City alderman. Mr Cox has suddenly decided he cannot bear it and brought a criminal-conversation suit against Mr Kean, which has brought as many spectators to the Court of the King's Bench as to Drury Lane. She prefers not to think about it: it has nothing to do with the Mr Kean she knows, the inspiration and goad, the galvanic battery applied to the dead nerves of her performances.

'And of course everyone is talking about it, from ticket-takers to third fiddle,' he snarls at her. 'Isn't it so?'

'I dare say. I don't listen to such things.'

'You know, Miss Smithson, this pretty-please touch-me-not act is all very well, but it will wear thin when you get older, you know.'

'Mr Kean, I'm not *The Times* or the King's Bench, so please don't use me as if I were,' Harriet says lightly: thinking, That will hurt later.

'Palpable hit. Sorry. But look here, you don't read the gossip and you don't listen to it – tell me, Miss Smithson, what *do* you do?'

'I'm an actress. And that's enough. As for private matters –' she manages not to say *affairs* '– that's what they are, private.'

'Ah, but they ain't, not for the likes of us. If you're a gentleman with five thousand a year and a correct set of opinions, all parcelled up and deposited with your family lawyer, then you can talk about private. All the difference, Miss Smithson. This England is a very small place. And they make it smaller with their damned hearts of oak. Narrow, hard little hearts, that's what. D'you know, in America people ask why I'm not a lord? Ha! They'd as soon ennoble a Billingsgate fish-fag. Well, I'm just giving you a warning. When we play tomorrow, there may be a certain – hostility.'

'Preferable to indifference.'

He grins, very wolfish and Richard the Third. 'I've hopes of you yet. "In time we hate that which we often fear." Do you know *Antony and Cleopatra*? Marvel if you do. Our prig-public won't suffer it. Too much passion. You know why they love us, and yet hate us? Because we *dare* on their behalf. They let us take them so far, into the dark woods of their selves, and they like it – into their passion, and their lies and greed, their beauty and mortality: so far, but no further. They get frightened, and want to hurry back to counting the sovereigns and bullying the servants and letting their minds go blissfully empty. It is, if you like, seduction, and they're shocked at themselves for enjoying it, and they whip down their skirts and scream names at you. That's why art is dangerous. What's the matter?'

'Nothing.' She calms herself. 'I'm glad you said art, Mr Kean. I was just thinking of some words of Dr Johnson's – something about dancing dogs on tables—'

'Johnson, old pension-grubbing humbugging Tory. Art, art, cling to it, Miss Smithson, they'll take everything else from you. Ah, can you imagine what *The Times* would say to us now? – alone together in a darkened theatre? Another innocent female entrapped in the wiles of this – now what did they call me? *Obscene mimic.*'

Harriet smiles. 'I'm not conscious of any wiles, Mr Kean.'

'That's because I'm not extending any. No, I'm not for you.' He studies her. 'I wonder who will be.'

'As you say, Mr Kean, I prefer to cling to my art.'

'What you prefer has nothing to do with it. Fate, Miss Smithson. Ever have your fortune told? I did when I was nine or ten.' He draws a brandy-flask from his pocket and takes a deep draught, then examines his outstretched hand. 'There, takes off the shakes in a second. Nine or ten – not entirely sure when I was born, which is a novelty. Usually it's the day of our death that lies hid from us. Nine or ten years, and been on the stage so long I had the experience of twenty. An old witch at Bartholomew Fair took my hand and told me my fate – and she was a veritable witch, Miss Smithson, even the biggest fairground brute wouldn't dare cross her for fear of a curse that would cramp his guts or turn his hair white. You smirk, of course, you don't believe in witches.'

'I never smirk, Mr Kean.' *Be assured, they believe in you.* 'What was it she told you?'

He yawns as if suddenly bored. 'Fame and riches and crossing the sea and the love of many women. All of these would come to me.' He drinks deeper. 'And falling. Beware of falling. It might be as well if you left me now, Miss Smithson, as I intend getting drunk.'

He extends a hand: she shakes it. 'Well,' she says, 'beware of falling.' The echo of his laughter follows her, grating and forlorn.

Mr Kean, if not a witch, is an accurate prophet. When they open in *Richard the Third* the next night, there is a certain hostility – very certain. But the hisses and boos that greet Kean's entrance are comparatively genteel beside the ribaldry. Richard's love-making is a gift to the gallery. 'Tell Alderman Cox he's at it again!' When he offers Harriet's Lady Anne his sword the wits go wild. 'Go on, girl, take hold of his weapon!' Harriet reckons she makes about one line in ten heard. When the final curtain falls her throat is raw and Kean, who has had recourse to the brandy between acts, is spitting drunk.

These things have momentum. By the time Harriet plays again with Kean, a week later, Drury Lane has become a Roman amphitheatre. You come to yell at the savage sport.

The piece is Massinger's *A New Way to Pay Old Debts*, and in the green-room Kean is serene and expansive. Sir Giles Overreach is one of his greatest roles, and will surely overcome any amount of nonsensical demonstrations. 'When I first played it, no less a man than Byron was overcome − literally overcome. He confessed to me that he almost fell down in a fit. That was when he presented me with a Turkish sword, genuine article from Damascus, magnificent thing. We dined together often after that, you know − before the miserable canting sheep-wits of England drove him out. Ate like a bird, by the by − fearful of putting on flesh. Drink, though, that was a different matter.'

Byron, though, that was a different matter: that was the old days of the Regent and rakes and transparent ball-gowns, and now we do not breathe that air. When Harriet walks out on to the stage that night, she breathes the new air: close, sour, poisonous.

For a while they contend against the uproar. Then the oranges start flying − actually from a box on the right hand − and one nearly hits her. Kean stops in mid-speech, stands protectively in front of her with a grand and reproachful gesture. His partisans clap and cheer. Others reach for the fruit. Mr Elliston, approximately as drunk as Kean, stumps on to the stage and begins to orate. 'Seldom in my long career have I had occasion to reprove the patrons by whose generosity we poor players, we who are, as the poet has it, such stuff as dreams are made on, are enabled to eke out our substance . . .' Unsurprisingly, this is soon drowned. A young man who vaults through the orchestra and on to the stage, brandishing his cane and yelling, 'Kean and liberty!' gets a better response. Elliston manages to restrain him from climbing into the box and giving the orange-thrower a thrashing. There is a lot of gallant pointing at Harriet from both gentlemen − insult to the fair sex and so on − which at last gets the noise down to market-day level. Somehow the play limps on.

And Harriet, wretched and unnerved as she is, feels − well, she feels almost bored. Because there is nothing more boring than stupidity. She remembers the little girl sitting with her guardian in the theatre at Ennis, squirming and appalled, and wonders if she was right after all.

Harriet's twenty-seventh birthday followed a successful benefit night at Drury Lane, so she ventured into extravagance and gave her mother and Anne supper at Grillon's. It was not a greatly uplifting occasion. Women dining in public without men were looked on as at best eccentric, at worst as sluts; and Harriet certainly felt herself looked on. Mrs Smithson drank freely of Constantia wine, becoming picky, very nearly quarrelsome. 'Twenty-seven. Lord, I don't understand it. Twenty-seven, and still no prospect of a husband. I know, my dear, it's not for lack of opportunity. You attract a deal of notice, only you don't know how to bring it on. I can't suppose you're cold, not considering your parentage. I don't know: in our day we had more feeling, I think. Lord, didn't we have feeling!' She had developed this maundering way of addressing an invisible and ever-agreeing companion. Anne gazed at her with bottomless disgust.

Twenty-seven: Lord. Harriet didn't understand it either – the fact of the years, the fact that they mattered. What was one supposed to do? Make a plan – by thirty I will be such-and-such? Take stock? But she was always doing that: the insecurity of her profession demanded it. Just now, for instance, she must balance the success of her benefit with the fact that Drury Lane, and she with it, were in the doldrums. Elliston had staggered apoplectically into bankruptcy, receipts were plummeting, and Harriet's wage was down to three pounds ten a week. Mr Kean had shaken the sanctimonious dust of Albion from his feet and gone to tour America: his imminent return to the London stage was announced, but there were whispers that he was a wreck now, crow-voiced and stumbling. The first ladies of the company still kept the plum roles, such as they were, and a desperate note had entered the voice of Harriet's supporters in the press, calling for her to be given Lady Macbeth or Rosalind, to let her prove herself.

She was at present in rough seas, then – or becalmed, whichever way you looked at it: her future, a surrounding fog. But through that fog, a poke of light, from a most unexpected quarter. There were plans afoot to take an English company to Paris.

You are not telling it right.

Pardon me – I mean no disrespect, and of course you are telling it, everything, everything that happened – but what you are doing now, I quite understand it, is what the artist must do, that is intensify it. Build it up, roll the drums. And yes, how else can you convey that time – the time when my life stood at a halt, when really nothing was happening? There is the hardest task of art, to portray nothingness – or rather, mere inexpectation. That's what I mean, I think. I didn't know, you see, what was to come: I had no idea. We never do. Just another thing happening to you, on you go, wake, dress, somehow live. That's what you must remember.

You want me to take up the story? I don't know — I am not equal to much. I am not equal to myself, as it were. But — well, I can speak briefly, if it will help.

The business about the light through the fog — well, yes, it was at least something new, a prospect of sorts, and I did feel that the English stage was — pressing in, suffocating. Dull, in truth. But my first feeling was, this is not a propitious venture. More interesting than promising. I remembered Joseph in Boulogne, getting by, playing chiefly to the English abroad. As for Paris — I think I imagined it like London but fifty times more difficult to please. Or else absolutely indifferent.

But there was a manager in Paris, a Monsieur Laurent, who wanted an English theatre season and was prepared to pay for it and to procure all the royal permissions and licences and whatnot. Apparently Mr Cooke had taken his celebrated Frankenstein's Monster to Paris with great success — but then, you know, that was a mime role. A different matter, I thought, to give the Parisians Sheridan — or Shakespeare, which was what began to be talked of. Shakespeare in Paris? But those who knew said there was a little mania for things English in Paris now — people read Byron and Walter Scott and found it all prodigiously romantic. And the French theatre, they said, was horribly stately and stiff and hadn't changed since Louis XIV.

And then Mr Kemble of Covent Garden, Mr Charles Kemble that is, was mentioned as a possibility for the company, and then as a probability. The curious thing was becoming real. There was a large company wanted, and I remember several of us at Drury Lane putting our names forward as a sort of dare: let's see what happens. Then there was some trouble about Monsieur Laurent securing a theatre: the Théâtre-Italien wouldn't have us, after all, and the whole scheme looked to be falling to pieces. By that time I had signed my contract. Thought so, thought I. It won't come off.

But Monsieur Laurent was nothing if not determined, and at last came to terms with the Théâtre Royal de L'Odéon. I trembled a little, because of its fame — and also, forgive me, I was not good at French, and when you say it with a proper French accent it comes out as O-day-oh, or, as I heard it, Oh dear.

Shortly before we left for Paris, Mr Kean made his return to Drury Lane. Once again I was Lady Anne to his Richard. It was— He was not well. I don't intend saying any more than that. I don't intend saying anything more at all, really. Well, this: he gave me fifty pounds. It was for my Lady Anne, he said, who always made him more of a Richard. This is why I don't like to tell of myself — this second-hand retailing of compliments — and in a moment I shall have done.

Only this: 'You'll do better in Paris, Miss Smithson,' he said. 'Better than here. Better than anywhere. I see it.' And his eyes flashed. Oh, people's eyes are always flashing in novels, it is the stalest thing and never happens in life. Except Mr Kean's did.

I still wonder about that second sight of his. But now I'm doing it. Building it up, rolling the drums. Forgive me, let me exit now, gracefully.

Charles Kemble was the gentleman, as far as such a thing was possible, of the English stage. Decently married, son at Cambridge, decorous, judicious with the booze, he was welcomed by society in places where Kean would only have been tolerated as an exotic (peep in at him through the bars, but don't feed him). With his Byronically black hair (scurrilous rumours of a wig) and fine figure he looked younger than his fifty-odd years, which enabled him to perpetuate his famous Romeo; and he had the hawkish, profile-loving Kemble nose. Unfriendly critics said that was all he had. But he was the great name of the nascent Paris company, and at a preliminary gathering on the neutral ground of the Haymarket he moved among them in seigneurial or even royal fashion, the much-acclaimed legs modestly disguised in trousers.

Pleasant, though. 'Miss Smithson,' he said – he knew her, he knew everybody, 'I am delighted and honoured that you will be joining our benevolent invasion of our Gallic neighbour.'

She wondered if he had said the same thing to everyone. She had had a glass or two of wine. 'You don't think, Mr Kemble, that they will hate us?'

He paused, as if this thought had never occurred to him: then smiled. 'We must ensure,' he said, very royal-progress, 'that they do not.'

He passed on. The legs, even in trousers, looked splendid. But, Harriet thought, it would take more than that.

5

Paris: Harriet realized to her shame, as the *diligence* lumbered out of St Denis on the last stage of the journey, that she knew next to nothing about it.

She dredged up memories of Mrs Turner's schoolroom, but got little beyond the facts that it was the capital of France, that it was renowned for its luxury manufactures, and that some king or other had said it was worth a Mass. Oh, and twelve years ago Wellington and the victorious Allies had occupied it, with the result that the French hated the English unto death.

Yet they had met with nothing but courtesy on the long journey from Calais. Nobody had spat at them or cried *À bas Villainton*. Anne, however, considered this only a matter of time. Those French who were not atheists were Papists – it was hard to say which was worse – and the food at the inns, oily salads and *fricandeau* of veal, no better than poison. Everywhere she carried a square of flannel to interpose between her behind and the pollution of French chairs and coach-seats. At the last stop an old woman, observing Anne's twisted figure as she got down from the *diligence*, had murmured 'Ah, *la pauvre!*' Anne's schoolroom French, like Harriet's, was equal to that. It gave a last shake to the fizzing bottle of resentment. She stared relentlessly at Harriet, unless Harriet met her eyes: then she jerked her head away. It was you who brought me here. It will not be forgotten.

Mrs Smithson, however, was in high good humour. A late withdrawal had secured her a minor place in the company: she had ceased to tipple, started to rouge, and was a woman of the world once more. Her flow of anecdote had somewhat exhausted the politeness of their travelling-companion, an elderly Walking-Gentleman named Bampton, who had been feigning sleep for the last five miles. He was familiar with Paris, and opened his eyes when they came to the customs-barrier.

'Can you tell me, sir,' Harriet asked him, 'is Paris bigger or smaller than London?'

'Smaller,' he yawned, rubbing his jowls, 'by some distance. Still, this is, for better or worse, the capital of Europe.'

And suddenly they were in Paris, or Paris had stolen up and surrounded them. One minute the view from the window was of tramping shepherds and old crones bent double under bundles of kindling: the next it was brick and stone and beggars with outstretched clawing hands and young men in cast-off liveries crying, *Milord, milord, service, service?*

'Merciful heavens,' clucked Mrs Smithson, laughing distressfully, as the coach stopped at what seemed an arbitrary space in a swarm of people, horses, dogs, carts, carriages, 'whatever is going on? It must be a feast or a fair or something. What *is* going on?'

What was going on was Paris: a roar and a rumble, a stink, a whirl, a sort of unending civil battle for a stake in the urban space. 'Parisian hats,' marvelled Mrs Smithson, 'did you ever see so many feathers?' Beneath the Parisian hats Parisian skirts were casually lifted to avoid the moving streams of gore from butchers' stalls. Anne clung to Harriet like a vicious monkey as they tried to find a cab-stand. It seemed the Parisians had not heard of pavements: you hopped from doorstep to porch while the wheeled traffic bucketed and buffeted past you like a chariot-race. Once Mrs Smithson was pinned against a wall by a cow.

Lodgings had been arranged for them in a *hôtel meublé* in the Faubourg St Michel. Harriet could never quite work out how they had got there. Her painstakingly recollected French bore no resemblance to the gobbling argot of the *fiacre*-driver. She wrote it down: yes, he knew. Then came rattling, lurching terror. Then he got lost. '*Quelle rue est ce-là?*' Harriet enquired, with prim hysteria. Shrug. The street didn't have a name. Beyond the main thoroughfares, medieval mazes turned in on themselves: crazy timber struts blocked the way. Harriet saw a neat space between two cadaverous buildings with a cloud of dust rising, as if a house had just that moment fallen down. By the time they found the place, Harriet and her mother were both laughing wildly: there was nothing else for it. Anne stared down the obsequious hand-rubbing proprietor of the tall squeezed house and penetrated their rooms by inches, sniffing for garlic. 'Rue,' she said. 'Rue this and rue that. Rue, oh, yes, we will, we will indeed.' The grim pun cheered her up for the rest of the day.

What was going on was Paris, and the next day the company manager, Mr Abbott – a genial workhorse from Covent Garden who tackled the world, and his roles, with a perpetual smile of apology – showed Harriet and her mother some more of it. Dutifully they saw the monuments of a recent past more full of slaughter and business than the most melo-dramatic five-acter: the site of the Bastille, the place de la Concorde where the guillotine had stood, Napoleon's rue de Rivoli, straight as a cannon-shot. But Paris was a court city again now and its grandest sights reflected it. The strollers among the fountains and orange-trees of the Jardin des Tuileries looked more finished and frigidly noble than anything in St James's. No West End mansion was more exclusive than the townhouses of the Faubourg St Germain, each a small palace round a courtyard guarded by a *porte-cochère*: absolutely no entry. In the Palais Royal the windows of restaurants permitted glimpses of riotous gilt and velvet and mirror. People either looked through her or took in her English walking-dress with a comprehensive glance and a hitch of the lips. This place was entirely self-sufficient: entirely, superbly unimpressible. She had a vision of a vast castle, and a little motley band of attackers standing before it with slingshots.

First sight of their theatre. 'We are really very fortunate to have the Odéon,' Mr Abbott said. 'Second of the royal theatres in precedence. Well, theoretically.' And he renewed his apologetic smile. The Odéon, on the unfashionable left bank, reminded her of Drury Lane with its pediments and pilasters, but it was smaller, and the *place* in front of it was relatively empty. An elegant backwater, she thought. Inside, a rehearsal, or a rehearsal of a rehearsal, was being scrambled through with the usual obstacles of unfamiliar acoustics added to by uncomprehending French workmen and the apparent absence of a prompt-box. 'It will come round,' Mr Abbott said, smiling and perspiring. 'I am convinced it will come round.' Above, the auditorium ceiling glittered with an allegory of the zodiac.

'"The fault, dear Brutus, lies not in our stars, but in ourselves,"' Harriet said, looking up.

'Quite so. *Julius Caesar* never quite seems to *go* nowadays, does it? Insufficient plush, perhaps. My most recent communication from Mr Kemble suggests – only suggests – that we may introduce Shakespeare with *Hamlet*. I don't know. It *may* go. What think you, Miss Smithson? Have you played in the Dane?'

'Many years ago, in Dublin. I was Ophelia.'

'Ah. Well, there's not much for the female performer in *Hamlet*, after all. One gathers that the French are very classical in their tastes, which means everything fearfully formal and restrained and not even a poke in the eye allowed on stage, so one wonders what they would make of *Hamlet*. Jolly gravediggers and a heap of corpses at the end. Still, that's the Bard for you. It *isn't* all pure and marble, that's the point. The other possibility Mr Kemble mentions is *Romeo and Juliet*. Fewer corpses, at any rate. But the difficulty there, as he says, is the lack of a suitable Juliet. Well, it will come round. What do you think of the sound here, Miss Smithson? I fancy it's unequal. Those boxes swallow it up . . .'

What was going on in Paris, Harriet thought, was a fantastic gamble.

Never mind the talk of this very great interest in the English company among the young, among the students and artists and *bohémiens*: never mind the clamour for tickets: she was experienced enough to spot the firework of novelty. Walking about the streets – as, vaulting her fear, she began to do after the first few rehearsals – Harriet's awareness was all of difference: it thrust at her like a head wind. Her understanding could pluck only the odd word from the heavily accented French around her, a needle in a linguistic haystack. She looked in at the open fronts of coffee-houses, attracted by the little stone tables, the baskets of flowers: but the grim proprietress at the raised counter, enthroned like a priestess amid bowls of lump-sugar, scared her away. Water-carriers toiled by. You had to buy water, like milk or tea. Tired, she hailed a *fiacre*, which was dawdling by her as if hoping for custom: the driver grimaced and jerked a thumb at the closed blinds of his vehicle and then, seeing Harriet's nonplussed expression, performed a hideous mime to suggest that there were lovers inside. Along the Pont-Neuf traders occupied incredible niches of commerce: they gave new ribbons for old, they exhibited learned owls who selected your playing-card with dainty cruel beaks, they invited you to step into a booth and have your dreams interpreted. 'Have you dreamed of a cat, have you dreamed of a dog?' No, only of dusty prop-rooms, only of dead fathers coming to life, only of witches. She tried to buy tisane but could not understand how much was asked: the tisane-seller threw up his hands: she backed away, collided with a youth, tried to apologize, was answered with what must have been scabrous swear-words.

She began to despair. She longed to cry out: Don't you understand me? Don't you see me? Don't you realize I have feelings? And then out of despair came a kind of liberty. No, in a word, they don't. I am in a world entirely without expectations of me. Here I might just begin to exist, perhaps, if I took off all my clothes or stabbed someone in the street. Otherwise, everyone is quite sealed off. She walked behind a curtain of mirrors.

Then, a little mystical with fatigue and loneliness, she perceived that everyone did. Perhaps for a lucky few life was a broad boulevard, but for most it was a narrow blind alley of conventions and accepted ideas. In a way it was easier, skulking along there: you knew that the French were this and the English that, women this and men that, and you never had to dare the high dark walls.

And yet you feel, surely. You must feel: this conviction she kept touching like a precious door-key in the pocket. Never mind appearances. She saw the proprietor of the learned owl, his day done, thrust a sack over the reverend bird and curse it for struggling: as if he had no feeling. But you have to look beneath. We spend so much time lying and dissembling: actors, who do it for a living, know that best. Professional liars. Harriet thought: I want to tell the truth, nevertheless. I want to scale the walls.

What was going on in Paris? Something. Something exceptional.

Mr Kemble, tardy messiah, is detained in England for some days yet, and the opening night for the English company cannot be postponed. So, Mr Abbott makes decisions, or melts into them. Shakespeare needs a Kemble, so Sheridan's sturdy old *Rivals* is to inaugurate the season at the Odéon: Mr Abbott as Captain Absolute, Mrs Smithson as Mrs Malaprop, Miss Smithson as Lydia Languish. It will go. Yes, a comedy of manners relying much on a close understanding of English language and society, but still.

And it does go, in that there is cordial applause, and nobody shouts about Villainton or throws things, and five thousand francs' worth of tickets are sold. The French audience file politely out, and the newspapers say some complimentary things (though not about Mrs Smithson, past her best and generally agreed to be a disaster. Harriet tries to shield her from the news, picturing Joseph's face, all epic disgust). *She Stoops to Conquer* is next, another pleasant comedy. Receipts are respectable, but down. Lately a giraffe has arrived in Paris from Africa, and the exotic beast has been quite the rage in society: one must, my dear, see the giraffe. But you don't go and see it a second time. A firework, thinks Harriet: up it goes, and down comes the burnt stick.

Mr Charles Kemble arrives at last and, rather high-handing it over Mr Abbott – who only smiles harder – gathers the company about him in the cramped green-room of the Odéon and delivers a homily.

'Ladies and gentlemen, you may know that Monsieur Laurent – our . . . shall I say benefactor? – together with Mr Abbott and my humble self, have agreed upon *Hamlet* as the piece with which we shall introduce the true English drama to our expectant friends of Paris.' Freshly barbered, nose heroically to the fore, legs at concert pitch, Mr Kemble inspires.

141

'Before we set our rehearsal in train, I would ask you to consider, in serious though not solemn wise, the task and prospect that lie before us. We are to present one of the glories of our dramatic literature to a people who, let it be said, have long been convinced of its inferiority to their own. The scoffings of Voltaire still linger in the minds of those we seek to entice and enthral: the fertile genius of our native poet is still regarded as uncouth by an audience accustomed to the stately periods and chill correctness of Racine. The splendid burden placed upon us is to over-come those prejudices: to open their eyes to the beauty, the strangeness, the sublimity of the prince of tragedies. Ladies and gentlemen, we must give *Hamlet* to the French!' He strikes a defiant pose, to a murmur of appreciation, which nearly, but does not quite drown his concluding sigh of 'God help us.'

Casting: no time to dither about it and, besides, in *Hamlet* the prince is everything. Claudius, Mr Burke, Gertrude, Mrs Vaughan: old stalwarts. For Ophelia, Miss Smithson will do very well. Apart from her little songs, which always make a charming interlude, there is not much to the part; and though Miss Smithson's singing voice is only adequate, she does have beauty and a certain look of youthful innocence: there have been too many raddled Ophelias who look as if they would understand every one of Hamlet's dirty jokes, and some he didn't know.

So, rehearsal. Concentrate on the big scenes, with Hamlet at centre stage, the nobility and melancholy. Grandeur, dignity. Nothing to offend sensibilities. Dress: Mr Kemble in black doublet and tights makes several of the ladies moan low. But in costume he begins to find things with his voice, light but intensely musical, things that make Harriet stop seeing him and start seeing Hamlet. Harriet is all in white: Mr Abbott grunts pleased approval at the two of them in the Mousetrap scene. Looks rather well. Something is gathering. But not quite gathered up.

After rehearsal, Harriet goes back to her lodgings and, asking not to be disturbed, shuts herself in her bedroom. Anne stations herself at the door like a cat at a mousehole: but for once, she is not let in.

Hamlet – well, first, forget that. The old warhorse, the glory of the tragic stage, the magnificent distillation of the Bard, and whatnot. Forget every-thing. Above all, forget past performances, in which the prince stalks imperiously around a cast of nonentities, milking his great speeches, while Claudius rolls his villainous eyes and Ophelia trips on with the flowers to trill tra-la.

Instead, live there. Elsinore, wherever that is: somewhere foreign, but remember that to people living in foreign places there is no sense of foreignness. Look at Paris, where ladies hawk and spit. Home is what you are used to, and Ophelia is used to the court of Elsinore: it's where she feels warmth and that opposite of skewed sickness, which is elsewhere. And she lives with her father, whom she loves in spite of his frailties, as one does: perhaps even loves him for them – who can say? Dark battlements, and an arras, and a ghost walking. Yes, but every place has its dark battlements, and an arras is only a place to hide as everyone has hidden at some time: and what house, what life lacks walking ghosts? This is her world, and she loves it though she stands a little on the edge of it, not quite understanding, feeling that it goes on somehow beyond her. Oh, yes: I know that.

And she knows, or begins to know, love. You don't need a lover for that: only human blood, bones, breath. The love is not for her, beyond her again, above her, not to be considered: isn't that love's definition? (And then it turns nasty and brutal in a choking smell of dust.)

Harriet walks about her room, Ophelia's room. She must have one, though you don't see it in the play. She reports sewing in her closet when Hamlet came to her in his madness. Sewing, and thinking. There is a loneliness in it. Ophelia is a lady of the court, but she must often be in the background, silent, deferential: her garrulous father will hardly let her speak. When that happens, you must make sure that what you do say carries weight. No mincing and hesitating. Her brother too, Laertes, very forceful, very quick to hand out advice to her. All these formidable beasts prowling and strutting around her. But she isn't a mouse, that isn't right. A mouse wouldn't dare to love. Nor would the prince see anything in her. He is a thinker, and a melancholy one: he must sense some affinity. There is much going on in Ophelia, but she must not express it: a simmering pot, tight-lidded. And think of the way a pot, just before it comes to the boil, goes quieter. Think of that when the madness approaches. (Don't consider the madness yet: fear its coming.)

It isn't the weeping outside, but the weeping inside.

Harriet walks about her room. Ophelia walks about her room: a graceful gait but a soft tread, accustomed to walking respectfully behind others. But she looks them in the eye, Polonius, Laertes, Hamlet. No girlish head-lowerings: that suggests a certain worldliness, a demure shame. True innocence is direct. I am innocent. It means not knowing.

And then comes the knowledge when her father is killed. Death is knowledge, and knowledge is death. *I cannot choose but weep to think they would lay him i' the cold ground.* That's what they do. What you love is buried in the ground. And you see it later – a gravedigger carelessly turns up skulls. We are ghosts or bones. You might go mad thinking of it. You might go mad thinking. *Lord, we know what we are, but know not what we may be.* What does it mean to be mad? Just move over there a little: where the memories clamour, and are more real than the real. You step on to another path. But it's serious, surely: over there different rules apply, but they are still rules. The mad boy in Ennis, loving and talking to his broom. If madness had no rules, he wouldn't have howled when the boys took it away and made sport with it: he would have laughed too. The mad may laugh, but not at everything.

Serious. Forget the pretty Ophelias, warbling away. Madness is not pretty. But it may be beautiful. Look at the concentration of a small child, making a doll or toy soldier walk along the rug towards some crucial event. There is beauty in the intentness of the fiction. The art, if you like. Ophelia sings as the child plays, because in the narrative of her broken mind it is important. She is not singing for the audience. She doesn't even know an audience is there. She is behind the curtain of mirrors.

Pain and madness, madness and pain. The pot boiling over at last. But not in rage and violence: Laertes can do that, seize his sword and slaughter his way to relief. But Ophelia can't do that: she wouldn't be Ophelia. I can't do that. I must live and die as I am. The water, not the fire. *Good night, ladies; good night, sweet ladies; good night, good night.*

Tuesday, 11 September 1827. A muggy evening in Paris. In the little place de l'Odéon a throng of carriages. Inside the carriages – though not among the young men who have come on foot from the less fashionable *faubourgs* to queue early for places – a certain amount of grumbling: at the dreadful press of traffic, at the lateness of the performance, which will apparently not be short – interfering with Paris society's favourite visiting-hour, half past nine. And all of this to see some barbaric gallimaufry of ghosts and murders. Well, that's what I hear. Still, it's the new thing. And frankly, my dear, it can't be worse than the Théâtre-Français, where lately I am bored half to death. My God, did you ever see such a crowd?

Tuesday, 11 September 1827. A muggy, not to say stifling evening at the Théâtre de l'Odéon. When does it begin? Later the company, still half stunned, agree that it was during the Mousetrap scene: that was when you really began to be aware of it, the mutter and murmur, the creeping tremor of emotion in the auditorium. All agree that it reached its height at Act Four, Scene Five, when the mad Ophelia made her first exit. That was when it became almost frightening.

Harriet certainly feels it so as she stumbles into the wings with the noise ringing in her ears and a sensation as if she has just walked through a fire. 'My God, what are they saying?' she cries. 'Do they like it – or hate it?' And it is Mr Bampton, the urbane walking-gentleman with whom she shared the coach to Paris, who answers her in a rather hoarse voice: 'My dear Miss Smithson, you may be assured it is beyond anything. Beyond anything.' To complete her astonishment, she sees there are tears in his eyes.

Some reactions from the audience at the first night of *Hamlet* at the Théâtre de l'Odéon, 11 September 1827.

Monsieur Alexandre Dumas, twenty-five years old, clerk in the secretariat of the Duc d'Orléans: 'I am overpowered. I had high expectations, yes, in fact I came to the theatre at four to be sure of a place. But it was more magnificent than I imagined. No, not magnificent, that doesn't convey it, it suggests something grand and dull. This was nature, one felt it. Felt it. It has changed everything for me. I have tried my hand at short plays, but now I know where I've been going wrong. I've been going wrong everywhere, in truth. Truth, that's it. That's what Miss Smithson gave us. I must start again. I'm waking up, I'm Adam in the garden. God knows how I shall face dismal work tomorrow. Don't print that.'

Monsieur Victor Hugo, twenty-five, poet: 'You ask what I feel? About Shakespeare, about this performance, about Miss Smithson? In a few paltry words? Well, perhaps above all I feel vindicated. I have long contended that this is what we must have in our drama. Truth to nature. That means the liberty of inspiration, not the tyranny of old conventions. I'm sure that many of the audience tonight, if you'd told them there would be the ravings of madness on stage, and murder, and gravediggers jesting about death, and beauty and then *ugliness* – well, they'd have thrown up their hands in proper stylized horror. What a ghastly mixture. But there they were sobbing – actually sobbing. I wanted to cry out: "You see, you see?" But I was sobbing myself. Oh, at Ophelia. Great God, Ophelia.'

Monsieur Alfred de Vigny, thirty years old, ex-Guards officer, author: 'You may suspect me of a certain partisanship. I'm married to an Englishwoman, I know England. But in fact we are all partisans for what we believe and what we have seen tonight: poetry, beauty. It doesn't matter whether it comes from England or the South Seas. Though, to be sure, there is something peculiarly English in the feeling. Melancholy. Loneliness. My friend Monsieur Hugo spoke of the weeping, I think. That is what I take away. Ophelia weeping. The weeping inside.'

Monsieur Eugène Delacroix, twenty-nine years old, painter: 'Sublime. Sublime. I don't wish to say much, because it will take me away from that world and back into this dismal one. Carriages and umbrellas and chit-chat and, oh, God, it's seeping in already. Take me back to *Hamlet*. I want to be the prince again, I want to commune with the ghost, I want to be in love with Ophelia. As everyone is. And take that lamp away. I want the beautiful darkness back.'

Monsieur Hector Berlioz, twenty-five years old, musician: 'I can't speak.'

EPISODE IN THE LIFE
OF AN ARTIST

Second Movement: A Ball

Valse: Allegro non troppo

1

Moths are battering at the windows of the ballroom at the Bal de l'Opéra. Drawn by the candlelight. Fluttering like dancers.

The entrance fee for a public ball is one franc for men, fifty centimes for women. We needn't pay it. Just waltz straight in.

Note around you the fashions of Paris in the troublous reign of Charles X. (The last Bourbon king. Not that he knows it.)

Much white and silver for women, trimmings of blond lace, puffed sleeves, chignons and feathers. The men are anonymous. Dowdies in black.

Touches here and there of an unexpected influence, a certain *style à l'Anglais*. Tudor-queen waistlines. Walter Scott tartans.

No more than a fad, or so thinks the grandest *dame* of the English colony in Paris. Meet Lady Granville. Ambassador's wife.

No one more worldly, more unimpressible than she, with her look of a perpetual snuff-sniff. Seen it all, twice. Nothing can shock her.

Her mother was the spectacular Georgiana, Duchess of Devonshire, and her husband was once her aunt's lover. Bit of a scandal. Years ago now.

Nowadays she has to make an effort to find anything very interesting. Tonight, an exception. Look over there.

'Did you ever see anything more piquant? Just mark how they've dressed her! The famous Miss Smithson. *La Belle Irlandaise.*'

Her companions, both English, one gentleman, one lady, crane for a look. The man says, 'Exquisite.' The lady just stares.

'Exquisite, the effect, certainly – she must have had good advice since her triumph. A first-rate *modiste*. A good *corsetière*.'

'Mere clothes can hardly produce such an effect, Lady Granville,' the man says. He utters a sigh. 'Only nature does that.'

At the mention of nature Lady Granville shudders fastidiously, raising her eyes. 'Come, you enthuse. Unless you are jesting.'

'I was never more in earnest, Lady Granville – but surely *you* have seen her perform? Her Juliet? Her Ophelia?'

'My dear sir, we were at the first night of *Hamlet*, and very amusing it was.' He gives her a look. The lady does too.

'I hardly think,' the gentleman says, 'with respect, that such a perform-ance could amuse. The audience weep. The French are in transports.'

'Precisely what's so amusing, the way our good classical friends carry on. But *I* shed a tear. I admit it.'

'Now we have a confession – even Lady Granville was moved by Miss Smithson.' The gentleman smiles. Not very warmly.

'Certainly I cried a little, just as I would if I saw my housemaid die.' She fans herself. 'Who is that with her?'

'I do believe that is the tragedienne, Mademoiselle Mars – they say she is a great admirer. Attends every night. Drinking it in.'

'Oh, I'm sure that's what they say, and I'm sure that's what she would say too, of course. Thoroughly politic. Make up to your rival.'

But Lady Granville becomes aware that they are gazing at Miss Smithson, and not really listening to her. 'In truth she's quite *vulgar*.' Oh, talk to the wall.

Misty dawn over the stubble-fields outside Paris. Crunch of the gaitered feet of a farm-bailiff coming to inspect the sheaves. Snuffle of his dog. Autumnal croaking of crows. Gasp of surprise from the bailiff, and alarmed yip from the dog, at the man who lies as if dead on a bundle of sheaves.

Why dead? Something tomb-like about the posture, flat on his back, arms crossed on his chest. And surely no tramp or vagrant, this slender young man, cravated and tail-coated, with a mane of upswept hair. The dog yips again, and the young man opens blue, searching, terrible eyes.

'Monsieur,' falters the bailiff, hardly knowing what he says. 'Monsieur, how did you get here?'

The young man sits up, brushes chaff from his coat, stares around him with those eyes. Those eyes. 'How did I get here?' He utters a broken laugh, horribly at odds with the glaze of utter despair on his face. Well, a madman: no doubt of that. Hector Berlioz laughs again. 'How *did* I get here?'

How did he get there?

It begins with a cliché, or at least a commonplace. The arrival in Paris of *naïf* young men from the provinces, eager to make their way, more eager to make their mark, worried about by their families and forewarned against the temptations of the dazzling city. There are hundreds every year, enrolling at faculties of law or medicine, entering mercantile houses or banks or civil-service offices, scribbling and daubing in attics. Some few will make their mark: more will fall by the wayside, or drift back to the provinces, or settle for a goodish marriage, storing up Bohemian reminiscences for their disappointed middle age.

Witness these two, Hector Berlioz and his cousin Alphonse Robert, from the far-off Dauphiné: enrolling at the School of Medicine, combing the nearby shops for medical instruments and textbooks, settling into their lodgings in the student-haunted Latin Quarter: gazing out of their dirty windows at the crowded gables and chimneys and the strings of washing and then looking at each other and bursting out in delighted and amazed laughter: we're here: it's real. The morning hunt for cleanish underwear, the evening hunt for the cheapest café meal in the winding medieval streets. Alphonse a little concerned that they should avoid the unrespectable places, but Hector laughing it off. 'No one knows us. No one supposes anything about us.' Breathing deep at those words. Paris stinks of smoke and refuse, but for Hector it is pure ozone.

The study of medicine: it begins with a commonplace, Hector lurching out of the dissecting-room at the Hospice de la Pitié with his mouth full of vomit. The insides of bodies with their appalling rainbow of colours: the eyes still open, even bright. The eyes, the eyes. Never: never.

'Never,' he groans to Alphonse later. 'There's no getting over such a — a revulsion of feeling, you just can't—'

'Well, that's it, you see,' says Alphonse, in his diffident but somehow downright way. 'Feeling. I think what you need to feel is indifference.'

'That is exactly what is impossible for me,' Hector says, between gritted teeth, washing and rewashing his hands.

'Well, it's a pity. That subject cost me most of this month's allowance.'

'Body, you mean,' Hector says.

'Subject,' Alphonse mildly insists. 'It helps, you know, if you change the word. And they don't come cheap.'

Hector is shaken by a long, scouring laugh. 'No,' he gasps, 'no, I suppose they don't.' So he returns, jaw set, gullet clenched, to the dissecting-room. Just a body: just an assemblage of parts. Soon he is participating, soon his bare arm is in the chest cavity of someone who, perhaps, once put his hand there to still an excited heart or to swear a solemn oath – except that's exactly what you don't see. Be like the rats skittering under the floorboards, waiting for leftovers. Be indifferent. He feels old pieties draining from him as he saws and extracts. The Resurrection and the Life. Well, here I am, Mama: doing what you want.

Later he tried to convince himself – and, at the time, sought diligently to convince his father – that he really was trying to reconcile himself to medicine. The evidence was persuasive. He attended lectures, even finding fascination in the physics and the chemistry: he piled up notes: he passed his first year's examination. And if there had only been medicine in his life, if the sky had borne no star, then he might well have resigned himself to living under it. But medicine was what he had to do, whereas music – well, that was what he had to do, in the truest sense. And he had come from a place with a wheezing town band and a few plucky fiddlers in parlours to a city of music. The Paris Opéra was here.

And this is where the commonplace breaks down. Plenty of young students wile away their time at the Opéra when they can afford it. None approaches it quite as Hector does – with dry mouth, pain in his chest, maddening anticipation: yes, as a shrine. At the sound of an eighty-piece orchestra he hardly knows whether to stand, sit, or run away screaming. An aria rips into him like a scalpel. Sometimes people near him in the pit are rather frightened at the look on his face: have an urge, perhaps, to whisper, *It's only music.* Just as well they don't.

So much, Dr Berlioz, for your hopes of curing him.

La Côte St André: still the plain shimmers, the vines ripen, and change comes only on tiptoe. There is a new Berlioz son, Prosper: this should be their last child, Dr Berlioz privately considers, though such are Finette's religious views that there is no question of actually arranging it. ('Well, at least you've another boy to carry the name,' grunts Grandfather Marmion, 'if Hector doesn't come to his senses.' In response Dr Berlioz chews his lip. Often it bleeds.) Meanwhile Nancy – her hair up in combs now, first evening gown with shoulders perturbingly bare even under the fichu – grows more and more like her mother in looks. Firm in religion too, and thoroughly proper on social occasions. Only there is something sharp-edged and perpendicular about her, quite different from Finette who is all softness and talkative flow and amplitude (smothering as a downy pillow, one might almost say: though Dr Berlioz would not allow the thought, except perhaps during the secret carnival of opium). Nancy: she has a way of looking at you as if impatiently expecting a decision, and sometimes her father slinks from it.

Still, a difficult age. While Adèle, the younger, is yielding and tender-hearted: a sweet and yet not sugary girl. But then these odd glimpses of a determined and individual character – mere mentions of schooling, away from La Côte, have produced burning looks, even faint mutinous shadows of Hector. Chewing away at his lip and his anxieties, Dr Berlioz asks himself why this absolute unpredictability of our children should confound us so much: do we expect a little guidebook to appear at parturition along with the placenta? 'This is Child X: he will be awkward and temper-amental in infancy, will reveal pleasanter traits towards puberty, and then will make a sudden and even alarming spurt in intellect . . .' A whimsical fancy: Dr Berlioz dismisses it. It is the sort of thing Hector would think of, and with Hector the mind (which one . . . ?) must be continually on guard. There must be no seduction.

Fairness, yes. Though Hector's letters from Paris affect Dr Berlioz like turbid weather-fronts looming over the mountains, he sets himself to sit and read them without prejudice. (Like the lawyer he might have been, if he had not defied his own father.) Thus, the glowing accounts of Hector's nights at the Opéra, and the cool, cursory mentions of his medical studies, are not to be the pretext for hasty conclusions. Time will do its work; and, if not, other pressures may be brought to bear. (Hector cannot live in Paris without money: Dr Berlioz loathes the crudity of this, but he must keep it in reserve, like a gun in the cellar.) So, be bland in your replies: proceed gently. Unfortunately Finette does not see this. At the merest reference to music, theatre, arts, her splendid, sensual chestnut-crowned head raises in outrage. (How much better human life would be without beauty, thinks Dr Berlioz: it is far more unjust, far more arbitrary and tyrannical, than any despotism, it is the *ancien régime* of the flesh and the last supercilious enemy of reason. He believes this even when the last candle is out and Finette's bedded, tumbled languor stirs him.) Finette prays nightly for Hector's soul, and never more fervently than when his letters speak of Gluck, choruses, piccolos.

Alas, she does not trust him. Her son is potentially a spy in the camp, and must be watched in every way possible. So Nancy comes to her father in neat, pure, as it were double-distilled anger.

'Hector wrote me. Mama opened the letter first and read it. I wrote back to him. She unsealed *that* and read it. What *is* this?' Nancy plants her fists on her hips: one day strong men will quail at that. Dr Berlioz nearly does.

'My dear, Hector's far away, and your mother wants every little bit of news she can get about him, because she's his mother. It's natural, Nancy, though I can see it must have been upsetting for you.'

They look at each other. She is much too conventional, much too like her mother, ever to say: *You damned liar.* And he is too much the reliable father to say: *I'm lying, of course.*

'He is my brother, after all,' Nancy pursues. 'And don't you think I would tell you if I came across anything – disreputable?'

'Such as what?' In a way he genuinely wants to know: wants to hear someone else put into words his own dubieties.

'Being undutiful,' Nancy says readily. 'Neglecting his studies.'

'Oh . . . I think most students may be reproached for that at some time.'

'With Hector it's different, though, isn't it, Papa? It's different.'

Not for the first time, Dr Berlioz finds himself in a conversation with Nancy that he cannot see a way of ending. 'Should you not be helping your mother with the silkworms, my dear?'

She gives him another look, disappointed but resigned. On the way out she adds: 'I wish he would come home for a visit. Then we could really *see*. The point is, you can't tell anything from a letter.'

Uneasily Dr Berlioz realizes there is another thing Nancy has in common with her mother: she is very often right.

He goes to check his barometer. Though there is not a cloud in the sky, it indicates wet weather. It never seems to be right lately.

The Paris Conservatoire of Music is a building that, after the first few longing glances, Hector has preferred to shun. It's merely like rubbing grit into your eye to look at it when you have to hurry to a lecture on osteology. But now comes the discovery. From ten till three the library of the Conservatoire is open to the public. You can go in, take down a score, sit at a reading-desk and study it. If you are Hector, you can read the score of a favourite opera, learn from it, see it, hear it, live it. If you are Hector, you are lost.

Alphonse soon knows where to find him.

'Hector, what are you doing? You missed Thenard's lecture. Again.'

Hector looks up at him, vague as a drunk, his finger still in the score. 'Oh, I'll catch up. I'll copy your notes.'

'You said that last time.' Alphonse is the more anxious because Dr Berlioz, in a subtle way, has charged him with keeping an eye on his wayward cousin.

'Did I? Well, at least I'm consistent.' Smiling, Hector turns back to *Iphigénie en Tauride*. With a tiny sigh Alphonse glances round at the library shelves. He wonders how many scores there are: thousands, probably. Oh, they should never have let Hector in here.

Summer at Meylan: brilliant heat following a mild winter, and everything in the garden well forward, much to Grandfather Marmion's disgust. He is reactionary even about the weather, perceiving meteorological delinquencies. 'It isn't right. We'll suffer for it. Look at those delphiniums. That's the way it's going.'

Dr Berlioz is as patient as ever through the horticulture, at last remarking: 'By the by, Hector comes to us for part of the vacation.' Forcing himself to sound casual, he is so successful that he actually yawns. An interesting physiological reversal. 'Part of it. Around September.'

'Hm. I don't think Mademoiselle Estelle is coming to Meylan this year. Mind you, after a year in Paris I dare say he's forgotten all about her.'

'Perhaps. I shall be particularly glad to see him – well, anxious to see him also. After the rather perturbing letter I had from him.'

'Hullo, debts, is it? Nip that in the bud, Louis. I'm still having trouble with Félix in that direction. I tell him, "I won't settle them, you'll only contract more." Fool's old enough to know better. Now he's got a notion of marrying. On the lookout for a rich widow. Hence the moustache.' Grandfather Marmion laughs sourly.

'Not debts. At least, that is not what the letter's about . . . Music. He says he has tried his best with medicine, but all his thoughts are of music and he is now convinced that is where his – his destiny lies.' Dr Berlioz pronounces this thinly: there is a dramatic flavour about *destiny* that he finds distasteful.

Grandfather Marmion glares. 'And? Do you mean he's going to drop medicine because of this?'

'Oh, he doesn't say that in so many words. Instead he asks me to consider that after a year he should know his own mind. And that Paris has revealed to him his true – vocation.'

'Rubbish. Paris has revealed to him – well, look, that's what it is, he's been spending his allowance at the Opéra and whatnot, finds it all devilish exciting and wants to carry on doing that instead of working for his examinations. No, Louis. Pull him down from the clouds. Don't be soft on him.'

'I don't intend being hard, as that will only make him more stubborn: I intend being firm.' And clever, thinks Dr Berlioz: Hector is plainly growing, which means growing beyond him. He remembers teaching him chess, and the coming of that day when he had to stop trying to lose, and start trying to win.

'My dear Louis, this isn't a matter for finesse. Tell him the facts, which are that if he persists in this pipe-dream he will ruin himself, disgrace his family, spit on everything you've done for him, and break his mother's heart. It couldn't be more simple.'

As Grandfather Marmion is getting red in the face, Dr Berlioz bows a deferential end to the subject. Besides, he will not say those things to Hector because that would be to admit that, even for a moment, he thinks them.

Late September: the central courtyard of the house at La Côte St André is a brimming tank of amber light. Hector, seated there with bowed head, looks as if he is crowned with flames.

Nancy comes to join him. 'So,' she says, 'you've been quarrelling with Papa.'

He comes out of abstraction blinking like a sleeper. 'As it happens, no,' he says, stretching, 'or not exactly. I thought we might. Perhaps that's what was so unsettling.'

'You don't mean he's *agreed* to – to—'

'To my following music as a career? You can say it, Nancy, it won't profane your lips. Or at least, the *curé* will only make you say a few Hail Marys for it.'

'So you've become an atheist as well. This is what Paris does for you.'

'Does it show? I thought I'd hidden my horns. No, he hasn't agreed. He is simply – all benevolent understanding. This notion of mine is a piece of youthful enthusiasm, which on sober reflection I will gradually realize is not to be entertained beside the dignity and honour of a respectable profession, which is not to say that my love of music may not be pursued as an improving pastime, and so on and so on. It was like trying to wrestle with butter.'

She points her sharp chin at him. 'You would have preferred a row, then?'

'I would have preferred Papa, who is a reasonable man on every other subject, to see reason. But he won't. Oh, he's manoeuvring, that's what it is: playing Wellington instead of Napoleon, conserving his army, wearing the enemy down instead of going for the decisive attack. We shall be in the field a long time yet.' He stares at his hands. 'Bless him, he's also protecting me, in a way. From Mama. There's a look in his eyes that says, "Remember, she will not be so understanding." And he's also protecting her from knowing quite how lost and damned I am. What a delirious mess.'

'Well. I don't know what to think.'

'You mean you don't know whose side to be on?'

'Dear heaven, I hope it won't come to that. Sides – that would be a shocking thing for a family.'

'For this family, no doubt. There are plenty of families who hate each other very contentedly.' A wry smile: but he does not look as if this thought pleases him, not really.

'Hector, I do know how stubborn our elders can be. Sometimes I quite lose patience myself. And I can see that it is very hard on you – but truly, Hector, tell me: music, and the opera, and the stage and all of that, can it really be respectable? Isn't it rather – gypsyish?'

157

'My dear Nancy, when you see me in a headscarf and earrings, feel free to wash your hands of me.'

'I wish you'd be serious.'

'Do you really? Because, you know, that's exactly the trouble. I am serious about this, and that they can't or won't accept. It disturbs them.'

'You sound as if you actually like that.'

'Why not? After all, to be disturbed is to feel that you're alive.' His voice throughout has been cool and muted, and when he gives a shriek and claps his hands in front of her face she leaps right off the bench. 'There. See? Can't you feel your pulse throbbing now? Don't you know you're alive?'

'I think you're quite mad.' Not so much a reproach as a conclusion satisfactorily reached. 'What are we going to do with Adèle when you go back to Paris? She adores you, for some peculiar reason. She'll be in fits.'

'Tell her I will come back.'

'Oh, no doubt. But what will you be when you come back?'

'Well: whatever I was meant to be.'

Paris: with Alphonse, a sort of parting. They will not be sharing Hector's new lodging in the rue St Jacques. Both agree that they will get along the better for it. Visible but unspoken, Alphonse's relief at no longer having to be the responsible one and (Hector is sure of this) having to send back reports to Dr Berlioz on Hector's behaviour. Unspoken too but heart-felt, Hector's relief at no longer having his cousin's exemplary and shaming diligence always in front of him. Besides, the new lodgings are personally approved by Dr Berlioz, who knows the distinguished physician who owns the house – and so, probably, there will be another source of surveillance, though no one admits it. All these silent vacancies and untrespassed territories: life has become an antique map, with white spaces at its edges, haunts of debatable monsters.

No one to nag him about writing up his notes on nerve tissue – but, then, didn't he intend at least to try to be diligent, after the gentlemanly compromises of his father's last talk? Perhaps: but Dr Berlioz at his side, loving and persuasive, is a different thing from Dr Berlioz far away. The Opéra and the Conservatoire call to him: shout everything else gloriously down. And then there is the intervention of Providence.

If such a thing exists – Hector's mind is open – then it must enter into everyone's life at some point; just as even a stopped clock will show the right time twice a day. In his twentieth year, Hector and Providence finally coincide.

First, something that almost warrants the hoary old phrase, a bolt from the blue. Certainly in his most despairing moments Hector has called on lightning to descend on the School of Medicine, to cleave and incinerate it. Not quite that, but the effect is the same: for five months the Paris School of Medicine is shut down. A bubbling undercurrent of radicalism and revolt in the student quarters of Paris breaks out in anger at the royal government, which is busy sacking liberal professors and promoting reactionary clergymen. After a near-riot at the ceremony for the new term, a royal decree closes the doors of the School of Medicine. Alphonse comes to Hector distraught. How will they get on with their studies?

'You needn't worry,' he says, clapping Alphonse's shoulder. 'You're already far ahead of everyone else.'

'It's easy to fall behind,' gripes Alphonse. 'One loses one's impetus, and then the next thing—'

'The next thing, you end up like me,' Hector says, joyously laughing.

Alphonse peers at his incomprehensible cousin: somehow Hector always makes him peer and squint, as at an uncomfortably strong light. 'Well, aren't you worried?'

But Hector is not hearing him, Hector has a new voice in his head. Here is the second chime of Providence: he has met a man who believes in him.

Follow Monsieur Jean-François Le Sueur on his favourite walk through the Tuileries gardens, and if your fancy is sufficiently alive you may catch the echoes of history flickering around him like the shadows of the plane trees.

This upright, stiff-cravated old gentleman with the splendidly carved profile – somehow suggesting the knight in a chess-set – is currently the director of the Chapel Royal and professor of composition at the Conservatoire. But he has arrived at this calm eminence after riding the great tides and surges of the past thirty years. He, too, was once a young man from the provinces – from Abbeville, where his father was a peasant farmer – with a world to conquer and no weapons but belief and talent. The Revolution was made for men like him; and he made the music of the Revolution, vast, bold republican hymns to be sung by choirs drawn up like opposing battalions. Still, he had a losing battle against the entrenched diehards of the Conservatoire: we want no upstarts, we want our salaries. On the brink of ruin – and Monsieur Le Sueur knows about Providence too – came salvation in Imperial shape. Napoleon Bonaparte was his greatest admirer and patron. The Emperor made him director of the Imperial Chapel – even found him a house. At a nod from Napoleon, Le Sueur's operas, kept from the boards by claques and cabals, became the triumph of triumph-enjoying Paris. Though Monsieur Le Sueur has long made his peace with the new royalism, he keeps a shrine to the Emperor in his heart. Someone to inspire, to uplift, to awaken you to grandeur: that's what everyone needs.

As well as teaching at the Conservatoire, Monsieur Le Sueur takes private pupils, and one of them has introduced him to this curiously interesting young man named Hector Berlioz. For Monsieur Le Sueur, of sturdy Norman stock, everything about him is *piquant* – from his name to his striking look of an unkempt eagle, from his benighted goats'-cheese homeland to the hopeless cantata, which he tremblingly presented as evidence of his work.

Hopeless, at least, in an academic sense. 'You don't know what you're doing,' he told the young man. 'You lack even the most elementary principles of harmony.' The eagle did not flinch. 'In spite of that, there is fire here, motion. Yes, there is promise.' Yes, he would take him as a private pupil.

There would be much very basic work to do first of all. 'I rather feel,' he joked to his wife, 'that I have engaged to tutor the Noble Savage in civilization, from the loincloth up.' But now something unexpected has happened. Not only has young Berlioz made rapid strides, he has become something more than a promising pupil to Monsieur Le Sueur. Inspiration works both ways. Odd that he should mention fire at that first meeting, because Monsieur Le Sueur finds his mind kindling at the very thought of Berlioz: he warms his hands at him.

'Ah, so you are a lover of Virgil.' The lessons spill over, merge into talk: not chat but exploration. 'We are few these days.'

'Oh, I have my father to thank for that. He put Virgil into my hands when I was young.'

Piquant too, this airy reference, from a stripling of twenty, to *when I was young*. But Monsieur Le Sueur only smiles inside, for he is a rarity: he remembers what that is like. He takes note, too, of the way Berlioz mentions his father. There is a story here, though he lets it come out gradually, by itself.

'The death of Dido – God, what a moment! What a subject for music, if it could be done!'

'I don't doubt that it could be done. There is nothing music cannot do. But it would require the purest, chastest form of expression, allied with the freest and most flexible rhythm – such as I believe indeed characterized the music of the ancients, if we could but recover it . . .' This is a hobby-horse of Monsieur Le Sueur's, one that he acknowledges he is inclined to ride a little too long, but young Berlioz never looks bored. Those china-blue eyes never tire or fade. Indeed, Monsieur Le Sueur confides another amusing oddity to his wife. 'Do you know? I find it entirely impossible to imagine Monsieur Berlioz asleep.'

Nor is his pupil afraid to disagree with him. Sometimes the study of fugue or canon produces a great snorting sigh, as of the physical blowing away of dreary dust. Yet Monsieur Le Sueur never senses any slackening of respect. As for his association with Napoleon, his young pupil thirsts to hear of it. The summons to the Emperor's box at the first night of his opera *The Bards*: the arrival next day of a gold casket inscribed with the Emperor's compliments: yes, all true, though modesty should forbid his speaking of it. 'Indeed, you shall see the casket, if you like: come to dinner.' Partly the prompting of Madame Le Sueur, who on seeing the young man arriving for lessons at the house in the rue Ste Anne remarked that he needed feeding up. (Monsieur Le Sueur, reading between the lines, is already charging him very reduced fees.) Partly, also, simple pleasure in his company. Sometimes he wonders whether the tritest thing of all is behind it: the father looking for a son. At that thought the two boys he lost in infancy seem to rise before him, their last nightshirted agony transformed into reproach. So he is on his guard. Besides, Berlioz has a father.

Ah, that prickly complexity. Always his pupil speaks of his father in the most respectful, and indeed affectionate terms. And yet when he does so, he seems to be picking his way across stepping-stones, through a mire of unpleasant truth.

'I hear, Monsieur Berlioz, that the School of Medicine may be reopening soon.' Sunday, on the way back from the Chapel Royal, where Monsieur Le Sueur takes his pupil into the orchestra, shows him the music from the inside. 'Presumably the diseased body has been appropriately purged. Is that what one does to a diseased body? You're the medical man.'

'Am I?' Berlioz's face goes glazed and hard: then he turns passionately to Monsieur Le Sueur. (How do you turn passionately? All Monsieur Le Sueur knows is, Berlioz can do it.) 'What would you say, sir? Do you suppose my future lies in medicine?'

This, Monsieur Le Sueur thinks, is a great responsibility. Really he should not answer, or not unequivocally: strictly a matter between Berlioz and his father, and so on. But Monsieur Le Sueur is a child of the Revolution, when tyrannical fathers were toppled and men sprang untrammelled on to the chariot of their destiny. Also he feels he has a greater responsibility, to what is inside his pupil. Which he has a growing suspicion is genius.

'I do not think so. Unless, that is, such were your desire, and I have seen enough of your application to believe that you would do very well in medicine – *if* that were your goal.'

'Dear God,' says Berlioz, brokenly, 'you – can you doubt that I hate it, I loathe and despise and detest it—'

'Just the one hate will do,' says Monsieur Le Sueur genially, 'and I do not doubt that at all. Only I must tread carefully on matters that are not my province. But speaking as a musician and a teacher, I say medicine, no: music, yes.'

Berlioz suddenly looks sapped, reduced, as if about to faint at his feet. 'Thank you,' he murmurs, 'thank you, sir, and –' all at once the eagle is back' – 'and, actually, I knew it.'

'I should hope so. Well, I take it that you will not enrol again when the School reopens. I also assume, or rather infer, that this may cause certain difficulties for you.'

Berlioz chuckles aridly. 'Monsieur Le Sueur, may I tell you something? At home in the Dauphiné, I was trying to talk to an aunt about music, about the arts, about this adamantine provincial belief that they are all the devil's work. And I said, driven to extremes, what if Racine were in the family – what if that noblest adornment to our culture was born here, and wanted to follow his art, what then? Her answer was unhesitating. "My dear, a good name counts more than anything."'

'Dear Lord. She's a prodigy. You must bring her to Paris and exhibit her.' Monsieur Le Sueur coaxes his pupil into laughter. Formerly he has suspected exaggeration in these hints about his family: every young artist, after all, considers himself raised among brutes and Philistines. But seeing the struggle in that gaunt face, Monsieur Le Sueur believes it. 'The problem is,' he goes on briskly, 'one of perception. It is simply not seeing that the life of the artist, properly led, is one worthy of the highest respect and honour, just as much as any vocation or profession.'

Berlioz draws a deep breath. 'Oh, to hear someone say that. To hear you say what I believe. I don't know – I wish—'

'Many believe it, we are not alone,' says Monsieur Le Sueur, hastily. He may be wrong, but he fears some terrible wish surfacing out of his pupil's emotion: along the lines of *if only you were my father*. No, no. 'Ah, my friend, I wish you could have witnessed the great ceremonies of music we had in the Revolution. The uplifting of the spirit, the consecration of emotion. No talk then of art as a mere distraction . . . I think, by the by, Monsieur Berlioz, I might write to your father – should the need arise. Simply to state the case, that I believe music offers for you a much more productive future than medicine. I flatter myself that such a testimony from a Chevalier of the Legion of Honour may have its effect.'

And at that his pupil looks almost ready to sink with gratitude.

Almost. Because there is a witchy will-o'-the-wisp light about his eyes that seems to say: *You don't know the half of it.*

On the reopening of the Paris School of Medicine, Monsieur Alphonse Robert enrols at once. His cousin Monsieur Hector Berlioz does not. Crossing the Rubicon: sometimes it does not mean doing something, but not doing something.

It is soon after this (Hector, remember, is still sitting on a stack of sheaves in a stubble-field several years in the future, and we are catching up with him) that life takes such a turn that he has difficulty believing he is living it. Only reality can be so unreal. It would be much more bearable, it would make much more sense, if it were art.

Now there's an idea.

2

THE PRODIGAL: or, *Filial Ingratitude*

Opera in three acts

HECTOR BERLIOZ *tenor*
DR BERLIOZ *bass*
MADAME BERLIOZ *mezzo-soprano*
NANCY ⎫
ADÈLE ⎭ *sopranos*
FÉLIX MARMION *baritone*
MONIQUE *contralto*
ALPHONSE *baritone*

OVERTURE

ACT ONE

Scene One

(The Paris lodgings of Hector Berlioz.)

No. 1 Duet

HECTOR

No, no, my friend, be done with these persuasions.
My mind's made up: no medicine for me.
Speak one more word, and you'll put me out of patience.
At last I know what it feels like to be free!

ALPHONSE

Well, well, my friend, I'll say no more about it;
I know you think I'm merely speaking in your father's place.
Yet he only wants the best for you, even though you doubt it –
And so do I, and that is why I put the doctor's case!

HECTOR

The best for me? A life of pills and plasters?
When music calls me with a siren voice?

ALPHONSE

But sirens tend to lead men to disasters:
Bear that in mind before you make your choice.

HECTOR

It's made!

ALPHONSE

I know.

HECTOR

It's made.

ALPHONSE

'Fraid so!

HECTOR, ALPHONSE

It's made and I'm afraid there's nothing more to say!

HECTOR
Cheer up, my friend, and take a glass of cider –
It's all I can afford – but just pretend that it's good wine.
Great prospects lie ahead of me – I see them, spreading wider!
In Music's temple stands an empty niche – and that is mine!

Recitative

ALPHONSE
But tell me, does your father know you haven't enrolled again at the
School of Medicine?

HECTOR
I have, as it were, insinuated the information.

ALPHONSE
And what does he say?

HECTOR
Alphonse, you're not drinking your cider. Try holding your nose when
you take a sip.

ALPHONSE
I've tried, it doesn't help. Hector, this is troubling. It's one thing to talk
about music—

HECTOR
And another to give your life to it, which is what I am going to
do.

ALPHONSE
But nobody in La Côte St André gives their lives to music. They don't
even give a *sou* to a beggar. Not without calculating the interest.

HECTOR
We're not in La Côte St André, thank heaven.

ALPHONSE
Your family are.
(Enter Félix Marmion.)

FÉLIX
Somebody mention family? Well, nephew, I said I'd look you up in your quarters, and here I am. Devilish flight of stairs for a man with a foot full of cannon-shot. So, how goes it? Gad, you're thin. What is it – in love, are you?

HECTOR
Nothing like that, Uncle. What brings you to Paris?

FÉLIX
Affair of great military importance. Charming woman with exquisite shoulders and a fortune in the funds. But come on, what's yours like, hey? Don't tell me it's not love: I know you young rips.

No. 2 Trio

FÉLIX
Nine times out of ten
When a fellow has a yen
For a pretty *midinette*
Who is playing the coquette
And he's languishing in sighs
For those killing almond eyes,
When she's caught him in her mesh
He begins to lose his flesh:
His voice turns weak
And his sunken cheek
And his shrunken calf
And his hollow laugh
And his pasty skin
And his fiddle chin
And his hawk-like nose
Proclaim his woes:

It's always love that does it,
Yes, it's always love.

ALPHONSE

Though it may be true for some
I confess I find it rum
That a student's life is viewed
As incorrigibly lewd.
When you've got to make ends meet
It's the shoes upon your feet
And the cheese upon your knife
That dominate your life:
And you read all night
By a taper's light,
And you madly cram
For the next exam,
And you spend your days
In an eye-strained haze,
And you waste away:
So I would not say
It's always love that does it,
Yes, it's always love.

HECTOR

If the dart should fall on me
I've no doubt that I should be
Quite as skeletal a swain
As ever nursed his pain:
Yet from a different plight
Come the symptoms you recite –
Neither study nor romance,
Nor the opium-eater's trance,
Nor the fumes of wine:
At a higher shrine
I pronounce my vows:
Only art can rouse
In my curious heart

That delicious smart
Lovers talk about:
So I beg to doubt
It's always love that does it,
Yes, it's always love.

ALPHONSE
So I can't agree
HECTOR
So I just can't see
FÉLIX
My boys, trust me —
ALPHONSE, HECTOR, FÉLIX
It's always love that does it,
Yes, it's always love.

Recitative

FÉLIX
Well, I'll believe you: no doubt you don't want me telling tales. But,
Hector, on that subject, I gather they're worried about you at home.
Something about not settling to your medical studies. Is it true?

HECTOR
No, Uncle. There is no question of settling to them, I have given them up.

FÉLIX
The devil you have! Well, now, my boy, this is serious. Youthful enthusiasms are all very well — but your father's paying for you to have a
proper profession, and be a credit to your family. That's what you've
got to think of.

HECTOR
But, Uncle, I have a destiny I must follow. Didn't you feel the same
when you followed Napoleon's drum?

Jude Morgan

FÉLIX
Well, that's different: let me tell you how it was.

No. 3 Aria

FÉLIX
When the Emperor crushed the Prussians,
I was there,
A young lieutenant all wax and straw.
When the Emperor crushed the Russians,
I was there,
A young lieutenant, and not so raw.
I followed him to Spain, to Cadiz:
Where I saw what gallantry is:
And I followed him to Borodino –
For I didn't know then what we know:
I was ready to do it all again,
But to borrow a phrase from the naval men,
You must trim your sails to the wind, my boy,
You must trim your sails to the wind.

When the Emperor abdicated,
I was lost,
With nothing to believe in any more.
When the Emperor abdicated,
I was lost,
With no occupation – and I was poor.
And the King was climbing back on his throne,
And war was all I'd ever known:
So I reconnoitred my position,
And applied for a new commission.
I was ready to do it all again,
For to borrow a phrase from the naval men,
You must trim your sails to the wind, my boy,
You must trim your sails to the wind.
When the Emperor escaped from Elba,
I was thrilled,

170

For my hero was going to make a stand.
When the Emperor escaped from Elba,
I was thrilled,
And I rushed to join his loyal band.
And I followed him to Waterloo,
Where I saw what English squares can do.
When the smoke had cleared, I made a vow:
I shall have to be a royalist now:
I was ready to do it all again,
For to borrow a phrase from the naval men,
You must trim your sails to the wind, my boy,
You must trim your sails to the wind.

Recitative

HECTOR
You put it very well, Uncle: but you won't change my mind.

FÉLIX
I didn't suppose I would, my boy. Well, I must go: the charming shoulders await. Gad, I can't decide which one is the prettiest . . . But, Hector, all I will say is: think of your mother. Your mother, Hector. *(Exits.)*

ALPHONSE
The concierge has just brought this letter up.

HECTOR
From my father. *(Reads.)* So. I am summoned home.

ALPHONSE
You mean invited.

HECTOR
Summoned. Sternly. Fatally.

ALPHONSE
Oh, Lord. I was afraid it would come. You'd better pack. Hector, try and – well, never mind. Good luck. *(Exits.)*

No. 4 Aria

HECTOR
Papa, do you recall
When you and I read Virgil side by side?
You showed me beauty then,
With never any hint that beauty lied.
I don't believe it does, Papa –
I don't believe it can.
I know I can convince you that I am the man
You wanted me to be,
If only you could see
That every man has a star,
A light he must pursue –
After all, who taught me that but you?

Papa, do you recall
Aeneas leaving Dido for his fate?
And how we almost wept
Not just for Dido, but for Dido's mate,
Whose lot was bitter too, Papa,
In sailing off alone,
Forsaking love for glory – it must turn the heart to stone.
That's not how I would be
If only you could see
That every man does what he must
And not what he must do:
After all, who taught me that but you?

Scene Two

(The parlour in Dr Berlioz's house at La Côte St André. Enter Monique, the housekeeper.)

Recitative

MONIQUE
In all my years, I've never known such unhappiness in this house. Quarrelling and shouting from morning till night. The master all black looks, the mistress in tears, and Hector roaming about like some caged wild animal. By the Virgin, I dread waking up to it. I don't know all the ins and outs of the matter, but all I can say is nothing's worth this much pain. Oh, here they come. I don't even dare ask what they want for breakfast. *(Exits. Enter Hector and Dr Berlioz.)*

HECTOR
Papa, I still can't believe it. Thank you – a thousand thank-yous. I must be dreaming—

DR BERLIOZ
Not on this occasion, though I believe you spend half your life in that state. Well, no more of that. As I said, I'm simply weary of this endless dispute. It's grinding me down, which was perhaps the intention – no, I take that back. But moderate your thanks, Hector, and remember what I'm offering you.

HECTOR
My freedom.

DR BERLIOZ
That is precisely the wrong way to describe it. A trial, that's all. You will still have your allowance, and you may study music for a time – a limited time. After that, we shall see.

HECTOR
Oh, we will!

No. 1 Duet

HECTOR
I shall conquer, you will see:
There are prodigies inside,
All bursting to be free,
And they will not be denied –
Ambition is another word for hope.

I shall work hard, you will see –

DR BERLIOZ
If the music does not serve
Have something in reserve—

HECTOR
I shall live on bread and air—

DR BERLIOZ
As I said to you before
You can always try the law—

HECTOR
For your generous faith in me
I shall carry everywhere!

DR BERLIOZ
These expressions are wild
You argue like a child—

HECTOR
Ambition is another word for hope!

Recitative

DR BERLIOZ
Well, I have done: perhaps when you get back to Paris you will think

more coolly. Yes, I suggest you go at once, for this reason: I have not told your mother of my decision. You know that, where I am rationally against music as a career, she is ferociously against it. To avoid any more scenes, pack your bag and slip away, and I'll explain to her later.

HECTOR
Thank you, Papa – though I know you don't want to hear that.
(Embraces him and exits.)

DR BERLIOZ
Not want to hear it? No, no. But I would wish to be thanked for doing something I approved. Which is a sort of vanity, perhaps. 'My freedom,' he says. The young use words so easily. They have not yet felt the strength of them, the complexity of them: their strange bitter taste.

No. 2 Aria

My freedom – is that what it is?
That prevents me from relishing his?
All my life I have planned and projected,
And now here I stand,
With no map in my hand,
With no charts to guide me,
No compass beside me in this unknown land,
Is that why I feel unprotected?
My freedom – is that what it is?

This freedom – how much have I known?
While I shouldered my burdens alone,
I sought always to carry them lightly;
I wanted to spare
Those I love from a share
In the weight that soon bows you
And cripples and cows you and silvers your hair.
Do I envy my son – even slightly?
This freedom – how much have I known?
(Exits. Enter Hector, Nancy and Adèle.)

175

Recitative

NANCY

But you were packing your bag. I saw you. What does it mean? Has there been a decision?

ADÈLE

It means he's going. He's going!

NANCY

Hush, Adèle, stop crying. There have been quite enough tears here lately.

ADÈLE

Not from me. I like it when Hector's here. It's when he goes I cry.

NANCY

And it's when he arrives that other people cry. Well, Hector, you must confess it looks like that. Unless you can tell me different. Unless you can tell me exactly what's going on.

HECTOR

Dear Nancy, you're the one who should be a lawyer. Very well, but not a word to Mama. I'm going back to Paris to study music. For a time. Papa permits it. Again, for a time – but isn't it wonderful?

ADÈLE

Oh, you're going to be a musician! Oh, shall you play the piano?

HECTOR

I doubt it, I loathe the instrument: tinkle, tinkle.

ADÈLE

Well, it doesn't matter: you're happy, so I'm happy.

No. 3 Trio

NANCY

It matters very much, Adèle,
As you must surely know.
For certain things in life are high
And certain things are low.
And certain things are proper,
And certain things are not.
And some paths lead to heaven,
And some to – where it's hot.
And in this due proportion
We may trace the Maker's hand,
And we must treat with caution,
What we do not understand.

HECTOR

It matters not a jot, Adèle,
That's all you need to know.
Attend to what lies underneath
And not the outward show.
According to the custom
All artists live on gin,
And anyone who steps on stage
Commits a mortal sin.
And in this dead convention
You will find the soul's demise –
And it's my firm contention
That it's all a pack of lies.

ADÈLE

I don't know what either of you mean:
I can only judge by what I've seen,
Which isn't much – but still
I can't think ill
Of my brother, or another,
Doing what they want, for where's the harm?

NANCY
The harm is very real, Adèle,
At least, potentially:
A man of solid character
Should live prudentially.

HECTOR
My character's not solid –
To that I can attest –
Indeed, I thank the stars for it:
Fluidity is best!

ADÈLE
I don't want Hector burning
In the flames of you-know-where,
And all because of learning
To play the flute, so there!

Recitative

NANCY
You're too young to understand these things, Adèle.

HECTOR
And you're not, dear sister?

NANCY
I understand very well. And I'm not setting myself against you: I'm only thinking of our reputation, of the family – well, above all, what Mama will think. When she knows that you have been allowed to take up music—

MADAME BERLIOZ *(entering)*
She hears. She knows. Nancy, Adèle, leave us. *(They exit.)*

HECTOR
Mama. I had hoped you would learn—

MADAME BERLIOZ
When you are gone. When you can no longer look me in the face.
Providence has decreed otherwise, Hector, for which I raise my
thankful prayer. You will not go back to Paris, Hector: not like this.
You have beaten your father down, but I am fortified by a resolution
he cannot know, the resolution of my faith. I will not see my son
disgrace himself in the company of fiddlers and harlots, and place
himself outside the salvation of Holy Church. I forbid it.

HECTOR
Mama, you can't.

No. 4 Duet

MADAME BERLIOZ
No? Then let me beg, let me implore,
Upon my knees, a sight you never saw –
Your mother, yes, she kneels before her son,
And when her little sinful life is done,
She hopes to stand before the Seat, and say,
If rapture has not torn her voice away:
'If anything may spare me in Your sight,
May it be this: I strove with all my might
To save my son from blackening his soul
And return it to his Maker pure and whole.
For this on earth I may have earned his hate –
But care not, so I bring him to Thy gate!'

HECTOR
Mama, please stop it, let me go –
It's like an evil dream to see you so.

MADAME BERLIOZ
No dream, my son, these are your mother's hands,

The same that wrapped you in your swaddling bands,
The same that I would thrust into the fire

Before I'd see you have your sick desire!
Renounce it now, and join me in a prayer!

HECTOR
It's madness. Get up. You should have some air.

MADAME BERLIOZ
You refuse your mother, kneeling.
Already dead to filial feeling.
Then, go!

No. 5 Aria

Go on, my son, the Paris stews await,
Make sure you speak our name to every whore,
Go on, my son, and take a mother's hate –
Yet no, because you are my son no more.
When the filth is all around you,
When the actresses surround you,
When you breathe corruption in at every pore –
Go on, my son, forget your trail of woe,
Or glory in it – God knows which is worse.
But still remember – everywhere you go,
You carry with you, this: a mother's curse!

(Enter Monique, Dr Berlioz, Nancy and Adèle.)

Recitative

MONIQUE
I told you, I knew it wasn't just the usual quarrel.

DR BERLIOZ
What goes on here?

MADAME BERLIOZ

Ask your son. Or, rather, ask who lives here: a respectable family, or a circus troupe?

ADÈLE

Oh, that's easy. It's the family. Though it would be nice to have the circus – clowns and things—

NANCY

Be quiet, Adèle. Mama, you're crying.

HECTOR

One artistic accomplishment that is not forbidden.

DR BERLIOZ

Adèle, Nancy, go out of the way, my dears.

MADAME BERLIOZ
No, they shan't.

No. 6 Act One Finale

MADAME BERLIOZ
Let them know, let them hear:
Let them learn the worst, then let me go.

DR BERLIOZ
Oh, Finette, this wasn't meant to be.
Dry your eyes, my darling, come with me.

MADAME BERLIOZ
Don't touch me, don't speak:
How could you be so weak?

DR BERLIOZ
Finette, you're overwrought, you'll make yourself ill—

HECTOR
Mama, in spite of all, I am your son still—

MADAME BERLIOZ
Get out of my sight!

HECTOR
I will, I will,
Only please say I am your son still!

DR BERLIOZ
You'd better pack. You'd better go.

MADAME BERLIOZ
No, I shall leave for Le Chuzeau,
This place has been defiled.

ADÈLE
But why, Mama? I want to know—

MADAME BERLIOZ
You cannot know, you're just a child.

NANCY
You cannot know, you're just a child.
But still, Mama, consider, he's Hector just the same.

HECTOR
This is just a dream. Any minute I'll be waking.

DR BERLIOZ
A nightmare, rather – a nightmare of your making.

HECTOR
Papa!

DR BERLIOZ
I know, I know. I must share your blame.

ADÈLE
Mama, he's Hector just the same!

MONIQUE
Nothing but trouble since he came!

MADAME BERLIOZ
A filthy stain upon our name—

MONIQUE
He is your boy, ma'am, just the same—

NANCY
Just the same, he is to blame—

MADAME BERLIOZ
That boy is not my son, he is my shame. *(Exits.)*

HECTOR
Mama!

DR BERLIOZ
Go back to Paris. There's nothing to be done.

NANCY, ADÈLE
He can't go like this!

DR BERLIOZ
It's done.

MONIQUE
Now see what you've done!

ADÈLE
What has he done?

NANCY
Adèle, have done.

HECTOR, DR BERLIOZ
What have I done?

MONIQUE
My poor mistress—

DR BERLIOZ
Monique, have done.

HECTOR
She cursed me. She actually cursed me.
I'm dreaming—

DR BERLIOZ
No, the dream is done.

ALL
The dream is done.

End of Act One

(The work is unfinished.)

3

Well, Dr Berlioz might say, with judicious austerity, well, that is a version.

He would even admit that art by its nature must simplify, heighten and dramatize. He knows that: the thing is – the tragedy is, perhaps – that Dr Berlioz is not a blinkered Philistine. And he might well concede that his wife's laying a mother's curse upon Hector (a painful affront to his rationality) is indeed the sort of thing that belongs in a libretto rather than in the plain daylight of ordinary provincial life. He might even tell you the sequel: Finette storming off to their country house at Le Chuzeau, he and the girls and Hector following her there in the hope that she might at least bid her son farewell. How they came upon her in the garden, reading in the shade, looking so beautiful and so much his wife that his heart leaped: how she looked up, gave a terrible betrayed moan, and ran away from them into the fields.

What Dr Berlioz might point out, though, is that this is not the end, because unlike art life has no ends, nor even any true consistencies. He might tell you that Hector's next visit to La Côte was, to begin with at least, cordial on all sides, that his mother covered him with kisses: that life began again. And yes, there were more storms before his departure. He will even admit that this was because he felt Hector might have come to his senses at last, and was disappointed to discover the opposite. Then another bargain: one year, starting this day, to prove himself as a musician, or else abandon the whole idea. (Hence, more tears and reproaches from Finette.) Dr Berlioz, if you were to press him, might even admit that one thread in his tangle of feelings about Hector and music is the suspicion that his son will fail. There are far too many second-rate artists in the garrets of Paris, dreaming of great things and doing mean ones. Further than that Dr Berlioz would not care to go.

He might admit that, instead of pitched battles, he settled subsequently for a war of attrition, through that year and the next. Late deliveries of

Jude Morgan

Hector's allowance, reductions in the allowance, threats to cut it off alto-gether – yes, these were part of it. And yes, of course it made him bitter. It is bitter to feel that no one understands you. Finette – well, she fights the same war, but with different war-aims. What if Hector were to succeed, though – what then? Will he have vindicated himself – or will he have proved his infallible father wrong, and laid up a new store of bitterness?

There you press Dr Berlioz too far. And as to whether a curse, once pronounced, can be undone, on that subject Dr Berlioz has nothing to say.

Sunday, 10 July 1825, parish church of St Roch, rue St Honoré, Paris. First performance of a Mass for full chorus and orchestra by Monsieur Hector Berlioz, pupil of the Chevalier Le Sueur.

Who sits alone, hands knotted on his stick, in an inconspicuous corner seat, so as not to fluster his pupil, and to observe. Monsieur Le Sueur has heard a great deal of music in his time, so much that on hearing a new piece he is, as it were, several steps ahead of the composer: he foresees the next cadence, awaits the return of F major, glimpses future chords like landmarks on the horizon, while his learning greets the influences: Gluck there, hullo, Haydn, good God, Piccinni. All this happens as his mind navigates the course of his pupil's Mass. If it were all that happened, he would not necessarily be displeased – there is satisfaction in compe-tent craftsmanship, especially from so young a man with so little training. But other things happen. The landmarks disappear and reappear in unex-pected places: he is taken along puzzling paths that open up into unexpected vistas. There is simply more, more even than there should be – but no matter: his pulse quickens, he sees the tic of it in his veined hands, finds they are gripping the stick as if to save him falling from a high place. He is aware of tears. He dearly hopes his pupil will not suffer the reaction he had after his first successful performance – the ashiness, the empty boom, the feeling of climbing a flight of stairs, then finding they disappear up into darkness.

Later, at the rue Ste Anne, he pries Berlioz from the admiring cluster of Madame and Mesdemoiselles Le Sueur and embraces him. Searchingly he looks into his pupil's face: sees a bewildered, naked expression, like that of someone plucked from shipwreck or flood.

'Now I shall tell you. I believe you have genius. This is only the

186

beginning. We must think of the future. The Prix de Rome – yes, you must enter, that must be your goal. The Conservatoire, you must enrol for formal studies.'

A tremulous smile. 'But, Monsieur Le Sueur—'

'Hush. I know what you're going to say. But they *must* listen now.'

'A Mass.' Madame Berlioz carefully folds and lays the letter down. Usually, of late, they are screwed up or tossed aside. 'Well, that is not something to – there is honour in that. A church work. Apparently it was – noble, uplifting. Well.'

'Does that mean I can tell my friends about Hector now, Mama?' asks Adèle.

'Oh, Mama, don't let her,' puts in Nancy. 'She will only make a great romance out of it.'

Nancy: a young woman now and – odd how it sometimes happens – unfortunately finished. There is the crossroads of adulthood, and the various routes to follow and the things that you might take with you: decisions of identity. Nancy possesses intelligence and adaptability and wit, which she has taken with her, but for some reason she has left warmth by the roadside. Odd: because the choice does not seem to make her very happy. And she finds something increasingly irritating about Adèle – with her openness, the leaping look in her eyes: something, perhaps, Hector-like.

'You may,' pronounces Madame Berlioz, 'mention the Mass.'

'A Mass,' says Grandfather Marmion. 'Quite well received, it seems. My neighbour sent me a cutting from a Paris newspaper. Why didn't you tell me, Louis?'

'It is a subject,' says Dr Berlioz, taking an unprecedented interest in a calceolaria, 'on which I have nothing to say. Is that blackfly?'

'No. Hey, well, doubtless there'll be no stopping him now. You should have nipped the whole ridiculous folly in the bud, Louis, as I told you. The only other recourse is to stop his money altogether.'

'I'm aware of that.' A hot day at Meylan, the garden shadows like ink and the dragonflies riding the air: but Dr Berlioz is frozen, frozen.

'A Mass. Henri the Fourth said Paris was worth a Mass. But, I wonder, what's a Mass worth in Paris?'

An equine coughing resolves itself in Dr Berlioz's numb mind as his father-in-law's laughter. He realizes that he has never before known Grandfather Marmion to make a joke. And having lately taken two (or was it three?) grains of opium, Dr Berlioz almost feels like laughing too. In a way.

From the church of St Roch to the Théâtre des Nouveautés is only a short distance physically – but what a difference. From deep solemnity and antiquity to a brand-new building put up with brand-new money and where – well, let's follow that old man down the rue Vivienne to the theatre, because he works there, and perhaps he can give us an idea of what goes on.

Quite a sprightly old man indeed, and with an incisive profile that suggests more the keenness of youth than the chiselling of age. Fine head of grey hair too – so fine that one suspects a wig. Follow him into the well-appointed dressing-rooms of the Nouveautés, and your suspicion is confirmed, as off comes the wig – you may have noticed that he has shed the stoop too – and, in fact, this is nothing less than a young man disguised. A lean and striking young man, whose flamboyant bushel of hair actually springs up bristling after its imprisonment. Quickly he gets into his costume – a sort of spangled bandit affair – exchanging a few muttered words with his fellows, similarly attired, which suggests they are the male half of the chorus. From the auditorium, a blast of music, though of a very different kind from the stately strains lately heard at St Roch. What link can there be between them? Only this young man, Hector Berlioz, who on the strength of his serviceable voice has been engaged as a chorister at the vaudeville Théâtre des Nouveautés for fifty francs a month.

The disguise implies that he would rather not be seen coming here, so perhaps we should avert our eyes from the spectacle of him marching out on stage with the spangly bandits singing, *Boum boum tra la la la.* Well, his chief concern is that no word of his nightly occupation should get back to his family in La Côte St André, and he does have a large circle of acquaintance in Paris now – including a young fellow from his home town, Antoine Charbonnel, a chemistry student with whom he is sharing cheap lodgings in the Latin Quarter. Charbonnel supposes that Hector teaches pupils in the evening (the wig comes out of his pocket only when he reaches the street-door), so no tales can be told there. And we are not likely to reveal his secret – which would, after all, be the bitterest gall to his father (or would Dr Berlioz find, in the midst of his disdain, that nasty little pleasure of *I told you so*? You decide), whereas Madame Berlioz would simply be prostrate with shame. So Hector may admit us into his confidence after all.

And, after all, he is the first to enjoy the joke of the Nouveautés. He can give you a thoughtful analysis of the relative merits of the pieces in which he appears: he is still undecided whether *Grandma's Young Man* is surpassed in brilliance and sublimity by *Mr Jolly the Singing Bailiff*. As for the jigging pot-pourris of fashionable tunes that comprise the music, he cannot disguise his wince, but he can give you a fine impression of the principal singer, a lady with a bosom that could take on all comers, and who is sometimes so very near the right note that, as Hector confesses, you feel like applauding the sheer effort. The essence of Hector is the unexpected; and you tend not to expect so molten, driven, and susceptible a man to have a sense of humour.

And much of his current life he takes lightly. The meagre diet on which he and Charbonnel survive – bread, cheese, leeks, whatever is cheapest at Les Halles at closing time when the poor remnant is sold off – he lightens it by imagining it is the austere diet of the ancient Greeks, fuel of virtue and heroism. He carries raisins in his pocket and eats them one at a time to still the growling stomach. Certainly he might eat a little better if he were to forgo his visits to the Opéra. But there is food, and then there is food. And what he gets there he thrives on: he becomes mighty. Some members of the Opéra orchestra are a little afraid of that threadbare hawkish spectre leaning out from the cheap seats, and calling damnation on them when they miss a phrase or depart from the score. He is, they conclude, a little mad. Everyone is a little mad about something: but Hector's little madness is potent and purposeful.

That's why he can put up with the Nouveautés and the raisins: in his intense inner life, they are the frame round the picture, and who looks at the frame? Sometimes he does feel faintly savage, especially when he leaves the theatre after some particularly puerile confection has been applauded: or even after the Opéra, when the piece has goaded him with cheap tricks and repetitions. (He is a little mad about Rossini, who rules the Opéra nowadays: crescendo, bass drum, cymbal, perfect cadence. Friends suspect a certain jealousy of the successful Italian, the musical Midas, though they know better than to say so. Don't start anything with Berlioz: he'll still be convincing you when dawn breaks.) At such times he is unapproachable, brooding in a café corner over his own scores, turned cylindrical from being repeatedly stuffed into his pocket. There is a completed opera there, which he has found he can get staged with about as much ease as he can drink the Seine dry. And in this, perhaps, he differs little from other students, bruised and longing, who lurk about the Latin Quarter fondling their unsung masterpieces. Yet there is a difference about the way he handles them. A sort of defiant daring, a risk: as if they were explosives that might go off.

As for the Nouveautés, again, expect the unexpected. Rather than a low point in his fortunes, this is a stage of liberation. That fifty francs a month is money he earns, and for which he does not have to thank his father: just as well, as Dr Berlioz has reduced his allowance to that same sum, in a last, Waterlooish attempt to win the war. For Hector, the benign dream of independence looms. (For Dr Berlioz, perhaps, the nightmare?) Not that this means the thread joining him to La Côte St André has loosened. It doesn't work like that. A stretched thread, growing tighter and thinner, hurts you the more you try to hold on to it: and Hector still tries.

But he is going to be a musician, and that's all. He is fortified by Monsieur Le Sueur, who insists he enrol at the Conservatoire and compete for the French composer's Holy Grail, the Prix de Rome (and Monsieur Le Sueur has already decided he will pay the competition entrance fee if need be). And if that means skulking down the rue Vivienne in a grey wig, so be it. After all, the true artist must be a chameleon, Protean, able to enter into any feeling or situation. These are the ideas that are circulating in the bloodstream of Paris just now; and the name given to the various strains of infection is Romantic.

Monsieur Hugo the poet is particularly catching, and as he is part of a whole circle of writers and painters, the doctors of culture must be on their guard against the spread of the contagion. It is all, messily, to do with expressing emotions truthfully, even to their extremes, which means reproducing nature in art even where it is not neat and biddable and classic. It is spontaneous and awkward. It has no reverence for models. It sees no point in artistic rules if they do not serve the truth in the heart.

It wants to replace marble with flesh. It is, confusedly, political. It is, some-times, silly and incoherent.

But you can't ignore it, and above all you can't deny it, because there are some people who don't even contract the germ: they are born with it. Witness Hector, who belongs to no circles or salons but who has the devil's or angel's mark on him, indelibly. When somebody finds it, under the hair or on the shoulder or somewhere else, look out.

He doesn't know what he is – of course he doesn't, because no one does. If he is anything, he is a bundle of sense impressions: the continued but ignorable nag of hunger and outworn, chafing clothes: the continual, and beautiful, and maddening brain-sound of music, grinding splendidly at you like the opposite of toothache: the murmur of self-disgust at his brief emulation of Charbonnel, great lover of the Parisian-female-available, which has left him with a hatred of his flesh and a passionate pity for her: the pounding of his heart that comes upon him for no reason, and seems to lead like stealthy, muffled timpani to some grand *tutti fortissimo* that never comes.

And sometimes before sleep he looks at the sky – just looks at it, doesn't commune with it or hail it or apostrophize Diana in it but just looks at the damn thing – and he can't see, in all that pointless endless room, a single star.

By the by, he also sometimes beguiles his bewigged route along the rue Vivienne by observing the English. Because this is the Little England of Paris. There is an English bank here, and an English bookshop tanta-lisingly full of Scott and Fenimore Cooper and Byron and English newspapers, which look funereally solemn beside the garrulous splashi-ness of the French press. Tantalising, because though he has very little English, translation has made this world a permanent feature of his mind. There is a *Waverley* Overture among his pocket incendiaries; his imagi-nation roams Byronic landscapes. And even the language, overheard and uncomprehended, seems to call him in some way beyond the literal: bristling with consonants, oddly rhythmic, refusing to be smooth. *No* he understands, and he finds in it something misty, regretful, beside the clipped and decisive *non*. He has, very faintly, a sensation of exile, which is strange as he is in his own country. And occasionally he studies the faces of the English people there, strolling, framed in carriage windows. Remnants of wartime animosity still caricature the English as horsy ganglers with bad complexions and giant teeth, but Hector sees no such grotesques. Once or twice he glimpses beauty, melancholy and pale.

And sometimes, on his way home after the theatre through dark streets, he has an urge to shout at the top of his voice: 'You're asleep!' Literally true, perhaps, for many people, but perhaps he doesn't mean them.

The Prix de Rome: win it and you're made.

That is, your country bestows on you its highest laurels, gives you a comfortable stipend, and sends you off to Rome for three years to develop yourself as an artist. When you return, you will justify the Institute's faith in you by producing work that carries on the proudest tradition of the nation's culture – and so on.

Rome: of the five annual prizes, four are for painting, engraving, architecture and sculpture. Plenty of those in Rome. What there is for the winner of the fifth prize, for music, is a different matter – but let that rest: there are other anomalies to be faced first.

Charbonnel, a breezily vigorous young man with a pugilist's face, grins all over it when he hears what Hector has to do.

'So they shut you up in this place for three whole weeks. And you can't go out.'

'Of course you can't go out, it's – it's like an examination.'

'Ah. And you can't see anyone?'

'I believe they let you go out to the courtyard in the evenings, and you can see visitors then. But only if— You're not taking this seriously.'

'Oh, but I am.'

'Well, only if you don't bring anything, gifts or whatnot – and if you write me a letter, they read it first in case it's got something in it that might be construed as cheating . . . All right, it's not that funny.'

'Oh, it's wonderful. The academic mind. They really think I'm going to smuggle you in a tune. PS Hector, look in the bottom of the box and you'll find the chord of C sharp minor.'

Hector throws the breadboard at him. He is laughing himself, and he wants to laugh more – except that for him it is, in spite of everything, extremely serious.

In spite of the dusty, lofty, Louis XIV atmosphere of the Institute of the Academy of Fine Arts under its chilly dome, where you expect to hear the jangle of ghostly harpsichords and be tapped with fans by spectral ladies in ringlets. In spite of the endlessly ceremonious welcome to the four candidates in the committee room, where they perch on brocaded chairs clutching their notebooks and waiting to be given the words of the cantata they must compose to order over the next three weeks. In spite of the suppressed squeaks of disbelief at the appearance of the Permanent Secretary, an ancient fumbler who makes his way to the desk by a very circuitous route – He's never going to get there, Hector thinks, his legs are going to take him back out of the door – and who proceeds to dictate the libretto to them in a voice like dry moss. In spite of the libretto, a drear piece of fustian on, of all brilliantly original things, the death of Orpheus. In spite of the equally ceremonious ushering to your solitary room under the dome, where the commode sings its own noisome song and you are cautioned about using too much of the music-paper.

Another time you would laugh, but this is how you win the Prix de Rome. And Hector does not even wait to unpack his bag before seizing the music-paper, sitting at the rickety desk, and plunging.

Grandfather Marmion: 'Well, at least this shows you were right all along, and I hope now he sees it.'

Dr Berlioz blinks, haled back from long distances. 'Hm?'

'I say you were right. About Hector.' Blast the man, you can never tell what he's thinking nowadays. 'This folly of his. Now he can't deny it. You were right.'

'Oh, that, yes. Yes.' Dr Berlioz walks on, stumbling a little on the lush turf. Funny thing about being right: it's never, really, as nice as it should be.

Result of the music section of the Prix de Rome of the Académie des Beaux-Arts, 1827. First prize, and winner, Monsieur Guiraud. Second prize, Monsieur Gilbert. Third prize, Monsieur Despreaux.

As for the fourth competitor, his cantata has been withdrawn. Odd business, as the judges agree: one doesn't really know what to say. For one thing, he altered the text, cut bits out, added his own. Then it was all arranged for some sort of fantastic orchestra when the candidate knows very well it is to be performed before them with piano accompaniment – and what an unholy row *that* made when the pianist tried to do something with it. One feels, indeed – sure you concur with me on this, gentlemen – that the Academy is being somehow mocked. All in all, one wonders how he got here.

Hector on the sheaves, staring through the cloud of his own breath at the great smudge of dawn-stirring Paris: how did he get here?

The failure of the Prix de Rome didn't kill him. He went on with his studies at the Conservatoire, addressed himself once more to the Byzantine bureaucracy that determines whether a new opera may be put on in Paris or not (*not* being the usual case). He learned to love leeks and raisins again. Nothing changed, perhaps – except a new self-belief, which is indistinguishable from loneliness. Moments in life when you hear, like a stone dropped down a well, that single bleak echo: for you, my friend, this is how it's going to be. Get used to it.

And when the English theatre company came to Paris, soon afterwards, he didn't stand stricken on the road to Damascus. Rather, he was passionately interested and excited in the way of many of his friends and contemporaries – the people who are beginning proudly to style themselves Romantics, wearing the badge in defiance of solid newspaper-reading opinion, which characterizes them as long-haired, pathological, unhealthy and probably unpatriotic misfits. The fact that the company would be performing Shakespeare merely quickened his interest, as the same creaking academicians who wanted him to make Orpheus die discreetly and correctly have always loathed that messy northern barbarian. Hodge-podge of comedy and tragedy. No polish, no classic restraint. For which, Hector would say, thank God.

Still, he didn't know what to expect, when he took his place at the Théâtre de l'Odéon for the first night of *Hamlet*. He was aware of heat and stir and something like a tide of concentration bearing him up, but he was aware, too, of a sore place on his heel where his boot-sole was worn thin, and of a flourishing wen on the back of a nearby neck, and of his debts. There is a truism in the nature of the unexpected: you don't expect it, whether it be the heart-attack, the religious revelation, the earthquake. Hyperbole, perhaps, but with Hector from now on even the greatest hyperbole is an understatement.

So, the curtain goes up. But it also goes up on his life.

★ ★ ★

'Berlioz, just what is wrong with you?'

Charbonnel addresses him from a great height. Opening his eyes, Hector has the impression that the stocky chemist has been painted on the ceiling, like some classical allegory. Sturdius, the god of Common Sense. Hector utters a laugh, which surprises him as much as if birdsong had come out of his mouth.

Charbonnel sniffs. 'Well, it's not brandy. Look, for God's sake say something. At least tell me why you're lying on the floor.'

'Am I?' Hector lifts a neck that feels as if it is made of unyielding bronze. 'Oh, yes. Well, to sleep.'

'To sleep. God knows our beds are lumpy enough, but surely preferable to the floor.'

'Too comfortable. I don't want to be comfortable.' Hector sits up: the room does a mad waltz around him.

'Sleep you do need. I'd suggest food and a change of clothes also, though no doubt you'll say something cryptic and peculiar to that as well. And just where were you last night?' Charbonnel grimaces. 'Now I'm sounding as if we're married. Look, there's a scraping of coffee, do you want it?'

Hector shakes his head. Funny thing, the head: really everything is there, mind, expression, the looks that make you an individual: even lust and hunger. The signal starts elsewhere, but the head acts on it. No wonder the Jacobins chopped off heads: that's the end of you. Now he is laughing again.

Charbonnel shrugs. 'I don't know. I wish you'd tell me what this is all about.'

Hector wishes it too, but that would mean using words; and they have, in the true sense, failed him. For this they are inadequate in a faintly disgusting way – as if you should try to describe a sunrise in numerals.

'Denmark,' he says. 'That's where I was last night.' And he has a feeling that he is going to be sick again.

It is Hector's cousin Alphonse who finally gets some sort of sense out of him.

'It's the English theatre at the Odéon,' he tells Charbonnel. 'It's given him this tremendous – excitement. And especially that actress they're talking about, Miss Smithson.'

'Oh, I heard about her. What? He fancies he's in love with her, does he?'

'Something like that.'

'Well, so is everybody, from what I've heard. Is that all it is?'

Alphonse gives a small sigh. He is embarked on a successful medical career, is gleamingly booted and stiffly cravated, and it is all very odd being back in the Latin Quarter with its seething emotions and uneven table-legs propped with half-Bibles. Still he retains his imagination; and sometimes he finds something a little obtuse, a little La-Côte-St-Andréish, about Charbonnel. 'The thing is,' he says, 'it's different for Hector.'

Who appears at his bedroom door, looking dreadful. As if someone had attacked and beaten him up – or rather, Alphonse thinks, as if he has somehow done it to himself.

'I am in love,' he says, in a grating, clockwork voice, 'with Shakespeare.'

'Hate to tell you,' says Charbonnel, 'but he's dead. And a man.'

'No, no, he isn't,' Hector cries, folding his knuckles before his face, beating them against his bared teeth. 'That's exactly it, you see. Mind you, nothing is exact. Nothing ever is. That's what we must learn. That's what I've started to learn. We're all asleep, you see.' He makes a courtly bow of valediction, and is soon heard being sick again.

Hamlet was the first thrust of the blade. After that he was staggering around, wounded but upright.

At the time, in the Odéon, he was lost to everything, you could have set light to his clothes without him noticing: later, as fragments of last night's dream suddenly visit the mind at midday, he recalled that several people left the pit after Ophelia's last scene, distressed and stumbling. He saw it through, but he understood. In essence, after Ophelia he couldn't move. When he did grope his way out of the theatre, he hit his elbow a shattering blow on the door-jamb; but the pain occasioned in him only a mild surprise at the continuing existence of his body.

He dreamed of Ophelia, wept, laughed: plunged his whole head into a bowl of cold water to tell himself, *Come on, stop, end it*. He roamed the streets, trying to tire himself, until his thighs and calves burned and his breath was a guttural sob; but his mind was in charge, and it kept on beating and flashing like a beacon through smoke. He retched. He had sudden electric fancies that he was about to see her, in front of him, around the next corner: Ophelia. He knew Ophelia was an Irish actress named Harriet Smithson but, then, he knew that his hand was an assemblage of small bones, muscles and nerves – and what did that say about it? Ophelia, Harriet: Harriet, Ophelia: you couldn't separate them, and if you could there would not have been that hush, those moans at her appearance.

Yes, he had fallen in love: Hector would agree to that if he could make his mouth work. And no one needed to say it, he could hear the voices already: 'Smitten with an actress, eh, my dear fellow: well, she is uncommonly pretty to be sure: try your luck at the stage door, you never know.'

All a grubby irrelevance. The beauty that exists for everyone is a mere concurrence of opinion. Hector was experiencing the private, painful and baffling apprehension of the beauty that is the person you love, applicable to crone or witling. Except, as Alphonse said, it's different for Hector.

Because when he sees and hears Ophelia, everything is transformed. If he had gratified his family and become a doctor, he might well still have fallen in love with Ophelia – but she would not have affected his views on the treatment of quinsy or the physiology of digestion. Whereas Ophelia and Harriet invade not only what conventional romance calls the heart, but everything that matters to him: every last village and outpost is taken. Napoleon never dreamed of such a conquest.

In lucid moments – admittedly few – Hector can even analyse it. Here at last is theatre where you don't applaud the acting, the grand style, the technique – because you forget they're acting, of course. And here at last is art in which true expression of nature, with all its lopsided emotion and passion and absurdity, matters much more than the rules: (oh, the rules, the bloody double-damned rules: and here is another oddity, Hector who is usually vivid but decorous in his speech finds himself in his desperate nocturnal rambles muttering the obscenest *f*s and *b*s, as if he would throttle language in his extremity).

All of which, after all, should be an inspiration. Instead, Hector finds himself dry, empty and mocked. The music that is always shifting like ever-sculpting sands in his mind turns into the caw of a parrot or the thump of a press. He is an ancient city, spectacularly ruined, extinct.

And the announcement, after *Hamlet*, of *Romeo and Juliet* as the next production of the English theatre, strikes Hector as a warning. Don't go. You're already half mad with it. Miss Smithson is to play Juliet. There is a rush for tickets. Whatever you do, don't go.

Charbonnel, trying to make a meal out of bread, lard and mustard: 'Where are you going?'

In answer, only the frantic clatter of the staircase.

And that is what has brought him here, to the fields outside Paris. *Romeo and Juliet* was the killing blow. After Ophelia, Juliet: love ineffable, intolerable: love like a sword. He has been roaming about with it pierced through him; in delirious moments he can feel the bloody hilt. He has walked and walked, along the Seine, up to Montmartre, back to the city, until his feet are bleeding and he falls and sleeps wherever he finds himself. He has haunted the place de l'Odéon to see her arrive at the theatre, and turned reeling from the sight of her stepping out of her carriage, feeling the savage sword twist inside him. He has not been to see another performance, even though everyone is talking of Miss Smithson's triumph and the season is to be extended: he knows he would not be able to bear it. He is already overflowing with the beauty and sorrow, the love and death.

The appalling simplicity of it is this: he no longer knows how to live. The future before him seems no more negotiable than a sea of scalding lava.

Hector climbs down from the sheaves, assures the farm bailiff he is not a madman and tests his legs. Well, that's something: he's not going to faint. Nor, for a wonder, be sick. He breathes complex autumnal air, listens. A remote tessitura of birdsong.

'Why do the birds sing?' he asks. 'Surely not for us.'

The bailiff backs away a little. 'I don't understand you, Monsieur.'

'Ah, but they understand each other.' He begins plodding across the field towards the city. 'Art,' he calls back suddenly, 'can speak to art.' The bailiff's dog growls at him.

By the time he reaches the Barrière de Vincennes he is so out of breath that he can only gasp it out to the customs-officer. 'Art can speak to art.' The man shrugs his shoulders and waves him on: no duty payable on insanity.

Much later Hector will deny that he ever said, around this time: 'I shall write my greatest symphony on *Romeo and Juliet*, and I shall marry Harriet Smithson.' Perhaps he didn't. Still, no smoke without fire.

PART THREE

Portia

1

The two lives of Harriet Smithson.

At nine o'clock in the evening of Monday, 3 March 1828, she took her final bow of the Paris season before a packed audience at the Salle Favart. It was her benefit night. In the boxes, a glitter of *duchesses*. In the pit, people standing, yelling, calling her name. *Smith-son*: somehow the awkwardness with which the French tongue tackled it made the sound more yearning, more moving. Others shouted the French version of her first name: *Henriette*: so close to *Harriet*, yet with a moan about it, like a prayer. Some were still hoarse from weeping at Juliet's death. She had heard the sobs.

And while she bowed she remembered standing helplessly beside Mr Kean at Drury Lane among the flying oranges and dirty jokes. For life to turn about like this, with such completeness, must mean something; but there was no thinking what it might be, no time to think. Scarcely time to feel: the exultation, the fear, the delight slipped like beads through your fingers. The applause kept on, waves of it engulfing her and receding and then coming again, until it felt exactly like standing with your feet in the sea: the tide makes it feel as if you are the one who is moving, being drawn inexorably forward; down the beach, the stage, towards her turbulent public.

In the green-room, astonishing gifts. From the Duchesse de Berry, a great Sèvres vase. (How will I get it home? Where will I put it? What if I break it?) And a gift from – actually a gift from – Charles X, King of France, a purse of money presented by an actual flunkey on a tasselled cushion. (Do you thank the flunkey? Tip him?) From the auditorium, more cheers: Mr Abbott was making a speech of thanks.

'Unctuous as ever,' Mr Bampton reported to her. He was still in costume as the Apothecary: not the aptest of roles for the world-weary gentleman. He always handed Romeo the poison as if it were an indifferent Burgundy. 'Practically on his knees with gratitude. Mind you, with such receipts, who can blame him? Special mention for you, my dear. "A talent that has grown before our eyes", no less. True enough, of course. And to think they wouldn't even have given you a sniff of Juliet before this.' The actorish acidity was a mere reflex, and Harriet hardly noticed it. 'They're calling for you, by the way. Shouting the house down.'

'I'm not allowed to go on, am I?' In Paris there was a police regulation against actors taking curtain-calls. She had spent fruitless hours trying to work out why.

'Well, not unless they start a riot. You know the French. Any excuse for a barricade. What *are* you going to do with that vase?'

She could not go on again, but she could listen to the acclamations; and when she left the theatre, in her own carriage, the street was so full of people cheering and jostling to get a look at her that the carriage could hardly move along. Which she didn't mind: she found herself quite without impatience, even without a sense of time. She sat back, settled her wrap about her, gave the odd wave through the window, and simply occupied this moment. She considered some questions: whether in this triumph lay vanity and pride: whether it was deserved. But they didn't need answers, because without time there was no urgency; and above the Paris roofs, the stars were shining on her.

The two lives of Harriet Smithson.

At eleven o'clock on the evening of Monday, 3 March 1828, she was in her lodgings on the rue Neuve St Marc trying to fend off the frantically beating fists of her sister Anne while her mother, drowsy with wine, made ineffectual shushings.

'I hate you, I hate you. You don't love me at all, you don't care. I've been so ill, Harriet, so ill that if only you knew you would never have left me tonight, but you don't care at all, you don't . . .'

'I do care, I do. And I'm sorry you were ill, but it was my benefit. I can't miss that, and you know it, Anne.'

'She hasn't been ill,' Mrs Smithson grumbled. 'Naught but bad temper.

Don't you know, you silly girl, that you wouldn't have that pretty frock if it weren't for Harriet and what she does?'

'Pretty frocks don't look pretty on *me*,' Anne said, with a scorching look. As so often, she seized on the saddest of truths: sometimes she even seemed to hug them to her. 'If she's gadding about all hours because of that, then she needn't trouble. I don't want them.'

'I never knew such an ungrateful girl,' said Mrs Smithson, reflectively, as if mentally reviewing and comparing a whole list of ungrateful girls in her experience.

'I can't be here all the time,' Harriet said, 'because when I'm acting—'

'You're not acting when you go off to these parties and balls and receptions and—' Anne smacked her lips disgustedly, as if even the words were foul. 'Unless, of course, you're acting up to the *men* there, which no doubt you are. That's why they're all making such a great fuss of you, Harriet, because of what they want to *do* to you—'

'Stop it. Stop it now, and don't ever speak to me like that again.' It was the sharp ferocity of Harriet's tone that made Anne stare in reddening silence. Not, no, not the slap across the face that, God forgive her, she had so nearly given.

Anne limped into her bedroom, pitched herself on to the bed. Harriet followed and pushed her sister's hair back from her face. Anne was crying convulsively, silently: square-mouthed and scarlet, like an infant. 'I want–' a shuddering gasp '– to go home.'

We have never had a home. Harriet had developed the knack of internalizing the true replies, the replies you couldn't make to Anne. 'I know. But we need to be here for now, because we're doing so well. Some time we will go back.' To oranges and Princess O-me? And the dusty smell of the prop-room? No, keep that down too.

'No, we won't. It won't happen. Because you're going away from us.' Anne wrenched herself into a sitting position. She looked white, exhausted: ill. Perhaps she really has been ill, Harriet thought, while I was bowing and smirking. The guilt was like an old tiresome friend knocking at the door: you know you'll let him in. Anne plucked gloomily at Harriet's fingers. 'You're not ours any more.'

No, I'm afraid I'm not. How can I be? When I walk down the rue Vivienne I see my portrait in the window of every print-shop and bookshop. They tell me even the hairdressers are offering *la coiffure à la Miss Smithson*.

I'm not yours, I'm not anyone's now, I'm the public's. 'No, no. I'm always yours. Think about it. Haven't we been together through so much? And now we're together in this, which is – which is very strange, and so I can see it's difficult to get used to. It is for me too . . .'

Not working. Bleak, dark-rimmed eyes lacerated her. You could no more cajole Anne than you could knead a brick. Harriet cast about; and then she thought of the flunkey with the cushion.

'And besides, Anne, we saw this happening, you and I. I can tell you now – Mama wouldn't understand. You remember at school, when we used to invent such stories about us?' A blink: very well. 'There was one in which we rescued a prince from a dungeon. His wicked uncle put him there, I think – there was always a wicked uncle.' Twitch of unhappy lips: good so far. 'And when we had rescued him, and delivered him to the true king, we were given a reward. This is what's so absolutely curious – you'll hardly believe it – but that has come true, just as we used to imagine it.' Now this next part was a lie, and Anne's memory was almost infallible and she pounced on lies and made you suffer for them: still, try it. Harriet opened her reticule. 'Look. It's a purse full of gold. Go on, undo it, look. That's exactly what the king in our story gave us. And tonight at the theatre the King of France sent a servant round with this – a purse full of gold.' Anne's too-knuckled fingers groped, found: the unreal coins spilled on to the coverlet. 'Doesn't that show? Oh, Anne, doesn't that show . . . ?'

Harriet couldn't say, or even imagine, what is showed exactly: but. 'Fancy,' said Anne, a smile dawning. 'Just fancy. Gold from a king . . .' She turned on Harriet a look of wincing shyness: it meant one of her rare attempts at humour. 'But didn't we also have a story where you ended up by marrying a wizard? You don't see many of *those* about.'

'Oh, well,' Harriet said, laughing with relief, 'you can't have everything.'

So, success. Anne presently went to bed, placated, affectionate: saying, fancy. Harriet went to bed much later, having drunk the remnant of her snoring mother's wine, and having looked again at the purse of gold. The trouble was, it wasn't a fancy. This was really happening, and in her first dozing half-dreams she was standing far out on a promontory, surrounded by enticing sea, and it was a splendid place to be – only she kept turning, turning, and wondering, wondering.

★   ★   ★

In the morning Anne was thin-lipped and silent. The weathervane had turned again. The Bible lay open on the table, always a bad sign. When Harriet pinned on her hat – Parisian, a fabulous creation of velvet and plumes – Anne turned her back and stared out of the window.

Harriet was almost out of the door when Anne spoke: 'Where are you going?'

'To see Mr Abbott. About starting a new season.' She hesitated. 'And to see about my carriage.'

Anne did not look at her, but her chin grew sharper. 'I don't know why I'm here,' she said.

Perhaps, Harriet thought, perhaps so that my head won't be turned.

Or perhaps it already had been. It must change you, wearing these clothes, stepping into this carriage, knowing that people would crane in to look at her and wonder where she was going this evening. A ball, a salon . . . Yes, probably: what they couldn't guess was that she still felt dry-mouthed with fright when she entered the ballrooms. Mademoiselle Mars was helping her, coaching her in basic French: still, this faint feeling that she was an imposter among the gilt and pier-glass, that somewhere among the turning ostrich-feathered heads was one who knew it and need only smile thinly and point a finger for everything to fall away. When she got down to look at her portraits in the print-shops it was not so much gratification as reassurance she sought.

Or perhaps just vanity. Again the voice of Anne in the wilderness: looking through the book of prints by Monsieur Devéria, representing Harriet in her triumphant roles, Anne had closed the volume and pushed it aside with a shrug. 'But none of them are *you*,' she said.

Ophelia. Juliet. Jane Shore. Desdemona. But they are me, she had wanted to say, or I am them. Not a thing to say to Anne, who would only blast her with some bleak truth. Such as: *They don't love you, they love who you pretend to be.*

Unanswerable, except by the admission: *Of course. It can't be me, because there isn't anything to love.*

She met Mr Abbott at his hotel in the rue de Rivoli. Success had altered him only to the extent of a jewelled cravat-pin. His habitual apologetic smile seemed to refer to it: forgive this, a weakness.

'Encouraging news from London. It looks as if we will have Macready, though he wants a hundred pounds a week and he's fussing about details. I'll go over as soon as the receipts are banked, try to ginger him up. We can't drag our feet if we're to open in April. Oh, and he wants *Macbeth*. Very much his style of thing, you know. Ever act with Macready?'

'Years ago. He wouldn't remember me.'

'Hm. Well, he might *say* he does, you know.' Mr Abbott offered a small smile, as near as he ever came to malice. It was true that Harriet's triumph had changed her past as well as her present. After the public reaction to her Ophelia, Charles Kemble had offered her Juliet with magnanimous grandeur, like a king in disguise doffing his old cloak. 'Yes, Miss Smithson, Juliet: it is the role, I am convinced, that you were born to play: I have long thought so.' It was better to be amused than bitter about it. And now William Macready, the Tsar of Covent Garden. Kean, Kemble, Macready, the three emperors of the stage, and I shall have been empress to them all. She savoured it, if only to keep off the flittering bat-wings of Anne. And something else.

'Lady Macbeth,' she said doubtfully.

'Who else? You'll be splendid, my dear Miss Smithson. The crown of your triumph. At the price of a few bruises. Macready does tend to pull his ladies about rather.'

Ophelia. Juliet. Jane Shore. Desdemona. All roles that called for pathos and pity: sometimes she almost felt a vampire's exultation, feeding off the moans and shudders beyond the footlights. Lady Macbeth was a villain-ess, and powerful.

Mr Abbott observed her tactfully. 'The most difficult of Shakespearean ladies, I always feel. I remember Mrs Siddons in the part: eloquent, noble – but perhaps too noble. One felt she would never have even touched those beastly daggers. Never fear, Miss Smithson: I have no doubt that come April, you will have *jeune* France besieging the stage door once more.'

'Oh, Lord, not too much besieging, I hope,' Harriet said. 'It is very awkward when they – well, when they declare themselves ravished, and all of that.'

'Ah. Not more letters from the musical gentleman?'

'No, thank goodness.' She had received many complimentary letters, but this from a man with a French name that struck her as even more peculiar than most had been a rather terrifying annunciation. He was madly in love with her, he beseeched her to have pity on him, he was stricken with passion. And he seemed to demand some response – other than the obvious one: *But you don't know me, and I don't know you, and it's absurd.* In the end she had got the company treasurer to despatch a cool note stating that she could not reciprocate his feelings. It was even more absurd to feel guilty about that. 'It must have been a – a momentary enthusiasm. If not, then perhaps Lady Macbeth will kill it off.' They're making a great fuss of you, Harriet, because of what they want to do to you. Out, damned spot.

At the coachmaker's, she very nearly decided against it. It was a whim that had come to her the other day, and Harriet very rarely acted on a whim: caution, caution. But on getting down, she heard someone murmur, awestruck: '*Voici La Belle Irlandaise.*' And vanity, or whatever, rallied. She wrote down the English words she wanted painted on the panel of the carriage, extravagant result of her salary soaring to five hundred francs a week (but justifiable – think of Anne, unable to walk far). '*My kingdom for a horse.*' The coachmaker repeated it back with such an exotic array of vowels that for a moment she thought she had written something else. Like *Out, damned spot.*

It was true about Macready: he made a grabbing, pinching, bruising Macbeth, and as he had the unusual habit of attending full rehearsals, Harriet soon felt like an overripe fruit. Mild Mr Abbott, as Macduff, was petrified at the sword-fight. Once out of character, however, Macready was all punctiliousness. 'Miss Smithson. My thanks, madam, and my compliments.' He stalked away, sniffing: a stiff-backed martinet with a long, pursed face and unquiet eyes, watched by a frustrated Harriet. She could not make anything of Lady Macbeth, and he was unamenable to discussion. Would not Lady Macbeth, in this scene, be less resolute than— 'My dear madam,' he interrupted her, lifting a peremptory finger, 'these cogitations will help neither your performance nor your peace. You must remember that the stage is, all in all, damnable. You must keep a part of yourself inviolate from it, or it will damn you too.'

'Always says he hates the theatre,' Mr Bampton told her. 'Only forced into it when his father lost his fortune. Well, of course, he has to say that, doesn't he? How else could he get his enormous dignity on to the boards at all? I accidentally brushed against him in Two three. Gave me the very devil of a look. As if I were a sweep's boy. So, how long did he stand staring at Banquo's ghost today?' A sharp imitation of Macready's statuesque immobility. 'One of these days the carpenters will come along and shift him.'

Harriet did not much care for Macready's stately style: still, she realized he was the best thing in the relative failure of *Macbeth* before the Paris public. The witches produced giggles, the scenery looked oddly tropical for Scotland, and Lady Macbeth was nothing, nothing at all. *A momentary enthusiasm*: her words came back, like Banquo's ghost, to haunt her suppers at Tortoni's. Yes, go on, spend while you can, while it lasts. Vanity, vanity.

What she needed was a spark. It came with the arrival of Edmund Kean.

The Parisians had been clamouring for him: Shakespeare and *la belle* Smithson had made *Romantique* the confession of the new faith, and now the last prophet must come among them. The original Romantic of actors called at Harriet's lodgings as soon as he arrived, looking like a seedy ostler, his voice a croak.

'Stairs,' he rasped. 'Infernal stairs. In a better world, I would be carried everywhere in a litter, like an Oriental potentate. Don't stare, this passes. Give me a brandy and you'll see it. How d'ye do, ma'am, and what do you think of this prodigious fledgling you've hatched? You keep, I'm sure, a little restorative brandy . . .' His voice gave out. Mrs Smithson, who kept more than a little, flew to her cabinet. Anne withdrew to her own stony corner.

It was true: the drink did restore him, visibly – a landed gasping fish dropped into water. Quite as visibly, he could not do anything without it now. A spark, where once there had been a blaze; but it was enough for Harriet.

'Conqueror of the French.' He kissed Harriet's hand gently: a contrast with raging Macready. 'A second Wellington, except that you're not a stiff-necked toadying old despot. Unless you are – unless it's spoiled you – let me see.' Those eyes still mesmerized, but they gave away, painfully, too much: it was like looking into an exposed and beating heart. 'No, I think you're still Miss Smithson, at least. Your fame is . . . What's that unlikely phrase? . . . bruited abroad. Bruited. What a curious little wagless docked-tail of a word, never use it otherwise. Yes, your triumphs are reported in London. With a well-bred sneer, of course. I may as well warn you that they will hate you for them.'

'Will they?' She supposed, then didn't suppose, that he was joking. 'Why?'

'Why? Because they didn't appreciate you, and if the rascally French do, then the rascally French must be wrong, of course. You've been away from England too long, Miss Smithson, you've forgotten how to breathe that special English air of cant, envy, hypocrisy and costiveness. They need a good purge, they need a national dose of rhubarb, but they won't get it. I'll trouble you for a drop more of that excellent medicine, ma'am: and let me compliment you as a hostess, as a man who knows what it is to be offered dismal cordials by simpering Lent lilies who expect to be *thanked*.' He raised his glass, with quite genial irony, to distant Anne. 'So. What do they think here, what do they really think, of Shakespeare?'

Harriet swept up scattered thoughts: it was disquieting, Kean here, Anne here, her two worlds brought grindingly together. 'They – they love it. Yes, they love it – even when they don't understand, or something seems strange to them or even repulsive, you still know that they are fastened on to it. They won't let go, unless – well, unless you let go.'

Kean emptied his glass. 'It sounds too good to be true. But I'm still thinking like an Englishman, who goes to Shakespeare as if it were an irksome duty. I shall leave in a moment, ma'am, otherwise I shall drink all your brandy.'

Her mother fluttered. 'Oh, you needn't trouble about that, Mr Kean, I'm sure there's plenty—'

'I'm sure there isn't, for my requirements.' He growled it, but the old growl was soft, even self-mocking. Perhaps the tiger had grown too used to the chain.

At first he was dreadfully erratic. He gabbled through speeches to save his broken voice for the big moments, then threw them away. He fell back on stylized gestures and overused the sardonic laugh. 'Which is he now?' someone muttered at rehearsal. 'Hamlet mad or Hamlet sane?' Audiences were politely puzzled.

Harriet's pain was sharpened with understanding. She knew what he was doing: waiting for the moment, looking for the powder-train to receive the spark. She knew because this, she realized, was what she did. It was a disquieting discovery: lifting the carpet to find a gaping hole in the floorboards over which you had been blithely stepping.

Shylock saved him. It was the role that had made him, the role he had rescued from years of cheap burlesque. Unusually, there was a full rehearsal. At the end, no mutterings: only a held-in silence.

'It will go,' he said to Harriet in the wings, wiping himself with a towel: without drink he was in a perpetual dripping sweat. 'Old, embittered, lashing out from his corner. That's what I'm good for now. Congratulations on Portia, Miss Smithson, you have made her very nearly not an unbearable prig. All that can be done with her. Apt casting, though, since you defeat me at the end.'

'Don't say that.'

He grinned unhealthily. 'I have mastered the art of the uncomfortable compliment. Miss Smithson, if ever woman stood in the position of Portia, it is you. The prize of Paris, waiting to be won. The caskets ranged before you. Who will step up to choose? Who will make the right choice?'

'Thank you, Mr Kean, I don't want to be a prize.'

He tottered away from her. 'Want has nothing to do with it.'

After a successful *Merchant of Venice*, Kean left Paris in June, without saying goodbye.

Occasionally Harriet's right ear would close up: sleeping in an awkward position, perhaps. It always righted itself quickly. It was one of those things you immediately forget. When it pops up again, you greet it with mild, surprised irritation: oh, yes, it's this. Until it becomes more frequent, or worse.

So with the young musician with the odd name.

She ended the Paris season as Desdemona to Macready's Othello: battered, but victorious, again the house rising, again the great baying and wailing of her name. She checked her balance at Périgeaux and Lafitte, the one bank trusted by the cautious English. Plenty there, but it would diminish. She must look ahead, calculate. A talkative beef-faced man of business named Turner was often there, and at Gallignani's, and he agreed. He had contacts throughout the theatrical world of the Continent. He knew everybody. He knew her brother Joseph. He knew the musician.

'Bair-lee-ose,' he instructed her. 'Remarkable young talent, in his way, which isn't everybody's. One gathers he is always at loggerheads with the academies. But he had a whole concert of his own music put on at the Conservatoire Hall last month. Couldn't go myself. Enterprise, though, remarkable enterprise. That's what's needed in Paris. Things in your way, you know, regulations and stuffed shirts. Young blood coming up. Oh, I'm not surprised he wrote you, ma'am, he's one of those who saw your first Ophelia, never got over it, so they say. Striking-looking fellow. I'll point him out if we ever come across him.'

'You needn't do that,' Harriet said. 'I don't quite like the thought of . . .' She didn't finish. The thought of *not being got over*. It wasn't that she didn't believe it. It was believable as Ophelia mad with grief, Laertes leaping into the open grave, Othello killing with passion. It belonged elsewhere. Perhaps Macready was right: keep yourself inviolate.

'Well, to be sure,' Turner went on: he made do with any reply. 'But look here, ma'am, I hope you don't think of an early return to England, after such a season?'

'I don't particularly want to go back.' She smelt oranges and prop-room dust. 'No, I don't.' I don't, but Anne does. Out, damned spot.

'But there's nothing in Paris for now, of course there isn't. After the races everyone leaves for the country. But don't underestimate the provinces, my dear Miss Smithson. And Holland, now – I have a lot of associates in Holland. If you'll allow me to look into the matter . . .'

She allowed him. It seemed to her that she needed a Turner, with his confident bustle and excellent French. Mr Abbott, who had informally managed her affairs till now, was too inclined to strike while the iron was lukewarm. Having Turner as her agent meant, she soon found, more mentions of the remarkable Bair-lee-ose, but it meant no more than the ear trouble: oh, it's this.

Summer tour of the French provinces: execrable coaches, wonderful landscapes, and audiences somewhere in between. In one or two remoter towns she felt she had wandered into one of the old caricature prints in which John Bull laughed pityingly at his benighted neighbour: harpies in sacking aprons and wooden shoes lined the muddy streets alongside bottle-nosed *curés* and starveling youths spitting green fountains, all grimly staring at the actors as if they would have fetched the faggots and kindling at a moment's notice.

At Le Havre Charles Kemble and his famous legs joined the company. After the strain of Kean and the chill of Macready his mannerliness was rather a relief. That she did not entirely trust him was a separate matter.

'One wonders,' he said, after a dismal response at Rouen, 'whether the appetite of the French is becoming jaded for our fare.'

'Or whether the fare is not rather ill-cooked nowadays,' Harriet said. Home engagements and responsibilities had reduced the company, and Mr Abbott had filled the gaps with any old stuffing.

Kemble's well-bred eyebrows went up. 'Indeed.' He would not contradict a lady: but, she felt he did not really heed her opinion. As if she were still a serviceable walking-lady, instead of the company's biggest attraction. The club remained closed to her.

She did not think of herself as stubborn, or inclined to powerful feelings; and the resentment, or pride, that she carried with her on that tour surprised her when it crept out. The occasion was Charles Kemble's offer of a three-year engagement at Covent Garden, at an initial salary of twenty pounds a night.

'As I've remarked before, I believe the enthusiasm of the French has run its course. In London, whatever the vicissitudes of individual theatres, whatever the shifts in taste, we have our feet always set upon firm ground.'

'When I left, the taste was shifting decidedly towards pantomimes and acrobatic horses.'

Kemble shuddered fastidiously. 'It is a great pity. But a tendency that those of us who have a care for the integrity of the dramatic art may contest with all our might, Miss Smithson, and I should be honoured if you would take up arms in that crusade.'

All very persuasive, and a year or so ago she would have leaped at it. But still this offer did not guarantee her against being cast as the Princess O-me or Second Gentlewoman. And she had heard rumours about Kemble's beauteous young daughter, a princess in waiting groomed for the succession. And . . . Yes, very well, perhaps my head has been turned after all. I do have a neck like everyone else. France made me. England put me in the prop-room, among the dust.

'Absolutely the right decision, my dear Miss Smithson,' Turner said, when the company returned to Paris. For a moment it occurred to her that he never questioned any decision, but she let it pass. 'You shall have a score of such offers. Besides, I hear Kemble is hock-deep in debt at the Garden. Quite right to turn him down, quite astute. Europe is your field, ma'am. And your greatest admirer will be glad to hear of it, I know.'

'Oh, Mr Turner, please, not your Monsieur – Monsieur Berlioz again. What *is* the matter with him?'

'The matter, my dear Miss Smithson, is that you are his idol! I know no other word for it. Yes, I've talked with him more than once of late, I find him vastly interesting. You and Shakespeare have set him to learning English, by the by. Le Sueur, who is a great man at the Conservatoire, has the highest of hopes for him as a composer. This is the point, ma'am – you as an artist have inspired another artist, which I think rather affecting and splendid. Pray don't take it as anything distasteful or disreputable. Believe me, you are his holy of holies.'

'Well, I don't find that very comfortable either. But if I have helped this gentleman with his musical career, then I wish him well. All the same, I shall make sure my maid –' my maid, Lord, listen to me '– knows that no letters from Monsieur Berlioz are to be accepted. It will only encourage wrong notions in his head, and be no kindness to him.'

'Absolutely, of course.' Turner did not question that decision either.

'Harriet, I'm sorry – but you did say we would be leaving soon.'

Anne had been quite severely ill with a septic throat; and, as often, illness had mellowed her. It was as if illness was where she really belonged, whereas in the half-way house of limping, indifferent health she could only be unhappy. Now she looked almost timidly at Harriet from her convalescent cocoon by the fire.

'Yes, I know. And we will. But I've agreed to do this one performance at the Opéra-Comique, and I can't escape it. And it's not for me, it's a benefit for the poor, so surely even the Bible must approve that.'

Unfair to hit back at Anne when she was laid low, but Harriet was soured by the unsuccessful struggle to get approval for a new winter season in Paris: she and Mr Abbott had suffocated in the tendrils of royal committees and theatrical commissions. In Paris, Mr Abbott had concluded with uncharacteristic coarseness, a horse couldn't shit on the road without a certificate. Turner had secured her an engagement in Amsterdam, but after that it would have to be England.

'I was only wondering,' Anne said.

'I doubt you're fit to travel yet anyhow,' Harriet snapped, 'so there's not much sense in talking about it.' What a nice person one could be, she thought, staring out at the icy street, if only one were always happy. Even the view of the rue Neuve St Marc affected her unpleasantly now, since Monsieur Tartes, the owner of the house, had informed her that the ridiculous Monsieur Berlioz lived in an apartment just on the opposite corner of the rue de Richelieu. Oh: it's this. And more. And getting worse.

And here now came Monsieur Tartes, tapping and insinuating himself in, no doubt bringing more unwelcome information. But no: only to enquire after the young *mademoiselle*. He was a little grey-headed sidling man with a look of birdlike attentiveness. For some reason Anne, even when well, liked him. While they cooingly conversed Harriet took the opportunity to slip out: to breathe pure air, banish her mother's snores and the smell of horehound, walk out her disappointment. But she slithered on frozen mud, and the thought of that unknown apartment inhibited her. Furious with everything, turning back, she concentrated her fury on the deluded musician. In this state she stepped back indoors, and met Monsieur Tartes in the hall.

'Ah, Miss Smithson, I was hoping to have a word with you . . .' He spoke in French, but luckily his ingratiating manner made his speech slow enough to follow.

'I hope it is not about the previous subject.' She answered in French, which gave her a feeling that at any moment she should twitch her robe and sweep out like a queen of antiquity. It was the only time, in fact, that she felt stagey. 'And I hope it is not another letter. I thought I had been clear about that—'

'No, no. No more letters. Monsieur Berlioz understands that. Absolutely, Madame.'

Monsieur Tartes had got to know Monsieur Berlioz or, probably, the other way round: she hardly cared any more. All that mattered was that the deluded musician now had another advocate, living directly beneath her lodging. It was Monsieur Tartes who had tried to press into her hands an anguished letter of avowal, written in English, begging for one word in reply. Or that was what he said it contained: she didn't want to see.

'Only I have again been talking to Monsieur Berlioz, and I engaged to speak to you once more about his previous letter—'

'As I told you, Monsieur Tartes, one is not obliged to reply to such a letter, least of all from a stranger. It is altogether absurd.' She turned towards the stairs, then felt bafflement tug her back. 'Why does he persist in this? It makes no sense. I really do not understand how he can believe . . .'

Monsieur Tartes made some wincing birdlike bobs. 'To be fair to Monsieur Berlioz, it appears he has reason to believe his suit is not quite hopeless. He often speaks of your agent, Madame, Monsieur Turner, who seems to encourage him – saying that you are always interested to hear about Monsieur Berlioz, and—'

'Mr Turner will say anything,' Harriet burst out, 'just for the sake of talking.' We always learn things too late, she thought, with a kind of mental crackle – or, rather, realize we knew them all along. She drew a long breath. 'I fear Mr Turner has given Monsieur Berlioz quite a mistaken idea. For this I blame him, not Monsieur Berlioz. All the same, your friend must know, sir, once and for all, that I cannot entertain these advances.'

Monsieur Tartes was almost at right angles in his sympathetic interest. 'Then I should say to him, Madame, that his suit is impossible?'

'Yes.' She put her foot on the stairs. 'Nothing is more impossible.' How cutting it was in French. *Il n'y a rien de plus impossible.* She meant it, and yet for a moment she seemed to feel the blade-like slicing into the shrinking flesh.

Eventually something like that troublesome ear gets better on its own. Often, after a last flaring-up: and then, gone.

For Harriet, at the rehearsal for the gala benefit at the Opéra-Comique, only one little gluey tickle when she sees a galley-proof of the programme lying on a chair. Upside down she reads, idly: '*MISS SMITHSON and MR ABBOTT of the celebrated English Theatre present scenes from Shakespeare's* Romeo and Juliet: *for the first time ever,* opéra-comique *by M. AUBER, entitled* La Fiancée: *Overture upon Walter Scott's* Waverley, *by M. BERLIOZ.*'

Well – after the jolt – in a way she is pleased for him. His star is rising.

This is, perhaps, what he needs. Plunge deep into your art, and a lot of useless clinging things wash away: she knows that.

So the rehearsal — the most powerful scenes only, culminating with Mr Abbott's Romeo cradling the dead Juliet in his arms, and her usual effort to disregard the agonized quivering in his stringy biceps and dismiss the suspicion that she is getting too fleshy, and to ignore the sooty fishing-nets of cobwebs depending high above her and the somewhat winy scent of Mr Abbott's breath though it is never, thank heaven, anything worse and nor does he ever choose these moments thrustfully to intrude on her notice a more authentic reaction to the passion of the moment in his breeches: and then, from nowhere, the final and incredible flaring-up.

It begins with a hideous shriek that brings Juliet back from the dead and the rest of the company peering round the wings. Afterwards they establish that the young man who walked into the theatre at that moment, and had a sort of convulsion at the sight of Mr Abbott and Miss Smithson rehearsing, was the composer Monsieur Berlioz, arriving a little early to rehearse the orchestra in his overture. They establish that after he had blindly butted and threshed his way out of the theatre, he came back at last and did his job. And there is a general chuckle at the susceptibility of artists, in which Miss Smithson — some say — is heard to join.

At the time, however, there is no doubt about Miss Smithson's galvanized start at that cry, and her stammering injunction to the company: 'My God, did you see him? Look out for him — dear God, look out for that one. The one with the mad eyes.'

2

Some thoughts about eyes.

Oh! tell me not of sorrow's seal,
It chills, but cannot quench the soul;
Say not life's cup no sweets reveal,

There's still some brightness in the bowl.
Can all be dark that life supplies?
Whilst earth can boast of SMITHSON'S eyes.

Verse extracted from the *Dramatic Biography* of William Oxenbury, Harriet's admirer and contemporary at Drury Lane.

Dr Louis Berlioz: 'Orbs of aqueous matter linked to a complex of nerve tissue.'

Colonel Félix Marmion: 'Orbs, yes. And, by God, they dazzle you. If the bigger orbs down below haven't already done so. Sorry.'

Mrs Constance Smithson: 'Oh, Lord, I was always told I had the prettiest eyes. A gentleman wrote me a verse on them once, all about lamps and stars and things like that. And when I first met my husband at the Gloucester country assembly, and this was in the days when gowns had just begun to be *very* revealing – well, that's another story.'

Miss Anne Smithson: 'They're where you can really see the lie – if you look.'

William Shakespeare:

Love looks not with the eyes, but with the mind,
And therefore is winged Cupid painted blind.

3

I feel this is rather unfair. You ask me to speak just at the moment when there is not much to say – that is, you have had the important moments at your disposal, and now I am to fill in the rest. The uninteresting interim. That's not to say I quarrel with the way you've done it so far, not at all: if anything, you have underplayed it. Perhaps necessarily. In essence, if I were to tell the story entire, it would not be believed, it would be flaming romance. And this is a cunning stroke of yours, passing the torch to me now, so that any criticism will not rebound upon you. Well, I will go along with it, as much as I can. Remember, you tax me: the sum of me will soon run out.

Yes, England. I came back with a sort of defiant reluctance. I wanted to show them what I could do as I had in Paris — yet from the start I doubted I would be allowed to. Mr Kean was in the right of it: to be a favourite of the French is not the way to win English hearts. The London newspapers were very satirical about me. They had got hold of a private letter in which I spoke of my warmer feeling for French audiences over English, and printed it: so, I was practically a traitor, smuggling military secrets through Calais in my reticule.

Well, I returned to Covent Garden, and played Juliet — at least there was no quarrelling with my entitlement to such roles now. Opinion was divided. There was some rapture: some indifference. Probably, yes, my head had been turned, or swelled: I was used to all rapture. I'm sure I was a very mopish, discontented creature when I set out on the summer tour. There were no pictures of me in the print-shops of Newcastle: audiences did not weep or shudder in Leamington. I suppose I held my turned or swelled head up by thinking: This is not the real way of it. This is a pause in my true life — a tedious halt at a dismal inn while the horses are changed, then huzza, on with the journey. A very dangerous way of thinking.

Meanwhile the patent theatres were staggering under the weight of debts. Covent Garden was saved when Mr Kemble introduced his daughter, Fanny, to the stage. Sensible economy: in a family concern you can, as it were, live on board wages. But more than that, she was a great favourite with the public. Did I begrudge her success? Please, you know I am — was — an actress, you know better than to ask that. In truth, though, I did not, whereas I should have if I had been sensible — for here was a door closed on me: but I still had my sights set upon the glories of Paris, I was still dawdling expectantly at the inn.

Oh: as for my strange admirer, I forgot all about him. There: just as well I have the narration of this part, after all. You, I suspect, would be working in little hints and foreshadowings. Whereas in life we don't know: we don't know. I forgot about him.

Likewise even upon my return to Paris. It was an odd engagement I went there to take up — but when had my association with Paris ever been anything but odd? Who in their right senses could have predicted any of it? I may even have thought: If it seems rather mad and improbable, then it must be meant for me. It must have been this sense of a destined end – there, now I'm doing it, you have infected me – that enabled me to overcome the objections of my sister. Mama was feeling her age now, and did not mind anything as long as she was taken care of. Anne – Anne was different. However, there we were in spite of all, and there I was on the stage of the Opéra-Comique. The piece was an opera in French, which included a role for a woman who did not sing or speak French at all, only English. Yes, I know. What shall I say? In spite of that, we did very well. Which made it all the more galling when at the end of the run the managers of the theatre disappeared with the takings.

I did what I could. With a French dictionary at my side I composed letters to various authorities looking for redress – looking for the seven thousand francs I was owed, in other words. I was even prepared to petition the King, the same who had sent me the purse of gold. But this was the year 1830, and the month was July. I remember only the concierge advising me not to go outdoors, some gunfire that sounded like fireworks, a lot of noisy brassy bands, and later, when it was safe to go out, seeing that a lot of trees had been chopped down and a lot of houses were flying tricolour flags. I think I was not even surprised that there had been a revolution: one felt that the French simply tended to do that, as the Scots have Hogmanay. But during the fireworks the King with the purse of gold had been toppled. So that was that. I tried petitioning the new King, Louis-Philippe, because they told me he had seen our Shakespeare: but no good. Bigger fish to fry just then, one presumes. I have been a little sceptical of revolutions ever since. If you have seen the celebrated painting of Monsieur Delacroix reflecting that event, with the large and bare-bosomed lady leading some eager fully-clad gentlemen into battle over the barricades – well, I hesitate to say this, as Monsieur Delacroix was among those young artists who took their inspiration from my performances (you see why I don't like telling this? turned head, swelled head) – but I always imagine at the edge of that picture someone gloomily trailing about trying to get their back-salary paid, and not thinking about their heroic profile at all.

Luckily I still had friends in the Parisian theatre. They arranged for me a benefit at the Opéra. Maria Malibran sang, Madame Taglioni danced. It was beautiful and magnificent, and it enabled me to pay my creditors, and the doctor's bills for Anne, who fell sick with a dreadful fever that we feared was the cholera, and our passage back to England. Also it made me dislike, all the more intensely, the thought of going home. In spite of my struggles with the language, I felt France was where I belonged: my own country seemed a place of exile.

Probably this discontent was part of the reason I did not thrive on my return. My own acting – whatever made it go, I mean – was always a mystery to me, and the only times I tried to speak about it I talked sheer nonsense: but one thing I do know – when my heart was not in it, I was miserably bad. Apt, then, that I should end up, after a long, provincial trudge, back at the Royal Coburg. The tone of the place had not improved: suffice it to say that there was a special dressing-room for the performing goat. I was also enabled, or forced, to renew my acquaintance with Mr Frank Cope. Let me record my satisfaction that he was still nothing more than a Walking-Gentleman, whereas for all my difficulties I was a leading actress with a famous name. As a corrective against vanity, I shall also record what he said – not to me, for we did not speak, but in careful earshot: 'Oh, Lord, have you seen La Belle whatshername preening? All because a parcel of Frenchies went tail-on-end for her. Can't she see that they don't understand a word, and it's just her bubbies they're looking at?'

I find it hard to say when my decision was made. At least, the first part of it – that I would go back to Paris – had never been, as it were, unmade. But against that stood the seeming impossibility of getting a company to mount another season there. Mr Macready was unwilling, Mr Kemble was taken up with Covent Garden, and Mr Kean was, alas, not to be relied upon. Prospects might have been better had someone been prepared to take on the wearisome work of organization – all the business of grants and censors and permissions – but Mr Abbott, for one, had had enough of that last time. I suppose my decision was forced on me by my own unquenchable desire to recapture those soaring evenings in the Paris theatre. I had taken all the alternatives out of the box, and there was only one thing left at the bottom.

I would have to manage my own company.

My mother said, 'Of course, dear, the very thing.'

Anne looked at me long and hard, then went away to think. When she re-appeared, she said: 'If it's your company, does that mean there isn't some man in charge?'

'Assuredly,' I told her: I remember feeling surprised, even charmed, at the ease of my victory. 'There is no man in the case.'

I think, in all ways, that I have said enough.

It was the same Paris: surely it was the same Paris.

'Well, yes and no,' said Mr Bampton. He was one of the few members of the old company she had been able to engage: also one of the most distinguished, which said a lot. Daily he brought her the news and gossip from Galignani's. 'Rather trying times of late, one gathers. Political situation as volatile as ever: someone took a pot-shot at poor Louis-Philippe. Then there was the cholera. It's died down now, apparently, but everyone's on the *qui vive* for the first signs. They say that at its worst there were corpses ranged all along the Pont-Neuf. Some churches are still draped in black. And the rich have been rather slow to come back from their country houses. Self-preservation, you know. Still. Things can only improve. So. What *are* we to do for scenery?'

'I don't know. I shall work something out. I have another appointment with the director of the Théâtre-Italien tomorrow. I hope he will talk a little more slowly. Why do the French speak so quickly?'

'Because they're speaking their own language.' He was very loyal, Mr Bampton, helpful in many ways, but you had to accept the acerbity. 'By the by, I've asked everywhere after your Mr Turner, but he seems to have dropped quite from sight.'

'Oh . . . never mind. He wasn't greatly to be trusted anyhow.' No, but he spoke fluent French and he had all the push and confidence that she lacked. Or that she was beginning to fear she lacked. She tried, grimly, proudly: I am Miss Smithson, she told herself as she waited in the anterooms of secretaries and ministers, I am La Belle Irlandaise: when I am on stage I make people weep and tremble.

But she wasn't on stage, not with the lawyer who made incomprehensible cavils about her company's contracts, looking at her as if he tasted something metallic in his mouth: not with the printer who made a misspelt hash of the posters and handbills, and shrugged, his back to her, when she protested: not with the newspaper editors and reading-room proprietors who took a few of the handbills with a dubious nod: not with the banker who drew her account-sheet across his desk towards him with a single disdainful finger.

And nor, except in a literal sense, was she on stage with her own company, most of them strangers, few inclined to enthusiasm or inspiration. In rehearsal they waited about stolidly for her to direct them. When she did, they looked mutinous. When she told them simply to follow the emotion of the moment, they looked baffled. The scene-shifters watched with interested, crooked smiles, as if observing the progress of a bet.

And, of course, all of this was because she was a woman. Actresses did not manage their own companies. Hence this continual scramble over hedges and ditches. Harriet comforted herself with this thought for a while, but eventually she found a hollowness in it. It's not the fact that I'm a woman, it's the fact that I'm me.

'You should be sharp with them,' said Anne: in a curious way, an ally. 'These people will lead you a fine dance if you don't. You should put your foot down.' And also in a curious way, Anne with her invincible belief in her own rightness and her fearful temper might have done it better. In an even more curious way, she had all the characteristics of a successful theatrical manager.

But opening night was approaching, and then it would be different. Then she *would* be on stage. Then she would be reunited with – well, at the end of an exhausting and dispiriting day, her head jangling with tax-bills and irregular verbs, Harriet over a couple of strong, indispensable brandies would think of it as . . . a reunion with a lover. And they never went wrong, did they?

'I suppose one can never recapture novelty,' said Mr Bampton. 'By its nature, you know. Novelty, newness. Same Latin root. There, my education wasn't wasted after all.'

'I don't,' Harriet said, thick-tongued, desperate, 'I can't . . . I can't believe that – that we only ever succeeded in Paris because of novelty. Don't you remember the way they used to . . .' She stopped, staring down the dark well of her mind at a pitiful reflection of herself: living on past glories, at thirty-two.

'Mm.' Mr Bampton left a polite pause. 'I fancy we are, in a way – or I should say you, Miss Smithson, above all – are victims of our own success. One gathers that after our Shakespeare, the choice dramatic spirits of France picked up their pens and set to work on their own account. Really we should be flattered. You must have heard about Monsieur Hugo mounting his *grand pièce romantique* at the Comédie-Française with Shakespeare coursing in his veins. Practically a riot at the first night, it seems, but they won. The new men, the Romantics. Delightfully French, isn't it, the way they're prepared to go to the barricades over a play? All long hair and fancy waistcoats, apparently. But you see my point. When we first came here, the theatre was absolutely dead, and we, somehow, Frankensteined it back to life. And now, well . . .'

'It was a first night, and a little lumpy and sticky in the way of these things,' Harriet said firmly. Or she meant to: she had a drizzly suspicion that her firmness came out merely shrill. 'We shall do better. We shall do better.' Oh, yes, that's right, say something twice and it makes it come true. She dearly wished for brandy, but it wouldn't do to be seen tippling in the green-room. That was the trouble with being a manager: they were always looking at you.

Polite notices, and a few of the old rhapsodies at her own performance: meanwhile she conned the receipts, compared them with expenses, held her head and wished herself elsewhere. Her mother had stayed in London this time, sharing lodgings with an old crony from the Dublin days: her absence made Anne all the more present. 'Are you sure they haven't made a mistake?' Anne needled. 'A deliberate mistake, I mean. They'll try to swindle you, you know. You're too weak, it's written all over you.'

Harriet wanted to leap up, bang the table, shout at her: she was prevented only by the realization that she was turning into her father. Instead she said: 'It's not a mistake. At least – not the accounts.'

Anne refrained from further comment, going to bed early, resolutely, a witness and martyr.

And then the old impassable paralysis came over Harriet, the same that had once sent her trailing numbly and resignedly around the Drury Lane alleys, knowing that she could not go on and that it was all a terrible wrong-turning and there was nothing to be done but regret such a cataclysmic error as believing she could be an actress. This time nothing cured it. She postponed and then cancelled performances, giving out that she was ill. Not a complete untruth: whenever she pictured going on stage, she was seized by dry retching. She lurked in her rooms at the Hôtel du Congrès. Her mistakes swarmed about her like gnats – including these expensive quarters, which had seemed more fitting for a manager. Season: should have started earlier or later, more chance of securing a competent company, bigger audiences. Repertoire: should have started with something other than *Jane Shore*, nothing new, not even Shakespeare. Publicity: should have sought out the journalists who had lauded her last time, prepared the ground, stirred up excitement. Finances: should have found someone else to put money into the venture, instead of using (losing) her own. Character: inadequate, and hence responsible for all the rest.

Responsible. Cold sweats doused her, while Anne moved about quietly and cheerfully, humming.

It was a dream that pricked her back to life – or, rather, what she made of the dream. A huge hourglass the size of a barrel was thrust, brutally, into her hands, and she desperately sought for somewhere to put it down in a world denuded of surfaces. The hourglass was a horrible and inimical thing but it needed her. When she woke she was actually weeping at the strain on her arms.

She thought for a moment of going to one of the dream-booths for an interpretation: but, really, no need. The salient thing about hourglasses was that the sand in them ran out, drip drip, before your eyes. While she lurked and agonized, that was what was happening to the money. Drip drip.

Harriet dressed, put up the *coiffure à la Smithson*, which was actually all she could do with her thick recalcitrant curls, got ready to go out. Anne was seated at her favourite window overlooking the gardens of the Tuileries, which she watched with a sort of dark anticipation, as if waiting for someone to fall over or hurt themselves: waiting for disaster. When she saw Harriet in her cloak, her eyes kindled, as if it had come at last.

'It went, I think, a little better,' Mr Bampton said, calling at her hotel the day after the second performance. 'I felt that the reaction was . . .' He seemed to be searching for a positive word for mild, tepid, lukewarm, and gave up. 'Well, we must see what the reviews say.'

'I can tell you what the receipts say.' Harriet let the papers fall to the floor, sifting, fluttering. There was a little sleet at the window. Poetic correspondences. Perhaps they were meant to compensate for ruin.

'I wonder whether we might profitably drum up a little support among the English community. I know a clever young fellow at Galignani's, writes for their newspaper – great admirer of yours. Understands the art of priming and puffing, so important in Paris. If you'll allow me to introduce, we might enlist him.'

'Very well. Anything.' Anything, rather than sitting here with the gnats and the figures. 'Let's go to Galignani's.'

'Now?'

'We may as well.' Why not? One thing, now, seemed emptily equal to another. She would have gone for a dip in the icy Seine if someone had proposed it. Volition had left her. It was almost comforting. Put the thread into my hands, and I'll follow wherever it leads.

The young journalist, very English, very red and stammery at meeting Miss Smithson, had the unlikely name of Schutter. Certainly, to be sure, anything he could do, notices, distribution of complimentary tickets: above all, word of mouth, get them talking, the Parisians loved to talk. Mr Schutter loved to talk, and Harriet's head began to buzz and ache. Shut up the shutters. Bring down the curtain. Kind, though, eager. Could he call on her at her hotel? Yes, anything: you decide.

She rode back in a cabriolet with Mr Bampton. The wheels skidded on a crust of slush and horse-droppings. *My kingdom for a horse.* The vain carriage had long gone, also the money she had got for it. Probably, in fact, it was a simple matter of her luck running out: there was, as Bridget had always hinted, only so much of it to go round. Drip drip. She wondered if she should drink brandy when she got in. Well, if there was any, she would: no need to decide. Keep hold of the thread.

Mr Schutter called and called again, peppering her with ideas. Shakespeare, that was the key: audiences were jaded, they needed shaking again with that terror and pity. Perhaps a different theatre, less imposing, more intimate. Certainly, to be sure, anything. There was a letter from her banker, pained and regretful. She did not know what to do with it.

Anne ordered dinners and dealt with the laundry, fuming. She liked life abrasive and difficult: this ghostly passivity of Harriet's was no good to her. 'What's wrong with you? If you're ill, you should see a doctor. If not, you should make an effort.'

'You decide.'

Sunday, and Mr Bampton called about a little matter of salaries.

'Blood from a stone, Mr Bampton. We must wait until the new year. A new season.'

'That's what I thought. But as to the matter of the new season . . .' He studied her face. 'Well, never mind.'

The maid, unpaid likewise, sourly announced: 'Here's another one.'

Mr Schutter, unbearably fresh-faced. He bowed to Anne, who regarded him suspiciously. Here we all are, thought Harriet: what next?

'Miss Smithson, I have come to urge you to – well, to attend a concert this afternoon.'

Harriet was still trustfully keeping hold of the thread; still, she could not quite believe it was meant to lead there. 'A concert? What on earth for?'

'This concert,' Mr Schutter pursued, 'is an occasion of particular significance. That is, in all ways, as the composer is the most remarkable figure, and the excitement surrounding it is – but forgive me, the significance, Miss Smithson, as I was saying, is for you. Believe me, all of artistic Paris will be there. It is an event you simply must grace with your presence. An event – an opportunity. And I have secured a box.'

'A box?' said Mr Bampton, perking up. 'I'm rather fond of music myself.'

A concert, a box. This decidedly made no sense – but, then, she had stopped looking for or expecting sense. 'Mr Schutter, I fear I'm not in the vein for listening to music,' she said weakly. You decide.

'Still, publicity, you know, Miss Smithson,' Mr Bampton said. 'Always helps to show yourself at these occasions.'

'And you're certainly doing no good moping about here,' snapped Anne. 'You need something to shake you up.' She mimed the shaking, untenderly.

Even Anne: well. Decided, then. Still, it meant getting out of her chair, and she was not sure she could manage that.

'Where is it being held, sir?' Mr Bampton asked.

'Great Hall of the Conservatoire. Magnificent venue.'

'Magnificent,' echoed Mr Bampton, very much wanting to go. As far as Harriet remembered, it was he who in the end almost lifted her out of her chair. Then she was in a cabriolet with the two gentlemen, and in a moment of mild alarm putting her hand to her head: but, yes, someone had given her her hat. The cabriolet rattled and slithered, following the thread.

'Here's the programme,' Mr Schutter said. 'Very detailed as you see, but then it is a work of unusual scope and dimensions.'

The motion of the carriage made it difficult to focus her eyes on the flamboyantly printed words. GRAND CONCERT DRAMATIQUE. Something about an orchestra of one hundred musicians. Imagine the cost of that, said her manager-self. EPISODE DE LA VIE D'UN ARTISTE. Episode in the life of an artist. She wished French was always so transparent, helpful. *Symphonie fantastique*. Fantastic Symphony. Well, that was appropriate: description of her dreamlike life just now. Or nightmare, perhaps. *Donné par M. Hector* BERLIOZ. The carriage, bucketing in a pothole, shivered the name out of her sight for a moment.

'Mr Schutter,' she said, nearly dropping the programme, 'it says – doesn't it say Monsieur Berlioz?'

'Indeed, indeed. One of your greatest admirers when you first played Paris, you know – well, of course you know.'

'Yes.' Tickling in the ear. Oh: it's this again. But she couldn't believe . . . 'But that was rather a long time ago.'

Very English Mr Schutter gave a very Gallic shrug. 'The impression has remained, one gathers. Monsieur Berlioz himself gave me the ticket. Quite the coming man in music, it seems. Won the Prix de Rome, you know, but beyond that – well, no doubt you'll see.'

I'll see. That sounds better: just follow the thread. Monsieur Bair-lee-ose, the lost nuisance. The one with the eyes. The impression has remained. It was the same Paris, surely it was the same Paris: for the first time, instead of a doleful no, she thought it was, after all: because, oh, it's this again. Concert of his own music at the Conservatoire: quite a coup: one thing she did know, though she was generally unknowledgeable and useless, was that getting anything staged in Paris was a feat. Fantastic Symphony. Yes, very like life. You'll see. Umbrella sky of winter afternoon. Crawling and cramming of carriages outside the Conservatoire. Interesting to be on this side of the fence for once: inside the hall or theatre, dressing and preparing, you know nothing of this, whether there is a crowd gathering or a storm or, worse, an indifferent smattering – only what the ticket-takers dart in to tell you, which is usually fibs. Music. I know nothing about music. Well, rhythm, perhaps, the music of speech, the turn and throb, or I used to. *I have no joy of this contract tonight. It is too rash, too unadvised, too sudden; 'Too like the lightning that doth cease to be Ere one can say "It lightens" . . .'* Is that music? It always felt like it. Juliet. Her Juliet always loved in fear, love was the needful crossing of a tightrope. At the other end, beauty, but still there was the terrible plunge beneath. I am dressed, am I not? Not sure. Not sure of anything.

In the Conservatoire Hall at last, among a soft roar of voices, and up some intimidating stairs amid red plush and plaster medallions. Feeling of a mistake, deep-rooted, needing to be rectified: daughter of Irish barn-vag wrongly transformed and translated. Squired by two odd gentlemen, a superannuated actor and a twitchy young journalist: could one ever, truly, have predicted this? But never mind that, follow the thread.

Emergence – no other word for it – into their box, their eminence: a cringe of bright lights, and below a shuffling, burbling vastness of people. Sit, shrinking. Eye them from above, feeling that you should not be above, and take in what you can: glossy hair, wraps sliding on bare shoulders, serious whiskered profiles leaning in conversation across intervening fans and skirts. An upward draught of humidity and humanity. Strange how we gather and cluster regardless of room, like gulls on a cliff. Strange how, now that she is here, the gulls are all turning their heads and gazing up at her, ruffling their wings, excitedly cawing. Is she that much of a joke now? She finds that all the time she has been clutching the programme, like a small child with a new toy, and to shut out the attention, to shut up the shutters, she diligently reads it.

The French language puts up a screen between her and the meaning, but only a thin fire-screen – you can still feel the heat on the other side. When music with a programme has been played or, rather, administered to her before, it has usually been tricksy music that sounds like birds or coach-horns. Instead, she is to eavesdrop on the soul of a young artist who has seen at last, from afar, the woman who realizes his ideal of beauty, and who haunts him in the shape of a theme or *idée fixe* ('Fixed idea,' says leaning-over-her Mr Bampton, annoyingly, unnecessarily), but he cannot have her, though her image pursues him even through his opium-induced dreams, as in despair he has taken opium to relieve himself of this unbearable passion and . . . Actually, this is all a mistake, I shouldn't be here: how to get away? Impossible, as she is hemmed in by the gentlemen, and below the flexible necks are still turning towards her. And while I sit here, stupidly aware of its being Sunday afternoon, and having no money, and my walking-dress is creased and not fit to be seen, and I am trying to fan myself with this wretched programme which is about *me* – meanwhile, the hourglass is drip-dripping. Soon, presumably, he, Monsieur Berlioz, the young artist with the soul and whatnot, will join that enormous, stealthily preparing army of musicians down there, swapping chat in the cello forest; and then it will begin. Army indeed, bassoons uplifted like pikes, trombones primed and ready to fire.

'You see, Miss Smithson,' offers Mr Schutter, 'this musical work is directly inspired by you. The references—'

'Yes, sir, I understand them, I thank you.' Crushed as only a young pink-cheeked Englishman can be. Another time, the guilt would leave her like a cored apple. But now, this is something that requires, God knows how, her attention. She fiddles with the programme. A young artist, feeling this and that . . . Five movements: she'd thought symphonies had four, but of course this was different, this was Berlioz. Bair-lee-ose. All this time, still existing, still dreaming, still – what? Still the ridiculous nuisance? Something has shifted. First movement, *Dreams, Passions*. About me, for me. God in heaven. Second movement, *A Ball*. 'Still the image of the beloved haunts him . . .' At the end, as far as she can work out, he imagines his beloved transformed into a witch. Please, not the witches. How does he know? How does he know anything, and why has he been thinking about me all the time? She fans herself distractedly. This is not *me* in the programme, he doesn't know me. Or does he? Can't say with confidence I know myself – the swell-headed fool who sailed into Paris with her own company and promptly lost all her money. If you knew yourself, you wouldn't do such things. Can't trust myself. Can't trust this. Too wild, too strange.

At her ear Mr Schutter is pointing out notabilities in the audience. 'Observe – three seats from the end, fifth row, Monsieur Hugo, another of your admirers, and quite the rage in the theatre now. I've approached him about translating one of his plays into English. A *quid pro quo*, in a way. And there, two rows in front, gentleman with the curls and dark complexion, Monsieur Dumas – they do say his grandmother was a Negress. Another theatrical young lion – your creations, Miss Smithson, no less! And now – oh, there she is, Madame Dudevant – little dark woman, mannish dress – George Sand, as she styles herself. Shocking reputation – yet rather plain, I find. Oh, and there – just coming in, you can't mistake him, long thin scarecrow of a fellow, Paganini. That is the actual Paganini. Did you ever see such a face? Utterly demonic. They do say—'

'Please, Mr Schutter, I'm rather hot, and I can't follow all this . . .'

'Sorry, sorry. Still, you know, quite a notable gathering. You see why you had to come. Even leaving aside the . . .' He coughed with a nod at the programme, crumpled now and damp in her fingers.

I can always leave. Fourth movement, *March to the Scaffold*. 'He dreams that he has murdered the beloved . . .' Go to a dream-booth: interpret that one. She doesn't know whether she is still holding the magic thread: presumably. No rational reason could have brought her here. A music-stand tips over and falls with a noise like a gunshot: she jumps in her seat. Elsewhere, a woman laughs in a careless bray. Wish I was that woman: different world for her, different moment in life, incidental only, went to the concert, Monsieur Blanque told me the funniest story. Is there a close-stool nearby that a lady may use? Paris is more generous with such things than London, but not much. Not that I need to go. Feel as if I have no body at all, only breath and heat. Floating. Wish I had dressed better. Who for? Chandeliers blazing. Dark, these winter afternoons. Need to be a child to live in them at all: curl up with a book, opposite her guardian's comforting shoes, fire crackling, no tomor-rows.

This is not right. Just when she is about to turn to Mr Bampton and say she wants to go home, there is a stir below, which resolves into applause. Below, directly below: she is, she sees, right above the platform, god or goddess-like, and there a bald grandfatherly man with spectacles perched on a ripe plum of a nose is taking snuff. Jerk of grandfatherly head as someone bounds up on the platform and shakes or seizes his hand. Someone not at first recognizable because she can't see the eyes but, yes, the unmistakable forward sweep of hair, the jagged profile. Mr Schutter redundantly whispering, 'That is—'

'I know.'

Sudden sharp glance upwards by the young man (Bair-lee-ose) as if he has been warned of something plummeting from the sky: what, where? His head turns, roaming: stills and fixes: he has seen her.

He has seen her. After a moment he turns, fidgets with a score, edges himself about: changed. Perhaps it's the height – me up here, him down there – but she feels for him pounding pity. Not with lofty condescen-sion – the Reverend Dr Barrett might call it Christian pity, which involves an opening not a closing of the heart. The young man still feels, it seems, the same thing. For me – but that is the least of it. She is moved simply by his unchangefulness. You have to change, accommodate, bend, that's what the world is about. She can't, as witness the disaster of her company, born of a stupid refusal to recognize that the past is gone and the case altered. But to be a winner, you have to. Alas for him that he won't, yet bravo for him too.

Rippling of the bare shoulders and sculpted heads: the snuffy spectacled man is on his feet, assuming a position of authority. The troops with their bows and horns coming to attention: a feeling of peculiar obedience that affects you too. The young man (*there is no man in the case*) seated still on the platform adopts a tense, crouching posture, as if about to run a race. Bronchial chorus from the audience, sheep-like bleats and drones from the tuning orchestra. Mr Bampton crosses his legs and sits back: absolutely delighted to be where he is, one good thing, then, to come out of it. Glance again at the programme: the artist sees for the first time a woman who realizes the ideals of . . . a woman who . . . Oh, yes, but only words. And now comes the tum-ti-tum. Only music. Only a play. All pretending.

Baton lifts: then the silence is breached.

Thought, with the battalion of musicians, it would be immediately loud. Instead shadowy, stealthy, beckoning. Feels as if someone is murmuring in your ear: compelling things, but also things you may not want to know. Makes you tense. The orchestra stare balefully at their music-stands while their fingers dance, lips perform pursed and difficult kisses. Ghosts rise and lament. Then everything is wiped off like chalk from a slate. A tune arises in solitude, except not a tune as she knows it: it won't straighten out, it limps and persists and longs (like Anne, like Anne). And now a frantic heartbeat, excitingly not quite regular. (Another fireside, another father. 'It's in the rhythm, you see? Like the pulse in the wrist. You feel it and don't feel it.' *Give me my Romeo. Gallop apace, you fiery-footed steeds.*) And now the music is galloping and breathless, dragging her like a barbaric chariot. Stops. Lifts you up, gently. Keeps taking you by surprise, and why not? Mr Kean, just when you thought you had his measure, plunging into quietness, or driving the mad words at you. Acceleration, blazing flourish of that limping, longing tune now straight and healed (unlike Anne) and now you know why so quiet at the beginning, because when this huge orchestra sounds the charge you almost feel it pressing you back in dazed defeat. Emphatic chords: Harriet who has had to sing ditties in many a minor performance knows enough music to recognize those, common chords. In fact she twitches at the sound of them, usually a cue to go on or off. And surely the ending – but instead a boat-like rocking, down and down, denies the hurrah, sinks you back into the slow doubt of dreams.

Beside her, Mr Schutter hunched in attention, jaw working: but Mr Bampton high-eyebrowed and rubbing his chin dubiously. Is it not right? What should I do – sneer, look bored? I can't, I'm not, though I don't understand it. Dying away. Below, she sees the tousled head and high shoulders. He made this. Enough to think of for now, to marvel at. He made this for me, no, a step too far, draw back from it.

In the orchestra, wiping of mouths, stroking back of sweat-damp hair. Not, she gathers, easy. (Oh, that attraction of the easy: hide in your lodgings and drink brandy.) Second movement, *A Ball*. Now she is instantly charmed: twinkling and tinkling, waltz time and harp and the suggested swish of slippered feet. Not so long ago, me, at the Bal de l'Opéra. Sea of skirts parting for me, whispers. La Belle Irlandaise. Cinderella transformed. Oh, yes, this is me: she sways a little. But it's *all* about me. The longing tune materializes, interrupting the smooth dance. Oh: it's this again. All about me. Her guardian, long ago, telling her playful stories: 'Once upon a time there was a little girl who had a little pair of boots, and do you know what the little girl's name was?' Delighted yelp: 'Harriet!' But that was childhood. This can't happen now. It shouldn't be about me. I can always leave. Pecking flutes and plucked strings question that. How can I move with no body? But that's why I'm so insubstantial, I see it now. I'm part of his dream. Flicker in her vision: presentiment that he was looking up at her just then.

Spacious pipings, a suspension of time: third movement, *Scene in the Country*. Is he from the country? I know absolutely nothing about him. He must come from somewhere. Surely nowhere like Ennis, though this country of his is slow and roomy and earthy like that. Mr Schutter exchanging with her an intimate glance – intimacy of shared experience only, surely; still, hope he is not going to start being lover-like. Why hope so, or rather – as I don't find him handsome or anything like that – why hope so with such desperation? Smell of prop-room dust, perhaps. But then there can be elements of your own self that become dreadfully boring, more boring than they would be in other people. Her tune has risen again like a mist from the musical meadows. Do I even follow him there? Dear, dear. Best to laugh, inside. It's not the weeping outside, it's the weeping inside. And the drums hint at a storm.

Much coughing and muttering after that. Expert audience-taster, she would tell Berlioz (in another world, that is, where she and Berlioz would speak) that they didn't take to that piece, modifications needed. Not that she knows anything about it. She felt at peace, whereas now – Fourth Movement, *March to the Scaffold* – she is all unease. Tread of impending death, snarls of brass, bassoons low and suggestive, all chuckling cruelty. He dreams that he has murdered the beloved . . . Crowd of instruments baying their excitement at the execution. Good receipts. Standing with Mr Kean among the jeers and flying oranges: the love of hate. You hear the head go plunk into the basket. Oh, horrible. She can always leave – makes an indecisive movement, in fact, but hemmed in by men. There is a man in the case. And, oh, God, here comes, Fifth Movement, *Dream of a Witches' Sabbath*. Not the witches—

You do not believe in them? Be assured, they believe in you.

Here they come fluttering and circling down from guttural darkness of basses. Skirls and shrieks. Witches, not gloomy and lurking, but loving it, full of themselves. How does he know? Bridget appears at her side, pippin-cheeked, eyes shining with vindication: See? I told you. The beautiful ones are the worst. Her tune skips horribly in, wicked and jubilant: this is what it really sounds like. Oh, he knows me. She is nudged and cajoled by barks and howls while a great unholy jig proceeds and invites. Not quiet, oh, not quiet now: the chandeliers tremble, the naked shoulders forget themselves in the blast of it. And perhaps this is really the truth of it, these skeletal caperings and mockings: with the *Dies Irae* twined into it all, from the Mass for the Dead; expect no more, Harriet, expect no fathers from the grave, no Reverend Dr Barrett, no William Smithson, only rattling bones now. Death is, first and last, a grin. Oh, Monsieur Berlioz, this is not kind. Yet it is all about me. And true. The maniacal dance, the happy fury, stamps beyond breath and spends itself in a last brass-throated roar that smashes apart temple doors and levels the cities and challenges the following ear-ringing, stupefied silence.

Uncertain breaths, murmurings, a whole orchestra of them; and then, applause. The young man stands, turns into visibility. He looks, as well as triumphant, a little sad and frightened. People are turning to look up at her box. There she is. *Symphonie Fantastique*, Fantastic Symphony. Sunday afternoon. At home, Anne brooding, and pages of desolating accounts, and the maid smashing the china from spite. Here, this. Perhaps once in your life you are presented with an occurrence that is so unlikely, so pregnant, so surely fictional that there's nothing to be done with it except recognize it. Harriet, shrinking back into the box as if she has never had hundreds of people looking at her before, joins in the applause, a little late. Not sure how to clap. How do you do it? Oh, yes, that's it. Oh, yes: it's this. Soon, her palms sting.

Soon, she stings.

4

Anne: 'And what's that you're writing?'

With a deep breath Harriet summons the old patience: a well that just might run dry one of these days. 'A note of congratulation to Monsieur Berlioz, on the success of his concert.'

'Mr Bampton says it wasn't music at all. He says it was an unholy mess.'

'I thought you didn't like Mr Bampton.' Before sealing the note, a single flicker of hesitation. Then the wax hisses.

'I don't like anyone much.' Anne makes it sound like the most pitiful of her illnesses: which perhaps it is.

From Berlioz, an ardent note of thanks in reply, begging to be allowed to call on her. In contrast with his language, his handwriting is clear, neat, scarcely sloping: restrained.

Now comes the real decision: now comes the remembered smell of prop-room dust. Now, do you want to breathe that air all your life? A waltz tune shimmers about her as she fastidiously mends a pen, stirs the ink. Anne watches her, ominously not saying a word.

'Mademoiselle Smithson.'

'Monsieur Berlioz.'

And perhaps it ought to end, or pause, or freeze here, to let the moment resonate in its significance, its sheer unlikelihood. In a sense it nearly does end here, because her French and his English are equally inadequate: how are they to proceed? But it is Harriet who recovers herself, and asks him in schoolroom French to be seated. Only when the moment has gone does she realize how beautiful it was. Which makes no sense: but since the concert she has stopped looking for sense. It seems a misdirection of energy.

Mr Schutter is there, to make the formal introductions, and Anne for propriety – besides which it would take an armed guard to keep her out – but Harriet finds she is quite able to ignore their presence. For one thing, there are Berlioz's eyes, deep-shadowed and keen, not the sort of eyes from which you can lightly look away.

'Allow me to congratulate you once again on the success of your concert. It was a greatly memorable occasion.' The French for this she has rehearsed. From now on she is on her own.

'Oh, Mademoiselle Smithson, to hear that praise from your lips – I cannot express the satisfaction it gives me. Whatever success I may have had, whatever I may have in the future, it all begins with you – you were the source and inspiration, though I fear this is not a strain in which I should continue, painfully aware as I am of the clumsiness I have shown in the past in expressing my admiration—'

'Monsieur Berlioz, please – I must ask you to speak a little more slowly . . .' She is not the only one, she thinks, to have been rehearsing.

'I beg your pardon.' Suddenly he smiles, with a transformation of the tense eagle looks: wry, ready to be amused, younger. 'I'm rather over-excited. Which was exactly what I told myself not to be, coming here.'

'Why?' Simple language makes you, she finds with faint alarm, very direct.

'For fear you would send me away. If I behaved as I used to. But I won't allude to the past any more. Tell me, will your company open again in the new season?'

'I hope so. To pay the debts of last season.'

A demonic twist of scorn crosses his face. 'The dear public. They change their tastes as they change the trimming of their bonnets or the tying of their cravats.' His own dress, she notes, is not so much Bohemian as, somehow, proud: spare, well-worn, but well-brushed coat, polished boots. He is slender, small-waisted. Long, bony, unringed fingers. All the extravagance is in that face, and the wild chestnut hair. 'As for the Parisian theatre, it has learned its lesson so well from the English that now it is afraid of you as a rival. The artist who leads the way is like a link-boy with his torch. Once he has got them safely home, they toss him a *sou* and forget about him.'

'Is that how it is? A sad prospect.' Sad: yet an absurd burst of happiness in her, at that word *artiste*: at being able again to take it seriously, to believe in it.

'We must make them see. We must make them hear. As you did with your first Ophelia.' He crouches forward as he did on the concert platform. She seems to see, hear, a torch lit and blazing at her. 'We must make them feel.'

'We,' pronounces Anne, 'are not sure that France is the right place for my sister's career after all. There are many other possibilities.'

Berlioz bows politely in Anne's direction; but it is to Harriet that he says: 'It would be a thousand pities if you were to let them win.'

'This is very well for you, sir,' she says, with a slight smile, 'for you have—' She has to drop into English, and looks at Mr Schutter to translate. 'You have all Paris at your feet.'

But Berlioz understands that, and gives a high shout of laughter. 'Oh, Mademoiselle Smithson. Forgive me, but if only you knew the whole story.'

Mr Schutter puts in then with some eager comments, as an aspiring playwright, on the state of Parisian theatre, which makes conversation general – or, rather, divides it into three, as Anne raises her fearsome banner of silence. But something has begun: in an interchange of looks, a slow relaxing of postures: in something as simple and powerful as interest, which opens continents, which maps the stars.

If only you knew the whole story. She lies awake, thinking about stories. Her guardian's stories of kings and parliaments: the stories of escape and enchantment she would invent for Anne: the stories of the Prince of Denmark and the star-crossed lovers of Verona. She thinks of her own story, fascinated by the realization that she has one, rather than that random drift and collision called life. Fascinated by the thought that his story, whatever it is, has proceeded alongside hers, to coincide at this particular, peculiar point. Perhaps it has meaning: perhaps not, like the definite face in the curtain-fold that you can't see at all the next day. The Berlioz who bowed to her in her lodgings was no longer an incomprehensible presence but a man, a polite and personable man. Still, she was a little frightened of him: the intensity and otherness, the feeling that both he and his music gave you of standing on the heeling deck of a ship.

But she would be interested to hear the whole story.

He called every evening – every evening when she was not performing to her diminished and lacklustre audiences. It made quite a contrast.

She wondered what the Paris rumour-mongers were making of it. One thing only, probably. And she had Anne to point out to her, helpfully, what impression she was making.

'It's not just that you're making yourself cheap. You're turning yourself into a laughing-stock. He makes this public parade of you with his insane music, and you encourage it. We might as well set up as a bordello.'

If only they knew how much of it was talk. Which, when you thought about it, was always denigrated. Idle talk. Talk is cheap. Talk's but talk. All talk. Images of emptiness. Yet she was discovering how much there could be in talk: enough to fill the world. Enough to change it.

Probably they would not believe that she and Berlioz talked about Shakespeare, whom he worshipped. Probably also they would sneer if she asserted that the problems of language did not hinder them. Well, of course not, my dear: there's one language these actresses always understand. In fact, it made you attentive to every word. No throwaway remarks to fester afterwards: no possibility of misunderstanding, when you had to stop each other to make sure you had the meaning exactly. And later you reviewed it in your mind, getting more from it, like a piece of music or a role newly learned. Remembering, the mixture or *mélange* of English and French would resolve itself into one language: a new one to Harriet, who had spoken millions of lines into theatres, but had never talked to anyone so much in her life. New and strange; but she felt she didn't have to give it a name, yet.

– When I came back to Paris, I had no expectation of finding you performing here again. Absolutely none. And yet when I heard – somehow I wasn't surprised.

– Weren't you? I fear everyone else was. I'd been away too long, and thought I was still the queen. But here come my woes again.

– I don't mind, I like your woes. What a beautiful English word that is. Let me see if I can say it: 'For never was a story of more woe . . .' Ah. Help.

– 'Than this of Juliet and her Romeo.'

– I still turn *th* into *z*. It spoils it.

– No, no. Where had you been? When you came back to Paris. Was it to your home – La Côte . . . ? Ah. Help.

– St André. No. Well, yes. I went to stay for a while after I escaped from Rome.

– Escaped? Were you a prisoner?

– The most miserable and helpless of prisoners. In the Villa Medici. That's where they send you as your punishment for winning the Prix de Rome.

– Now you're confusing me, Monsieur Berlioz. You must be serious.

– About the Prix de Rome? Impossible. Well, it's an award given to you by the nation for writing music that settles the listener into a nice, comfortable sleep. They set you a cantata text that always starts with rosy-fingered dawn. Or dawn with its rosy fingers. Then somebody classical dies – Orpheus, Cleopatra, Sardanapalus. I know because I entered it four times before I won. I'm not proud of it, because when I won I wrote obedient trash. Probably the three times before that I wrote trash, but it was *my* trash.

– I don't believe that.

– No? Why so?

– Because – because I know with that sort of thing you can't pretend. Like when I had to play the Princess O-me – it's no good simply walking through it, you have to try to believe in it a little—

– The Princess O-me?

– Yes, Monsieur Berlioz, don't laugh. The life of an actress isn't all Ophelia and Juliet, you know. I'll tell you about it some time. Now, why did they put you in prison?

– Oh, that's the prize. No, to be fair, the Villa Medici has its charms. They send you there for a term of three years, and give you money, and you mix with a generally pleasant set of fellows who have won prizes for painting and whatnot, and you get all your meals and your laundry, and in the meantime you're supposed to develop your art. Water it at the never-failing spring of the Eternal City. Except the music in Rome is an atrocity. There's nothing, nothing. Beautiful monuments and picturesque country and abundance of life – but your ear starves. I'm sounding ungrateful.

– No: not if you mean it.

– I love the way you answer me. Like Ophelia. The heart speaking. I'm sorry, ignore that. It's just in Rome it's all yelping about *amore* and madonnas and decrepit chanting, and no one knows anything about Beethoven—

– I'm afraid I don't know anything about Beethoven.

– But you don't pretend. That's what infuriates me – the pretending. In Grenoble—

– Wait, Monsieur Berlioz. I was in Rome, now I'm in Grenoble.

– My fault. That's what the critics say about my music: I don't prepare my harmonic progressions correctly. I jolt you.

– Sometimes a jolt is what makes you feel alive. I remember . . .

– Go on.

– Well, I don't like to talk about myself.

– And I do, too much. Go on.

– Oh, I was just remembering Mr Kean—

– Kean!

– I love the way you echo me. You never saw him? I wish you had – when he was at his best. The first time I acted with him, he gave me such a jolt I was almost ready to hate him for it. But then I understood why . . . Now, Grenoble. Slowly, please, Monsieur Berlioz.

– Slow is very suitable for Grenoble. My sentence in Rome was finally over: so, bags packed, hopes high, and over the Alps to France. Paris was my ultimate goal. That was where I could begin my life as a musician again. Begin my life again, in fact. I stirred and woke like Frankenstein's Monster. Ah, you see, Miss Smithson, I am steeped in your literature. But as my road back took me to the south-east, and I hadn't seen my family for so long, I made my first destination La Côte St André. And it was delightful to see them again, my father and mother and Prosper and Nancy and Adèle and – well, especially after our earlier difficulties. Which I think I may have mentioned.

– You have mentioned them, though I don't think you have told me the whole story. But all that must have changed when you won the – won that prize?

– To a degree. To a degree . . . Sorry, it's all rather difficult. Also tedious. Well, I had a warm welcome. At last I felt – I felt accepted for what I was. I thought: Perhaps it's all right after all, perhaps the two worlds can be brought together. Sorry again, if you don't know what I mean: I'm not sure I do. Only after a while I grew tired of the local talk and the state of the wine harvest and who had been repairing his mill and how much it had cost. So I went to Grenoble to see my sister Nancy, who was married now – actually I walked, which was upward of thirty miles—

– Now you're joking with me. No, you're not. Wait, let me remember. Two sisters, Nancy the eldest. Go on.

– I love the way you say, 'Go on.' People usually beg me to do the opposite. Yes, I used to be rather close to Nancy. Mostly she disapproved of me, but she was always prepared to tell me why, which is something. She had married Monsieur Pal, a lawyer, much older than her. Nothing against that – but he was not only older than her, he was older than Methuselah, older than the stones of the world. He knew everything and nothing could surprise him. He had the sublime comfort of fitting absolutely into life, like a key in a lock. In Grenoble the lawyers and lawyers' wives meet over the game *ragoût* and exchange their knowledge of everything – they know exactly how many candles they are burning and how many are left in the store and Beethoven, yes, eccentric fellow, German, Madame Whatshername, well up in music, new pianoforte from Lyon, paid rather too much for it to my mind, well, she played over a piece of his at Madame Thingummy's and really, though one could say it was interesting, little laugh, you could scarcely call it music, and then Beethoven would go out and in would come the desserts and goat's cheese and everything was everlastingly settled . . . Then I would end up in a black mood, and be dismal company, and my family would wonder why I ever came to see them. And this is my woes again. No more. Miss Smithson, I haven't asked – I have hesitated to ask – your mother. Previously she travelled with you . . .

– Oh, no – I mean, yes, she is quite well, only she chose to stay in London this time. But Anne came to – to help me, and keep me company.

– I see.

– She is very – we are very close, necessarily, and it is difficult to understand . . . Well, Monsieur Berlioz, you are very knowledgeable – I think I never introduced you to my mother.

– It would have been strange if you had, as I was only that madman haunting you like a second-rate ghost. I learned it, of course. Everything about you was famous in Paris then. And still is—

– You needn't flatter me like that. I do know.

– And it will change. This I know. I should be honest and add that I enquired. More than that, I – well, this will sound ridiculous and unbelievable, but when I came back to Paris this year I actually took the set of lodgings on the rue Neuve St Marc that you and your sister had just left. Which I didn't know. The concierge told me, and I . . . Oh, I know, it's mad, and everything appears mad to me now. And yet not mad. I hope you don't think I'm mad, Miss Smithson.

– I would not be sitting here with you now if I thought that . . . Are you generally thought mad?

– Oh, yes, it's a received opinion. I think I'm a supremely rational person, but then perhaps everyone does. We all have our reasons: God, we have our reasons.

– Tell me, after Grenoble. As you have your Grenoble face on now.

– How can you tell? Miss Smithson, the things you see – oh, I'm sorry.

– It doesn't matter. I am a little – proper about such things, touching hands and so on. It's nonsensical as one does it on stage all the time but there it is entirely professional and one feels nothing—

– I should go. I never meant, I'm so sorry—

– No, don't go. Monsieur Berlioz, sit down. Please. You were telling me – after Grenoble.

– Well. If you insist. You know, you are the most – sorry again, I won't do that. So, I came away from home, the despair again of my parents, and of Nancy. Hasn't changed his ways. God help him. Or damn him, literally. The difference was my sister Adèle. As a child she was always on my side but, then, that's what little sisters do for big brothers: only now she's grown, she's more, she has the most remarkable sweetness of temper and – oh, that sounds cloying. I can only describe it as that easiness you feel with someone who never has to have things explained. There's never that look like the snapping of a latch on a door. *What* do *you mean?* I know I'm trespassing on forbidden ground, but I'll say it, I am reminded of you. Anyhow, the day I left, it was raining as it can only rain among the mountains – and I went with Adèle for a long walk, sharing an umbrella, and we said nothing, nothing at all. And I felt as if I'd had the most beautiful and rewarding talk. And the rest of the family said we were fools and well suited. And then I came back to Paris. And then I heard that you were here. What's wrong?

– Nothing . . . Nothing, Monsieur Berlioz. I can't – I can't talk the way you do. I just wanted to say how strange life is. And as soon as you say that, it isn't. It's merely a commonplace. Perhaps the words spoil it. But it is, though: stranger than we can ever imagine.

– It wouldn't be worth living otherwise.

– Don't say that.

– No? Why not?

– Because it frightens me.

Two lives of Harriet Smithson.

Foremost, the cold daylight of managing and rehearsing (and rehearsing, too, the appeals to bankers and ministers' secretaries, and if only they worked like the speeches of Portia: the quality of mercy decidedly does not drop upon her like the gentle rain) and prodding her company towards a new season and Shakespeare and perhaps, perhaps after all, a rise in receipts and a diminution of debts. Include in this her life with Anne, which is just as exhausting and burdensome, as Anne mounts to a higher pedestal of resentment and jealousy: over him, of course.

'I've heard he has fits. He absolutely has fits and no one dares go near him. And this music of his is only some ghastly noise that people listen to because it's a novelty. The Paris Opéra won't have anything to do with him, that's well known. He's quite mad. He's a by-word for it.'

'What a lot of by-words there are in your vocabulary.' Increasingly Harriet lacks, or cannot summon, the soft answer: after so many years, you run out of them.

Then Anne in a new triumph: waiting in ominous, amiable silence until the candles are lit and their meagre supper is on the table, and then plopping a purse of money in front of Harriet.

'What's this?'

'Three hundred francs. He gave it to me. He called when you were out. *That* makes a change. Must be something in this, I thought. And here it is. He wants to help you, is how he put it, and I wasn't to speak a word to you about it. Of course I know what that means. You poor fool, he's trying to buy you now, can't you see? Can't you—'

Anne doesn't finish, as Harriet in a gesture so unlike her that she feels as if she is demonically possessed, throws the purse at her face.

'I'm sorry . . .' Harriet dips her head in her shaking hands, smelling greasy cutlets. 'I'm sorry.'

'I'm not.' Anne's voice is flaky-dry. 'At least now you're being truthful. About me. About how you see me.' With steady hands she helps herself to potatoes.

– Tell me, for God's sake, tell me. Henriette—

– Very well. The money. Anne told me. She—

– But she swore she wouldn't, it was something to help you without you knowing, she agreed—

– I know. And you must understand that, with Anne, these things are different. I know what you meant, and I will even take it as well meant. But you must swear, Monsieur Berlioz, never to do anything like that again. Else I shan't ever speak to you again. I do mean it.

– I know.

And so, the two lives: this is the other life. Berlioz coming to see her, evening after evening, and the long talks, and even the difficult abrasive moments like that one: still, it is a thing that goes on and must go on. Anne has written her mother in London, and in reply comes a letter to Harriet of blurred sternness: what is this? Heaven knows, it's high time, but this, dear me, such an entanglement . . . Harriet hates that word, thrusts from her mind its rubbery, knotted images. Almost without knowing it, she is preparing a new ground to walk on: a place where no one else will understand her.

She first occupies it, perhaps, when he tells her one evening – after a long, tense silence – that there has been another.

And Harriet, even before he goes into detail, thinks: Thank God, thank God there's been another. The news makes the smell of the dusty prop-room vanish at last. Why this should be is a matter for the other times, the other life when he is not sitting opposite her, when they are not skimming glances like stones on water and beginning to speak and then laughing apologetically no, no, you first, and shifting about in their chairs in such a way that they present curious mirror-images of posture and recognizing them and then shifting again: put off the why for another time, and listen to the story he tells her that plainly hurts him so much and truly does not hurt her at all. It was after his first desperation for her, when he was only that odd nuisance on the edge of her vision: when he finally won the Prix de Rome, and new horizons shone, and he hoped to leave behind his impossible Ophelia. (He speaks of her as Ophelia or Juliet quite without archness, naturally: she welcomes it, as Ophelia is something, Harriet nothing.) At that time he fell resolutely in love with Camille Moke, the pianist, and she with him. They became engaged. The glass was set fair as he set off for Rome. More than that, Camille Moke cured him of Harriet. (His head droops as he tells it, his voice cracks with shame: if only he knew how she likes to hear it.) Mademoiselle Moke got hold of some gossip about Harriet – that she was like all actresses, that she was compromised. The name of her agent Mr Turner was mentioned. (Dear God, Mr Turner! – whose talking used to give her a headache, whose eager teeth always revealed what he had had for dinner that day.) This was why, in his *Symphonie Fantastique* (she prefers the French for that otherworldly experience – keep it at a distance) he represented her as turning into a witch, and so on . . . She hurries him past that: he takes it as insult to her, which it was not, and hangs his head lower, and hurriedly tells her of his going to Rome, and the way his ardent letters to Camille never seemed to elicit a reply, or else the reply was mysteriously lost. And now he ignites (she waits for these moments, not wanting to, warning herself against it, but still she relishes this gathering of his shoulders, twitch about his lips, expressive unfolding of his splendid hands) and makes her laugh – about something that really shouldn't be funny, that some people would never make funny because it's about themselves (I never could, she thinks, all my life has seemed like a dark valley closing around me, please, someone, lead me out of it) and tells how he learned that in his absence his adored Camille had become engaged to a wealthy and elderly manufacturer of pianos (Monsieur Pleyel – she's seen that name above piano lids, and never thought about it, how strange life is, and I'm frightened still) and in his jealous fury he decided there was only one thing to do, which was to go back to Paris and, of course, murder Camille and her fiancé and then shoot himself. ('In that order,' he adds, sparking.)

With anyone else you'd think: He's making it up. Having a maid's costume made so that he could gain entrance to the house – 'I made rather an attractive girl, in an old-fashioned country-cousin way. The dressmaker was quite charmed with me.' The journey by coach via Genoa, with brigands in the hills, pistols at his side, the maid's costume in the coach-pocket, revenge like a storm of hornets in his head. And then the sudden beauty of Nice, where sunlight on waves told him the truth: that he did not want to kill, that he did not want to die. So he stayed for a holiday in Nice, composing, sunning himself back to reason. No, he isn't making any of it up, but she suspects he is throwing a veil over the real hurt, the betrayal. He is abject at the end, he seeks something from her: absolution. Harriet gives it readily. She, too, feels glad and shriven, though she cannot tell him why, or understand her own belief: that the only true love comes second. First time round is the pricking of the flesh and the dazzle and the self-exaltation. In the second love, it's the person you see, not the image of love. It's me.

Thank God.

Love: the meeting-point between familiarity and unfamiliarity. The voice is no longer strange to you, in fact you hear it in your dreams; yet when you encounter it again in reality you are still struck by it. There is always that little bit more to it than you thought, like the scent, like the crook of the knee, like the chuckle: like the ache, like the ache.

– Do you know *Othello*?

– Not well. Not like *Hamlet* and *Romeo*. They were the doors that let me in and closed behind me . . . Tell me, please. You've been so quiet. Tell me of *Othello*.

– I . . . The absurd thing is I feel stupidly shy of telling you when I'm not on stage.

– Then you are on stage.

– No. I mean, I can imagine it, but you are too near me.

– Very well. I shall withdraw to a distance. Enough?

– Monsieur Berlioz, that is not nearly enough.

– Ah, when you have that look – amused but, oh, stern – it makes me want to, I don't know. Yes, I do. Die at your feet.

– I am strongly averse to people dying at my feet, it makes a dreadful mess. Anyhow, you mustn't speak so, it's dreadful. Oh, you'd better go, I'm fit for nothing today. I am *not* crying.

— I didn't say you were. Miss Smithson, what is it? Harriet — Henriette, pardon me but I have to say it that way—

— You don't have to do anything. Please, now I'm lost, you must go.

— No. I want *Othello*. Give me *Othello*, tell me why *Othello*, then I'll go.

— You never keep still, do you?

— Someone said that to me once before . . . And no, to be sure, never keep still, it's the golden rule, it keeps the deadness off.

— Sometimes, Monsieur Berlioz, I'm still quite frightened of you.

— Hector, Hector. Why frightened? Never mind. *Othello*. I know he is the great general. His bride, Desdemona — you. And he is not worthy of her. Is that right?

— Oh, I don't know. Talk of that another time—

— Tell me when.

— We need more candles, it's dark. Please, don't . . .

— I'm sorry, I'm sorry, but I didn't think it was wrong or out of place — see? Just this. Your hand, my hand. Look at them together. Look, Henriette, it's not bad, it's beautiful. I believe—

— Oh, you'll have to believe for both of us.

— I can do that. Tell me about *Othello*.

— It's only a part of it. It's because of hearing about you, and Italy, and your family, and how strange and sad it all is. 'My story being done, She gave me for my pains a world of sighs: She swore, in faith 'twas strange, 'twas passing strange, 'Twas pitiful, 'twas wondrous pitiful.' That's Othello, telling how he won Desdemona. 'She thanked me, And bade me, if I had a friend that loved her, I should but teach him how to tell my story, And that would woo her.' Do you know, I have always found that part of it most unlikely . . . which goes to show something . . . Where are you?

— Over here. I've drawn away to the proper distance. My God, I couldn't take advantage of that. It was—

— Well, come back.

— Gladly.

— Only not too much back, if you understand me.

— No, I'm afraid I don't. Language can be a great barrier.

*　　*　　*

– Hector, I'm still frightened.

– You're too beautiful to be frightened.

– That doesn't mean anything, that's just lovers' talk.

– Ah . . . !

– Yes – well, yes, I love you, Hector, I do. Will you be satisfied with that? Yes . . . And so I'm frightened.

– Good, so am I. I'm terrified. Magnificent terror – waking up from a dream, except when you wake up the dream is all around you. My beautiful Henriette . . .

– Yes, I am . . . That is, not the beautiful part, but I am yours. I don't know how it happened. Only – think for a minute, Hector. Here we are, and we must – we must take stock.

– Take stock? Ah, of how many candles there are?

– Well, that too. In fact, I know, there aren't any. I don't know why I'm laughing. I don't know why I'm crying. Oh dear – I'm sorry – you must understand, I'm not used to this—

– Only the tears, Henriette. Only to kiss the tears.

Taking stock: so they do. And soon it is clear that there is no smooth, straight road opening before them, even if for a moment it felt like it.

Taking stock. Harriet Anglo-Irish, Berlioz French. Harriet Protestant, Berlioz (nominally) Catholic. Harriet deep in debt, Berlioz with very little money. Harriet in the insecure profession of the theatre, Berlioz in the insecure profession of music. All of which makes the road bumpy and stony enough: but then there are their families.

Harriet says nothing to Anne of their altered relation: but fastidious, hawk-eyed Anne, who can tell at once if a curtain has been rehung or a mantelshelf clock moved an inch to the right, perceives and pounces. 'So. He's won. You're going to throw yourself away. I can tell, Harriet, don't lie, I can tell, I can smell it on you, I can smell the dung-heap already.' For now, that is all: but Anne is girding herself for a grand campaign. She starts eating large meals and going to bed early. She will need all her energy.

Meanwhile there is the Berlioz family of La Côte St André: vivid and dismaying presences in Harriet's mind even from what Hector has told her, and she suspects he has softened the outlines. And bit by bit he feeds her the wormwood truth. His mother – an estimable woman in many ways, strong-minded, much beloved, but, yes, violently opposed to all forms of the arts. Which one most? Well, it has to be the theatre. His father, now, a man of much more liberal opinions and independence of mind . . . The fact is, in their separate ways they hated and resisted his adopting the profession of music. They have only reconciled themselves to it because he has left them no alternative; and because, at least, he has done nothing worse – like proposing to marry an actress.

'It's a sad blindness. A mania, even. Whereas I'm supposed to be the one who's mad . . .' He tries to smile, but she recognizes the look about him when his family are invoked: haunted, stooped, as if some winged and relentless thing were digging its talons into his shoulders.

Still the two lives, as her company begins the new year with a new season in a new theatre in the rue Chantereine and by concentrating on Shakespeare begins, a little, to fan the old interest, if not exactly to a blaze: still the juggling and struggling, still the dragging chain of responsibility. And yet this life – she can't help it – has a faded, bleached look beside the glowing colours of the other. Hector: love. Love and its great trouble.

'He refuses.' Hector says it breezily, offhand, while going to the window of her new and cheap apartment on the rue Castiglione – as if mentioning that it's raining, rather than telling her his father refuses his consent to their marriage.

'Oh.' Not a great surprise: but, then, she doesn't quite understand, as she learns when she adds: 'Perhaps he will come round – do you think?'

Hector's smile is grey, directed at the floor. 'I think perhaps it's different in England, Henriette. Here, if a father doesn't consent to his son's marriage, then it implies disinheritance, and in return the son takes legal action—'

'Slower, Hector, please.'

He transfers to her the ashy smile, shifts to English. 'By law your father makes you not his son. And you fight him with law to stop him. And everyone suffers.'

No answer for that but an embrace. Slowly she is ceasing to shrink from these and even beginning, shamefacedly, to hunger for them: that warmth, that pressed tick of hearts. Still there is this about their embraces: the feeling of clinging together on a precipice, toes groping at crumbling rock.

★   ★   ★

It is miserable and grinding, the family opposition: but she wants to, must, know it all. So: his father is solidly, patiently opposed, and waits for time to bring Hector to his senses. His mother despairs, prays, weeps. His sister Nancy disdainfully supposes it one of his tasteless enthusiasms. His sister Adèle loves him and believes in whatever he chooses to do. (Adèle. Timidly, Harriet recites the name to herself, like a charm.) His grandfather refuses to speak his name. His uncle Félix, who should carry more authority than anyone as he has lately been in Paris, called on and talked to Hector, and had even – to Harriet's alarm – been to the theatre to watch her perform, is equivocal: but on the whole, against it. She hardly needs to press for reasons, though she does as she must know all: and here is the grubby unsurprise. An actress, therefore a loose woman. A failing actress, therefore looking for a new opportunity. A bankrupt actress, therefore angling for a marriage. Well, now we know the worst.

Hector doesn't yield. He has a look now, even on entering a quiet parlour, of being ready to fight to the death immediately. Harriet can't join him up there – he is used to the world holding him at bay – but she tries to match him. She rallies her company, pushes them to make something of *Hamlet* and *Othello*. There are appreciative reviews: the old and golden days seem to revive. A flush of hope (treacherous: caution, caution) impels her to take a cabriolet instead of walking, and stepping out of it she thrusts her foot into the skirt of her own dress, pinned against the running-board like a tucked-in bedsheet; and then the unheralded sensation of falling forwards while her leg remains completely uninvolved, back there, making cracking sounds to itself. Then the – if you can call it that – the pain.

Anne the nurse. 'You poor dear,' she croons. 'You must suffer.' She makes it sound like an imperative: or else.

And this is the worst thing, this is the nadir, when that serviceable forgettable convenience, the body, lets you down, and you remember all those times when you walked on straight legs and breathed easy air while trivially fretting, not appreciating. For Harriet the worst thing has a worse thing: while she cannot move, she cannot act. So Miss Smithson's theatre company slithers off the edge and disappears into final insolvency.

Meanwhile she lies flat and understands at last the hemispheres. This throws her right back to her schooldays in Dublin, and the long, cool schoolroom and the globe, and her incomprehension. Western hemisphere, eastern hemisphere – what? Now, I see. One is dark while the other is light, but they are both part of the same whole. When my leg hurts so much that I swoon, then I sleep and the leg wakes: when I am feeling stronger, I sit up and live while the leg sulks and dies. One or the other.

'I'm sorry.'

'And indeed you should be. Deliberately breaking your leg in two places – I know it's exquisite, but you should restrain yourself from indulging in these pleasures.'

'Oh, you know me. Ever the pleasure-lover. Hector, I can't believe – I don't know what I'm going to do—'

'Hush, hush. Give me your hand. What you are going to do is heal—'

'Am I? Like I was before?'

'Of course.' Only a momentary hesitation: and she could have imagined that. 'And in the meantime, all Paris will rise to your aid.'

'All Paris? Goodness.'

'You're tired. I hope, by the way, you hate it as much as I do when someone says to you: "You're tired." Look, there's going to be a grand benefit for you, it's settled. Liszt is going to play, you've heard of my friend Liszt—'

'And I love the way you can't pronounce his name. Litz. It's a French thing. Sorry. It's the only chance I get to feel superior.'

'Minx. Also Chopin, whom I can pronounce better than you. Also Tamburini from the Italian Opera, Grisi, Mademoiselle Mars . . .'

'All Paris.' She wants to weep, but she is not sure what for, exactly: too many alternatives. 'Thank you for doing this, Hector. It must take up a great deal of your time—'

'Henriette, don't ever thank me for anything. Everything in me is yours to begin with, always has been. My life is yours. Do you understand that?'

She laughs weakly, touching his face. 'I've just had my sleeping-draught, so no, not really.'

But she does understand: which is why she is still a little frightened.

While Hector forges ahead, proceeding with the legal action against his father, raising money, discussing marriage contracts, Harriet mentally dawdles. The immobility forced upon her by her broken leg becomes both excuse and symbol. Yes, yes, but we can't do anything yet. Not up to it.

That is the key, perhaps: inadequacy. She is sure that she loves him, but not sure that they mean the same thing by love. Speaking different languages, indeed. For him, I am the great love of the ages, to be thundered out to posterity by a hundred-piece orchestra. How can I meet that, with my little penny-whistle of emotions? Different when I'm Juliet or Ophelia. But really I'm someone much smaller. I hope he realizes that.

So she hesitates and prevaricates, referring to their many obstacles while really baulking at the obstacle of herself. Money: the benefit raises six and a half thousand francs, but she owes still more, and she refuses to let him become liable for her debts. Family: the conflict with the fearful clan of La Côte St André grows more bitter and deadly. Her injury: it is slow to heal, and the heartbreakingly expensive doctor cannot say for certain whether her leg will ever be quite the same again, and she can only consent to marry if she can continue her career on stage . . . She wishes she could stop herself doing this. It is unfair to him – and it gives ammunition to Anne, who already has every artillery piece trained on her.

'It's because I stand outside it that I can see,' Anne says, in one of her more emollient moments. 'You can't, Harriet, because your head's been turned. But think about it. There are all these very good reasons why you shouldn't marry him, and you know them yourself, and you talk quite sensibly about them. And yet still you persist. Now, imagine if all those reasons were suddenly removed. Wouldn't you still hesitate? Of course you would, because in your *heart* you know it's madness. I'm trying to save you from yourself, Harriet, don't you see?'

'Yes . . . Please, don't talk any more, Anne, the pain's rather bad today . . .' Awful consequence of the leg: no longer can you get up and walk away from Anne. Of course she would always follow you, but at least you snatched a few seconds' respite.

'I'm sure it's not that bad.' Anne, veteran of pain and disablement, is scathing about this callow young pretender of an injury. She sighs. 'I don't know. I'm not sure I can save you from yourself, Harriet: you're simply so weak. But may God damn me if I can't save you from *him*.'

This hatred of Berlioz is ferocious, primitive – biblical, indeed: only smiting him hip and thigh or smashing him like a potter's vessel would seem equal to it. When he is there she snorts and grinds her teeth: when he is gone, she vilifies him with great thoroughness and imagination. At first he is painstakingly circumspect, makes vast allowances: soon, inevitably, he bites back. It really begins after he brings, only as a possibility to be considered, a draft marriage contract, and Anne seizes it and tears it neatly up in front of his face.

'Miss Anne,' he says, after a deep breath, 'you have no right to do that.'

'You have no right to be here. You have no right to come creeping in, destroying people's lives. You think you've won, but you haven't, not while I have breath in my body. Don't talk to me of rights. Looking like the holy innocent. Everyone knows you're a lunatic and a charlatan. And riddled with the pox—'

'Anne, stop it,' Harriet begs from her sofa of pain, thinking: I should do more, I should rise up to defend him, but I can't. Peep of the penny-whistle. 'Anne, it's disgraceful . . .'

'I can assure you I'm not riddled with the pox,' Berlioz says gently, dangerously. 'The rest I can only protest against, and hope to prove otherwise. But as for destroying people's lives, Miss Anne, I think you are wrong to use the plural. After all, there is only one life you are concerned about, and that is your own. You pretend to speak for Henriette, but you speak only for yourself. Not out of love. If I thought it was love I would respect it, but it's only wanting to dominate and have your own way and be spoiled for ever.'

'Go to hell.'

'Probably I will, and I dare say I'll meet you there. Listen, I don't mind what you say about me, though I don't particularly like it; but it's knowing that whoever I was, you'd act in just the same way – that's what sickens me. I don't know whether you make other people unhappy because you're unhappy: once I would have been troubled about that, but not any more. Everyone has a story, Mademoiselle, everyone has a reason. But not everyone drops poison in the well because of it.'

Anne, head back, eyes fixed, looks somehow to Harriet as if she is burning, burning alive. But her voice is firm. 'You miserable foreigner. You miserable whore-chaser. If I had the strength, I'd throw you out of the window.'

And now she leaves them alone. While Harriet, perhaps because her mind is always running on her hopeless accounts, thinks: I shall have to pay for this too, in the end.

It is summer before she is able to take her first teetering walk on Berlioz's arm. They go to the Tuileries gardens. Her relief at being freed from Anne-haunted imprisonment is dabbled with anxiety. Something like the old fear of being looked at returns. And no doubt they are being looked at: La Belle Irlandaise, not so *belle* any more, and her lover the mad musician: well, well. The midday sun throws shadows like welts across the smooth turf.

'The third *sommation respectueuse* has gone through,' he tells her. 'The legal action against my father. No doubt La Côte St André can talk of nothing else.'

'What will happen now?'

'Well, that's the end of it. It's simply an insurance – if he does go all the way and disinherits me.'

'It's horrible.'

'It's horrible that families should be so idiotic and fanatical, but there it is: we can't let that stop us.' He is firm and brisk today: she feels unequal to him.

'Perhaps they need more time to – to get used to the idea.'

He stops and faces her. 'But it doesn't matter what they need. It's our needs that I'm thinking of.'

'Yes . . . I suppose that's what we must do.'

'You've become too accustomed to sacrifice, Henriette.'

'Perhaps I have . . . But what about you? Think of what you'll be sacrificing.'

'If I marry you, you mean?' It's always he who says the words. 'Well, what? The good opinion of my family? I lost that when I became a musician.'

'More than that. Hector, my debts now amount to fourteen thousand francs. We – I don't see how we can live.'

'That's the question everyone has to face every morning when they open their eyes. How to live? And somehow you answer it.' He gathers her arm closer. 'You think we can't afford to live. I say we can't afford not to. Do you think Romeo and Juliet would have changed anything?

Trust me, Henriette. I shall arrange concerts, I shall shake the ninnies at the Opéra and strike their heads together until they put on a piece by me . . . In the meantime, there's always journalism. Didn't know I was a writer, hm? Oh, nothing much. Little articles – music criticism. But there are possibilities there.'

'Surely that would take time away from your composition.'

'Oh! not much. If it was a review of a new Rossini opera, I wouldn't even have to go to it, since they all sound the same. My dear Henriette, it's all *no* with you today, isn't it? That melancholy English no. Which I love. As I love you. But I must insist on a *yes*, by way of a change.' His face came close to hers, all sharpness and intelligence: it pressed her like the rays of the high, unsparing sun. I, I am all shade. 'Unless it's you who wants more time?'

'No . . . no, I'm just tired. My leg's starting to ache now. Could we sit down?'

The time will come when you can't use this leg as an excuse for things, she told herself, as they sat down beneath the light-sifting trees. The time will come – but let me lean on him, for now.

When the time comes, it is in a flurry of disputes and despairs. Though not quarrels: they don't have those, any more than Romeo and Juliet.

She is prepared to admit to herself that it is largely her fault, or that of her demon indecision. Perverse demon: it rallies just when a new hope is offered. From London comes a letter from her mother, full of the same rambling disapproval: enclosed with it, a brief note from her brother Joseph. *Harriet – ignore all this – go on, take your chance, live. Send Sister Misery to me, I'll try and deal with the unholy pair. Opening for me in Dublin perhaps. Who'd have thought, etc. Go on, go on.*

So, here is an obstacle removed: what to do about Anne, which has been gnawing at her even though Berlioz has told her she must live for herself for once, that she has done enough . . . And the demon seizes her more fiercely. No, she says again – knowing she has said it too often, but helpless – no, this is too fast, they must wait, he must wait.

'Henriette, why? In God's name, why?'

'You don't believe in God, you told me so.'

'Don't say that's the reason. You're hiding, Henriette. Don't, please. Step out into the light where you belong.'

'I don't know where I belong. If I knew that . . .'

He makes himself sit down: it is as visible as if someone has pushed him. 'Do you want us to be apart?'

'No. No, of course not, and, anyway, we're not going to be . . .'

'Aren't we?' His jaw narrows, breath puffs from his nose: that's when men are about to cry, she notices, or part of her does – the actress, perhaps. The artist, God help her. She wants to stop it all now, bring down the curtain on this scene. She cannot. 'Aren't we? Then how are we to go on? Because I swear to you I don't know how to bear this. Weeks and then months and – what next? Years? Truthfully, I would rather be apart from you than suffer like this. At least then I would know where I stood. I mean it, Henriette. It has to be one or the other.'

Terror hits her, panic: it is as if the whole room has tilted like a heeling ship. It gives her words she has never thought of uttering. 'You mean you'll desert me? Is that it? Do you mean it's all been a lie? You don't love me.' She flings herself up, tries to locate the door in the sinking room. 'You don't – you don't love me . . .'

'Is that what you believe? Tell me, is that what you believe?'

'You're deserting me, that's all I see – what am I to believe? What, Hector?'

'That I can't – live – without you.' The held-in sobs almost make him retch the words out. 'Can't. And don't care to.' Suddenly he goes down on his knees, faces the chair, drags something from his coat pocket with shuddering ancient hands.

'What are you doing? What is that?'

'Opium.' He shivers the grains out of the bottle on to the chair-seat, fumbles them into suckling lips. 'A little helps whatever ails you. A lot – that helps. That can help most of all. What are you to believe, Henriette? This. When I talk of love – and living –' wincing, swallowing '– I mean what I say. Not that I can't live without you. Just that I don't want to.' Swallow. 'Don't want to.' He begins to laugh, sobbing, pressing his fingers to his closed eyes as if to force them back into his skull. 'I'm sorry. Shouldn't have done it. Sorry.'

Amid the screams, the slappings that turn to wild embraces, the forcing of emetic down his throat, the vomiting, the madness – amid this, several things happen. She watches the demon shrivel and depart. She looks at her own love, a naked thing violently ripped of its covering. She finds him: Hector, the man, the creature of flaws, just as helpless and absurd as herself. She lays her hand upon the confirmation that she has shrunk from: life is not going to be cosy and biddable, that's not the way it works. She discovers her leg has stopped hurting, and knows that is not the end of hurt. She knows there is one ending she cannot contemplate. She senses the curtain going up. A beginning.

Later, some days later in tenderness and calm: 'You're still hesitating.'

'I'm still hesitating. Can you bear it, Hector? Can you bear – me?'

'Yes. I shall fetch you, to go to the *mairie* and register the marriage. Then the banns . . . You see, I don't give up. I'm a force of nature. I'm a wind, I'm an earthquake—'

'Oh, I know that.'

Anne: 'Well, you've doomed yourself. Hey-ho. My sister has doomed herself to a life of unhappiness, and I'm expected to rejoice—'

'No. You're not expected to rejoice.' Here, at the last, Harriet grants herself a moment of cruelty: perhaps she is owed it. And perhaps it is a way also of obliterating the guilt: yes, scribble over it with nasty words, then it can't be seen. 'Only, what's the difference, Anne? What was my other doom? Any happier?'

Anne hardly ever shrugs, probably because it emphasizes her deformity. But now she hoists her asymmetrical shoulders with forceful, even French, expression.

She says: 'Witch.'

After all that, there should be this. And there is.

Cool and quiet – she likes that – in the chapel of the British Embassy in Paris: she and Hector standing about like schoolchildren, waiting to be beckoned forward, almost imperceptibly nudging each other, shuffling. Witnesses hovering, one of them his friend (and how one dreads the beloved's friends) Liszt, or Litz, all cheekboned and hair-swept, with a look in his deep-set eyes that seems to say: Go on then – show me. Go on. Loves himself, thinks Harriet. Nothing shall profane those magnificent long fingers, except the downward dew of compliant women. How boring rakes are, she thinks. They are only performing in front of their own mirrors: while the women who receive them are merely seeking to have that mantle of sauciness partly thrown over them, as if anyone cares.

Very wordly thoughts, considering she is not at all worldly (least of all in these matters, and she is simply terrified of the coming wedding night – but let it go. Cool and quiet). Also jumping to conclusions: Liszt has after all been thoroughly courteous to her. Just this suspicion that everyone here privately feels they are celebrating a great mistake. Even the chaplain, bending plumy eyebrows upon them in headmasterly fashion, as if admonishing a pair of truants. And Anne, of course, funereally dressed, working and threading her bony fingers: suggestive of one of the Fates itching for her scissors. Then there is the absolute killing absence of anyone from his family. But none of these should matter, none of these must be allowed to matter, beside Hector.

Her husband-to-be stands straight and braced as a sentry, handsome in velvet collar and scarlet cravat. Exceptionally handsome, in fact, which perhaps she should have noticed before now, but he has been too much an overwhelming force in her life for such details. You don't trace the shape of the lightning. He is contained and sombre, but she understands that: so emotional a man, standing on so emotional a height – if he lets go, he will fall. Yes, he matters, he must matter. Indeed, does he understand how much he must matter to her in the future that is opening like a bright, piercing eye? Too late for such thoughts: now they stand before the headmaster, now they must speak the vows. Cool and quiet. Hector's hand and hers mazily find each other, like two drunks. Sonorous Oxford vowels deliver her to marriage. Harriet, filler of theatres, can hardly voice the responses. Hector kisses her. She weeps and hides in him.

And there should be this, and there is: a honeymoon of perfect beauty. They have rented a house at Vincennes. October mists on the Seine like blue cobwebs, honeyed sunlight steeping the fruit trees in the garden where they pick their own dessert. A lazy autumn wasp floats obligingly away from the apple in her hand, declining to sting.

At night the fears rise, are faced, and transmute into tenderness. He is still Hector: there are no barbaric transformations.

'You have never . . . ?'

'Never.'

259

And at first she is the trembling, pained, bewildered learner. Then there is a curious exchange, as he groans and collapses and seems, sweaty and helpless, to need tending, to require her energy. She caresses and murmurs, counting his vertebrae. Other looming and fascinating discoveries: that bit of his jaw that she always saw as sharp but is actually soft and rounded, exactly shaped for her kiss . . . And so on. Harriet, a private person, would surely prefer no more. There is always a time for the curtain.

And there should be this, and there is: an idyll.

Prophecies of doom still surround this marriage, even though the prophets themselves are silent or banished. Anne departs for England, escorted by Mr Bampton, last of the defunct company. She is gloomily resigned. 'I warned you,' she says. When Harriet kisses her goodbye, she visibly jumps as if at the touch of a ghost; as if she considers Harriet to be effectively dead. There are letters of congratulation from Berlioz's Paris friends, from Chopin and Hugo and Liszt – but then they, too, are of the benighted artistic set, as his parents in La Côte St André would surely say. And from them, not a word – as if Hector, too, is gone, deceased. Only his sister Adèle secretly sends a letter full of girlish warmth. Hector declares: 'She is my family now.'

But here they are, Hector and Harriet Berlioz, in the beautiful spring of 1834 – Italian weather, Hector calls it – living on two floors of a vine-smothered house on the hill of Montmartre, above the city: above the clouds, in a way. No one, perhaps least of all themselves, predicted this – content.

For Harriet its purest expression is in the walled garden where she sits under a plum tree, listening to the nightingales that sing day and night. Content: stillness. There have been other things and other times, effortful and restless, but there is always this to return to, the still centre. There have been two concerts, one a disaster – including her own stiff-legged and tentative performance as Ophelia – the other a success. They are chipping away at the mountain of debt, she looking to a return to the stage, he working furiously at journalism, at a possible symphony for Paganini. But there is always this, there are always the nightingales. Sometimes she descends the slope with Hector to Paris, but more often visitors join them here. Liszt and Chopin sit and talk in the still garden: Liszt flamboyant and tigerish and full of himself, yet sometimes appearing to Harriet touchingly young, almost a lost child: Chopin immaculate and exquisite and somehow dry, never quite looking down his long nose at you but surely capable of it. Sometimes she loses the thread of their talk, but there are still the nightingales.

Thus, in spite of all muttering omens, they have found a life. Also initiated one. Under the plum tree, Harriet listens not only to the nightingales but to the strange new song of her body. Alarming, sometimes, in its leaps and swellings; but there is a blessing in the solid shape of Hector's cousin Alphonse Robert, now a well-regarded physician, and a frequent caller. The first time she sees his stuffy, benign face, she thinks: *Friend.* Often he is a sharer in the garden stillness, reliable hands folded on his waistcoat, patiently answering her anxious queries about the pregnancy. Is this right? Should this be happening at this stage? And is it usual to feel . . . ?

'My dear Madame Berlioz, nothing to worry about. All of this is quite usual.'

Hector reaches out for her hand. 'Nothing,' he says proudly, 'is usual about my wife.' *My wife*: he loves to say the words. And—

And really, this should be an ending. Surely here curtain, applause: home, satisfied, cheered. The end. A thousand pities – the first of a thousand – that it is not.

Oh, you are cruel.

I don't mean to be.

Probably no one does. Everyone has their own good reasons. But the result is the same.

I was just trying to show how it was and—

Oh, you show it very well. Dear God, yes, I can see it, the garden in Montmartre, the trees, my own hand on my own round belly. Hector. So – so let me look at it for a while. Fix it there. Let me gaze . . . And then I may – I only say may – let you go on.

Interlude: Chopin

Where are we? Paris – the Paris of the July Monarchy, of Louis-Philippe the Citizen King, in the year 1836 to be precise – ah, but which Paris? There are many, and they keep shifting.

For one thing, there is a continual convulsion of building, demolishing, rebuilding, improving. You are always being confronted with the new. Gas-lamps along the principal streets, above an even more welcome innovation – pavements. And amid the old huddle of cabriolets and *fiacres*, elephantine horse-omnibuses forge their way, crammed with shopgirls, clerks, dancing-masters, craftsmen on their way to ornament another new building with ironwork and stucco.

Or the elegant shopping galleries – they're new: step into one of the new emporia of 'notions', where you can buy an ebony-handled, ivory-headed back-scratcher. Get it monogrammed if you like. Pretentious? Why? Everyone can have a monogram if they like. If they can afford it. That's the point. The aristocratic mansions of the Faubourg St Germain still stand, more lordly than ever behind their barred *porte-cochères*, but even they must adjust to the times. In the salons the old names and titles may, if broad-minded enough, mingle with artists and thinkers, or bankers and speculators and money-men generally: another shifting. The membranes are becoming porous. The comfortably married stockbroker taking an ice-cream at Tortoni's after the Bourse closes may exchange a nod with an old-money *comte* fresh from a duel or an assignation; or he might decide to relax in a café instead, among students and journalists and officers of the National Guard balancing their shakos on booted legs; or he might decide to visit one of the many registered prostitutes.

Not quite so easy to find them now, though heaven knows still easy enough: they are no longer permitted to solicit in the streets, and the traditional bordellos of the Palais-Royal have been closed down, likewise its gambling-clubs. That venerable arcade of indulgence, where you could dine in the restaurant on the ground floor, buy a trinket for your wife in the shop on the first floor, nerve yourself with brandy in the café on the second floor, and spend the rest of your money in the brothel on the third – that belongs to another age, on which bourgeois respectability frowns.

Of course, you can only change the appearance of these things, not their essence. Alongside the wall-posters informing travellers of coaches to Brittany and the Midi are advertisements for pills and powders, all sovereign remedies for venereal disease. It's all still there if you want it: under the Seine bridges slender young men come out of the darkness like blades to invite you to *le sodome des quais*. The old city of mud is still there alongside the new city of light. The corner coffee-seller with her trestle and battered urn and ancient cups, her weathered cheeks and mittened claws, is as poor and ignorant as she ever was, and still has to fetch her water laboriously from the public fountains. In the Latin Quarter or the Faubourg St Martin, you can see the old oil-lamps strung across the narrow street between a jutting buttress of medieval Gothic and a timbered baker's shop: go a little further, and you find no light at all – a dark warren of pistol and cudgel, fights over tickets for bread and soup, sexless bodies slumped in doorways.

It's all there: the whole of the world, literally – for there is no city more cosmopolitan. An average boulevard stroll will take you past one German scholar, two English servants, and three Polish exiles. Or take the salons – as that is the social sphere to which we are headed: you can talk Italian politics at the salon of the Princess Belgiojoso, or Russian politics with Princess Lieven. Elsewhere you can talk philosophy, literature, art, music. Especially music. You can talk of the latest productions at the Opéra, where the names of Meyerbeer and Halévy rule, and vast spectacles are the fashion: chorus of ghosts of lapsed nuns (in nightdresses), processions of real horses. (If you run into the composer Monsieur Berlioz, he will be delightfully scathing about these: though some detect the flavour of sour grapes.) You can talk until dawn, for this is a city of late hours: a garrulous city, where the *petite poste* delivers letters seven times a day, so clandestine lovers can quarrel, make up and fall out again, all between breakfast and dinner. And a city of celebrities, like the one you are about to visit.

Well: no darkness or cudgels here – the rue de la Chaussée d'Antin, very fashionable, very carriage-and-pair. The apartment into which the manservant ushers you is – only the old chestnut will do – exquisite. Candlelight facilitates an elegant conversation between polished floor and silver-grey wallpaper, white silk curtains and oyster-coloured brocade. There are Sèvres vases with hothouse flowers, chairs in Renaissance style, and a lustrous Pleyel piano – but not too much of anything: air and light prevail. A discreetly agreeable scent of cologne emanates from the gentleman who comes with feline noiselessness to greet you: Monsieur Frédéric Chopin, musician, social lion, catch.

He is very slight: not much more than five feet tall, narrow-shouldered, with light, curled hair, pale eyes, a strong nose. Small, delicate hands gesture gracefully through the conversational commonplaces. He has a thin, effortful voice, which you must strain to hear. Certainly, yes, Monsieur and Madame Berlioz, he knows them pretty well. Holds them in high esteem. Not sure what he can usefully tell you. As you are to accompany him to Liszt's salon this evening, you may possibly see Berlioz there yourself, though he tends to devote himself to domestic life nowadays. And work, of course: the man works devilish hard. If you will be so good as to wait a moment while the valet brushes his hat and gloves . . .

—One thing I can tell you, which doesn't seem to occur to anyone else: Berlioz isn't really French. Hence his struggles. Oh, yes, there are these successes, but before heaven, he has to fight for them. And the critics are savage. Paris is a tide – sometimes it bears him up, but more often he has to swim against it.

Not French? you ask.

– Oh, by birth, by blood. But it takes more than that, oddly enough. I may as well add that I – Polish-born, with only my father French, and my homeland many miles away – yes, I am accommodated by Paris much more neatly than Berlioz. I may as well add further – how tedious this adding is, it makes conversation a very abacus – that Berlioz's music does not endear itself to me. Forgive it. My tastes are exacting, perhaps whimsical. I still have the highest admiration for his originality of mind and his generous character. Which brings me back to my first point . . . Ah.

The hat is presented for inspection first, then the gloves: pale lavender suede, and scented. Chopin's hands enter them voluptuously.

– Shall we go? My carriage is at the door. Actually, you know, I don't usually talk about such things. There is quite enough chatter in the world. Pardon the discourtesy, but who are you really – posterity, the Reaper, what? Never mind – don't answer that. As it happens you find me in confessional mood. I shall indulge it.

A very well-appointed and well-sprung cabriolet, you notice; and Chopin notices you noticing.

– Nice, isn't it? I seem to detect some – not disapproval, but disappointment. Images of the starving artist, perhaps. Starving but full of integrity. Well, this artist has an aversion to starving. In consequence of which, I teach, and play at selected gatherings. The pupils I teach are very well placed in society, where a piano teacher who arrived in a hackney, dressed like a lawyer's clerk, would not be welcomed. But there, you have heard about it, no doubt: do I really charge twenty francs a lesson? Yes. And do they leave the money tastefully on the mantelpiece? Yes. And it enables me to live, and to work. Life and art, and how does one direct or destroy the other – these, perhaps, are the questions you want to raise. Probably you would do better talking to Liszt about them. He's the one for ideas. Lots of them. You may hear tonight, by the by, a deal of airy talk about the People: ah, the People, and what our art can do for them. As if there were anything in that salon the People would want, except the food on the table. As if it is the business of art to be anything but itself.

Chopin coughs nasally, the pale, troubled eyes watering.

– Forgive me. Damp night air never agrees with me. Forgive me also, I'm rambling. So: Berlioz not French. Well, look: when I first came to Paris five years ago, I considered myself entering a sort of home. Not just my father's birth, but the presence of many exiles like myself, and above all a sort of spirit to which I responded. It is the centre, and I could see no other location but the centre as being worthwhile. If you will be so good – a little more room . . . ? Thank you. Again my whim. I always require a little space around me, otherwise I lose myself. Well, when I arrived, I was proud of my paternal French, which as you can tell is fluent. Imagine my surprise, as the cheap novelists say, when Parisians informed me benignly but firmly: *Ce n'est pas français.* It isn't French. Little lapses of grammar, imperfect vowels. I was wounded. Very stupid of me, but there it is. Certainly, now I am received in the highest society, and I do pretty well: but still, it isn't French. I have, and I say this only for information and with no emotional pleading, I have no home.

And this, you ask, is the same for Berlioz?

– Quite so. Likewise, and adding to the difficulty, Madame Berlioz. Whom I find absolutely charming. And, with respect, you may look at me all you like as I say that. What else would you have? I esteem him, and marriage to Miss Smithson made him happy. This is enough, surely, for anyone.

Did you ever see her perform, you ask, as Miss Smithson?

– No. My friend Delacroix did, and has never ceased to rave about it, and I respect his opinion . . . But these things are all rather difficult, are they not? Taste is individual, and therefore private, and therefore, to me, sacrosanct. Oh, to be sure, many people said the marriage was folly, and so on. They always will. People like to pretend they *know*. They need it. A great weakness, it seems to me. I am happy to say I don't know anything, and I mistrust anyone who does.

The carriage swings into the rue Lafitte, smooth, well lit, abode of merchant princes. Chopin peeps out.

– Well, you have tempted me into the two greatest sins: talking about myself, and going on too long. I can tell you this about Madame Berlioz: she is a devoted supporter of his music, with all its risks. The last time he hazarded everything on one of his expensive concerts, she said she was prepared to sleep on straw – and though she is an actress, she is not a theatrical woman, and I have no doubt she meant it. So, put me down as their well-wisher. Liszt, I know, was doubtful about the whole attachment from the beginning. He warned Berlioz against it – toils of a manipulative woman and so on. But if I may be frank – and even if I mayn't – Liszt, I feel, would never do anything actually stupid, in the sense of harming his self-interest: in the sense of daring, hopeless, unretractable. Liszt might do something *carefully* stupid. He knows how to choose his scandals. There, now you have made me unkind to a friend. Anyone would think you were trying to fix my personality in my words. My dear whoever-you-are – don't you know that for a musician, that is impossible? The world is wide, and breath is only air. Only air.

You get out at the Hôtel de France, and ascend the stairs – Chopin insisting that you go first – to the most brilliantly notorious of salons, that of Franz Liszt and his mistress, Marie, Countess d'Agoult. She is a married woman who not only left her aristocratic husband for Liszt but has had a child by him and is living with him openly; and they carry it off. Outside the salon, the usual servants yawn over cards. Within, the *maître d'hôtel* yells your name and that of Chopin into an indifferent babble. *Salon* suggests the murmur of cool cultured voices, but this is very noisy: there is a strong smell of wine, and Chopin waves an irritable gloved hand at the puffs of cigar smoke. Vital, though, undeniably. Liszt, at six foot the tallest person in the room, is noticeable immediately: ornamented waistcoat, backswept locks, lithe as a sapling, animated in talk. Noticeable, too, is Marie d'Agoult, cameo-like beauty somehow emphasized by a cheek-scar, and luminously blonde; and less assured. (More to lose.) Beyond that, take your pick: poets, parlour-politicians, bluestockings, musicians, radical riders of various hobby-horses, all vociferous. A piano awaits among the hubbub.

At your side Chopin sighs.

– Well, one must circulate. Oddity as you are, I'm loath to leave you: Liszt has been threatening to introduce me to this extraordinary woman they have in their ménage. You know the one who calls herself George Sand? Have you read any of her things? Shocking stuff, apparently. And I have a strong suspicion that's her – there, by the fireplace – this affectation of frock coat and trousers, dear God, it must be her. And a cigar too, how pretty. Do you think that's really a woman? More to the point, do you want to go somewhere else? We could always slip out and . . . No, I suppose not. Liszt's seen me. Oh, well: no escaping my fate.

EPISODE IN THE LIFE
OF AN ARTIST

Third movement: Scene in the Country

Adagio

1

Adèle Berlioz felt herself to be, by nature, a younger sister. Though it was only temporal accident that had made Nancy eight years her senior, and they would surely have remained their essential selves if their ages were reversed (a religious point on which the *curé*, and still more her mother, would have sternly assured her, though she had sense enough not to raise it), still she felt the difference was expressive, and definitive.

When she went to stay with Nancy and her husband Camille Pal in their pleasant well-upholstered house in Grenoble, Adèle always enjoyed herself. Camille, a successful judge, was all avuncular playful politeness, and Nancy made sure there were plenty of parties for her, and sent the maid to dress her hair after her own fashion – which was very resolute, with a high pompadour crest and two precise ringlets like fish-hooks. And part of the enjoyment was in the sheer difference in their situations, which Nancy herself seemed to like to emphasize. With soaring eyebrows and wry lips she lamented the unreliability of servants, the wayward temper of her little daughter Mathilde, the tortuous difficulties of social invitations. She made it all appear terribly taxing, while conveying also that she revelled in it: that it suited her. Meanwhile Adèle basked in the irresponsible privileges of the guest. Occasionally Nancy would make a pointed reference to Adèle's own future – you'll find out about this, this

271

is what it's like to be a mother, to run a household, you'll see – yet Adèle detected a certain lack of conviction. Which was unsurprising: because she was the eternal younger sister, she could never rise to Nancy's eminence. At least, she would never catch her up. If and when she became a wife, Nancy would be an older wife, with a new set of things that only she understood.

Adèle liked Grenoble well enough, but she was glad to get back to La Côte St André: she felt more herself there. She opened the pomade-sealed grave of her hair and let the exhumed black curls fall loose around her face. Which she did not much like. Adèle had strong dark brows, the Berlioz nose, full lips, clear olive skin – the kind of looks that are called striking. Given a choice she would have preferred Nancy's prettiness, though the question did not much exercise her. She was no tomboy – she had been a frail child, did not ride, and she still hated having to help her mother with the silkworm crop, shuddering at the touch of the yellow cocoons and the knowledge of the dead grub inside. Yet there was something unconformable about her that set Nancy's ladylike head shaking. A good deal of the time Adèle moved in a world of dream and reflection. She liked walking – rather than strolling – and she could spend an afternoon rambling about the fields and orchards at Le Chuzeau, gazing at the shimmering plain and the far brush-strokes of mountain, listening to the thrumming of the wind in the poplars and the cry of quail and the lonely wail of a shepherd's pipe. And when she got home it was with no sense of time having passed, and no real memory of what she had done. She would discover a burr on her skirt or an oak-leaf on the sole of her boot and think: Oh, yes.

Nor was she habitually temperamental, but when she did fly into a passion, of excitement or anger, it quite possessed her; and her mother would urge the *curé* to earnest talks on the subduing of the spirit. Adèle did try. But she could not help picturing her spirit as something like the silkworm in its cocoon, curled and sensitive and doomed to a pitiless baking. The worst time had been when her parents first proposed sending her away to boarding-school. She had screamed and sobbed and hurled herself about. It was embarrassing to recall: yet she felt strongly that she had been right to refuse. The separation from home and the familiar, just then, would have been unbearable. Other girls lamented the country dullness and longed for the smartness of Grenoble; but to Adèle this quiet corner of the Isère valley remained fascinating. It was as if she were made of it, of its limestone and terracotta, its walnut and vines, and to leave it would be a literal uprooting. No city street could have intrigued her more than the sight of the travelling puppet-show in the dusty square, or the *colporteur* with his basket of cheap almanacs and books of cures and lives of saints: not just these but the crowd gathering around them, the brown-legged women in looped-up skirts and shawls and clogs, the whiskered veteran, detained from *boules*, with the campaign ribbons drooping from his too-large coat, the stripling boy letting his oxen stray while he strained on tiptoe for a look.

And several years later, when she boarded at the Convent of the Visitation, she was happy enough: it was a different time. She had almost mystical feelings about time and its rightness, which gave her a special sort of patience. When Prosper, her excitable young brother, was looking forward to the New Year's gifts from Grandfather Marmion, he could hardly contain himself. 'Don't you want to know what you've got? How can you bear it?' But Adèle said, quite honestly: 'I can wait.'

Perhaps, though, that was simply her being the older sister. In her dreamy way she became interested in this question of relative standings: she even envisaged those around her as something like figures on a chessboard. Towards her father there was one overwhelming relation: she looked upward. He was wisdom, knowledge, kindness, decision: he worked in her life like a sort of benign law. Yet as she came of age she found another aspect becoming prominent. She liked to visit him in his study at the end of his day's work, and simply be there. Sometimes she talked, but she sensed that he valued a little quiet – her mother was so voluble – and often she simply sat with him, or browsed around the bookcase, or mended pens. Eventually he would draw a deep breath, as if refreshed, and take her arm to lead her to dinner. The king, in fact, needed her too, in certain incommunicable ways.

It did not alter his relation to her mother, which was one of infinite indulgence; nor Adèle's to her mother, which was one of finite adoration, with duty making up the gap. Towards Monique the housekeeper she stood at a different angle of fondness, mixed with the comic: she could always make long-jowled, unsmiling Monique laugh, and played up to it. But the most significant relation of all, because it was at once so simple and so complicated, was towards her brother Hector.

Put Hector and her together, indeed – not necessarily even in the same physical place, but as propositions of personality – and the whole pattern of the board changed. The *question* of Hector had been enormously significant since she was a small girl. Hector was a question asked of the Berlioz family, and Adèle had been at first bemused, and later passionately engaged by their failure to answer it. She had always loved and admired him; but when, with the beginning of the troubles, she realized that the others did not – or not in the same unconditional way – she assumed the new and fierce role of partisan. She became, as it were, Hectorized. And it freed her. Here was a ground on which she could stand. She had never been sure of anything, in the way Nancy was sure of the proprieties and her mother of the Church. But she was absolutely sure that what Hector did was right, when everyone else thought it was wrong.

The painful scenes of his abandoning medicine for music were long past. Dr Berlioz, in particular, had revealed a reluctant, wincing pride at news of his son's achievements. Still, one felt that they were only waiting, almost morbidly, for the disaster they had predicted. When it came, Adèle felt her feet planted even more firmly on their common ground.

'But this *isn't* some sudden freak of his, as you call it. Miss Smithson is someone he has loved for a long time.' The news of Hector's impending marriage had come. Her father was stiff and thin-lipped, her mother hysterical, Nancy disdainful. But what united them was utter rejection. Adèle fought alone. 'And even if it were a hasty decision, still he is a grown man who knows his own mind.'

'She is an actress,' her mother said, 'a common little actress, for whom he conceived some ridiculous moonstruck passion. That in itself is regrettable, but I am woman of the world enough to know that it happens. But to propose marriage to such a creature . . . I can only think of it either as a bad joke, or a determined attempt to sink us completely in shame and degradation.'

'I cannot believe,' Adèle said, 'that Hector, or anyone, would fall in love simply to disoblige his family.'

'You're as absurd as he is, with all this talk of falling in love,' Nancy snapped. 'Really, you know nothing about the matter. As for Hector settling to anything seriously—'

'She has trapped him,' mourned Madame Berlioz. 'That's what it is. I see it. In his madness he has made wild promises, and she has capitalized on them, and trapped him.'

'What for?' Adèle cried. 'His money? He hasn't got any. She must know there's nothing to hope from his loving family *there*.'

'Adèle, this is wickedness,' her mother said. 'Tonight you must pray to the Virgin for forgiveness—'

'You are misguided, Adèle. Like Hector.' Her father beat a clenched fist softly on his knee. 'We must wait. It's madness, as you say, my love, and time will show that to him. He cannot keep this up.' He had grown very deaf of late, and had developed a habit of repeating a remark, as if for his own stony ears. 'He cannot keep this up.'

Adèle knew, and faithfully believed, otherwise. Her father grew more grim and thin-lipped as the battle went on, avoiding Hector's name altogether, but she gathered he had turned to harsher weapons than time. Soon the only letters that came from Hector were addressed to Adèle. She was sorry and yet not sorry. She thought the story of Hector and Miss Smithson was a beautiful one: if it was strange, that made it more beautiful. She and Hector wrote copiously. It was the only thing she could do for him, and he seemed to value it. He tried to describe Miss Smithson, to her intense interest; and he dwelt on the openness and truthfulness of her nature. He emphasized this, of course, because she was an actress – but he had no need to for Adèle's sake. Adèle had no opinions about actresses. In some ways, she had no opinions at all: they seemed to her very restricting things to have.

When she knew the date and time of Hector's wedding to Miss Smithson, she made sure to mark it. She sat alone in her bedroom, looking at the clock, thinking good wishes. It was rather dreary and sad, but she felt it was important. Her father was in his study. Her mother was making laundry lists. Dispassionately the clock ticked away.

That evening her father suddenly said, almost in a sprightly way, as if telling some amusing piece of local gossip: 'Of course it won't work. He'll desert her in the end.' Most unusually, he smelled of brandy. There were, possibly, tears in his eyes.

Grandfather Marmion was categorical. Marrying a foreign Protestant actress, against the wishes of his family, was the last of Hector's follies he would countenance. He was out of the will, and henceforth no grandson of his. 'I give up on him. He's not worth a *sou*.' He took a *sou* from his pocket and spun it. And Adèle thought, for the first time: How stupid. To illustrate it like that. She was nineteen years old, and discovering that her elders were often fools.

After that she carried the flag alone for a long time. News from Paris was a smuggled commodity: she and Hector had to make a special arrangement with the post office in La Côte St André so that she could receive a portrait engraving of Miss Smithson – or Henriette, as she was learning to think of her. She felt no surprise at how happy he plainly was. The surprise was that her family took no notice of that fact. It was as if happiness was a negligible thing in life. Only from her father, once or twice during their quiet colloquies in the study, did she infer anything different. 'Well,' he would say, in that sudden brisk way, 'as for Hector, we must hope for the best. Yes, there is always hope.'

The change began when Hector's wife was expecting a baby. 'Oh, I'll believe that when I see it,' was Nancy's sharp response, as if an actress could somehow, cunningly, pretend that as well. But Adèle heard her mother and father having long, unimpassioned, tender-sounding talks at night, with Hector's name in them; and she allowed herself to feel hopeful. When the news came that Hector's wife, after a long and exhausting labour, had presented La Côte St André with a grandson and nephew, a little, perfect and thriving Louis Berlioz, the change was complete. The part of Adèle that had awoken when Grandfather Marmion tossed the *sou* had some acid comments to make: Oh, now it's all right, now there's a grandchild they can call their own and who has some of their precious selves in him, oh, it's all show and sentiment. But otherwise she felt hugely relieved and delighted. When she was appointed the baby's godmother, her cup was full. And still came the long, warm letters from Hector in Paris: through them she shared in her godson's first verifiable smiles, first teeth, first haircut.

In the meantime, Adèle grew terrified.

This in itself was not a new sensation. Adèle knew herself to be, in certain crucial respects, a contemptible coward. A strange dog in the street could paralyse her. Sometimes even a casually promised introduction to someone she did not know would skewer her with dread. Throughout her childhood she had suffered nightmares of fantastic vividness and point, and occasionally still did: she had trained herself to scream only through her teeth, retchingly. Her propensity to fear was what her mother would have called her cross: but she thought of it more as a hidden brandy-bottle, or even a murdered corpse – don't get too comfortable in your skin, because there's always that: that's the real you.

It was something to do with Hector's account of Henriette's labour, and how he had feared at one point he would lose her: the blinding drama of it all. Birth and death. How were you supposed to face them? How did people do so? Other people seemed to have been given some mysterious preparatory lessons, and she had somehow missed them. The silkworm shrank further into its cocoon. Adèle grew restless and mopish. Nancy was critical.

'Really, Mama, one never knows what to say to her. She is sensitive to the slightest thing.'

'I am *not*,' Adèle cried, and ran off to her room, where she took out and reread the latest letter from Hector. More and more, this was where she lived: in the mind, in the imagined household in Paris of Hector and Henriette and little Louis: where she felt no fear.

When the news came that Grandfather Marmion was mortally ill, she was as much chilled as grieved. Here came the terrible test. Appalling realization: the world had a tendency to diminish. Always there had been Grandfather Marmion with his verse-letters, his gardening, his testiness – above all, the summers they always spent with him at Meylan, among the maize-fields and crags, beneath an unfailing blue sky. It was all going to go. The chess-pieces not only moved to strange new oppositions: they could be swept from the board altogether.

Her mother went to Meylan to be with him: Uncle Félix, his son, was hastily summoned from Paris. In the study with her father, Adèle looked at the clock and thought how different this was from Hector's wedding. You couldn't watch for its coming, but it had its appointed moment just the same.

Her father sighed. 'Poor Finette,' he said. And later this struck home to Adèle. Her mother was losing her own father: this meant looking at the board from an entirely different point of view. It meant, in fact, putting yourself out of the question for now. Madame Berlioz's faith had inculcated in Adèle the habit of examining her conscience before going to bed. That night, examining, she reproached herself. Her fear was really an aspect of selfishness. In the morning, when the news came that Grandfather Marmion had died, she still recoiled in fear at the knowledge; but something was beginning to change. She and her father went to Meylan, and she set herself at once to comfort her mother. This perhaps was selfish as well, since it diverted her from having to think about the dead body upstairs, but never mind.

Uncle Félix was making free with the brandy, his moustaches quivering, a sad half-smile playing about moist lips. 'Y' know, before the end I told him how his garden was thriving, how forward the flowers were for March. And do you know what he said? "Damn the flowers." Isn't that a curious thing? God bless the old warhorse. You never know, do you? We can never know.'

'Would you like to see him?' her mother asked Adèle. 'Just for a moment.'

Curious thing. 'Just for a moment': as if the time mattered: as if one didn't want to intrude, or tire him. But her mother, in her rapid, flustery way, talking and not waiting for an answer, succeeded in sweeping Adèle up the stairs and across the dreaded threshold. And there it was: the picture of death. It was bad, it was horrible; but you assessed the badness of it, you made an internal adjustment, just as when your menses began you assessed the signs and readied yourself – faint grinding, sharp stabbing, or deep, miserable ache. She didn't overcome her fear, or conquer it. She found it wasn't like that. If anything, you had to make friends with it. Above all, it prepared you for the next time; because the menses always came, the blood always flowed.

After the funeral Nancy came to stay for a while at La Côte St André, and began taking the family in hand. What was to be Prosper's future? Her husband had some ideas, if they were stuck. And Papa – why didn't he get about more? – he hardly stirred, it would do him good to get over to Grenoble, have some different company. And on that subject, what about Adèle? She was becoming quite countrified, buried here. It was high time she was properly introduced to society.

In other words, Adèle thought, what was to become of her? There was plenty of fear still in that idea: indeed, perhaps all her fear had its root there.

'And have you heard that Hector has a commission for a Requiem?'
Adèle put in. 'An official state commission for the grandest of works. Isn't
that wonderful?'

'It certainly is a considerable honour,' her mother said.

Nancy sniffed and shrugged. 'Well, he's chosen his path, and that's that.
It's *you* we've got to consider.'

Nancy marched upstairs and reviewed Adèle's dresses like a sergeant
with an unpromising set of conscripts. 'Dear, dear. That one will do well
enough – for the rest, thoroughly provincial. We must do some shopping
in Grenoble.'

'Isn't Grenoble in the provinces?'

'Grenoble,' said Nancy sharply, 'is not lacking in fashion. We do not
look to Paris for everything, not by any means.'

The experiment in 'getting Adèle out' began with the winter season.
By then she had frocks in what she was assured were the latest modes
and had been coached in the latest dances by Nancy herself, who knew
very well how to lead. At the Pals' house in Grenoble she could no
longer relax, play games with little Mathilde, and dream the time away:
she was on campaign. 'You should be dressing!' Nancy would cry, coming
upon her reading or brushing Mathilde's hair. Dressing was a tremendous thing: you had to begin it hours before the occasion that demanded
it. Like a vast engine, the social life of the mountain-girt town was
ceaselessly chugging round. You had to be minutely attentive: even to
the trifling morning call at the high-walled, lustrously mahoganized
house of the leather-dealer – who was not quite the thing, you understood, but his wife was a charming woman with good connections in
the Church, worth remembering, and besides, also calling there was the
sister-in-law of the town's senior banker, and *he* would very likely be
at the party this evening, so there was a connection to bear in mind,
especially as his elder son was unmarried. Though there was talk that
the younger son was more favoured, the elder having revealed opinions too markedly royalist. Or too liberal, or too Jesuitical . . . or something. Adèle found it hard to keep all this in her head: the social
distinction between officers of the Grenoble regiment and those from
outside, the different branches of the law, the precedence of brides
going in to dinner . . .

'And try not to talk about Hector,' Nancy counselled her. 'Yes, yes, I know all that, you needn't flash your eyes at me. Just consider that not everyone is interested in such things, and they have a perfect right not to be so.'

The great engine whirled Adèle around. At night in a twitchy, weary, unsatisfying sleep she dreamed of starched white shirt-fronts, winking silverware, the shining bare shoulders of ladies swept by goose-pimples when a mountain draught bent the candle-flames: she tasted mutton and onion-sauce and smelt cologne and heard tinkling pianos and voices, endless voices including her own, talking of servants and vintages and Fenimore Cooper and the trouble with the Lyonnais and the outbreak of the malignant sore throat and the opening of the new railway in Paris and who had fifty thousand francs a year . . . And waking she tried to fix in her mind an image of the farm at Le Chuzeau, brightness in the air and earth-scent rising from her footfalls.

Before her departure Nancy and Camille – or Monsieur Pal as she always called him, in the genteel way – dined alone with Adèle and took stock.

'Well, you can't say you've lacked for introductions,' Nancy said. 'The question is, what have you made of them?'

'A difficult question to answer, perhaps,' Camille said genially, 'since it all must be rather a blur. Lord knows, it has tired me out.' But he chomped indefatigably.

'I dare say, Monsieur Pal. Still, it's different for a young woman in Adèle's situation. This is a time for taking notice. And being taken notice of. Now I observed Monsieur Taupin being particularly attentive to you at Madame Beauvallet's. What did he say? What did you think?'

Adèle searched in her mind: which starched shirt-front was that, and at which dinner? 'I really can't remember,' she said lamely.

Nancy clucked her tongue. 'You must remember Monsieur Taupin. His father is a partner in Taupin and Lavoine, the second oldest banking firm in the Dauphiné.'

'Oh. Did he have that written on his shirt-front?'

Camille Pal chuckled indulgently, but Nancy was rigid.

'I don't see why I should go to all this trouble if you're not going to try.'

'Well, I am, or I thought I was. But I don't know what's meant to happen. Do I write it down in a little book – do I allot points? And, besides, they all seem the same. The men, I mean, which I presume is what it's all about. Mostly they are very agreeable, but beyond that . . .'

'Agreeable – that's a start,' Nancy said, perking up. 'You see, it's quite simple really. You consider – merely as a first step – which you find the most agreeable.'

'Oh – well, Monsieur Suat. He was very nice.' Monsieur Suat – young, tall, thin, fair hair, ears with a slightly elfish point, grey eyes, rather beautiful gravely listening face. Yes, he was very nice. But beyond that . . . where do you go, where is the path? Adèle couldn't imagine finding it.

'Monsieur Suat?' her brother-in-law said. 'Where did you meet him?'

'I don't know. Wait, yes, I do. It was here.'

'You remember,' Nancy told her husband. 'Dinner, Saturday. Your cousin was ill, and we needed to make up the numbers.'

'Oh, yes. Oh, well, Monsieur Suat, decent fellow to be sure. Still, you could do a great deal better than that, my dear Adèle, take my word for it.' And Camille filled his roomy mouth with food, as if his word, once given, settled everything.

Nancy gave the full sigh of a busy and burdened woman. 'Well, we must try again, Adèle: perhaps in the new year. I shall talk to Mama.'

But talking to Mama became a different thing, soon after Adèle's return home. Shortly before Christmas Madame Berlioz fell ill. Her pretty figure swelled and she lost her appetite. Her eyes receded into her face, so she seemed to peep out at you through a mask. Dr Berlioz devoted himself to her care, though she remained her determined self enough to reject his gentler treatments, insisting on emetics and vast applications of leeches. Indeed, she remained herself right to the end, passionately talkative, busy with her rosary, strong in opinions. Latterly she seemed to be trying to fit it all in: there were gaspings of religious fervour, exhortations to her husband to take care of himself, dwelling on the failings and beauties of her children, plunges into despair. Often these seemed powerful enough to lift her swollen body from the bed and back into life.

They did not, though. The time came – and Adèle reminded herself of the importance of time, the time that must come like the new year's gift – when Dr Berlioz closed his wife's eyelids, while Adèle and Prosper stood by, clutching at each other's hands. You don't overcome it or conquer it . . . Remember, look differently at the board. Every piece is affected differently. Prosper bubbling with an eighteen-year-old's angry grief: Monique on the floor, actually biblically on the floor in prostration: Nancy in her well-regulated house in Grenoble and due for the news and probably much less armoured against it than she pretends: Hector in Paris likewise, and with surely a special twist of feeling as his mother once cursed him from her door, and one suspects, in spite of later reconciliation, that such a thing never dies. And her father. The doctor, the husband, unable to fend off death. Is it better or worse, Adèle wondered, when you are the doctor as well?

She kissed her mother and stroked back her hair. It was still the same hair, it sprang and fell in just the same way. Incidentally, the wonder: when does that change? When does she stop being your mother, with these little ways? Adèle wept: that was all for now. Only afterwards would come the recognition of change, the new relation to fear.

2

'What I want to know,' Nancy said, enunciating as if for the deaf, 'is why, exactly, Marc Suat?'

'Exactly?' Adèle echoed. 'What – am I meant to give you a figure? Very well: my reason for wanting to marry Marc Suat is exactly five hundred and twenty-seven. There, is that exact enough?'

'Hm. One wonders, as you're so flippant, whether you're quite *serious* about this proposal.'

'Serious – what? Is one supposed to approach a wedding as if it were a funeral?' Adèle caught herself up with a gasp: saw again her mother's coffin descend, wintry light striking a last flash from the lid before the darkness. It was nearly a year ago, but still that day was every day. She knew Nancy was seeing it too. 'I'm sorry.'

'Don't be.' Nancy came and took her hand: an uncommon gesture. 'You think I'm being interfering and overbearing and that I'm trying to take Mama's place.'

'Something like that,' Adèle said, with a weak smile.

'Well, I do feel a responsibility. Because of my position. Yes, we have an elder brother, but it's no use looking to him for any sensible guidance. And as for Papa, he's so shut up in himself nowadays. If you can get past his deafness, all he'll talk about is his ailments and his bowels.'

'He started talking about them the other day when the mayor's wife called. In great detail.'

'Lord . . .' Nancy frowned away her laughter. 'Still, I have spoken with him about this. And though he's not going to stand in your way, he does feel, as I do, that you might do a great deal better.'

'I know. He's spoken to me too. At least, he urged me to think carefully before committing myself. He didn't put it as crudely as you.'

Nancy dropped her hand. 'All I'm trying to do is prevent another disappointment in the family.'

'I suppose it would be no use my saying I love Monsieur Suat, would it?'

'It depends what you mean. Obviously you're very taken with him, but then you've hardly thought about it, you've hardly looked around and given the matter of marriage the consideration it requires.'

'Is that what you did?'

'We're not talking about me. But if you like, yes. I made sure I knew Monsieur Pal thoroughly. I made sure I had no illusions. You know, Monsieur Pal is very concerned for your future too. We stand together in this, which is one of the things you'll have to learn about marriage. It's a union of interests. Lord knows, when Hector married that actress, Monsieur Pal was deeply worried for the effect it might have on your chances, because that sort of mud sticks to the whole family—'

'Nancy, please tell Monsieur Pal not to lose any more hair worrying about me. It pains me to think of him shouldering such a burden. Besides which, it is absolutely none of his business.'

'When it's a family question, it is. You are my sister, and who you connect us with is a matter of importance. Now Monsieur Pal has nothing to say against Monsieur Suat—'

'Which means he does. Come on, out with it.'

'You are quite violent today. The fact is, Monsieur Pal is very eminent in his profession, and no one is better placed to give a just assessment of someone like Monsieur Suat – his history, his attainments, his prospects.

And Monsieur Suat is a respectable notary with a small practice, no more. And unlikely ever to be more—'

'You know, Nancy, I really would have credited you with more understanding of human nature. You try to deter me from marriage to the man I love by saying that socially and financially he is no great catch, and that all in all the great Monsieur Pal looks down his long nose at him – actually, it's not a long nose, it's a fat nose. And this is supposed to make me stop and think, Oh, yes, you're right, instead of making me all the more determined to marry him.'

Nancy's sleek head went up. 'Oh. I see. So you want to copy Hector. That's it.' She slapped her hands together, as if dusting off something unpleasant. 'Even when he's miles away, he's a menace.'

I would rather copy Hector than you. It was the thing you didn't say but thought of saying afterwards. Anyway, it was only true up to a point. Adèle wasn't marrying Marc Suat to be like Hector. She wasn't even marrying him to be like herself.

What she hadn't said, and couldn't say, to Nancy – still less her father – was how passionately, drainingly in love she was with Marc Suat. She was in this condition every waking moment; and condition was an apt term, for it was like an illness. A healthy, compelling illness – well, that was why she couldn't speak of it, the words made no sense. She had even hidden the true intensity of her feeling from Marc: because she feared he might recoil from it. This was why her love was making her unlike herself. It was a plunge, a dream, an escape: it was untying the moorings and leaving the old Adèle on the bank. She wanted to subsume herself in Marc completely. They were watched and chaperoned and well-behaved, so there was little opportunity for embraces – but when it came, she thrust herself into his chest as if she would penetrate his flesh, occupy the same space in the world as him.

She knew this wasn't right. Yes, her nature was rhapsodical and romantic like Hector's: still, she was also the straightforward provincial young woman, made of the mountain earth, and if someone else had confessed such extremes of yearning and self-abnegation to her she would have thought: *There'll be trouble.* One person could not be all in all to another in quite that way: for one thing, it was unequal. That was why she had to be careful. She knew something very important, kept it in mind, and always regulated her behaviour by it: she knew she loved Marc far more than he loved her.

It was not a matter of outright degradation. That she could not have borne. Marc was kind, attentive, chivalric, loving: no difficulties there. It was just that she knew, when he looked at her, he saw only so much: when she looked at him she saw everything. And this she was quite ready to accept. It seemed to her highly likely that all marriages were based on an imbalance – there was always one who loved more than the other, even if only by a little. But this was something the couples themselves were unaware of; whereas she was lucky enough to have recognized it from the beginning, and was content with it. That was how she knew she and Marc Suat would do very well together.

Marc Suat: he wasn't any more or less than the slender, fair, polite young man she had first met at Nancy's dinner table. He had revealed no darkly fascinating depths or startled her with flashes of mercurial temperament. Rather, he was like the farm at Le Chuzeau, which you first saw in the distance as you walked out of La Côte St André, and then the road presented it to you from an altered angle, and then as you drew nearer the blobs of the outbuildings took shape and the red roof kindled and blazed. She saw him better. She saw that, open and conversible though he was, he always suffered a faint flushing – a toasting – of his cheekbones when someone new addressed him. When he spotted a book or newspaper that interested him, he made a sort of stooping dive at it, his slightly arched eyebrows going up like an eager child's. When someone was talking detestable nonsense about Napoleon or the Jews, he pulled himself in with a look of indigestion, and seemed to fix his inward gaze on a later time when the nonsense would stop. He had a unique graceful gesture for not knowing something – I don't know, and out went his long fingers. And you could see the veins on the back of his hands, faintly green (why green?) and the flecks of fair hair.

And he was from Beaurepaire, near La Côte St André, and he had studied law in Grenoble and had his house and office there and – well, what did all this matter? In Adèle's life, where she often felt as nebulous as a cloud, Marc stood out as a rock. And he seemed to have no fear.

They were due to be married in April 1839. Six months before, Prosper had departed for Paris and a private boarding-school. He was slow in his studies, and inclined to telling lies for no reason: Dr Berlioz despaired of disciplining him. Still, he made the decision reluctantly. 'Soon,' he said, 'I shall be all alone.' He spoke not so much complainingly as from a rooted and even defiant melancholy: this is coming, only a fool would deny it. From Hector in Paris came encouraging reports of his brother's progress. Then in the new year Prosper fell ill with typhoid. Within a fortnight he was dead. He was not yet nineteen.

'My poor Adèle. I wish I could protect you from these things,' Marc said. He was, thank heaven, still the man she had thought him, for he stopped at this – instead of going on, Monsieur Pal-style, to regret that it was impossible, that in this world of Providence, alas, and so on. Indeed he said little: he sat and prepared himself, sturdily, to listen. He was very good at that. Perhaps he expected torrents of words and tears. But Adèle felt dry and numb. Guilty, also: she had never been as close to Prosper as to Hector or even Nancy: she felt she had not properly known him. But that was how their pieces had stood on the board.

'Do you want to postpone the wedding?' he asked at last.

She was prompt. 'No. Please, no. Marc, just – just marry me.' Save me.

Dr Berlioz agreed to the wedding. 'Why should you delay your happiness?' he said. He scarcely mentioned Prosper's name. But he stopped eating; and only under scolding pressure from Monique did he take up the habit again, sparingly. Food was one of the things he had done with. It was as if he were lightening the load of self, as he went forward into solitude.

A month after their marriage in the church of La Côte St André, Monsieur and Madame Suat set off for Paris on a family visit. Adèle was to be the first to meet Hector's wife, the legendary Miss Smithson, the beloved Henriette of his letters, the dear sister-in-law of her imaginings.

She was excited, but almost superstitiously apprehensive besides. Marriage she had found blissful and unexpectedly exciting. Now to see Hector and Henriette and her little godson and Paris besides – it was like borrowing a great sum, and being told breezily not to worry about paying it back. You wondered.

(Nothing had changed, by the way. She was still the one who loved more. Occasionally she saw a tiny look of polite reserve about Marc: as if to say, My dear, we're married, we don't have to go to these lengths. So she was careful.)

Lots of people, especially from Grenoble, had warned her she would find Paris dirty and disappointing. But it was splendid: she thrilled to it, while cheerfully knowing she could never live there. Obviously it suited Hector. He looked somehow more himself, more Hectorish, than she had ever known him.

'So, you were the one who had the courage to undertake the epic journey,' Hector said, embracing her. 'I'm so happy to see you. God, I'm so happy.'

It was a little awkward at first. They both had spouses to introduce: Marc had known Hector slightly in La Côte St André, but he seemed a little bemused by his brother-in-law, the flamboyant hair, the fashionable cravat, the rapid speech with eyes glancing darkly at the floor, the absence of steadiness. The little boy, Louis, helped: a thrustful chatty child of five who rampaged about them, bringing everything he possessed and heaping it in Adèle's lap. She thought, touching his fair silky hair: I love him. She was afraid marriage had made her sentimental.

'He's completely uncontrollable,' Hector said. 'I don't know where he gets it from. Can I have been like that? Surely I was all obedience and decorum. You must ask Papa.'

'Very well, but you know he will be partial, while pretending to be severe. I shall ask Monique if anyone. But I imagine you were just the same.' As she spoke, Adèle met Harriet's eyes. It seemed natural – the sisterhood of indulgence: they both loved him.

And of that Adèle had no doubt, within moments of setting foot in the house. Partisan though she was, the atmosphere of doom surrounding Hector's marriage to his actress must have infected her: she had been secretly prepared for disharmony, grand airs – something uneasy and not domestic. Instead, this quiet, approachable woman in simple morning-dress: beautiful certainly, but not in the regal style – large, soft, shadowed eyes, tentative mouth, white skin: a little plump, but so deft in her movements she seemed weightless: her French fluty, halting. And a simple fondness in her looks, at Hector, at her son – the one thing, in other words, that no one would have believed: natural.

Their apartments too. The good Côtois housekeepers would surely have expected masks, harps, parrots, sherbet and dirty rugs: but the rooms were rather Spartan than otherwise.

'A thousand thanks for the tea-set you sent us,' Hector said to Adèle. 'Before that we had to borrow cups from next door if anyone called.'

'Hector, hush,' Harriet said; and then, laughing a little, 'Though it's true.'

'Monsieur Suat, I hope you're braced for a thorough course of sight-seeing,' Hector said. 'Henriette has taken great pains to arrange your entertainment for the whole three weeks. You will stagger back to La Côte drained, surfeited, and jaded, this we promise.'

'Hector exaggerates as usual,' Harriet said. 'I hope we can help make your visit interesting, but you will want time to yourselves. It must be your choice.'

'This is very kind. Certainly there are things – well, I would like to visit Prosper's grave,' Adèle said, and then thought: Oh, I have taken the wrong tone: not the right thing to say so early.

But Harriet, without moving, seemed to reach towards her. It's those eyes, Adèle thought: they reach. 'Oh, that was the most shocking news. I was so looking forward to getting to know him. It's so unfair – it's miserably unfair.'

'I remember thinking the same when Hector wrote me about your poor sister,' Adèle said.

Nothing about Harriet visibly altered: you just knew that she was rigid. 'Thank you,' she murmured. 'Yes, it was very sudden. A paralytic stroke. My brother said she didn't suffer long. She was never strong, but still I didn't expect—' She frowned, smiling. 'Stupid. As if one ever expects.'

'Hector told me how much you did for her. There must be some comfort in – in knowing that . . .' What is this nonsense I'm saying? Oh, I did a lot for her, so that's a comfort now she's dead. Greetings, Harriet: your sister-in-law is a fool.

But the vast eyes reached again: Adèle actually felt as if her hand had been seized. 'Thank you,' Harriet said urgently, 'yes. I try to find comfort in that.' And in that moment Adèle was fastened to Harriet, and Harriet to her – when they were both, as she realized, not telling the truth at all. The men stood by, beningly listening, mannish, not understanding in the least. Harriet, after a moment, smiled. The conventional image was of the sun coming out. But Harriet's smile, Adèle felt, was like rain. She understood why Hector loved her.

The itinerary for the Paris stay: Notre-Dame, the Panthéon, the tapestry factory of the Gobelins, the Tuileries gardens, the Arc de Triomphe, the Opéra. Prosper's grave.

The other, even more interesting itinerary: the journey around Hector, little Louis, and Harriet.

Hector was and remained very Hectorish, buoyant, quixotic and often absent: he had a big work of composition on hand. Because of it, he was sometimes not there even when he was there: a tic came over him and he looked right through you like a ghost. But there were talks: Adèle and Marc, by Hector's arrangement, had an apartment at the Hôtel d'Antin just round the corner. It was easy to be with Hector, take his arm, stroll as they used to in the country.

'This is strange, Hector. Oh, nice, but – strange. I keep thinking of Papa.'

'So do I. How is he? You don't have to answer that. I don't see how you could, really. I suppose he'll never come . . . ?'

'To Paris? I've tried to persuade him. But it's a feat if he goes to Grenoble. And when he comes back he roams and roams about the house, as if he's trying to put himself back into it . . . He does often talk of you.'

'That must make him roam even harder. Where's that damnable son . . .'

'No . . . No, I think he's proud of you, in his way.'

'Which isn't his way. Which is the point.'

'Perhaps. Only perhaps. Does it still trouble you?'

'To anyone else, I'd say no. To you – yes. If I could prove him wrong, and Mama, God rest her, and all of La Côte St André—'

'But you have. Look, Hector, look at you. Parisian, lots of smart friends who terrify me—'

'Rubbish. Who?'

'I'm speaking generally.'

'Sorry. I keep doing that in my music, apparently. A nice tune starts, and then the rhythm shifts and the shape goes, and I'm not like dear old Rossini. Never know where it will end. That's why, going back to your question. I do not, my darling Adèle, succeed. I wrote you about *Benvenuto*

Cellini. I exaggerated then, in the opposite sense. It was more than a failure. It was a bottomless, ineffable, gargantuan fiasco. They didn't just boo. They hissed and cackled and hooted and brayed. It was like Noah's ark in there.' His smile was tight. 'The critics exulted. Never has the august stage of the Opéra been so debased, et cetera.'

'Why would they exult?'

'My darling Adèle, I have enemies. Everyone does in the musical world of Paris, that's what makes it go round, jealousy and malice and plot. But I can proudly say I have more than anyone. Becoming a music critic has made it worse, of course. I do try to be kind. But if it's tired old claptrap I say so. Then I have grand ideas. *Grrrand*, as the papers put it. I refuse to believe that music should be no more than a lukewarm hip-bath. I try to climb too high. So people love it when I fall on my back-side.'

'But this is terrible.'

He laughed. 'It would be, if that were all. But I have my supporters. Henriette first of all – she supports me in everything I do, absolutely. There's Liszt, though he's off astounding the Italians at the moment. And, of course, Paganini.'

'Harriet was telling me that when she came in and found you with the letter in your hand she thought something terrible had happened.'

'Oh, I was in tears. Absurd to recall it now . . . It wasn't just the gift of twenty thousand francs – it was the belief in me.' His laugh was like a snarl. 'What prize cant that sounds. Luckily I had my well-wishers to bring me down to earth. One anonymous letter instructed me to blow my brains out. And there were plenty of critics ready to find reasons for the gesture. Paganini was trying to curry favour with the Paris public, it was all a stunt to get people to his concerts, and so on. I went to see him, to thank him. He's a piteous sight – a skeleton. And he can hardly talk for the cancer in his throat. He won't perform again. He did it, he said, because he admired my music and wanted to give me time to compose. Simple as that. But there, no one wants the truth when they can have a nice juicy lie instead.'

'Such a noble gesture – and I confess I had always believed him to be rather a shocking character. Dear me, you've caught me out in a preju-dice.'

'I should like,' Hector said abruptly, fiercely, 'to trample on every prejudice. If I had not married Henriette, I would have chosen the bastard daughter of a Negress and an executioner.'

'But you married Harriet,' Adèle said, pressing his arm, 'fortunately. Fortunately for all.'

'Do you really think so? Oh, I have no doubts myself. And you've always been on our side. But back home – Nancy, Papa—'

'I shall tell them what I have seen,' she said, 'which is a picture of contentment.'

He smiled distantly. 'She was my muse. Truly, my muse. And I married her. It almost seems as if such things shouldn't happen, doesn't it? As if some law has been broken. The trouble is, she was – she is a great artist herself. If you had seen her in Shakespeare . . . But tastes change. No English theatre is workable in Paris now, and her French isn't fluent enough for our stage. I tried to get George Sand to write a play specially for her, with the role of an Englishwoman in it, but nothing came of that. It seems – such a waste.'

'But I'm sure she's happy. She adores Louis, and she adores you.'

'Yes,' he said, with something like a wince. 'Odd, isn't it?'

'I don't think it's odd at all. But, then, you're another of my prejudices.'

'No, I just meant . . . well, no matter. So, what has Henriette cooked up for your entertainment tonight? The Opéra? Ah, my favourite place, so full of happy memories. No, don't worry. I'm over that. They'll listen one day. One day, Adèle.'

That night she looked with new eyes at Harriet: remembering that she had been a great actress, wondering if the memory pained her. Certainly she seemed very much at home at the Opéra: she knew everyone: in the lobby during the interval she introduced Adèle to a dandyish gentleman with curly hair, Monsieur Dumas. *That* Monsieur Dumas? Harriet smiled at her expression, and asked him for tickets for his latest play at the Comédie-Française.

'For you, Madame Berlioz, a thousand.' He kissed her hand.

'But then you wouldn't make any money.'

'Pooh, money I have,' he said, with a conjurer's gesture. 'The one thing that could truly make my life complete has already been stolen by Berlioz, bless him and curse him.'

Adèle observed the faint, nervous flickering of Harriet's lips as she tried to follow Monsieur Dumas' voluble French. 'Tut, nonsense,' she said at last. Adèle reminded herself to slow down when she talked. Harriet never seemed to have any trouble understanding Hector; but then that, she told herself, was the language of love. Marriage was definitely making her sentimental.

The opera, *The Fairy Lake*, was by Auber, the latest in a long line of successes: it had been running for two months. (Hector's opera had lasted four nights.) Adèle found it very pretty and tuneful. What Hector thought she couldn't tell: his sharp profile gave nothing away, and he made no comment. But at the end, during the applause, she saw Harriet's hand reach out and cover his.

'Hector was telling me,' Marc said that night, undressing, 'how much he earns for his journalism. Or, rather, how little. He must write like the devil to keep them on it.'

Marc was not – of course – one of those who thought Hector an irresponsible scapegrace who had married a harlot to spite his family: she would not be with him now if he were. Still, he was a Côtois, and this strange world rather baffled him.

'Well, that's only temporary. The gift from Paganini has helped buy him time to compose. And it's going to be something truly grand and wonderful – a symphony on *Romeo and Juliet*, a huge work with soloists and chorus—'

'They don't usually have those in symphonies, do they?'

'In Hector's, they do. It will be something entirely new. It will be the making of him.'

'Well, I hope so. He works hard enough. Must be difficult having to rely on the public. If you want to remain true to yourself, as Hector obviously does. I thank the Lord that I haven't got any talent.'

'Don't say that.' For a moment Adèle saw Camille Pal's supercilious face. 'You are very good at what you do.'

'No, I'm not really,' he said cheerfully. He put his arms round her. 'But, still, I wouldn't change places. Not with Hector.'

Not with anyone was, perhaps, the phrase she truly wanted to hear. But Adèle kissed him, and contented herself with content.

★   ★   ★

'I wonder when I shall see you again,' Harriet said to Adèle, on their last night in Paris.

Her great eyes were mournful: drowning eyes, Adèle thought, and blinked away the unpleasant image. 'Soon, soon, I hope,' she said, taking her hand. Such a beautiful hand: and so cold. You wanted to rub and warm it like a child's. 'You know I would love to welcome you and Louis to our home – show him off to his grandfather . . .You would be welcome,' she added, at Harriet's expression. 'I would see to it.'

'Thank you. It's meant so much to me, meeting you – especially as I was terrified of you.'

'Of me?' She laughed uncertainly. 'My dear Harriet, what possible reason could you have to be terrified of me?'

Harriet laughed, a little. 'Fear knows no reason.'

The *diligence* took four lurching, teeth-rattling days to get from Paris to Grenoble. Luckily Adèle enjoyed travelling with Marc, who did not grouse about dinners and bed-linen at second-rate inns or get cross with the other passengers. When I am a wise old grandmother, she thought, leaning against his shoulder, I shall recommend this as the measure of marital compatibility.

They were no more than twenty miles from Grenoble when Marc changed. She was chatting about little Louis, and what gift she could send him: a stick-horse perhaps, or a drum, though that might not be such a good idea with poor Hector in his study trying to compose—

'Yes, Adèle, whatever you please.'

'But then you would know better than I what little boys like – having been one yourself, I mean—'

'I said, whatever you please.' He turned his face from her. Muscles twitched in his long jaw.

She was silent, more from puzzlement than hurt. Was this what they called the first quarrel? If so, what was she supposed to do? Go into a pet herself? But there seemed so little to work with. Marc was staring into space and chewing his thumbnail. Not pleasant: perhaps she should seize on that. It occurred to her that they were the only people left in the coach: the others had got out at Lyon. So, was he one of those men who only showed his true colours when there was no one to see? But that made no sense: they had often been alone.

Adèle reached out for him. He jumped violently. His arm was stiff, the muscles bunched.

'I'm sorry,' he said, 'I'm sorry, I'm feeling a little – out of sorts,' and turned from her again.

Well, thought Adèle: is it because now we're going home, and he's married to me and the novelty's over and that's it? She could not quite believe it, but she felt edged with bleakness. Listlessly she sat back and looked out at the dark afternoon, the familiar perturbations of the Dauphiné sky. Lightning played over the rim of mountains: thunder had been rolling about the slopes for some time, though it was such familiar weather to her that she had hardly noticed.

'I hope the storm breaks before we get home,' she said: she didn't know whether she was speaking symbolically.

Marc started laughing into his cupped hands, in terrible snorts. Her nape prickled: suddenly she was afraid, of him, of what this might mean. Then she realized: he was sobbing.

'Forgive me,' he groaned, 'please forgive me.'

'I do. I do, whatever it is. Marc?'

'It's *that*,' he said, slumping back, his face red and creased, and flung a trembling hand at the coach-glass: at the bruised, flashing sky.

'Oh!' she said, and something went through her that was too sweetly piercing to be called relief. 'Oh, you mean the storm. We're in no danger, you know – the road doesn't climb high—'

'I know that.' His chest jerked as the thunder boomed louder. 'I know all about that. It isn't the danger. It's – my fear.' He gasped and tried to laugh. 'A fine thing for a man born and bred among the mountains. Like a sailor afraid of the sea – oh, God.' The storm was ripening. 'I'm so sorry, forgive me.'

'What a thing to forgive.' She found his hand. 'My dear, it doesn't matter in the least.'

'But it does,' he hissed. 'To know you have this . . . I've tried everything. I'm a rational man, and I've tried to rationalize this—'

'Fear knows no reason.'

'You are very good,' he said: but he shook his head, could not embrace her: he shrank into his own shame.

Somehow Adèle knew what to do. She took the seat opposite him, so she could look into his face, and so he could fix his eyes on hers while she talked. She told him about the fear in her life and her life of fear, telling it seamlessly, so that his glance and attention should never waver to the storm outside: she even invented some to keep the flow going, though that didn't matter – we are all, it flashed upon her like the lightning, artists. Presently he delivered his hands into hers, and as she talked and the thunder cracked she could feel the electric starts in his body, passing from his hands to hers. Soon he was locked on to her, in utter trust and dependence, and that, too, was frightening in a way; but you made friends with the fear.

Outside Grenoble the thunder died away. But they stayed in that position, leaning forward face to face, hands clasped. It was a position of balance.

PART FOUR

Desdemona

1

First there was her father killing her mother. Now there was her husband killing her.

'You're killing me,' she screamed at him. 'Don't you see you're killing me . . .' Her voice reverberated with the flat coldness of the small hours. The bedroom bore the characteristic signs of a row: water-jug upended, bed-curtains half torn down, a shoe lying where she had thrown it. He picked up a pillow from the floor, stood holding it perplexedly, as if not knowing what to do with it: as if it were their whole situation.

The door nudged open. Louis stood there in his nightshirt, solemn, vastly blinking.

'Papa. Papa, I can't sleep.'

'Papa. What about Mama?' she said.

Louis scanned her with dubious wide eyes. Her eyes. That, at least.

'Hush now.' Hector went and put his arms round his son's shoulders. 'Go back to bed. It's all right.'

'What's Mama doing?'

'Practising,' he said, without hesitation. 'Practising for a play.' He ushered the boy out.

Harriet slumped down on the cold boards at the foot of the bed, wrenched with spasms of wild laughter. The candle was guttering. 'A play. Oh, yes. A play . . .'

Hector came and stood gazing down at her. He looked dramatically thin, as if the shadows were eating him away. He had the pillow in his hands again. *Put out the light, and put out the light.*

'You're killing me,' she gasped.

'And what,' he said, 'do you suppose you're doing to me?'

'Loving you,' she suggested, and laughed again until the hot double-distilled tears ran down to her mouth.

Not that scene first. Roll up that drop. Who cares to see Romeo and Juliet ten years married and quarrelling past the point of exhaustion? Who wants to think of it as a thing that may be?

(And who wants to think of that house at Sceaux, where the birdsong was like needles and the old he-goat assessed her with his slanted devil's eye and the boy did not hide his smirk as he handed her the basket: that place in the bleak regardless sunlight where everything is to be faced? Not yet.)

Go back instead to this. Romeo and Juliet as they should be. Hector's triumph, the great work that Paganini's gift had enabled him to complete. Dramatic symphony by Hector Berlioz, *Roméo et Juliette*.

'But of course you can't have a dramatic symphony,' Hector said, the morning before the first performance, scratchy and restless. 'It must be one thing or another. Opera, cantata, symphony. Stands to reason. Told you, fellow's mad . . .' He thrust the poker into the fire, stirring too much and ruining it. 'Ah. Well done, Hector.'

'Why does everything have to be one thing or another?' Harriet remarked placidly. She was sorting through Louis's box of toys. Many had belonged to Prosper: Dr Berlioz had sent them. A sort of acceptance, she dared to think. 'Now take this. It's a toy soldier, yes, but to Louis it's also Gabrielle. That's what he calls it.'

They laughed. Gabrielle was the maid, a thick-necked countrywoman, potently moustached.

'Louis has the true Romantic sensibility.' Hector chuckled, kissing her hair.

Those laughs. You forgot them, like the good meal and the warm fire: incidental. Yet they nourished you. Only when they were gone did you realize, and feel the perishing.

In the lobby of the Conservatoire Hall before the performance, Emile Deschamps, Hector's librettist, bowed low to Harriet.

'Madame Berlioz, before it begins, let me salute the muse of our invention, the true and original Juliet.' His brow was spangled with sweat: there

were two hundred musicians in there, a capacity audience, and thousands
of francs at stake. 'I was there, you know – of course you know. Your very
first Juliet, at the Odéon. All those years ago. And now here we are –
who'd have thought it?'

'Yes,' she said. 'All those years ago.'

The piece was long, big, ambitious, difficult: Hector had worn himself
thin preparing and rehearsing it. Once again she was in a box over the
orchestra, but this time little Louis was at her side. One or two of the
louder passages made him tremble – he even seemed about to duck –
and the audience appeared puzzled at first; but when they broke into
spontaneous applause during the ball scene, she knew that everything was
all right. This time Hector had won. Now, as Paganini had said, they would
eat their words. Her heart lifted: it even rose clear of that dragging phrase:
all those years ago.

At the end there was a great roar. She remembered the sound, the
sensation of that: you felt you could almost lean into it and it would
support you, like a head-on gale. Louis bounced up and down in his seat:
Papa, Papa. All those years ago. Harriet was happy. But perhaps here,
beneath the storms of applause, is where you can hear the first faint grind-
ings and growlings of what was to come.

The last fragments of her career – the odd appearance at a benefit, a scene
or two from Shakespeare in some unlikely mixed bill – had petered out.
Curiously, the awareness that it was all over was chiefly prompted by
tributes, like that of Deschamps. While they were garrulously setting the
artistic world to rights, Hector's friends – Hugo, Vigny, Dumas – would
chivalrously refer to her. 'Now this, Madame Berlioz, you will confirm,
you who showed the way. It was your Ophelia which first – It was at
that time . . .' It was, it was. Her French never seemed to improve beyond
adequate, but she knew all about the past tense.

Of course she had her mirror as a helpful reminder. She had never
regained her figure after Louis, and now someone in the mirror was
playing Harriet as a fudgy, motherly woman past her prime, and playing
it very convincingly.

'You are as beautiful as you ever were,' Hector would say. 'When I look
at you, I see the fair Ophelia with whom I fell everlastingly in love.'

She did like to hear it. But some deep wisdom had begun to seep in, telling her that men found these things terrible easy to say. They came out with them obligingly, just as they opened doors for you or put up umbrellas. Sometimes they did it simply to make you be quiet.

She felt the need of a female confidante. When they were living in Montmartre she had made a good friend in Madame Blanche, a brisk, sensible woman whose husband kept the lunatic asylum nearby. But Harriet could not bear to go to that house: the moon-like faces of the inmates seemed to ask some searching question of her. There was still Adèle, her talisman and touchstone. It was she who had relieved Harriet of the feeling that she had done Hector a terrible wrong by marrying him. The warm, chatty letters still came from Grenoble: but Adèle was far away, and occupied with raising her own family. Hector's other sister Nancy had come to Paris some time after, and had been perfectly polite; but she had an air of making continual mental notes.

As for their going south to visit his family on their home ground – somehow the plans for that always foundered. Harriet shrank from the reception she might get – especially from Dr Berlioz – and Hector shrank from putting her through it. A faint grinding here, perhaps.

The one woman Harriet saw most of was Gabrielle. And she was increasingly convinced that Gabrielle despised her.

She kept her on because she was good with Louis. Sometimes, when she could do nothing with her riotous, baffling son, his yells would bring Gabrielle to the door. 'Come,' Gabrielle would say, holding out brawny arms. 'Come, little one.' And as she left the room Gabrielle would meet Harriet's eyes over Louis's happily squirming shoulders for a long, cold moment.

'Oh, she hates everyone,' Hector said dismissively. 'It's her hobby.' He was more impatient, or less patient, with household matters nowadays, now that he was so busy. Busy in the bad sense.

Roméo et Juliette, for all its success, had made a profit of one thousand one hundred francs. It was because—

'It's because it costs so much to put on a concert like this in damnable Paris.' Hector at his desk, chin cupped in his hands, worry-raked hair drooping like a fallen crest. 'You have to do everything yourself. You have to get the parts copied, and beg on bended knees for the one concert hall we've got, and you have to advertise so as to accustom people to the idea of actually coming and *listening* instead of going to the Opéra to rest their eyes on the scenery . . . God. Liszt says in Germany people genuinely like listening to music, instead of treating it as a mild insult.' He sketched a witchy figure on his papers.

'I know, Hector.' She laid her hands on his shoulders. 'But it was a success. It showed what you could do.' Some of his music was beyond her – in her secret heart she sometimes even wished for the easy tunes of his enemy Monsieur Auber – but then she was no musician and, besides, some of the language of Shakespeare eluded her complete understanding. No, in this she was steadfast, her belief unconquerable. 'So, it was worth it. Worth it if you hadn't made a *sou*.'

'You are a wonderful woman,' he said, reaching up to touch her hand, briefly, 'and a terrible businesswoman.'

'Lord, I know that,' she said, laughing. Yes: still the possibility of laughter.

She left him in his bare, frugal study to work: he had yet another article to write for the magazines, and it was plain how much he had begun to loathe it. Occasionally she heard him fluently cursing and even kicking his chair across the room. It was different when he was composing: then he was seraphic, gentle, even his movements dainty and delicate, as if he lived in a beautiful yet fragile world. A dream of eggshell.

But there was less and less time for that. Practicalities pressed. Though there had been summers in blissful Montmartre, now they needed to be established in the city, close to Hector's editors and publisher and, above all, the musical establishment of Paris. Which was something between an ogre to be slain and a chaste goddess to be seduced. Either way, a tough proposition. Their apartment was in the rue de Londres. London Street. When, she wondered, did irony cease to be ironic? Was that simply how life was?

There were debts, and household bills, and Louis's school fees – and then the illnesses. Louis's illnesses, but also, more frequently, hers. She began to dread waking in the morning, when some ominous sign might present itself – the thickened throat, the thundering head. The impending summons to the doctor, eager and frock-coated, fee on his lips.

'You never see a poor doctor,' Hector remarked; and the irony of that seemed to assail him so overwhelmingly that he couldn't say any more.

It was an illness that ignited the first real blaze between them. Hector had had to borrow to pay for the doctor. He carefully did not allude to it; but Harriet, with the fractious nerves of sickness, felt he was too careful.

She detected the martyr's sigh in his restraint. 'It's not my fault. I don't mean to be ill.'

He raised his head from thought. 'I know you don't.'

She was still in bed recovering, and even his being dressed and up appeared to her like an assertion of superiority. 'I'm sorry you have to pay for everything. It's not like me, it's not at all what I'm used to. I supported my family entirely by my own earnings for many years.'

'Yes,' he said, 'I know.' Her mind glossed that as: *Yes, I know everything about you now, and it's become very tedious.*

'It would be different if I could still work. If I could work, I could help, financially I mean, I could—' She struggled: her French grew hazy when she was ill.

'Contribute,' he supplied.

The lack of the word seemed like her last and most crucial lack just then.

'Yes, of course, that. You needn't be so pleased with yourself because you know the word. It's your fucking language after all.' (Yes, she knew that word, especially since Louis had gone to day-school and come home crowing it.) 'You should know, it's your damned country—'

'If only it was.' He came to the bed and sat by her, calmly, kindly, as if she only complained of her headache.

'I wish I could help, and I can't, and it nags at me – I brought you all those debts, and that's all, I can't do anything—'

'Damn. And there was I marrying you because I thought you'd bring in lots of money.'

She half smiled; but she felt there was still a sort of untruth here. 'Well, you must have thought I'd bring in *some*. Or else—'

'Don't say that. Don't ever say that.' His cheekbones showed, reddening. 'It's wickedness.'

'Why not?' She pounced, a raw huntress needing blood. 'Because that reminds you of what I was? An actress, and a very successful one, with a life of my own – that's what I was. And is that what you don't like to think of? You just want me to be your muse, is that it?'

'But you are,' he said, with a quizzical look. 'You were, and you are.'

'Oh, excellent. So that's all there is for me, then. To be a muse. What do muses do, except stand there looking pretty and inspiring? Is that my future? Oh, wonderful. There's my lot in life. To inspire pieces of music that nobody likes.'

She turned violently over and thrust her face into the pillow, already hating herself. There was a long silence. She was about to raise her head – to retract, to see even if he was still there – when she felt him lie down beside her. His arms went gently round her. She stiffened, relaxed.

'Well, what other sort of music would you inspire, Henriette, but the music that belongs to future ages? Would you inspire cheap ditties, or – or the music of the world to come?'

'Mr Modesty,' she mumbled.

He laughed softly, with profound regret, against her shoulder. 'I have to believe it, because no one else will.'

She submitted to his embrace: soon welcomed it. However, he did not take off his clothes and get in with her, as he once would have. The smell of horehound, probably. Don't read too much into it.

'Where's Papa?'

'God knows.'

'God knows everything. Gabrielle told me so. She knows everything.'

Gabrielle, of whom Harriet was beginning to be a little afraid, without understanding why. But fear knows no reason.

'Well, that must make Gabrielle God, then.'

'That's silly.'

Louis had a way of screwing his fists into his hips and studying her, as if she could never quite be trusted: my mother the trickster. She indulged a pleading memory of him as a baby, when she had first taken him out around the lanes of Montmartre and the women had stopped to look and admire, and she had idiotically said with ballooning heart and helpless indelible smile: *Yes, and he's mine!* That she adored him still, even more perhaps, did not seem to weigh in any sort of balance.

'Papa's in the city. He has things to do. He'll be back soon.'

'I want him *now*.'

'You can't have everything you want.'

'Why not?'

Why not, indeed? No doubt she should have come up with an answer – something parental and definitive. Instead it seemed to her a very good question. She looked distractedly around the parlour: tapestry chairs, fire-screen, bureau, gilt-figured clock, embroidered work-box. It was the bureau that tugged at her. Brandy-bottle there.

'Because,' she said, with a sudden illumination, 'once you get everything you want, you don't want it any more.' And vast dreadful vistas of understanding opened up so dazzlingly that she had to shut her eyes.

When she opened them Louis was grumblingly on his way out. 'I'll ask Papa.'

Yes (on the way to the bureau), yes, ask him, get an answer.

Paris, and musicians. There were plenty of them. And what they did was this: they played the game.

They obediently submitted obedient works to the Opéra, where crusted and entrenched musicians who had long ago learned how to play the game approved them if they were sufficiently obedient. And meanwhile they thrust their noses to the ground and went snuffling and wiggling after official appointments, director of this and custodian of that. It helped, when the time came, if you had a record of obedience. Monsieur who? Ah, yes, I remember him. I'm sure he remembers me. A nod and a wink. We gladly recommend the appointment of Monsieur Who, an ornament to the whatever – and so on.

Harriet knew some of the musicians of Paris, of course. Less so as she chose to go out less frequently. (Was it a choice? Or a fear? And what was she afraid of? But fear knows no reason.) Some were in Hector's position – unsalaried, making their living only from their music. Differences, though. Chopin, fey, elegant, taught piano to the daughters of wealth, who were in love with him: and played it in the salons where there was a mass wilting at the first premonitory whiff of his cologne. Liszt diabolically pounded and titillated the keyboard before packed, palpitating and paying audiences, mostly female, mostly yearning for his long fingers to do something comparable to their bodies. But Hector was no pianist. He needed voices and orchestra to speak for him. Which meant the Opéra: but that was a nest on which various fat fowls squatted, unyielding. Like Monsieur Meyerbeer, whom everyone (even Hector) said was a charming man. But he knew what he was doing. He charmed and even recompensed the critics well in advance, he deployed a well-paid army of puffers, and he kept his finger on the pulse (Harriet had heard a ruder anatomical comparison) of the public: so, lots of processions, trumpetings, choruses, big tense moments with the basses and cellos going judder-judder, and dancing nuns.

Every day Hector went out – or, if you like, sallied forth, to pelt the ogre and try to pry apart the clenched thighs of the goddess. Harriet, at home, unoccupied, thought: wondered; and read and reread the latest letters from Adèle. Christenings, wine-harvests, a small ring of known names. A desperate longing went spinning out from her, twined with recognition, with memories of Ireland and wishes of now. I belong there more than here, in fact, though they would dislike me. I am unequal to my own scandal. It was never mine. I'm tired.

'I can't always be here.'

'You're never here.' Of course, an untruth, but along this downward spiral you brush against many untruths that have, still, something more about them: they stick.

'What do you suppose I do, then?' He asked it with fierce expectation. A shifting of ground, which he reflected by prowling to the other side of the parlour. 'As this is plainly a great issue: what do you suppose I do, when I spend the day in the city, working and striving, and come home feeling like a corpse on end – what, tell me?'

'God knows.' God knows everything.

He looked at her askance, sourly, bored. Funny: you seek to provoke that look, to prove something, and how you hate it when it comes.

'No doubt I revel in debauchery,' he said shortly. 'No doubt, instead of going to Schlesinger's to sort out my deficits, or to the bank to raise a loan, I lounge about with loose women—'

'No, only one, I would think.'

'You know, Henriette, you are as I've always said a great artist. And here you're surpassing yourself, creatively. I have, as I've proved to you, no interest in any other woman. Do you follow me? In fact after I met you, I found it impossible, literally impossible, to think of any woman without boredom. And yet here you are inventing one—'

'You men get very tedious once you start on art.'

He shrugged and went away. That was when she began to know.

And yet she was his loyal defender, as when she accompanied Louis and Gabrielle on a walk and they ended up at the baker's – Louis clamouring for a tart – and while she hovered back invisible she heard the baker's inflicted opinions.

'Him? Him up there? He's supposed to be some sort of musician. *Some sort.* He never has any money. Hasn't even got a piano – you look.'

'You're referring to my husband, Monsieur Berlioz,' she said, stepping forward, 'who is the greatest composer in France, who has invitations from all over Europe –' (yes, but she hated and dreaded them, because he would go, and once he was gone . . .) '– and who does not compose trifling little piano pieces for second-rate amateurs –' (And yet hadn't she said, in argumentative exasperation the other night, *Why can't you compose some little salon things for piano and earn some money?* Had she? She certainly didn't mean it. But she was finding her memory patchy lately.) '– and thank you, in future we will take our custom elsewhere.' The baker stared: she stared back. For that moment, though he didn't know it, he was all of Paris.

So Louis did not get his tart. He bellowed, clinging to crooning Gabrielle. All Mama's fault.

Perhaps, she thought, as she sneaked a brandy before Hector came home, perhaps if she were still on the stage, and not so drearily familiar, Louis would love her more. It wasn't that he didn't love her. He just loved Papa more. An imbalance. In a way, Louis's attitude to her was like that of someone who had fallen madly in love, then begun to cool. She poured another brandy, to blot out that thought.

Hector's uncle, Colonel Félix Marmion, was in Paris, and took to calling on her. Harriet liked him, without quite trusting him. She suspected he was there on reconnaissance, and sending despatches back to La Côte St André. But he was a listener.

'So, where's Hector?'

'Where is he always?'

Félix sat back and smiled, examining his booted leg with satisfaction. Nothing ever seemed to discompose him. 'You're not in spirits, my dear. I don't like to see that.'

'Men never do. It makes you a nuisance.' (Memory of yesterday, when she had complained of never seeing him. 'I have to go and see Janin about another article, and then I have to wait on some minister's undersecretary to get permission to arrange a concert, and then I have to try to hire some musicians and find the wherewithal to pay them, and then when I get home I have another review to finish. Tell me, where is the little gap in all of this?' Little gap, she had cried, I used to fill it all.)

'True enough, I dare say. But come, you've been on the stage, you know the difficulties of the artist's life. That's what we always tried to warn him about.'

And about me. 'It's not the difficulties of the artist's life that worry me. It's the easy things.'

You didn't have to explain things to Félix. 'Women, you mean? My dear Henriette, that's not Hector.'

'It wouldn't be women. It would be just one woman.'

Félix twitched his moustaches, not disagreeing. 'Well, but this is entirely hypothetical. I'm sure you have no ground for such a suspicion, have you? Hector's a married man with a splendid son: that's enough for him.'

'Is it? When he comes home to a useless, housebound wife and a son who's been screaming for him all day? I can't control Louis, he doesn't listen to me, it's only Gabrielle he takes any notice of, and she tries to turn him against me, but Hector won't hear of her going because she's the first reliable servant we've had. Then I reproach him, and he goes into the study and he's even glad to get in there when it's his wretched journalism he has to work on instead of his music. What can I be to him? What am I?'

'Oh, my dear –' Félix comes out with it '– his muse.'

'I'm afraid the muse looks different when you see her across the breakfast table every morning.'

Felix shouted with laughter. 'Oh, Henriette. Forgive me, I'm not laughing at your distresses, not at all. You just put it so beautifully. Look here, Louis is at day-school now, that must make it a little better. And didn't Hector say something about his going away to boarding-school? Good idea, you know, it's discipline he needs. As for Hector, he has to make his mark, and I've lived in Paris long enough to know it's a city of cliques and place-seekers who get on by taking in each other's washing. He needs to spread his wings – and that's why this notion of Germany is such a sensible one.'

She swallowed: it felt as if a lump of ice were going down. 'So he's complained to you about that.'

'Mentioned it. Not complained. But I gather you don't want him to go.'

'I just – wonder how I'll manage without him.' (Memory of last night. Arms imprisoning his neck. Hector, Hector, I love you so. Kind look. 'My Henriette. I love you too. You should know that.' As if it were a simple sum, two plus two. You should know that.)

'Quite natural. Actually it's rather nice when you think about it – not wanting him to go. Plenty of women would jump for joy if their husbands went abroad. But I'm sure, you know, you'll manage perfectly well.'

'You speak of it as if it were a settled thing.'

'Oh, you're too quick for me, my dear. No, I speak sensibly, I hope: putting the reasonable case.'

'When I married Hector,' she said, 'I never thought I would have to be reasonable.' And Félix rocked with laughter again.

When did she first start looking through his letters? She really couldn't tell: that treacherous memory again. (Gabrielle coming upon her in the twilight. 'Master Louis has got a hang-nail. Won't leave it alone. It wants snipping. Shall I do it, or shall you?' Harriet had just been about to make for the bureau. 'You,' she said weakly, or from weakness.) She knew that after the first time there was a hiatus, a pause of horrified recoil: never, never will I do that again. Then at some point she was taking a candle into his study and yanking open the drawers and rifling through his letters with snatching unsteady hands. The papers slithered and crackled, as if in resentment, as if resisting: a paper-cut beaded her thumb with blood. She sucked, swearing. She could see nothing – or, rather, she could see too much, correspondence with publishers and impresarios and friends and acquaintances and family; and what, after all, had she expected? Something glaring written in giant red letters? Possibly after that she went away, visited the bureau again: at any rate she found herself eventually reading with careful attention a letter from Liszt, the all-conquering, who was on a triumphal tour through Germany and Russia. Much of it, typically, was about himself and his affairs: in both senses. There were hints of an estrangement with Marie d'Agoult. There were hints of other things: exhortations to Hector to follow his lead and tour Germany: commiserations: Hector must cheer up, it would all be resolved . . . Then back to himself again.

A noise made her rush to the parlour. Only, as it turned out, the jeweller who lived below slamming his door. But now she was back with the bureau, and now she had something to think about. Mistresses. Wasn't that the way of it, in Hector's circle? Liszt with his countess, not to mention rumoured others. Hugo with his actress (when does irony cease to be . . . ?) Chopin with that strange woman George Sand. Now that she thought about it, her married life with Hector seemed a freak, a sport. Perhaps in the salons they joked about it, like an inexplicable attachment to some old-fashioned coat. Perhaps he joined in. Perhaps, perhaps. But brandy had a way with *perhaps*: it stiffened its backbone and gave it ideas above its station. Brandy: *eau-de-vie*, as they called it. Water of life. How absurd she used to think that, when she could hardly bear the taste of the stuff. Water of life.

That night she turned on him. 'I can smell a woman on you.'

After the first sharp glare he seemed to gather himself: he reached for rationality with a suppressed sigh, as one reached for a coin for an importunate beggar. 'Where? Tell me where on me, precisely.' The reasonable case. He thrust out his chin, exposing his jaw and neck (that place she liked, but other times, other worlds). 'Here? Or the hands? Or my clothes? The cab I took home wasn't of the cleanest, I warn you, but still. Take a good sniff.'

'Oh, no doubt you'd be careful—'

'No doubt I would. If it happened.'

'You mean you *want* to . . .'

'Do I? I don't know. Obviously you know best, Henriette, what I mean, so I leave it to you. I'll only say this. If you wanted to drive me into the arms of another woman, then you have chosen the absolutely infallible way of doing it.'

His fury: she recognized it, as always, too late, for he did not simmer and rise and boil as she did. He took one step across a threshold to a place of cold, closed constraint, and was unreachable. Just at the point when she might easily have been argued and cajoled back into sense. They were never both in the same place at the same time. An imbalance.

He stalked into the bedroom, tugging at his cravat. 'I can smell it,' he muttered to himself. She couldn't tell whether he was echoing her, or saying something else.

2

Hector went to Germany, and everyone agreed that it was a good thing. After all, said Félix Marmion to Harriet, you don't want to hold him back, do you? And after all, wrote Adèle, more gently, let's be reasonable.

And, after all, she did survive. She had a friend in the bureau. She had Louis, who was fonder and more amenable – as if, in Papa's absence, he were manfully helping to shoulder Papa's burden. Hector sent her money – bills to be cashed at the Banque de France, with exact instructions on how to do it. (For heaven's sake, I know about this, I used to support my family – yet still she trembled at having to go out and do it, to meet the comfortable stares of strangers who understood what life was.) Hector wrote. He depicted it and shared it with her. Germany welcomed and applauded him: there were professional orchestras with musicians who could play their instruments, and audiences who did not chat during the slow passages. There were eminent musicians who supported him: the celebrated Mendelssohn, an acquaintance from his Prix de Rome days: Clara and Robert Schumann: the young lion Wagner about whom Hector seemed in two minds. There was the welcoming and cultivated court of the King of Prussia, where the Crown Prince and Princess talked knowledgeably to him about music instead of sending him to be cross-questioned by a junior minister for the non-encouragement of the arts. There were journeys by the astonishing new railway, a Mercury, an earth-girdling Puck. There was the repeated assurance that at the end of his six-months tour, he would be back with her.

And in the rue de Londres, there was this: Louis and Gabrielle overheard in the next room.

'What's this face? What are you mourning about? Come, come, tell Gabrielle.'

A hesitation. 'Just Papa.'

'Papa. Always Papa.' Indulgent, even approving. 'Well, what about him?'

'I just don't like to think of him so far away, all alone.'

And now a tilt in the voice, as of someone straightening up, speaking partly to herself, eyes smiling coldly at the distance. 'Bless you. Bless you, he's not alone.'

Probably Harriet imagined the witch's cackle after that. She had always had a strong imagination.

We're coming to the house at Sceaux soon. I know it.

Yes. But you know, that's how it must be.

How easily you say that! As if being told 'It must be' has never troubled you or pained you. As if you just accept it.

I'm sorry. Perhaps you would prefer to speak . . . ?

No. I've long gone past the stage of preferring anything. Only set down this, before you do it: all the time, I loved him more. And more, and more. An imbalance, as you rather coldly put it.

Yes, I've finished.

'The problem is this,' says Hector, or the new, remote, efficient Hector she doesn't like (suspicion also that he doesn't like it himself). 'This,' and he holds up the empty brandy-bottle.

Except she notices the little blood-like wedge at the bottom, and thinks: There's some left in there. I went to bed – at some point – thinking it was gone, and yet there's, let's see, one more measure there. And I didn't notice! She is so taken with this discovery that she loses for a moment what he is saying.

'. . . and if we are to have any future together, this is something you must overcome, Henriette. I'm not saying this like some dismal moralist. I don't care about drink or opium or whatever it is, it's because I love you, or the person you were—'

'Does she drink?' So quick, sharp and conversational that she catches him: oh, she catches him.

He sags. And again, you don't want to see it: it's like those hidden cupboards and slowly, creakingly opening doors in your dreams. But though you struggle and fight the bedclothes, you know you're going to look: you know revelation must come.

He says: 'Not much, as it happens.'

Funny: you want to ask more. If he wasn't your lover, you could elicit a stream of interesting anecdote from this. It might even make you laugh and sympathize so much that you'd end up in bed. But, but. The time is out of joint. And she hates: my God, she hates. She knows there will be a time – probably not far off – when she will not hate, she will find reasons for him and beg and plead and do anything to have their life back just as it was, and it doesn't matter that you've got a mistress, and as you've made me go about in your absence I've even picked up the name, Marie, Marie, of all the boring basic names to have, I'll bet she's your archetypal pretty woman who spreads her legs and likes to be taken to interesting places, oh, Hector, that was lovely, and never thinks of going there on her own, never thinks you can be a woman like me who had all France at my feet and it was *just me* . . . All this, but she doesn't say it: why bother? And in the meantime, as she beats her fists on his chest like any actress expressing loving despair, Harriet reconciles herself to her future. In fact, she's already living there.

The house at Sceaux, on a westward slope with a view of orchards and a windmill, reminded her at first of their idyllic home at Montmartre, even down to the walled garden with a seat beneath the trees. Hector had chosen it, for her convalescence, or banishment: this was one of the questions her flinching mind could not touch. Enough for now that it was like Montmartre, and so perhaps Hector had chosen it with that in mind, and so perhaps, perhaps . . .

'How long am I to stay there?'

'As long as you wish. You've spoken about wanting to go to the country . . . The air is very good there. Perhaps that, and the quiet, will help restore your health.' All his talk was like this now: a gingerly crossing of stepping-stones.

'You mean you want me to stop drinking.'

He sighed. 'Well, yes. If you can just overcome that—'

'If, yes, what then?' she said eagerly.

'You know we've talked about this. You know there can be no promises. But if there is to be any possibility of a future—'

'First the drinking must stop. Very well. I'll do it. You'll see. And I'll do it because I want to.' And she did: it was splitting her in two. The drunken Harriet had behaved very badly last night, screaming and cursing at Hector for hours: the sober Harriet even had a notion that she had spat at him once. Hard to be sure, though. The drunken Harriet was pulling further away from her control – soon, perhaps, to break away altogether, take on a riotous life of her own.

'Still no promises,' he said.

'Yes. And still no promises from you to stop seeing that woman.'

'No promises,' he repeated, with an ashy look. 'Only that I'll do what you're doing. Try.'

And the house at Sceaux was not, after all, like Montmartre. Her apartment on the ground floor, pleasant enough in the sunlight, emitted a penetrating damp smell after dark. Rats shifted behind the old wormy panelling. Nor was the garden as welcoming. The proprietor, a retired vintner with a miserly look, kept a goat there: big, old, shaggy and stinking. 'Take no notice of him,' Harriet was told, 'he won't hurt you.' But she could never be easy when that goat was near. The goat watched her. When she picked up her book or her sewing (yes, she had brought bags of sewing, which she loathed, but the idea was that the innocent domesticity of it would somehow rub off) and went back into the house, the goat turned his head and watched her go with deliberate attention. It wasn't the horns she feared: it was the look of evil wisdom. It was the feeling that he was somehow going to impart it to her.

We must live apart. This was the theme that had persisted through all the stormy, convoluted variations of the last few weeks. They came with her to Sceaux: she could not lose them. When she woke in the morning with a sunbeam lancing through the cracked shutter the words seemed to be written there in the dust-motes. At night, after the long, skin-crawling, dry-mouthed agony had brought her at last to the brink of sleep, they came as a final murmur in her dimming ear.

It was for the best, they made each other wretched, Louis was suffering, Hector could not work, she could never respect him now that she knew about the other woman – oh, the arguments were numberless, an enormous army against which no one could fight. *We must live apart.* The trouble with those words was, they made no sense to her: that is, they expressed an impossibility. She could not live apart from Hector – it was like saying black was white. Even hating him, as she did now, did not change that. Hating, she found, did not stop you loving – not at all. So the words that haunted her were at once unbearable and futile. She did not believe in them.

She thought Hector perhaps had perceived that, by the infinitely sorrowful questioning look he gave her as they said goodbye. It occurred to her that he actually wanted her to be happy; and for this, she must stop loving him. And this was beyond his power. That made her pity him, for she knew how bitterly conscious he was of his failures, and now here was another. How could they have arrived at a position of such hideous complexity? It just seemed to happen, as the strings of Louis's marionette, carefully laid in his toy-box, would always be hopelessly tangled when he took it out again.

So she had seized on this: the drink. A simplicity. Giving up drinking meant a change, and surely one change always followed another. So. Sceaux, and sewing. Sewing at Sceaux. In the unearthly tingle of continued sobriety, odd little near-jokes like this kept popping up in her mind. The youth who brought her provisions from two dingy little shops at the other end of the steep street had a missing front tooth through which he whistled endlessly and tunelessly. When she bit on an especially hard piece of gristle in the veal-and-ham pie he brought, she was convinced for a moment that she had broken a tooth. Now we'll be the same, she thought, and imagined opening the door to him and greeting him with a windy whistle. She burst out in a sort of laughter, until the echo of it in those empty rooms appalled her.

Hector wrote her from Nice, where his doctor had recommended he rest: he was gaunt, his face painfully alive with nervous tics. His tone was kindly, impartial – also, she thought, a little hectoring. (There was another one – but she didn't laugh.) He urged her to keep trying – as if, she thought, he suspected she had already failed. She fired off an indignant reply, telling him, truthfully, that she had not touched drink for a fortnight.

A fortnight. That evening, as she opened the window to let out the marshy smell and took up the hateful sewing and listened to the shuffling stomachy noises of cows being driven home beyond the garden wall, Harriet marvelled. A fortnight: that meant she had done it. And she hadn't even congratulated herself. The marvelling rose to pride, and then a pitch of angry assertion. To go a fortnight in this dreary hole without so much as a glass of wine was not merely a triumph: it was excessive. It was beyond what anyone could rationally expect. Excess, after all, was the problem.

The notion of rewarding herself for her efforts took hold. A glass or two of red wine before her bread-and-cheese supper appeared to her as so perfectly fitting that its impossibility struck like an insult. Her walks had not taken her much further than the end of the street – people stared so – but she knew there was a wine-shop just past the mill. She thought about it: pictured it, torturingly. Pipe-smoke and spit and a fat-armed *patronne* glowering behind the deal counter. A solitary woman – a stranger – a foreigner, walking in there and asking for a drink . . . She might as well proclaim herself a prostitute. Probably they would report her to the *mairie* and have her drummed out of town. The certainty of this did not so much quench her desire as fan it into white-hot righteousness.

She threw down the sewing. A beetle whirred in through the window, encountered the candle-flame, and fell with a click like a dropped button. Harriet stared at it for a long time, then rose and went to bed supperless: if not to sleep, to wait.

And in the end there was no difficulty. The boy added a bottle of wine to his list without comment – and why should he? Harriet thought: this was France after all, you had wine as you had bread or salt.

She kept it until the evening. She read a great deal, she sorted her laundry, she even had a long conversation in the garden with the old vintner, who cloudily informed her that France was a rotting corpse, which could only be revived by a Bonaparte. When the time came to light the candles, Harriet enjoyed a feeling of calm, warm ceremoniousness, rather like Christmas. She drank the wine with her supper. It tasted very pleasant. It tasted like wine. All the absurd portentous mystery dissolved before her pricking eyes: she realized that both she and Hector had been making altogether too much of this. Some time soon, she felt, they would both be laughing at it. Before she went to bed she noticed that the dead beetle still lay on the floorboards, but she decided to ignore it. For several hours she slept peacefully.

She woke before first summer light, woke with galvanic starts and strangled breath and a sensation of something grievously unfinished that must, must be done. When the birdsong began she lay and cursed at it: its shrilling, its pointlessness.

The trouble with the wine, she realized, was that it was not really her drink. So it had unsettled her. Better to be comfortable: to know where you are. And so that night, and the following night, she was much more comfortable with the brandy that the boy brought in his basket. She was more herself. This seemed important.

The day after that it was gone, so she had to ask him to get her some more. He studied her sidelong, his strawberry tongue wriggling between his teeth.

'I don't know,' he said, wiping his nose on his knuckle with sticky, leisurely enjoyment. 'I'm not sure I shall be able to get you any more.'

'Why? I have money. There surely can't be a shortage of brandy in Sceaux.' She was lofty, but was sure he could hear the busy thumping of her heart: certainly it was deafening her.

'I don't know.' He admired the back of his hand. 'It might be difficult, Madame. That's all.'

So she bribed him sufficiently, and when he came back that afternoon he grinned at her over his lifted basket as if they were sharing the most gleeful joke in the world.

However, he was gone, as all such annoyances must go: so the first glass of brandy told her, and the first was never wrong. The later ones couldn't always be trusted; though they often had interesting things to say. It was the middle ones, as it were, that were the sweet core of the experience. There, the mind lifted like a boat on a gentle tide: troubles did not disappear, but they stayed on the bank, away from you, and you could even look at them from a different angle as you drifted by. Around her the panelling creaked like an old man stretching. The faded striped chair that she had found so uncomfortable welcomed her, and sun like syrup filled the window and dripped along the floor to her crossed feet. How small and dainty her feet were: or perhaps that was because her body had grown so large. There was a cracked square of mirror in her bedroom, if she wanted to go and look, to do the gypsy dance, crouching and straightening and turning, of revelation. But I don't. Why should I? What can it matter? This also seemed important. Her skirts also seemed fantastically creased, as if she had lain down in her clothes lately. Which hadn't happened, and wasn't important. These things weren't, and it was important (there was another one) to remember this – like her guardian's shoes, so old and shallow and bunion-accommodating. Think of those, if you wanted an example of something: she wasn't sure what. The beetle, she saw, was still there. A sort of companion.

Now here was Anne presenting herself to her mind, but not too badly, as we're still in the middle of the drinks: not with guilt and anguish. Harriet was even able to apologize to her, for deserting her, for letting her down. She said it out loud: there was no one to hear. 'I'm sorry, Anne.' And for killing me? Anne put the question with her old elfin look over her bony shoulder. Well, surely that's – that's putting it too strongly. Is it? – I didn't live long after you left me. Yes, but you were never strong . . . – Wasn't I? I think there was a great strength about me. It stood up against you marrying that man – and wasn't I right?

'No,' Harriet cried, getting up and pacing around. 'No.' No, because we have – we have Louis, and we had years of happiness and, besides we still have each other and always will. In a way I don't expect you to understand – I don't know if anyone can understand. You might have once, Mama – not now. Mrs Smithson was a distant and vague shape, only the sketch that Joseph had given her in his last letter: living with her relatives in Bristol, drink given up for devotion, a poor relation sighing over her Bible. No, Joseph whispered, flickering into view, she never mentions you now. Perhaps Joseph might understand – but he was quickly fading, would not be addressed: he had gone abroad, shadowed by rumours of a scandal with another actor, and was lost to her. Well, I certainly don't expect *you* to understand, she snapped, as Frank Cope smirked at her from the armchair, crossing his long Walking-Gentleman legs. All I understand, he smiled, is that your man's found another skirt to lift, and that's what it all comes down to in the end.

She poured another glass, noticing with interest that this was the only time her hand did not shake. Precious fluid. Precious preservative. Were the words related? Her guardian would have known. That's what I've always needed, she thought, someone who knew things. Her father materialized sorrowfully: Did I, then, know nothing? Not a great deal, Papa, I fear. Not even yourself. But you did know Shakespeare, and for that I thank you. And you too, Mr Kean. Dead now these ten years and more. But what an exit, cried Mr Kean, vaporizing Frank Cope with his Mephistophelian breath and leaping into the chair to grin at her: what an exit, Miss Smithson, collapsing right in the middle of *Othello*, sinking there and then on the stage! Could anything be more Romantic? He cocked a hard gem-like eye about the room. And, my dear Miss Smithson, could anything be less Romantic than this?

I don't know about that, sir. Loneliness, longing, drink. Have you not heard my husband's *Symphonie Fantastique*? 'Episode in the life of an artist' is the subtitle. The artist goes through tremendous torments for love. He takes opium. He dreams he has murdered his beloved. *Put out the light, and then put out the light.* Harriet sought the bottle, laying her fingers against its coolness. *It is the cause, it is the cause, my soul.* Then, you see, under the opium he dreams of a witches' sabbath and she is one of them. Oh, no, not the witches. (Over in the corner Bridget nodded ominously.) 'This is how artists are, it seems,' Harriet announced, filling her glass. I should know, I was one, once. I know, growled Mr Kean, tenderly, as he left her. Wait, tell me something, Mr Kean, how could he do it? How could Othello kill her? *O, banish me, my lord, but kill me not.* Poor Eliza from Drury Lane sauntered sadly by, shabby heels dragging: they all do, she said, they all do in the end. *But I do think it is their husbands' fault if wives do fall.* Adèle, Adèle, what do you think? Can't you help me? But Adèle shimmered, holding out a helpless hand, fading. Harriet moved to sit down, missed the edge of the seat, hit the floor with a bump. It was surprisingly painful, so surprising she started laughing, or possibly crying. From outside came a rumble of wheels. Ah, here they come. Remember it, think of it: the place de L'Odéon packed with carriages, the theatre like a great stirred hive. Mr Kemble doing loud, nervous throat exercises. The prompter in a panic over his lost spectacles. Twang of gas and hot velvet and floor-chalk. The stage, where you lived, first, last, only life.

Along the floorboards late liquid light found the dead beetle and ennobled it with a shadow as long as a pencil. 'My audience,' Harriet said softly. No worse than Buxton out of season. The equivocal noise escaped her again. Come, stop it, the carriages are here, you must perform. You must be Desdemona, nothing else. How beautiful it was, that concentration, that shedding of everything.

'My mother had a maid call'd Barbary:'

(Gabrielle appeared scowling, but Harriet glared her up the chimney.)

'She was in love; and he she loved proved mad,
And did forsake her. She had a song of "willow";
An old thing 'twas; but it express'd her fortune,
And she died singing it.'

Her mind groped for the tune they had used at the Odéon. A drink might help her remember, but the table with the bottle and glass seemed to stand unreachable at the end of a titanic perspective. Not much of a tune, she was sure. Hector should set the words. Yes, she would suggest it to him. Oh, yes, here it came. Her throat felt like a rusty hinge as she sang.

'Sing all a green willow must be my garland.
Let nobody blame him; his scorn I approve—

'Nay, that's not next. Who is't that knocks?'

And somebody really was knocking. Life and art: just went to show something. Had she disturbed the old miser? Well, let him stew, let him go and boil his head. Not that you could stew and boil at the same time. Now she made a noise perfectly pitched between laughing and crying. A balance, you see, that's what's needed. Come, come, you're losing your audience.

'. . . Mine eyes do itch:
Doth that bode weeping?'

No response. 'Prompt, prompt, damn it,' she snapped. Her elbow was hurting: she realized it was because she had fallen on it. Prompt, prompt. And prompt he came, giving up his knocking and finding the door unlocked and coming in upon her there, Hector.

She found a moment to admire the way he navigated the room, stepped over the discarded shoes (when?) and the newspaper and the trampled sewing, the way his eyes swept over the table and the bottle and the glass, taking it all in. How tall he was, she thought, blinking up at the rigid pillar of him, though he was not a particularly tall man. That was the trouble with the later drinks, they made you inconsequential. She tried to say something. She tried to anyalyse the look they exchanged. Far off beyond the impassable mountains of estrangement she fancied there was a faint glow – of mutual recognition: of failure. But perhaps the time for fancies was past.

Prompt, prompt, damn it. Oh, yes.

'Kill me tomorrow: let me live tonight!'

Interlude: Mendelssohn

L ONDON. Easter vacation lately over, and the orchestra of the Philharmonic Society rehearsing in the Hanover Square Rooms for their new season. A long rehearsal, too: longer than they are used to, as may be seen by the disgruntled looks as they pour out of the hall into the chill dusk. A spring dusk – but recognizable as such only by the habituated Londoner.

Fog everywhere. Fog roiling up Regent Street, where it offends the lungs and spoils the curled whiskers of the fashionable gentleman descending the steps to his carriage for a dinner engagement. Fog stealing down Bond Street, where the jewellers and dressmakers, with a couple of hours' trading still left, are obliged to light the lamps early in the pilastered and curlicued windows. Fog densest in the poorest parts of the great city, skulking up the rotten riverside steps of Limehouse and infesting the narrow courts of Seven Dials: but fog quite at home, too, out west among the squares, saddening the trees in Hyde Park, and even darkening the already dingy and smoky apartments of Buckingham Palace, where the young Queen Victoria – rather hipped from the discomforts of expecting another little royal stranger – has been refreshing her spirits by singing over some favourite *lieder* by her favourite composer, Mr Mendelssohn.

Whom you are appointed to meet. He it is who has been rehearsing the Philharmonic Orchestra beyond their wont, and who is still in animated discussion with the leader as you wait on him in the lobby of the Argyll Rooms.

All apologies for his lateness, he darts at your hand, gives it the quickest of shakes, and presses you, if you will be so good, to walk a way with him. He is staying at Kensington, but as a prodigious walker he finds it no great distance; he is, besides, a little agitated – *agitato*, perhaps – and vigorous perambulation, he explains, helps to work the feeling off.

Mr Felix Mendelssohn is a handsome, athletic man in his middle thirties: well dressed, his richly dark and curling hair and whisker well barbered: with a high, luminous forehead, a keen dark eye and an incisive profile: much quickness and delicacy in his speech and movement, and withal perhaps a certain impatience, which may be responsible for those two sharp headachy grooves between his eyebrows. You are reminded a little of the illustrations of young Martin in the latest number of Boz's *Martin Chuzzlewit*, which you have been reading on the journey here. Mr Mendelssohn speaks fluent English, with only a faint buzzing on the sound *th* to betray his German origin; and he soon puts you at your ease, conversing genially as he strides briskly along.

– Not at all, not at all, he says, when you apologize for bearding him at the end of a tiring day.

– The fact is, I am never tired. Or, to put it another way, I am always tired. (Mr Mendelssohn's laugh is quick and abbreviated, as if to save time.) I would not have it any other way, of course.

You remark, as he nimbly guides you down a side-turning away from the press of drays and carriages, that he seems to know these streets like a native.

– I consider myself little less, he says, with a smile. – This is my, let's see, seventh or eighth time here. The English have been kind enough to take me to their hearts, and it is an affection I warmly reciprocate. I have even become almost fond of this (waving a hand at the fog). Alas, when my late father came with me on one visit the climate was something he could not abide. I remember the look on his face when the barber cheerfully said what a fine morning it was: the sky at the window was the colour of weak tea. I was able to assure him there was one thing thicker than an English fog, and that is an English pudding. These are quibbles. I may say I feel just as at home here as in Germany.

And the admiration of the English, you say flatteringly, extends to the highest in the land, does it not?

– You force me to a boast. Yes, I was most civilly received at the palace by the Queen and the Prince, who are thoroughly musical. The Queen was good enough to sing one of my songs, and very well. It was all charmingly domestic, no ceremony. It is a great *canard* that the English are an unmusical nation. Certainly musical education here is lacking. But not talent or taste.

And the orchestras, you venture, remembering the looks on the faces leaving the Argyll Rooms – are they satisfactory?

– I have yet to find a satisfactory orchestra anywhere. They all tend to be hidebound, they resist anything new. You have to coax them over fences like stubborn horses. And sometimes they will not jump at all, which I regret was the case today with the orchestra of the Philharmonic Society, usually excellent. I brought with me the C major symphony of Schubert, hoping to introduce this wonderful work to these shores. It was never heard in his lifetime – it lay undisturbed, unsuspected until my good friend Herr Schumann discovered it on a visit to Vienna, in a trove of papers belonging to Schubert's brother. What a revelation! To my regret, these players – (he jabs a thumb over his shoulder with surprising violence) – found the revelation beyond them. There is a repeated triplet figure in the finale which made them – unmanageable. They actually burst out laughing. So, I have withdrawn the work.

There always seems to be this resistance to the new and daring in art, you say – as, for instance, in the work of Monsieur Berlioz . . .

– Monsieur Berlioz, of course, yes, now, what can I tell you? Well, first let me record my great respect and esteem for Monsieur Berlioz as a man. I know few who are so cultivated, intelligent and sensible. I had the pleasure of renewing our acquaintance at Leipzig last year. Monsieur Berlioz was touring Germany, and I was supervising the Gewandhaus season, and so I was more than glad to assist him in setting up concerts of his works. A renewed acquaintance, yes – we first met many years ago, in the most piquant and memorable circumstances. Rome. I was touring Italy, and Monsieur Berlioz was studying at the Villa Medici after winning the Prix de Rome for composition, and not finding it very profitable. I quite understood that – in Rome one is entranced by all one sees, but the musician can only be disgusted by what he hears. We struck up a friendship – all the more gratifying, I think, because there were so many points on which we disagreed. I take it, from your original request, that you wish me to be absolutely frank about Monsieur Berlioz? Very well. Though I liked him and enjoyed his company, I found at first something rather theatrical about him. He was at that time engaged to Mademoiselle Moke, the pianist, but one gathers that all was not well in that quarter. This I felt he made rather a *parade* of. Forgive me. Generally I am not fond of those who talk a great deal of their feelings.

Perhaps, you say unwisely, that is what endears you to the English. Mr Mendelssohn does not smile.

– Perhaps so. Of course, Monsieur Berlioz was very young then. (Mr Mendelssohn, you estimate, must have been still younger: but you have a presentiment that he has never been young in quite the usual way.) I found his youthful enthusiasms excessive, but when he was calm he showed admirable judgement. He called at my lodgings most mornings: we talked of music and literature, we sang, sometimes we argued politely. For Monsieur Berlioz Bach was an old dry windbag who had nothing to teach us. Sometimes I would tease by saying, 'Your pupil, Bach.' He always took it in good part. When he was very melancholy he would lie face down on my sofa and listen to me play, murmuring to himself. When he was lively we would go riding in the Campagna, or walking among the ruins. Once we were exploring the Baths of Caracalla, and the sight of these sublime fragments of a vanished age set him to talking of the comparative characteristics of religions. It was often his pleasure to vex me in this way, knowing I was devout. *Am* devout. He suggested that these pagan relics would find a counterpart in future ages, in the disused shells of Christian churches. I disputed with him, of course, most hotly. He contended that the pagan system of propitiation and sacrifice, which I deplored, was no more absurd than Christian morality, with what he called its ridiculous belief that good or bad actions in this life have a determining effect on the afterlife. I confess I was so incensed that I scarcely looked where I was walking – inadvisable among those crumbling stones – and down I fell. Monsieur Berlioz, helping me up, laughed most heartily. 'There,' said he, 'there's my proof. Divine justice? I blaspheme, and you suffer.' Hm. After that we took care not to talk of religion. He is French, of course: they have this regrettable tendency to free-thinking.

It was suggested to me, you say, by someone I believe you know well – Monsieur Chopin – that Monsieur Berlioz is somehow not properly French, and this accounts for his neglect in his native country.

– An interesting notion, says Mr Mendelssohn. – Certainly when he came to Germany he received a cordial welcome. Audiences there are more inclined to investigate the – the unusual. Our orchestras impressed him, which is understandable. When I first went to Paris I was shocked by the thinness, the superficial quality of musical life there, and I know it has not improved . . .

Mr Mendelssohn stops and directs a sorrowful look at a nearby doorway. A baby-minder, a poor, patched, wretched old woman with a face like grey leather, exhibits her starveling charge and proffers a trembling palm. Shaking his head, Mr Mendelssohn strides on: then, changing his mind, dodges back and places money in her hand.

– One does not know quite what to do, he says, biting his lip. – One cannot pass by on the other side, and yet one cannot give to *all* the poor creatures one sees in this city: nor would one begin to relieve their distresses if one did. London is a monster, I find. There is in it everything that is fabulous and extreme. Well: Monsieur Berlioz, yes, Germany has treated him rather better. He admitted to me that the one thing he did not like about Germany was the constant puffing of pipe-smoke: this offended him. I could not help but be amused, considering the manifold indecencies that Paris presents on every corner.

Perhaps at this point, you say tentatively, you might raise the question of Madame Berlioz and . . .

– I have not had the pleasure of Madame Berlioz's acquaintance, Mr Mendelssohn says crisply. And I understand that she and Monsieur Berlioz now live apart.

Quite, you say. Wondering how to proceed, you become absent-minded. Mr Mendelssohn, with a civil hand at your elbow, prevents your getting run down by a fast hackney, though you still come in for a splashing. Across the street a costermonger, all corduroy and neckcloth, with the complexion of a boy and the eyes of an ancient Satan, laughs at you, calling you unthinkably obscene names the while. Recovering yourself, you ask: did Mr Mendelssohn never see her perform?

– Never. I did see Mr Kemble in *Hamlet* at Drury Lane, on my first visit here. I found it all rather showy and eccentric. But I am not a great admirer of the theatre. I heard, of course, about Miss Smithson's fame – who did not? And I much esteem her company for bringing the genius of Shakespeare to a people who had never recognized it. I was fortunate enough to be introduced to Shakespeare at a very young age. My sister and I always adored him. I have some music to *A Midsummer Night's Dream* in rehearsal now, which I hope the poet's compatriots will like. We presented it with the play in Berlin – where, alas, the play was not liked. What is this strange mixture – fairies, lovers, clowns? As if everything must be one thing or another. But the Berliners are very stupid. As for Miss Smithson, it always seemed to me a great pity that such gifts, and such a nature – for I understand she was both charming and modest – must be at the service of so hazardous and disreputable a profession. It seems to me hardly possible that a woman can have a public career of that sort and keep her character. One must lament the lack of early guidance that allowed it to happen. My sister Fanny showed great musical talent from childhood, but thankfully it was always understood that this must remain in the private and domestic sphere. Even I found myself long dissuaded by my father from adopting music as a profession – for the soundest of reasons. But Miss Smithson plainly was not so lucky.

And one must pity her situation now, you suggest – as it appears the separation is complete, and that Monsieur Berlioz has . . . entered into another association.

Mr Mendelssohn frowns, his lips thin.

– Well, I will say what I know, though the subject is distasteful to me. When he came to Leipzig last year, it was in company with a singer named Mademoiselle Recio. Marie Recio. Not a singer of tremendous ability – and whatever else one may say about Monsieur Berlioz, he is exacting in his standards of performance. So one naturally wondered. Herr Schumann had come to Leipzig to take up a post at the Conservatoire, and was eager to meet Monsieur Berlioz, and had some talk with him. Afterwards he told me that Mademoiselle Recio was *not* merely Monsieur Berlioz's concert singer – and Herr Schumann is the last man in the world for idle gossip. So. There it is. I regret it, as one must regret all such liaisons. And it surprises and saddens me. No matter what his other qualities, I do not think Monsieur Berlioz is a man who lightly conducts *affaires*: he is altogether too serious: he is not like Herr Liszt, for example, who freely takes moral liberties as he takes artistic liberties at the keyboard. Forgive me, you find me a stern critic perhaps.

You have the greatest respect for Mr Mendelssohn's opinions, you tell him: and on that subject, you have sensed a certain reserve about the music of Monsieur Berlioz himself . . . ?

– Very well, says Mr Mendelssohn, with a smile that is a little wry and also a little cross, very well, I shall continue with this unwarranted frankness, and say I do not like the music of Monsieur Berlioz. I have come across an admirable English word which I must use: it is *drivel*. I have even felt, after examining one of his scores, that I needed to wash my hands. And it isn't that I don't *want* to like it, as I'm afraid is the case with the audiences in France: I was always fascinated and touched by what he told me of his intentions for music, the new expressive devices he sought, the freshness of inspiration – yes, yes, absolutely, thought I. And then came this incomprehensible, nonsensical, lopsided mess of music, exaggerated effects covering up the weakness of technique . . . It is a great sadness to me. He toils on convinced that one day the world will catch up with his art, and all the time—

But is this not comparable with the Schubert symphony you have been rehearsing, you put in excitedly – a piece that conservative musicians still take against, only because they refuse to, as it were, open their ears?

There is perfect politeness in the attentive tilt of Mr Mendelssohn's handsome head, and yet you feel he does not much like being interrupted, or contradicted.

– The fact is, he says, with fine-drawn patience, Monsieur Berlioz lacked a thorough and proper training – leaving aside the question of how much talent there was to begin with. In this I was fortunate, as I am well aware: I was raised in a cultured home, where any gifts were recognized and encouraged and, above all, rigorously trained. Oh, I know what some people say about me. It has all been very easy for Mendelssohn, his family was rich, he had every opportunity, the public love him, he has the art of pleasing. As we are being frank, and as we are going to part in a moment, I may as well add that I sometimes wonder, in my secret heart, whether they would say these things if I were not in origin Jewish. Well, never mind that. Who gets their just rewards in this life? Who can say, who can decide? Monsieur Berlioz is a man who works fearfully hard, with little success. I am a man who works fearfully hard, with, thank God, a good measure of success: but still I work fearfully hard. At night I sleep badly – that is, my body resists sleep, it objects to it, it kicks and twitches and says, Come, come, you have your duties at the Berlin Academy, remember those, and then the commission for Birmingham, think of that, and then there are the concerts to conduct in Leipzig, you must those prepare also – (in his agitation Mr Mendelssohn, for the first time, loses his idiomatic English) – and it is a relief to be up, to be not resting. I miss my wife, my children. But I have to do it. Monsieur Berlioz is not the only one who is – who is driven. (Mr Mendelssohn realizes he is blocking the path of a wide-skirted, much-flounced lady, and hastily moves aside with a bow and doffing of his hat. She smiles on him.)

You thank Mr Mendelssohn for his information and his frankness, and say you are afraid you have wearied him.

– Not at all, he says, with a kind and sweet smile, seeming really to mean it: though you see all at once, horribly, as if someone had thrust a lamp under his chin, his pallor and the thrust of his cheekbones and the deep, round, troubling shapes of eye-sockets. – I remember, he says, with an apologetic shrug, I remember as a child my dear mother raising her head from her sewing, and looking suspiciously over her shoulder and saying: 'Felix, are you doing nothing?'

Mr Mendelssohn laughs, a full laugh this time, very attractive and, if you like, untrained. He darts at your hand again, shakes it and, having assured himself that you know quite where you are (Orchard Street) and will be able to get home, plunges into the tumult of London – adding only, in a peculiarly pained voice: If you see Monsieur Berlioz, please give him my warmest regards.

EPISODE IN THE LIFE
OF AN ARTIST

Fourth Movement: March to the Scaffold

Allegretto non troppo

1

'There is only one way to salvation,' insists the visiting *curé*. He holds up a sharp snuff-stained forefinger, impressively, or at least he thinks it impressive: as if *one* is a startling new idea that his hearer can never have come across. 'One way, sir. Do not be seduced by any of these free-thinking notions that offer the soul an easier passage. There is only one way a man may be saved.'

And Dr Louis Berlioz listens with tolerant attention. Possibly the long, gaunt, suffering face that perturbs him each morning in his shaving-mirror is the kind of face that excites a determined priest like this one, a visiting cousin of one of Dr Berlioz's friends in La Côte St André: the man has fastened on him, haunts him, seems to see in him splendid possibilities. Lonely godless man of science ageing, sickly, staring mortality in the face: what an opportunity. Dr Berlioz puts up with the — he privately relishes the pun — visitations. After seventy years' experience, he considers it unlikely that a bustling young fanatic in a snuff-covered *soutane* will have anything remarkable to convey to him, but he is prepared to try. What distracts him is the undeniable, the riotous growth of beard on the *curé*'s cheeks. Plainly the man has recently shaved, and just as plainly nothing but fire or castration would keep it down. This would make Dr Berlioz laugh, if he ever did laugh nowadays: that frantic celibacy, while sex keeps urgently sprouting from his face.

Why do we lie, wonders Dr Berlioz, when he is sufficiently well and sufficiently far from despair to do such a strenuous thing as wondering, why do we lie about so many things? Example, this young priest, who

333

lies in pretending to believe that human life has one simple answer – and it is far too complex for that, even if we were scuttling cockroaches it would still be too complex for that. Example, me, when I say that I miss Finette and life hasn't been the same without her: I loved her and love her memory, but I have grown older without her, and gone through other things alone, and if I saw her now I wouldn't know what to say to her. Example, Hector, when he came to visit us last summer, in the fearful heat that made his hair stick to his head and it altered him, made him look faintly furtive and untrustworthy, which is not like Hector at all, and he would say nothing to me of how he is living, and it took Adèle to hint to me about this woman he's with. And why this lie, when I always said it: when he married that poor Irish actress I said it – he will leave her for another.

That was why I was against it. Nothing to do with that poor actress: I pity her: and wish I had met her. I just knew.

The recent visit by Hector coincided with a concert of his music that was being performed at Lyon, thirty miles from La Côte St André. Adèle and Nancy went to it: Dr Berlioz did not. He is still not sure why. He has never yet heard a note of his son's music. He considers that he probably never will.

Why this should be is another unanswerable question, like why we lie. All Dr Berlioz can say is, that as we grow older, we want less: we enter the box-room, sort through the tempting lumber with a reluctant ruthlessness: set aside: choose. Or perhaps the image of a journey is better. The last stages of it are taxing and primitive, so the less baggage the better. There are many things Dr Berlioz now simply does not do: practise medicine: stir beyond La Côte St André: read, except for old familiar books known by heart: eat, except when forced by Monique. He does not take the tea with which the *curé* is thirstily refreshing himself in the intervals of his harangue. He can do without.

He cannot do without the opium: that is different. But he needs more and more of it. He has had recourse occasionally to huge doses, which seem to threaten a final oblivion – not that he much minds that: let chance have its way.

Hector looked drawn the last time he saw him, he thinks, drawn and somehow severe. His lips were tight as if he were perpetually biting on something: something small and hard and pungent, like a clove: like his pride.

Dr Berlioz understands that his daughter-in-law now lives alone in Paris, except when Louis visits her from school, and that Hector continues to support her. So she, too, is doing without. Sometimes he tries to picture her in her solitude, and it is then that he feels a curious link with the woman he will never see. He imagines that she thinks a lot, which further inclines him to her. He hopes that in the course of her thinking she does not regret. Regret is the surrendering of thought to its seducer and betrayer, emotion. That is Hector's trouble. It's not that Hector doesn't think: he has a wonderful intellect. But, reflects Dr Berlioz, with uncharacteristic crudity, it is always flat on its back getting poked.

Monique is there: more tea for the *curé*? And perhaps one of her curd-tarts? Monique venerates all priests. Certainly, certainly, whatever the *curé* wants. He will not get what he most wants from Dr Berlioz, of course.

'I will accept, sir, for the sake of argument,' says Dr Berlioz, suddenly, 'that there is only one way to be saved. But I put to you this counter-proposition: are there not many, many ways in which a man may be damned?'

The Damnation of Faust.

For weeks the Paris papers have been full of references to the coming première of this remarkable work by Monsieur Hector Berlioz, conceived during his recent and triumphant tour of Germany – and so on. One gets tired of these puffs. Paris is shivering under a miserable winter, stocks are down, the government is jittery. If I stir out for anything in this weather, it'll be a good show at the Opéra. And what *is* this Faust thing? Concert-opera? What does that mean, no sets or costumes? I dare say that sort of thing might suit the Prussians. Dreadful dowdies. And at the Opéra-Comique of all places – on a Sunday afternoon? Really, one doesn't . . . Have you seen the prices flour is fetching? Oh, something must be done. And I'll tell you what it is . . .

The Damnation of Faust. What is it? It is a vast work for two hundred performers – soloists, chorus, orchestra – on which Hector has been fever-ishly labouring for over a year, sometimes on coach and rail journeys, at café tables and in hotel lobbies, whenever a moment has presented itself. He has written the words too. And now he has had the parts copied, at enormous expense, and hired and rehearsed his forces, likewise, and hired the Opéra-Comique – the only place he could get – for a further, unthinkable sixteen hundred francs; and now, on this lightless December afternoon with dirty melting snow making a harsh monochrome of the Paris streets, soaking skirts and trouser-legs and upsetting carriages and souring tempers – now, he must take up his baton and mount the conductor's rostrum, and stand: or fall.

The Damnation of Faust: it is the Faust legend passed through the bubbling retorts and naked flames of Hector's imagination. In this version it is Faust himself, the lonely, proud dreamer, the overreacher seeking to venture beyond mortal scope, who stands at the centre: there is less of Marguerite, the innocent girl who loves and is betrayed by him. (But still she is there behind everything: oh, yes.) And once tempted by Mephistopheles, there is no way back for this Faust, no redemption from the diabolic pact. Defeated, he descends to the abyss. This Faust is damned.

The Damnation of Faust is damned.

Oh, they listen: they wonder at the strange blazes and chills with which Hector's orchestra afflicts them: they applaud the grand strokes: the critics prepare favourable notices. But the auditorium of the Opéra-Comique is only half full: less than half, surely. Every bronchial croak and shuffling of snow-numbed feet echoes around the space, like devilish laughter. Paris, in fact, does not give a damn.

Afterwards, having thanked the orchestra and singers, and seen Marie to a cab, and established in his mind a reasonable estimate – six thousand francs – of his ruinous debts, Hector walks home to the rue de Provence alone, through the slush that is beginning to freeze again under the December starlight. Everywhere around him people are slipping and falling: some laugh, some curse: others bend their backs and proceed with toe-clenching care and slowness. But Hector, thinly shod, striding, unseeing, takes no care at all; and does not lose his footing for a moment. A charmed life, you might say: or, that more ominous phrase, the devil's own luck.

The damnation of Faust proceeds by relentless steps. Hector wonders, in a blank, cold, frozen way, whether the same thing has happened to him.

Sure, unstoppable steps in the damnation of Hector.

First, inevitably, this: setting eyes on Mademoiselle Marie Recio.

No fanfares. A rather dull *soirée*, which his publisher has urged him to attend in the hope of seeing someone important from the Opéra, who is not there after all. The sort of evening at which music is not so much promised as threatened. A pianist simpers up and down the keyboard. Men compete with the heartiness of their laughs. A slender dark young woman is led to the piano. Her voice is pure-toned but nervous and unsteady. A *roué* in an elevated wig and malicious little spectacles leans over to Hector.

'Very pretty woman, eh?'

'Not really,' Hector says.

Not really: that's not what you'd call her. For a moment Hector meets a pair of arrestingly black eyes. Usually the eyes called black are dark brown, but not these.

The singing goes on, and wearies him. He turns his mind to the article he has to finish for tomorrow. Later, at some point, there is an introduction: Mademoiselle Whoever. She says something about admiring his music, but by then he is too tired and bored to listen.

He does not quite forget the eyes.

Another performance at the Opéra: Hector in his usual seat, notebook in hand, to prepare the usual review. (Once or twice he has had a dream about all the reviews he has written: he wrests open a door, and they come toppling down on him, not fluttering singly but in great bundles: he seems to hear his neck snapping as he wakes.) Donizetti's *La Favorita*. He struggles to find ways to express a fair opinion of it while disguising how much he loathes it and keeping off the flavour of sour grapes. Donizetti never fails.

He is too far from the stage to see much of the eyes of the singer playing the confidante: so he must remember more of her than he thought. He looks at his programme. Mademoiselle Recio, that was it. He knew that already, somewhere.

Another *soirée*, noisy and crowded. Across the room, Mademoiselle Recio is winding her way towards him. Very slim waist, long, flexuous arms: she seems to insinuate herself through the narrowest of gaps. Purposeful, very.

'Monsieur Berlioz, I wished to thank you in person for the kind notice you gave my performance in the *Journal des débats*. From so eminent a musician, to one who is a mere novice, it was more gratifying than I can express.'

'Not at all, Mademoiselle. I am happy to give a fine artist her due.' What is he saying? Mademoiselle Recio's voice holds up very badly under pressure, and her taste is erratic.

But then, of course, neither of them is saying what they are really saying. That is something else entirely, something like the perfume that rises from her trim bodice: dark, elusive, undeniable.

Another night at the Opéra, another review to write. Sometimes he feels that he could hardly bear this, if it were not for the fact that it prevents him thinking of the other thing. The other life, in the rue de Londres: Harriet: the unstoppable haemorrhaging of their marriage. Once he is out, he closes down all thoughts of that other life. Enough that it begins when he reaches the apartment door, and opens it, and the battle is joined. Keep it separate. It can be done.

It can be done, and probably somewhere in his mind he has taken note of this, and seen that it may have other applications. But he doesn't know it yet. He is surprised and puzzled when a man he knows bends over his seat and remarks: 'Here to see your favourite, eh?'

What favourite? He looks at his programme, and her name confronts him again. He finds himself adding to it, from private knowledge. Mademoiselle Marie Recio. Marie.

'We must live apart. Harriet, you know this can't go on. We must live apart.' He has said this so many times, in so many different ways – and, God help them, in so many positions, with her clinging to his knees, with him covering his head as she wildly bats her empty brandy-bottle about his shoulders, with both of them slumped exhausted in the powdery light of dawn – that the words have become both meaningless and bizarre to him. This must be how priests feel, intoning their paternosters and nomine-domines.

While he goes round the apartment picking up broken glass, bent at the waist and wearily deft like a gleaning peasant, Harriet rages at him about another woman. And taste this for bitter-black thrice-brewed irony (when does irony cease to be . . . ?) – there isn't another woman. Not now. Not yet. And with every snarl and wail, Harriet is making him want one.

Which is what men say to excuse themselves, of course. A sliver of glass slides painlessly into his thumb and shows him a little red gem: his own blood. He is oddly reassured to find that he has some.

He is lunching with Marie Recio and her mother at their apartment in the rue de Provence, and feeling very awkward. Marie's mother is a thick-set, warm-hearted, garrulous Spaniard, continually tripping back and forth to flourish before him mementoes of her homeland. See this, Monsieur Berlioz, and now see this. Marie is the result of a liaison – though not a marriage – between her and an officer of Napoleon's Peninsular army. All very romantic – or not, rather. There is nothing romantic about the cramped rooms with their guitars and *prie-dieu* chairs and the oily fish, which Marie's mother keeps urging him to eat ('Look at you two! Both as thin as shadows! What a pair you make!'), and the languorous, slightly bored gestures of Marie, who presents a bare sketch of a smile to her mother's reminiscences and traces patterns on the patched cloth with her fork and sometimes stretches and arches her long, smooth neck pleasur-ably, as a cat will make itself comfortable in an unlikely place.

Well, I should never have come, thinks Hector, trying not to choke on a fishbone: this is nonsense.

'You will hardly believe, Monsieur Berlioz, how much Marie has talked of you since making your acquaintance – you, one of the most distin-guished musicians in all Paris—'

'If that is so, Madame, then I am afraid there's a mistake somewhere – you have taken me for Monsieur Adam or Monsieur Meyerbeer perhaps. In Paris the only thing I am distinguished for is the number of unpleasant cartoons of me you see in the papers.'

Coolly Marie cuts off an explosion from her mother. 'Why do you talk like that?' she asks him, with her faint husky lisp.

He tries looking at the heavy-lidded black eyes. Apart from the usual stirring, he feels nothing: or, rather, he reads a language he does not under-stand. 'I exaggerate,' he says. 'But exaggeration is only a bolder statement of the truth.'

'That's not an answer,' she says, with her small, curled smile.

'I long ago gave up expecting answers,' he says. 'It's enough if the ques-tions are interesting.' Now I'm talking in epigrams. This is nonsense. How much of this damned fish is there? I ought to go.

'You don't value yourself enough,' Marie says. 'I wonder why.'

'On the contrary, I value myself rather too highly. Part of the trouble, or the whole of it, probably. I was thinking I really ought to—'

'How splendidly we're getting on!' cries Marie's mother. 'I don't like everything all stiff and formal, and neither do you, Monsieur Berlioz, that I could tell at once. So I know you'll forgive me if I leave my daughter to entertain you for now. On Tuesdays and Fridays I lend my services to a society of charitable ladies. We distribute tracts. We sew. We do not sew well–' a gurgle of laughter, already on her way to the door '– but we sew. I am so very proud to have you as my guest, Monsieur Berlioz.'

When she has gone, Hector stares at Marie, then at his plate.

'You needn't eat that fish,' she says.

'I've tried.'

'I know.' She gets up and walks out of the room.

Which is either some sort of Spanish indication that he has insulted her, or some sort of Spanish way of excusing herself. He sits undecided, wondering what the maid has done with his hat. This is nonsense.

When, after ten minutes, he goes down the little passage he finds the door of Marie's bedroom very slightly ajar: just the kind of gap, in fact, that she would be able to slip through. He finds her sitting on the bed in a rather demure position, slightly turned from him so that a crescent of light describes the curve of buttock and thigh, wearing only her stockings and a bracelet that she is dreamily contemplating.

His uncle, Colonel Félix Marmion, comes upon him in the Café Anglais on the boulevard des Italiens, delightedly trumpeting his name through the smoke.

'Well, my boy, how goes it? Shouldn't call you boy, but you know . . .' Félix Marmion's pointed beard and whiskers are appropriately and handsomely peppered with white: he always looks just right for his age. 'What's that you're working on there? Opera, maybe, something to make us sit up? Poor stuff lately, I thought.'

'I'm afraid the Paris Opéra is closed to me, Uncle. You look well.'

'Don't feel it, Hector. Damned foot plagues me at nights. For a *sou* I'd have it cut off. Mind, I'm the picture of health next to your father. Why doesn't he leave that pesty hole and take a cure somewhere, have a change of air? Oh, well, you know him better than I do. Isn't *that* an entrancing creature?' he says, nodding at a perfectly ordinary woman without interest. 'Oh, look here, I called on your wife the other week. Felt I should make the effort. I gather things are pretty well finished between you.'

'We are – looking to find a new accommodation of interests.' Now I talk like a lawyer. 'How did she seem?'

'Hm? Oh, the same, the same, I'd say. Curious creature. Let herself go dreadfully, if you don't mind my saying so. But, of course, you know. The main thing is, she's reasonably settled, she has the boy with her when she can, what more can a man do?'

Hector gazes at his uncle. He wonders why moustaches and beards always make the lips look so very red and wet. 'I don't know,' he stammers, 'I'm not sure what you . . . Of course I want to look after Henriette no matter what—'

'Of course you do. And certainly the less she knows the better. I always bear that in mind when I go and see her. She has the general picture, nothing to be gained by details. I'm sure you agree.' He gives Hector's shoulder a heavy, teeth-chattering slap. 'That's all I need to say. We're both men of the world, aren't we?'

Hector is not sure what he says in reply – something apt, no doubt: but inside he shudders, and the shuddering goes on. The last thing he has ever wanted to be in his life is a man of the world.

Certainly – and it doesn't matter, my God, it doesn't matter – Marie has done this before. She curls her bare tapered leg around his neck and pilots his head to the right place with the absent sureness of a baker kneading dough. Thank heaven for that. Thank heaven that – greedy though she is for him – he is for her only a familiar dish prepared by a different chef. When she sees him, embraces him, guides him into her, he is only a variation on an old theme. Thank heaven no burden of mutual adoration: instead they have the measure of one another, very quickly. No soaring flights into the blue: no crashing, thank heaven, back to earth – since you have never left it.

He finds himself wondering what would happen if a bird learned to fly, but didn't learn how to land. Think of that: think of that bird: what would happen?

He laughs. Marie, dressing – a great, a holy ceremony – turns with her supple hands cantilevering her masses of rich black hair.

'What are you laughing at?'

'Nothing. Not you.'

She turns back, resuming the devotions of the mirror.

She says: 'Never do.'

Now there is this: the house at Sceaux. Hector has nothing to add.

Except, perhaps, again, he is relieved. He has been given the expected thing, and he stows it away in his pocket, and moves on. Thought so. Just goes to show. Thanks for that.

Nancy and, to a lesser extent, Adèle write letters in support. Yes, we see. Of course, it's better that you live apart, all things considered. The fact of Marie is like the margin on these letters, a blank we do not encroach upon, for obscure reasons of form. Somehow, he is sure, they have heard or guessed.

And Hector, in the vacillating moments that occur during the separation agreements, like a nerveless sagging of the knees, can always fortify himself with the images of the house at Sceaux, that ghastly demonstration that Harriet is not what she was: that his Henriette is gone. So, be tough. Above all, guard against any suspicion that when Henriette lifts her brandy-glass, it is no different from Marie clasping his face and introducing her snaky tongue into his mouth. These things are not the same. Weakness, surely, varies. Surely.

There must be some sort of meaning or symbolism in the fact that Marie accompanies him to his southern homeland, as Henriette never did: but he is too dazed by the unreality of it all to work it out. Lyon wants him for two concerts, and he has four weeks to prepare. He will be close to his family: be able to see Adèle, Nancy, his father. They, and the provincial society he fled from, will hear his music.

He and Marie arrive in Lyon by Rhône steamboat: Marie fussing mightily about the unloading of her trunks and hatboxes. He has never known that a woman could have so many clothes, and so various, cunning bits and pieces with clasps and laces and ribbons: beside her he feels as primitive as a savage in a loincloth. And how important they are, imposing tremendous choices, requiring scrupulous orchestration. Curious that she is also so comfortable out of them. Unlike Henriette, who never liked to be naked – but shut the door on that.

They have rooms at the Hôtel du Parc. While Marie unpacks the sacred trunks, Hector goes down in search of air: in the heat of a southern July dusk he feels as if he is breathing wool. Taking a turn in the hotel court-yard, he finds himself noticing the provinciality of ladies' bonnets. My God. I'll be carrying a quizzing-glass next.

'Hector! I knew we'd find you!'

The woman stepping down from the carriage is Adèle, to his aston-ishment – which she laughs at.

'Well, you needn't look so shocked. You wrote me when you were coming. And quite by chance Marc had business in Lyon today, so I said, "Let's descend on him . . ."' She hugs and kisses him: Marc Suat smiles shyly. Hector cannot think why he wants to run a mile; he has been glowing with the thought of seeing Adèle again. Unprepared, probably. He realizes he always likes to be prepared for things nowadays, like a spy continually checking his disguises and false papers.

'I'd forgotten about these summers,' he says awkwardly, wiping the perspiration from his lip. 'Darling Adèle. You look so cool. And well, very well. Monsieur Suat – welcome.' Which makes no sense, as he is the visitor here.

'Child of the frozen north,' Adèle says, watching him, seeming to see a great deal. 'Well, you must tell us everything. What are we going to hear at your concerts? I have badgered absolutely everyone I know and some I don't and we shall *make* them a success. The trouble is it is the season when the good folk of Lyon retire to the country—'

'Good folk don't come to my concerts,' he says, pleased to find he is momentarily himself. 'And how are the little ones?' Their names, their names, you fool. 'Joséphine, and Nancy—'

'Splendid, and you shall see them – we shall all see each other, a proper family reunion—'

'Hector!'

Marie has a particularly sharp, possessive way of calling his name. But she has modulated her voice to a Spanish softness by the time she reaches his side and coils her arm through his. 'Oh, forgive me, you have company.' She smiles expectantly and inclusively round the three of them. Hector feels his throat jerk like rusty clockwork.

'Not at all, let me introduce – my sister, Adèle, my brother-in-law Monsieur Suat – they—'

'And I,' says Marie, with an air of successful social smoothing, 'am Madame Berlioz.'

He has been sitting a long time with his father in the musty, shadowy study at La Côte St André, though not much has been said. The window, with its shimmering square of outside heat, looks like the open door of a furnace.

'Louis,' Hector says, struggling on, 'Louis does very well. He's always talking about his grandfather, and how much he would like to see him . . .'

Dr Berlioz, hunched dyspeptically in his chair, waves a hand. 'I know. He writes to me. Very nice, but in a way I wish he wouldn't. I have to reply, and I don't know what to write. What do you say to a boy?' A great remoteness about that *boy*: as if he had said Eskimo. But Dr Berlioz, sinking fleshlessly into his shiny black suit, is now exclusively, almost professionally old.

'Just what you would say to a man,' Hector says, trying to smile. 'After all, when I was a boy you always addressed me as an equal.'

His father is very deaf now, which means repeating what you have said; and he has developed a way, once he has heard it, of frowning and shrugging it off: that wasn't worth repeating. Hector thinks: I can't talk to him, and loneliness hits and shudders through him like a stroke on a great gong.

'I can't move my bowels,' Dr Berlioz complains, staring at the blazing window. 'You have no conception of how wretched this condition is. I've tried everything. How is Harriet?'

The first time, Hector realizes, he has ever heard his father speak that name – and in the English form, too, which he never uses. He feels strangely wrong-footed: caught out.

'Her health is not sound. But she is somewhat better than she was. We have decided, as you know, that it's better if we live apart. Louis will spend his holidays with her, and I . . . Oh, she has an apartment in the rue Blanche now. She always liked Montmartre.' We always liked Montmartre. Another exoticism: thinking *we, us*. He never thinks in those terms of Marie and himself. But then, thank heaven. 'Well, I have been driving the orchestra hard in Lyon. I think they're a little frightened of me – but would you believe who is there, in the strings? The very man you engaged to teach me guitar, all those years ago. This must be fate. Or something.' He hesitates, trying to read his father's eyes, to see past their watery film of absence. 'A sign from the gods. Virgilian. Saying, Papa, you really must come to the concert if you can possibly face the journey.'

Dr Berlioz is a long time replying – or rather not replying.

'It may be an effect of the opiates, of course,' he says, shifting and wincing. 'The blockage in the bowels.'

After the first concert at the Grand Théâtre they dine together at the hotel: Hector and Marie, Adèle and Marc, Nancy and her husband, Camille Pal.

Who has grown red and pendulously jowled, almost wattled, with prosperity and self-importance. He has the defiant ugliness of the truly successful man. He pokes an authoritative ladle into the soup-tureen, sniffing, as if protecting them all against possible poison. *À propos* the concert, Monsieur Pal talks of expenses and receipts.

'Ten thousand francs was the aim,' Hector admits.

Monsieur Pal makes a rumbling sound. 'I doubt you'll see that. Of course, the season's against you. Now, in a winter season . . .'

'Oh, but the applause,' says Adèle. 'I thought it was a wonderful success. I've made my voice hoarse from shouting bravo. I do wish Papa had come. I shall scold him for it.'

'Your father must have a care for his health, you know,' Monsieur Pal says. 'For someone of his sedentary habits, a sudden change can be ruinous for the constitution.'

'Yes, thank you, Camille,' Adèle says, not looking at him. 'I think I can say I know my own father as well as anyone.'

'It may not be ten thousand francs,' says Marie, who has been presenting to each of them a face of reposeful attention: Hector fancies he can hear her purring at them. 'Perhaps we shall see eight. But the most important consideration is the expenses. Hector knows, I've told him, that he is too inclined to be generous in his dealings. Fiddlers and pipers should not expect such rates of hire, especially in the provinces. It's absurd. They should remember, he is the genius, they are the servants of genius.'

Hector, in a tense unhappy way, is interested to see what they make of this. Marc as ever seems mentally to be elsewhere: Nancy has her

345

characteristic look of of peering round a corner at something dubious, only more so: Adèle is nakedly torn between liking to hear him called a genius and not liking Marie. Monsieur Pal sits back behind his stomach with a look of indulgent admiration.

'You have a good commercial brain, Madame,' he says. They have settled on Madame as the term of address. 'First rule of business, minimize your expenses.'

'Perhaps I should write string quartets,' Hector says, to the soup-tureen.

'Do they pay?' asks Monsieur Pal, taking him seriously.

'When we go back to Germany – oh, you cannot conceive how much Hector is wanted in Germany – we shall be careful about these things,' Marie says. 'Or, if you like, *I* shall.' Her attempt at a girlish laugh is game, if doomed. 'Presumptuous of me, I know. But if I keep an eye on the practical matters, Hector has more time to devote himself to his art.' She distributes her smile equally amongst them. 'And that makes me happy.'

Hector almost feels like applauding.

'I'm not fond of the sound of a string quartet,' Marc Suat says ruminatively. 'I don't really know about these things, but I find it – well, rather stringy. Like celery.'

'Well, of course you will only have heard amateurs,' pronounces Monsieur Pal, with such evident condescension that Hector's eyes redly tingle, and he asks, in a voice probably too forceful, too forced: 'Come, Monsieur Pal, never mind the receipts and the ledgers, tell me, what did you think of the concert? Of the music?'

Monsieur Pal chews a large piece of bread at his leisure. 'Very loud,' he says. 'Remarkably loud. Of course, Beethoven is often loud, isn't he? Though I understand he was deaf later on. I wonder if that accounts for it. There's an interesting question for you.'

Welcoming him to Bonn, Liszt seizes Hector's hand in both of his, saying through a fixed smile of agitation: 'Here we are, then, the long-awaited Beethoven Festival, and smile with me while I tell you it's a heap of shit. That's it. They've had ten years to think about it but they've only just finished the hall, there's nowhere for anyone to stay, the Rhine stinks like a sewer, the orchestra are village idiots, and I've had to raise most of the money and make the damned thing work, and now they're saying I'm taking over and using the festival to publicize myself. You look tired. It's

Symphony

good to see you. Oh, rewards of art, eh? The spirit of Beethoven must be laughing in the Elysian Fields.'

'You pagan,' Hector says.

Liszt shrugs. 'Only on Tuesdays and Thursdays.'

Probably his best friend, Liszt is also the only truly famous musician who is his partisan. He does everything in his power – which is considerable – to publicize Hector's music, which he genuinely likes. Even if he didn't, he would still be helpful. Liszt is always going out of his way to do things for other people. He has the generosity of the pure egotist: he loves himself so intensely that he wants to share it with everyone. Take a piece of me, it's gold. Hector knows this, and it only deepens his affection. With Liszt you never have to plod through the dull mud of consistency. He and his sorcerous fingers have spent the last five years touring Europe and astonishing it, making crowds stampede, making ladies faint as well as other things, making moralists mutter about diabolism. And making a mint. But of course he wants to give it all up, he hates it, his mind really yearns to scale the austere ladder of the spirit, he's going to retire to a monastery.

'Lord, make me pure, but not yet,' Hector suggests, over wine, the first evening.

Liszt thinks. 'Well, there's a time for everything.'

Unchanged, still the fine-boned conversation-stopper who swept subtly into the chapel of the British Embassy to witness Hector's marriage to Harriet, Liszt has darkened, however, or mellowed (you can never tell for sure with him), like a good painting. He has been everywhere: Italy, England, Ireland, Spain, Poland: Russia, where he politely hinted that the chatting Tsar should shut up while he played. Numerous affairs, already legendary, but probably true. This has given him an occasional shy hesitancy: have I already said this, or done this, since I've said and done everything? What should I do now – is there anything left?

Hector tells Liszt about the ideas scratching at his mind, the Faust legend: the brilliant possibilities. But . . .

'Write it. Work. My God, you've got to. If it's there, you simply can't not let it out. What are you afraid of?'

'It's big. Expensive. The Paris Opéra wouldn't take it and, anyway, it's not an opera, it's something different . . . I suppose what I'm afraid of is Paris.'

347

'Think beyond Paris. Look at the Germans, how they listen to you, actually listen. Think beyond that, Vienna, Russia. Write for the world, not for Paris.'

'You're right, of course.' He knows he is going to write the Faust work: somehow it is already there waiting for him. Like the house in which you will one day live – or the grave in which you will lie, he thinks. It's Paris that prompts the ironic-macabre in him, because he knows also that he cannot look beyond Paris, not completely. The prophet without honour. Yes, Vienna, Russia, but he wants his own country to listen to him, he can't help it. It's like a marriage that you want to work in spite of the alluring foreign mistresses . . . Oh, God, no, it isn't. Slam the door.

'So, what are they saying about me in the unholy city?' Liszt asks.

'You're a flashy charlatan who has made an unmerited fortune by imposing on the debased taste of a sensation-seeking public. The usual, in other words.'

Liszt drinks the Rhine wine in deep draughts as if it were light beer. 'That bitch Marie.'

Hector suffers a shallow plunge of his heart before he realizes who this Marie is. Marie, Countess d'Agoult, the long-serving mistress and quasi-wife with whom there has been a bitter and well-discussed parting. 'Oh, well, it needn't be her. You know what the papers are.'

'Partly her, though, partly her. She's doing everything she can. Now it's the children she's using.' Liszt refills hugely.

'Ah. How old are they now?'

Liszt gives a charming shrug. 'Old enough. The fact of the matter is, she only wants them for one reason, and that's to turn them against me. They'll do no good with her, she's always angling for the men. Ah, man. The flawed beast. She wants to redeem us.' Liszt laughs cheerfully. 'Isn't that funny? They always want to do that. Been all around the town, twice, but they still see themselves as the Madonna, there to purify men's spotted souls. Forgive me, I'm bitter, I don't mean any of it. Except the bitch, which is what she is.'

'What –' Hector sits forward with deep, nervous interest '– what was it, actually? The thing that finished you. I always thought you and Marie were . . .' He lets that evaporate.

Always courteous, Liszt considers the question. 'Well, the touring. The offers. Always threatening to take me away from her, and so on. All of it, in a way. It's sad, really. All I had to do was turn myself into a completely different person and she'd have been happy.' He scowls suddenly at his drink, as if it has been thrust unwanted into his hand. 'She won't get those children. My mother will have them. She knows how to bring up children.'

Hector nearly decides to ask him their names – but he likes him too much. Lately he is always nearly-doing things.

The Beethoven Festival is, indeed, a shambles in many ways. Bonn is too small, thieves skulk around the heat-stricken crowds, and the attendance of the King of Prussia is complicated by a family visit from Queen Victoria and Prince Albert: royalty reigns over art. The unveiling of the Beethoven statue in bronze is to be the crowning moment, and Hector often looks up at the shrouded lump, and thinks how delightful and appropriate it would be if they whisked off the canvas and it was Schubert. In the end it is Beethoven, but facing the wrong way: the notables have to shuffle round to get a look at him. The ensuing concerts fare better, but there are many and noticeable absences.

'No Mendelssohn,' Liszt says. 'And I did ask him.'

'Well, Beethoven's only been dead these twenty years. Mendelssohn prefers them actually mummified.' Funny, Hector thinks, remembering Mendelssohn with lost warmth, how your most accurate darts hit your friends. He has the music of Beethoven still in his head, and it loosens his tongue like wine. 'Listen, Franz, you and Marie. Wasn't it also . . . Oh, for God's sake,' he says, at Liszt's handsome inquisitor's face, 'you know. This latest one, the dancer. Lola Montez – she can't really be called Lola Montez, nobody's called that, even the cheapest tarts in the rue Pigalle wouldn't dare . . .'

'No, of course, she's Irish, I think.' Liszt stands as straight and deferential as a waiter who will later spit in your soup. 'And she can't really dance, to be honest. Why does it matter?' He looks at Hector, really wanting to know.

'Irish.'

'Yes, no, who cares? Hector, my dear friend, if you don't mind my saying so, you're acting very strangely. Yes, yes, I know, nothing new.'

'Look, I know all about her.' His next tour of Germany and Austria approaches, which means Marie coming with him, which means leaving

Harriet alone, which means great toppling heaps of meaning . . . And Marie is having a tantrum about his hesitation, in such a pacing, nostril-flaring, stagily Latin way that Hector is rather charmed: charmed to find life unfolding with such predictability. It's comforting, like listening to Rossini. You know where it's going. He finds he is already, mildly, looking forward to the reconciliatory yelping sex that will follow the storm. 'I know all about her, as everyone does, and I don't see what the difficulty is. She's the past. She's old and fat and a drunkard, and you pay for her coals and her brandy, and that's it. Come on, what can hold you to her?'

'Nothing,' he admits. 'Nothing. Let's pack.'

'Now you're seeing sense.' She throws him a special look over her magnificent sloping shoulder.

'By the by,' he says temperately, 'do you think you'll ever grow old and fat?'

'Kill me first,' she says, burrowing in hatboxes.

'I'll remember that,' Hector promises.

Travels: Marie takes charge. She examines railway tickets and is forensic with hotel-keepers. In the registers she signs herself with a flourish 'Madame Berlioz', vigorously unpacks and dresses and is ready at once to meet and cross-examine the local impresarios: what publicity? Who are the important people in the press? How much, how much? Hector admires her toughness, in all ways. East of the Rhine transport is often erratic. The railway line to Prague is so new that workmen are still hammering at sleepers as the train starts. The Danube steamboats wallow and run aground: instead they lurch across the Hungarian plain in an antediluvian coach pinging with fleas. The foreign mistresses, even unimpressible Vienna, welcome him: no Parisian sneer to be seen. Meanwhile he dreams and scribbles *Faust*, breathing the visionary's rarefied solitude, standing with him above the abyss. Work, work.

At Prague Liszt turns up and listens with unashamed devotion to a rehearsal of *Roméo et Juliette*.

'So, what are you doing?'

'I'm writing it.'

'Excellent. You should always do what your heart tells you and never mind the rights and wrongs.'

'Now you sound like Mephistopheles.'

Liszt laughs, liking that very much.

Before the concert Prague lays on a celebratory supper for Hector at the Three Lindens, with Liszt leading the speeches. Journalists and musicians hammer their acclamations on the tables, then turn to some proper Bohemian drinking. Liszt, awash with champagne, gets into a quarrel with a music-lover over something that, in the way of drink, they really agree on.

'Well, we'll have to settle it.' Liszt staggers over and holds himself upright on Hector's arm. 'Come on, you can be my second.'

'You're joking. You're drunk.'

'We'll settle it. Right now, in the street.'

'I don't happen to have a sword about me. Maybe you could hit him with this.' Prague has presented Hector with a silver baton. Behind them Liszt's manager hovers anxiously. Hector pats Liszt's shoulder. 'Look, Franz, you've got a concert tomorrow. Better go to bed and—'

'Pistols,' says Liszt. 'Fellow over there's got some in his carriage.'

'What? Ten paces? You can't even see that far.'

Liszt laughs dangerously. His long fingers dig into Hector's arm. 'Neither can he. We'll stand closer.'

'No. No, I doubt either of you can even hold a pistol straight, but even so you might manage to kill each other, which would be a shame—'

The lightness isn't working. 'Why?' Liszt demands. 'It's clean, it's quick. Nothing shameful about it at all. Look how we treat women. Much nastier. We love and then leave and we kill them *so-o* slowly. By inches. Well, isn't it true?' Liszt gives the abrupt drowsy grin of the drunk. Hector feels cold and shrivelled. 'By inches. I'm thirsty. Where's the waiter?'

The next day Hector goes to Liszt's hotel, wondering how he will manage the concert: he was still talking about duels in the small hours. The manservant finally manhandles him out of bed with half an hour to spare. Liszt topples into his carriage looking like a waxwork. Hector follows him to the Sophieninsel Hall, which is full, expectant. Liszt strides on to the platform, now looking like the god of cheekbones, and plays so brilliantly, so demonically that the audience moan and gasp as if they were at a public hanging.

'No, I feel pretty well. A little tired,' Liszt says to Hector afterwards. '*You* look tired. Not sleeping?'

'You pianists are madmen.'

Liszt pouts humorously. '*Are* there any other pianists?'

'No, swell-head. Listen, Franz – what you said last night—'

'Yes, dear God, what did I say? All a blank. Capital party, though. I wasn't offensive to anyone, was I?'

Hector hesitates. 'No. No, not at all.'

In the pale watery light of a Normandy afternoon twelve-year-old Louis looks shyly across the laden inn-table at his father, who feels once again the shattering of his heart into a thousand pieces. It happened when Louis was born, when he cut his first tooth, when he first fell down and hurt himself and the precious blood flowed. That it happens so many times suggests that the shattered pieces quickly join again, which suggests something else. Hector calls for another dish of cream. Yes, put it there, fill the table so there's no space left, no room for the guilt.

'The principal tells me you're doing very well. Very conscientious, very respectful.' He smiles. 'Of course, what do principals know?'

Louis does not smile. Wrong, thinks Hector, he doesn't want you to be a boy with him, he wants you to be a father.

'I'm slower than the other boys.'

'Not all of them. And you work hard.'

'Some of them have private tuition. What's this?'

'Veal. Don't eat it if you don't like it.'

'I didn't say I didn't like it.'

'Some day soon,' Hector says, 'I might be able to afford private tuition for you. I'm writing a big work, which may—'

'It doesn't matter. I'm never going to be clever anyway. I might be like Great-uncle Félix and become a soldier. They don't have to be clever.'

'Time enough to think of that.'

'I had another letter from Mama. She's very sad.'

'Sometimes life is very sad.'

Louis gives that evasion the look it deserves. And this should be the trite moment when Hector sees his mother's eyes gazing out from the boy's thin solemn face – except he doesn't. As he has grown older Louis has lost any resemblance to Harriet. If anything, he looks more like his grandfather. Why do we obsessively seek out these resemblances? Another evasion, perhaps: trying not to face the responsibility of having made an individual, absolutely separate, absolutely unpredictable.

'You know, Papa, we must look after her. Whatever other things are going on.'

Hector moistens his dry mouth with wine. 'Yes. You're a good boy, Louis.' I'm not fitted for this, he thinks. In the ordinary business of life, where nothing is to be gained by being different, I have no talent at all. 'It isn't that your mother and I don't love each other, Louis. It's simply that we don't – we don't fit together any more. I know she's unhappy. But when we were living together she was even more unhappy. It's one of those things that doesn't have an easy answer.'

Louis nods, then reaches for the tart. 'Can I eat this now?'

'Of course.' Guiltily, Hector is already looking forward to the meal being over, to walking Louis back to his school, to escaping Rouen.

His mouth crammed, Louis says: 'I think I shall be a soldier.'

Before *Faust*, before the final damnation, there is this: a piece of irony worthy of Mephistopheles. Hector gets an official commission.

'A what cantata?' demands Marie, trying on a new hat.

'A Railway Cantata. From the city of Lille. For the opening of the new line from Paris to Brussels. Hail, Iron Goddess, that sort of thing.'

'Hm. They're paying you?'

'Oh, yes.'

'Then write it.' In the mirror the black eyes drill into his. 'What are you laughing at?'

'Nothing. Nothing at all.'

And now the filthy snow has melted and refrozen once again, so that Paris, under a murky sky, looks as if it is half buried in ash from some volcanic disaster; and the second performance of *Faust* has failed to fill even a third of the theatre, and Hector sits down to reckon up his debts. Yes, here is the reckoning.

'It's the only possibility,' he tells Marie flatly. She has shown signs of brewing up one of her tempests, but he is too weary to care. 'There's nothing else. There's nothing in Paris for me. Not now, not in the foreseeable future. I must travel or starve.'

'You could at least wait a while. There's going to be a new director at the Opéra, I have it on good authority, and if you can find out who in advance—'

'And woo them, and receive lots of nice promises, and then watch them put on nothing but Meyerbeer. Or hear about it, as I stand in the debtors' court.'

'Why Russia? It will be the most miserable journey – and dangerous.'

'Because Russia has offered me invitations, and I'm in no position to turn invitations down, even if they come from the Sultan of Zanzibar.' He takes her hands in his. An uncommon gesture: she does not like her hands to be imprisoned. 'It will be uncomfortable. Damnably cold, no doubt. But that's all. And it will give me at least a chance to work off some of my debts.'

'And what about your music? How will you compose, while you're riding in sleighs and conducting choirs of Cossacks or whatever they have there?'

'Compose, what for? One thing's certain, I'm damned if I'm ever going to spend another *sou* putting on a performance of my work.'

Marie observes him long and coolly, then frees her hands. 'And you think you're going alone, don't you?'

'I am going alone. It will undoubtedly be uncomfortable – yes, I know you don't care about that, but I do. Also it will cost twice as much for two to travel. It's as simple as that.'

Marie paces away from him. He can see her hovering on the edge of a tantrum: there is a pink glow at the nape of her exquisite neck. But Marie – no fool and no romantic – knows better than to fight a battle from such a disadvantageous position. She prowls back to him, jaw set, and jabs a kiss on his lips: a kiss that is more like some numbing sting. There, take that with you, don't forget.

'You won't abandon me like you did her,' she states: not a question. 'I'm not like that.'

'Oh, I know,' says Hector, who is already travelling through ice and snow, bleak and illimitable, beyond all touch of warmth.

EPISODE IN THE LIFE
OF AN ARTIST

Fifth Movement: Dream of a Witches' Sabbath

Larghetto – Allegro – Poco meno mosso

L ONDON, 1848. The farewell concert at the Hanover Square Rooms by distinguished musical visitor Monsieur Berlioz lately over: likewise the season. Theatres close, blinds go up at the windows in the western squares, and society decamps to the country.

Muggy, moist June weather. Not quite fog, but enough coal-dust in the listless air to make it feel so, and to set a bleary haze over the city that depresses the eye of distinguished visitor Monsieur Chopin, sitting at the window of his lodging in Dover Street and coughing blood into a handkerchief.

Poisonous weather, following on a mild winter. Typhus and cholera flourishing: undertakers likewise. Across the Channel, a deadlier fever rages: the Revolution of February has turned in on itself, and there is slaughter on the streets of Paris. A tang, a metallic sensation as of distant thunder.

Prosperous times at any rate for the druggist in his little dark shop in a little dark street off Covent Garden, who has just made his last sale of the busy day – twenty-four grains of opium to a Frenchman – and is reckoning up his takings. He assumed the man was French from his accent: a lot of them coming over here since the troubles. Not usually troubled with imagination, the druggist nevertheless noticed how pale the Frenchman was under his thick cowl of hair: as if he'd seen a ghost.

Which is very much what has happened to Hector, and he makes sure, as his quick steps take him away from the Garden, to give a wide berth to Drury Lane, where the apparition touched him.

What is Hector doing in London? Nothing much, now: in spite of the bloody reports coming out of Paris, he is considering going back. Nothing

357

much: though when he first arrived, back in November, he was going to do great things.

He got off the boat-train at London Bridge into the fog, and was met by the news that Felix Mendelssohn, adoptive Englishman, had died in Leipzig of a stroke at the age of thirty-eight. He mourned, and refused to see an omen. Everything, except the weather, was set much too fair for that. The magnificent impresario Monsieur Jullien was offering him magnificent terms to conduct the new Grand English Opera at the Theatre Royal, Drury Lane. After his labours in Russia, Paris had welcomed him back with her usual disdain, and the English offer was not to be resisted. Already the half-formed thought was in his mind, as he negotiated the fog-bound and endless warren of exciting streets: *I shall become an Englishman. Take that, France.*

The magnificent Jullien, magnificently moustached and shirt-fronted, even put him up in his magnificent house in Harley Street, and magnificently introduced him into London society. Here he was too thrilled and dazzled to peck at the crumbs of innuendo dropped by acquaintances about his magnificent host: hints to the effect that the magnificence was built on sand. He had come from one great city where the fevers of rumour and back-biting thrived: no reason to assume they were quite absent from London.

And yes, Drury Lane. He was silent the first time Jullien showed him around the vast theatre. A tribute: an obeisance to memory. Harriet had begun her career as a leading actress on this stage. It seemed dismayingly large. The cavernous auditorium seemed to growl with spectral voices. Brave, he thought. And they hadn't appreciated her. Spider-threads of sympathy went out from him, but he hastily gathered them in. Marie would be expecting a letter tomorrow, would probably be joining him at some point. Keep it silent; keep the door closed.

He was not much moved when, during the mild, sickly winter, he had heard of the Revolution convulsing Paris. If some good came out of it, which he doubted, he would be happy: but he felt as detached as if he were hearing news from Mexico. France stood aloof from him, and he could only return the compliment. Besides, he had more pressing concerns: the magnificent collapse of Monsieur Jullien's grand schemes, for which it turned out he had never had the money. The Drury Lane audience rose in generous acclamation of Hector and his orchestra and company, all of whom were living without salaries. Monsieur Jullien, magnificent to the last, went magnificently bankrupt in April – a development revealed to Hector in the most direct way possible, by bailiffs walking one morning into his Harley Street bedroom and sorting through his wardrobe.

'I may as well stay,' he said to Marie, when she joined him: he had taken cheap lodgings at Osnaburgh Street, where she stared in molten insult at the faded wallpaper and crazy rush-bottomed chairs. 'There's a chance of a few concert engagements. Actually, the English do like me, and I like them.'

She seemed to find some deep and detestable meaning in that remark. (Perhaps it was there: he was past caring.) 'Hector, you're a fool. If you'd let me come with you in the first place, none of this would have happened. I would have seen through that mountebank Jullien at once.'

'Would you? The trouble is, he is a splendid fellow all in all. He just had big ideas. I still can't hate him.'

'That's *your* trouble,' she snarled. 'You're too soft-hearted.'

He nodded. 'And after all you've done to cure me of it.'

This, then, is what Hector is doing in London. Marking time, now that his last concert is over, with its rivers of applause and trickle of receipts: realizing he has no money, again: realizing that his time here is over and he must return to France, where the barricades are building and the bullets are flying and no one, it is certain, is troubling themselves about the arts. Marie is confined to bed with one of the rheums and snuffles that seem to hang in the sooty air, and he is consoling or torturing himself with long walks, farewell walks if you like, about his old haunts in the city.

Haunts: significant word. Haunting Drury Lane in the breathless, shadow-stained dusk, he felt the presence of Harriet so strongly that for several moments he was immobilized. He looked up in keen suspension at the vaunting pilasters, the rumble of carts and forlorn cries of late street-vendors fading in his ears. It seemed then as if the membrane of time might split, and he would see Harriet, young, beautiful and beginning, come down those steps. And not recognize him, of course: that was before . . . but there lay the real enchantment of the spell . . .

He almost yelled when the woman's hand touched his arm.

'Sorry, sir. Beg your pardon, sir, didn't mean to fright you . . .' The woman looking up into his face with a mixture of natural timidity and professional boldness was a terrible broken-down creature, probably his own age, eking out the remnant of very good looks with rouge. Her bare, slack, bloomless bosom, like powdered tripe, quivered pathetically as she turned and tilted. 'I thought I'd take heart and speak to you because you've got a rare good face. Oh, yes . . .'

A corrosive whiff of spirits hit him. He shook her off, more violently than he intended: his heart was still hammering. 'No, no,' he said. 'No, my good woman, I . . .' Was that the right English phrase? She seized on his hesitation.

'Now, I know what you're thinking and, begging your pardon, you're wrong. I'm not asking what you think I am, sir – not unless that's what you're thinking too, in which case it's different, if you follow me. I just saw you admiring the old Drury, and I thought, I'll speak to that gentleman, out of old acquaintance, because you know I trod those boards in my time, sir, d'you believe me? It's long gone now, but you still might find somebody backstage who remembers poor Eliza and what I was going to suggest is we might have a drink on it. Mark it, so to speak—'

'You were an actress?'

'So I was, sir.' The bloodshot eyes explored his face, hopeful, doubtful. 'Mind, if you'd prefer that I wasn't, then that's very well too: we'll say that I wasn't, if that's how you like it. We'll have a drink on something else. Ask anyone, they'll tell you Eliza's not particular. It's up to you, sir – it's all up to you . . .'

Her hand was stealing towards him again: trembling, feeling priggish, he retreated. 'No, no.' Bloodshot eyes, but large and expressive and once probably beautiful and luminous eyes: no, no. 'You are mistaken.'

'Didn't mean to offend, sir.' An anxious, policeman-seeking look as she too retreated. 'Hope you won't consider—'

'Not at all. I must go. Please, take this – just take it.' He fumbled out a coin – what was it, a half-crown? English money was so unwieldy. He laid it in her hand, a surprisingly beautiful hand, the hand that had touched him from a ghostly past. It closed on the coin slowly, like an evening flower. He got away.

He got away, and in a wild whirl of emotion roamed about Covent Garden head down, cabbage-stalks squeaking like small killed things beneath his boots, and at last barged into a tavern and ordered brandy and drank it off and it did nothing, nothing at all, and he found then that he could not go on, could not continue being conscious in this way, could not go back to Osnaburgh Street and face fretfully dozing Marie and the trunks standing ready and the next cold compartment of the future with its iron door ajar.

It was a long time since he had dosed himself with opium. It had always been his father's trusty painkiller, and he had used it sparingly himself for minor illnesses; and in his young days, fascinated by De Quincey's *Confessions of an English Opium Eater*, and with the experimental excuse of the medical student, he had taken various recreational doses, and had some interesting experiences. But he had never liked the way it blunted certain sensibilities – above all, rendering music meaningless.

Blunting, though – oh, yes, that's what he wants now, an end to all the needling and stabbing that makes his brain feel exposed, like a pincushion for every thought and memory in the world. It is solitary too, opium, an intense and heavenly rejection of everyone and everything else: there is only the fascination of your own mind, performing its delicate arabesques of introspection. It calls a halt. In the castle in the wood the princess sinks into an enchanted sleep, the servants snore, the banners droop on the battlements, and you are free to inhabit the universe.

Knowing the time it takes for the drug to take hold, he steps into another frowsy tavern, and in an undisturbed corner takes his dose mixed with wine. It is a long way thence to Osnaburgh Street, and he intends walking it all – but after busily, exultantly marching through streets filled with hilarious sluggards who seem to be half paralysed, he is confronted with a desperate impossibility, and folds himself into a hackney for the rest of the journey.

In their lodgings a light is burning in the bedroom, where he peeps at a sweatily sleeping Marie: everywhere else is in darkness. A signal: come to me as soon as you're home, don't sit up, you have no other life. He laughs – in complete, lip-compressed silence: he finds this is unexpectedly possible – at the vanity and presumption of this. People simply don't understand themselves: how much truth there is in this, and how they hate to think it! But he doesn't mind the darkness, darkness itself is a kind of revelation. Walk about in it, and you can almost feel its soft pelt-like nap on your face. You can feel light on your face, can't you? Well, then. He lies down on the sofa, or rather he and the sofa meet in a mutual perfection of accommodation; and he falls down the welcome well.

Jude Morgan

(Scene, a blasted heath. Enter Hector.)

HECTOR
This desert place I know not. Yet the gleams
And far-off lashings, where the mast'ring storm
With rightful fury lays about the neck
And naked shoulders of th'unprotesting world
Do seem to prick my curlèd thought, and rouse
The snaily conscience from its thoughtless shell.
I know not, yet I know, this place, as doth
The blearèd sleeper catching in his arms
His beauteous vision, absolute to a hair,
But waking, straight forgot. Do I dream?
I feel the sapless sod beneath my feet,
A noisome wind benumbs my cheeks; and yet
I doubt me, this fled moment, whether sleep
Did not inthral me: nor if some dram
Or drowsy tinct, in thwart despair engorg'd
To haste the froward bridal of the eyes,
Incite my blood, and this phantasma make.
Or can it be that this is death – that thus
The soul is winnow'd from the flesh, unknowing,
And cast upon these sullen winds, t'affront
Its answer, ere the question scape the lips?
(Enter Three Witches, above.)
What shapes are these, that through the billow'd air
Descend, as swimmers breast the dark profound
To ravish ocean of her bedded sweets?
If wracks they seek in this the liken'd deep,
Then here a wrack behold: no chargèd bark
Nor hopeful argosy was ever broke
And shiver'd by the blast, and downward thrown
Beyond oblivion's gulph and marge, as I.
Yet naught of worth, if treasure do they seek,
Will fishers pick from out the stavèd ribs
Of this my founder'd hull of bones: naught,

362

Except the tarnish'd orts of bootless dreams
And gawds of vain ambition. – They approach.
My heart misgives me. Something hides their faces
From my sight, as a megrim brands
Its paining bar of light upon the eye;
And yet I see their robes and tatters swarth,
And feel their beatings stir the vap'rous air,
As if the gorcrow should the eagle's size
Usurp, though failing in his majesty.
I hear them warble in a tongue unknown:
All that is unearthly speaks their form.
In these dark seemings may it be
That th'angelic hides? As the sun
On which we may not pale our tender eyes
Unless some interposèd cloud preserve
From killing with its many-pointed glory?
My tongue would give the yea that still my heart,
My prudent miser, charily withholds:
I find no warrant in my mortal life –
If it be expiate – t'admit my soul
Unfee'd to the cabinets of the blest.
And certes the coyest virtue could not lurk
Behind a veil so ghastly, unpropitious,
And obscure, as these same climatures.
(The Three Witches gather around him.)
Speak! What art, and what thy purpose here?

FIRST WITCH
Hector, on purpose to thee do we come.

HECTOR
My name! What bodes this? In that voice
Which shrills upon my shrinking ear
As if the screech-owl borrow'd human tongue,
I yet some minded accents faintly hear.
I do not know, and yet I know, that voice.
Beshrew thee, creature, what enchantments fell

And secretitious hast thou laid upon me,
That I should thus be cozen'd? What the spell
That taunts a man with shadows, dear and lost,
And baits him to the halter's length of tears?
What face behind that mystic visor? Speak!

FIRST WITCH

When first thou oped thine eyes upon the world,
This face, my son, was what thou saw'st; and these
The hands that on thy infant clay the first
And tend'rest impress set.

HECTOR

Oh, horrible!
Oh, sorcery the foulest, that can gloze
Upon the sacred matter of a mother dead!
This evil posture stint, this termless wrong
Forbear, thou ape of hate, I conjure thee!

FIRST WITCH

In this our region, Hector, no command
Hast thou: nor was it ever meet that I,
Thy dam, should hear thy hest. What subtle craft
Doth this translation compass, whence, and whither,
Regards thee not: know only that thy mother,
True and entire, through these borrow'd chaps
And with this charnel voice and hollow speakest.
I laid upon thee once a mother's curse:
That monstrous shoot I dew'd with tears of gall,
And saw it thrive, and spread, and skywards mount.
Thou walkest in its sickly umbrage yet;
But do not think I come to thee in pity
Of thy ruthful case, or would undo
What's done: no, no: I here my curse renew!

HECTOR

Be gone: nor plume thyself upon thy prize,
Nor count these drops that sweal upon my face
As aught but moist'nings from the boiling rage
That rattles on my heart, and threats to spill
In fury at this contumelious gulling –
What? In such sorry shifts as these,
And fair-day tricks, do th'immortal shades
Beguile the blank and indistinguish'd hours?
I plaud me that I reck'd the nether world
As naught perpending. And look not so
Upon my raining cheeks, you watchful hags,
Nor augur aught of import thence, as if
You might from summer's showers incidental
A general tempest auspicate.

SECOND WITCH

Thou man,
Proud, as I have known thee long, and prick'd
With high and vaunting sentiment: emulous,
And while thou climbest, holding in disdain
Those feebler spirits, who the baser slopes
Domesticate, and turn to kindly uses:
Know that I am France. In me the maiden
Who resists, and maugre all thy wiles,
Thy anxious suit repels, incarnate stands.
That I have ever scantly valu'd thee
'Tis true: to own thee as my proper kin
Mislikes me much as this my eldritch sister.
The land that bore thee hates thee. Know we come
To serve thee with th'unseason'd dish of truth,
Although the Lenten mess thy palate roil.
From me expect no comfort, for the reach
And utmost of my view no rearing prospect
Nor hopeful cresset's kindling can devise.
Cold misprision still shall be thy guerdon;
The native ear thy song shall still disgust,

And scorn shall ever clip invention's wings.
Oppugnancy thy meed shall still deny
And mew thy spirit where it sought to fly!

HECTOR

If spirit of my native bound thou be'st,
Look not for disconcertion of my nature
At this thy cruel vouch. I do not stare
Or muse, to know thee such a cacodemon:
To thee my heavy wroth is fast assign'd.
My substance sorely has declin'd in suit
To thy affections moonish and inconstant.
I know thy crackl'd laugh and fleering lip:
Thy glaucous eye, its bend more deadly cold
Than basilisk or fatal cockatrice
Doth nothing gast me. All my wonder is
That this thy figur'd shape no worser stands,
Nor blazon'd with devices darker yet
T'express thy loathly essence.

SECOND WITCH

                    Thou answerest
With bolster'd pride, as if the worst were o'er,
And takest to thyself no blame or taint
Nor ownest thou the smallest grain or scruple
I' the heapy balance of thy present doom.
Attend my silent sister, when she grants
Enlargement to her tongue incarcerate
And fetter'd down with adamantean grief,
And then we'll try thy hollow metal.

HECTOR

                           No:
In pity's name, no more: I fear that shape
In gauzy tires lapp'd, who shades from me
With vailèd eyes their undisclosèd beam:
Though fairer than thy sisters, I could wish

Thy favour grimmer-look'd than harpies foul
Or serpent-tress'd Medusa. – Touch me not!

THIRD WITCH
No hand is with a title interess'd
More licit, or from abrogation fenc'd
In such security, as this my hand
T'inclose thine. My husband, this I gave thee,
And eke my heart, my hope, my life, and fortune,
Parcell'd up within the same conveyance.

HECTOR
Oh, Henriette!

THIRD WITCH
             Aye, such the name by custom
Did'st thou call me; not mine own; but whiles
The alteration did from love proceed –
Love delighting thus to make anew
And meld its treasured gold in figures fond
And image personate – I was content,
No other name desiring. Yet in this,
Th'estrangement of my proper calling, lay
A token and a prophecy, whose terms
I came in time to scry through dimming tears.
For thou, who mad'st me in thy ardent thought,
And as a sculpted idol set aloft,
Condemn'd me to a hopeless task, and durance
Passing human potency: to be
In very truth what thou hadst vision'd me
Within th'unspotted glass and shrinèd crystal
Of thine art. And so my punishment –
Thy despite, and final cold forsaking –
Was for no other crime but that of nature:
For being what I am, a woman flesh'd,
Was I arraign'd, and th'execution sped.
I do not come to fret thee with reproofs,

Nor would I to the bending yoke thou wear'st
The carcanet of guilt subjoin; for love,
Howe'er envenom'd by betrayal's fang,
Is yet to its own poison antidote.
I love thee, Hector, still. Not in my words,
But in my sole continuance and being
Lieth thy reproach. For what I was,
I am: and what I am, I was: no more
Nor less of quittance do I seek from thee,
Than that you raise your blinded eyes, and see.

HECTOR
I cannot speak. No hell-pains do I fear,
Who feel an age of hell in every tear.
(The Witches rise, and dance.)

FIRST WITCH *(sings)*
Sisters three, who rule his fate,
Ere our charmèd powers bate,
First his mazèd sense astound
With a giddy aërial round.

THE THREE WITCHES *(sing)*
Rise upon th'incorporal wing,
Featly form the antic ring,
Hand to hand, with tunèd throat,
Weird resound the ghostly note.
To the region without end
Circling ever we ascend:
Let our necromantic cheer
Ever vex his trancèd ear.
Truth may lie, and lies may tell,
And well be ill, as ill be well.
(They exit. Hector falls in a swoon.)

La Côte St André. The hay harvest lately in, and the natural term of the
life of Dr Louis Berlioz approaching its end.

Baking July weather. As much dust in the streets, as if a Saharan wind had scooped up a portion of desert, and deposited it on the little town with its scorching breath. Dogs stagger into pools of shade, and horses hang their heads as if they could never lift them again, and prefer the teasing of the flies to the effort of shaking their ears. In the street outside the Berlioz house, people pause, look up: meetings are quiet interrogations. Any news? Do you know how Dr Berlioz is? Is he . . . ?

The bedroom where Dr Berlioz lies is mercifully cool. The shady eaves and stout walls of this house, so devotedly preserved by their owner, have always kept the discomfort of the southern summer at bay. But Dr Berlioz, who was always such a diligent consulter of his barometer, is no longer in a condition to notice the temperature.

When it was plain that he was not going to leave his bed again, Nancy called in the *curé*. Dr Berlioz took the sacraments. Or, at least, he acquiesced in them. Adèle, for one has noticed that in his lucid intervals her father still has the lonely, flinty look of a man keeping his own counsel, right to the end. But the proprieties have been satisfactorily observed.

And now there is nothing but the vigil. The vigil, of course, for Nancy, Adèle and Monique, at least one of whom is always by his side: but also the vigil of Dr Berlioz, watching the hours of his own death.

A doctor – another doctor – has been called in, but he has nothing to offer. For as long as he is capable, Dr Berlioz has continued to treat himself – with opium; when speech and grasp fail, he is still able to gesture for his dose, or signal with his eyes. Nancy is inclined not to give it to him, but Adèle overrules her. Monique bathes his face, and changes the clouts to which he is reduced. Meanwhile the opium sustains his decaying system. He is aware of shaking, and convulsing, and of doing something, fixedly, that used to be called seeing, which involves focusing his organs of sight on exterior objects, though he very rarely finds it has its former communicative function. What there is of his senses inhabits the velvet tunnel of the drug. Sometimes the tunnel seems to branch off into dark side-turnings, which he contemplates, but chooses not to pursue: though a fragment of his diminished awareness instructs him that presently there will not be a choice.

Short flarings, like the sputterings of a lucifer-match, show him the room and the people in it, and himself, and what he knows and remembers. Lying on his pillow, blinking, like a castaway waking on a beach, he finds Monique showing him an engraved portrait.

'Hector,' he says. And some time later, after he has listened long to the breakers on the shingle and the high blue humming of the sky: 'Hector?'

'He's still in London, I think, Papa. I've written him.'

One of the strange, incomprehensible beings who call him Papa has answered. There seems to be a requirement that his mouth – where is it? – should do something in kind. He gathers himself for the task.

'I shall write him presently.'

That, exhausting as it was, seemed to fulfil some purpose in this peculiar world he moves in now. He does not understand, but suppose he might eventually. It is all very new and strange. He closes his eyes. Sleep sweeps him up, runs with him, and flies him like a kite.

Now there is only this: he was just about to do something, and is irritatingly called away from it, and is trying to keep his mind fixed on it, and not forget, because it was important; but there we are. Opening his eyes is like opening the door to some annoying insistent knock. Three, what are they?, faces: three, what are they?, women: gathered round him. He finds a certain splendour in the way his tiny eye-muscles work, turning to them: one, two, three. But then he is terribly afraid of them, and is so grateful when the fear, and all of it, goes.

Montmartre. The battles of a second revolution lately over, the paving-stones plucked up by the rebels replaced in the Paris streets, the graves of the dead smoothed. Mild October weather, the sunlight steeping the Montmartre hill like honey through a comb. Everywhere, an unquiet peace.

In the garden of her house in the rue St Vincent, Harriet strolls with her arm through that of her good friend Madame Blanche. Cautiously they talk of what has been and what might be: both recall the spitting and stuttering of guns, and later the nameless stink rising: the way you could smell it even in linen that had just been washed. Harriet wants to show her the tree. During the violent summer she was walking past it when someone – a stray revolutionary, a soldier perhaps – fired into the garden. For a moment she thought the thudding bullet was in her, not the tree.

'Here it is.' Harriet probes her finger into the woody, surprisingly warm fissure. She can hardly believe it happened. 'I can hardly believe—' And then whatever it is she can hardly believe seems to whisk into the furthest distance, and leave her there with her body, which feels huge, graven, shockingly steadfast, as if she has exchanged her flesh with the pyramids: as if she has turned into a building.

She does something with her hand – withdraws it, possibly, from the hole in the tree. It has all become desperately chancy. You do this, perhaps: we'll have to see. She achieves a shuffling parade-ground turn, at last ending up face to face with staring Madame Blanche.

'I don't feel well, I'm afraid.' Spoken in an infinite, yawning giant's voice: though she feels like laughing, in a way.

'Henriette. Henriette, please, what is it?' Somewhere, at the edge of a doughy mass of flesh – mine? – a kind hand fastens.

'Don't know,' pronounces the giant, slowly. Awareness of the face, like a mummer's mask, half broken. Yet I'm quite all right. The actress, always prepared. 'I may have to go in, Madame Blanche. Please excuse me.'

'Henriette, what's wrong?'

Silly, shouted question: what's wrong? Surely nothing much, I feel quite myself. Indeed, doubly, trebly myself, as I am now three, identical and cheek by jowl, all calmly walking back to the garden door, and we, I, all three get there first, thank goodness, since there's a shutter closing some-where and I've lost that part to darkness. I, we, can just get in, and that will have to do, there's this wonderful slackness inviting me, and I really will. I'm dreadfully sorry, I really will have to lie on the floor.

No, truly, I do very well, this is all nonsense, I feel perfectly – I feel—

Yes. Yes, I will. But if he comes, and I don't know, you will wake me, won't you?

Please.

CODA: 1849

And now we see Monsieur and Madame Blanche again in their wall-papered parlour. But this time it is summer, and Madame Blanche is not going on, but returning from a visit. Her husband looks up expectantly as she unties her bonnet and persuades her grey kid gloves from her smooth, neat hands.

– So, my dear, asks Monsieur Blanche, and how does she do?

Madame Blanche hesitates. – In many ways, not well. No further seizures, but she is still weak.

– No wonder. She was lucky to survive the cholera at all. The figures in the newspaper today –

– Lucky. Yes: lucky, says madame Blanche, with an odd, distant look.

Her husband examines her, fondly, critically. – So it's true, then? He is with her?

Madame Blanche permits herself a smile. – Yes. He has been nursing her. Yes, of course, they are still separated, as man and wife. That's well known. But in another way they're not. He's there every day, at her side. Oh, I know he has that woman. Everyone knows that. But the fact is he's there, with Henriette, every day. And the look on their faces . . .

– My dear, you've become sentimental.

– Is the mystery of human love sentimental, Monsieur Blanche? Is that what you believe?

– You know very well it is not, he says. His smile is wry and tender.

– Oh, I can understand if people have a feeling of – disbelief. I felt it myself when he came back: oh, come on, I'm not a child, and so on. I don't know the whole history of it, but it's pretty clear to me that they would never do, together. They are just too . . . I don't know. And yet, he is always there, with her. And this I think is a different kind of love, which we don't understand – and now, if you like, you may accuse me again of being sentimental.

Monsieur Blanche is thoughtful. – Would you call them happy?

– In a very peculiar way – yes, says Madame Blanche, sitting down beside him.

– Sentiment, or the mystery of human love? Who can say? I wouldn't presume to say. I don't know.

At which Madame Blanche looks greatly refreshed, as if someone has opened a window on a stuffy room.

– *I don't know*, she says, delivering one of her dry kisses to her husband's cheek, is the best and purest sentence in the world.

We are allowed a glimpse.

Here we are again: the large, cool, neat room, the geometric rug, the fire-screen, the broad window with the *fauteuil* before it. The sad and immobile and fascinating woman is still seated there, and she gazes still from the splendid imprisoned eyes.

The difference is the lean, bony, sharp-featured man sitting beside her and holding her hand – beside her, physically, though there is something about his posture that suggests he is sitting at her feet.

The clock on the mantelshelf – the clock that has been for Harriet a terrible taskmaster, ordering her to look, look, at my slowness – is showing some late, admonitory hour: but neither she nor he gives a damn.

It's odd, how long you can do this – goes against every romantic idea, really: to have this emotion, you should be making fierce love or else pushing each other conclusively off craggy cliffs.

Instead, Harriet and Hector Berlioz are quietly sitting side by side in her Montmartre lodgings, and holding hands.

There can surely be no greater intimacy than this: the entire absence of illusions.

Harriet begins to speak. The repeated strokes have made this difficult for her, but Hector quietly waits: he knows that the best things are not easily said.

'We shall never be as we were.'

The struggle to get the words out gives them enormous weight.

'Yes,' he says, and in that word includes much. But – and he looks at, venerates her hand in his, that beautiful and unchanged hand: but. 'But in another way, we will always be as we were.'

Author's note

Harriet Smithson Berlioz died in March 1854. Berlioz continued to see her till the end. In October he married Marie Recio, who died in 1862. Louis Berlioz joined the navy in 1850. He was a captain when he died of yellow fever in Havana in 1867, at the age of thirty-three. This and the disastrous production of his masterpiece *The Trojans* darkened Berlioz's last years. He died in 1869, believing himself to be a failure. Subsequently, he was internationally recognized as the most daring innovator of Romantic music, his influence extending to Liszt, Wagner, Richard Strauss, the great Russian composers and beyond.